THE HOUR

Sara MacDonald was born in Yorkshire and travelled extensively as a forces child. She attended drama school in London and worked in television and theatre before she married, living abroad for many years before moving to Cornwall with her two sons.

By the same author

Sea Music
Another Life

SARA MACDONALD

The Hour Before Dawn

HarperCollins*Publishers*

HarperCollins*Publishers*
77–85 Fulham Palace Road,
Hammersmith, London W6 8JB

www.harpercollins.co.uk

A paperback original

Published by HarperCollins*Publishers* 2005
1

Extracts from *The Four Quartets* by TS Eliot reproduced
by permission of Faber and Faber.

A catalogue record for this book
is available from the British Library

ISBN 0 00 719429 3

Set in Sabon by
Palimpsest Book Production Limited,
Polmont, Stirlingshire

Printed and bound in Great Britain by
Clays Ltd., St Ives plc

For my beloved twin Nicky, with love.

Between midnight and dawn, when the past is all deception,
The future futureless, before the morning watch.
TS Eliot

ACKNOWLEDGEMENTS

I am indebted to Taschen GmbH Publishers for allowing me to quote from Harry Rand's book *Hundertwasser*.

I had not heard of Hundertwasser, architect and painter, before a visit to New Zealand in 2003. I became fascinated by his unusual buildings and ecological paintings. One painting, *The Garden of the Happy Dead* caught my imagination and so my book was born. A note on this painting is at the back of the book.

The New Zealand garden at the end of the book was inspired by the remote and beautiful garden belonging to (my son) James and his wife Susannah, an amazingly creative and resourceful horticulturist who, in true pioneer fashion are hacking and taming wilderness into a place of spectacular beauty.

I am very grateful to my two taxi drivers, Sebastian, (Christian) and Anwall (Muslim) in Port Dickson. They entered enthusiastically into my search for a past I would never have found on my own, for it hardly exists anymore, unless you look hard.

For purposes of this novel I have taken a few small geographical liberties with Port Dickson. The old rest houses, as they were, are gone and in their place stand modern red tiled, pagoda roofed houses. The lonely atmospheric road to Tanjung Tuan Lighthouse is now surfaced, but still lies through the jungle full of monkeys and strange birds and still brought me out in goose bumps. The steps from the beach have disappeared or perhaps they only existed in memory. The half moon curve of beach with spider crabs remains, but the sea is not as blue as I remember.

Despite seeing the west coast of Malaysia as it is now, in 2005, it remains the same as ever it was behind my eyelids. *That place, that time.*

PROLOGUE

Fleur treads water in the deep end as the twins slowly climb to the diving board. An older girl goes up behind them to make sure they don't fall.

Fleur is laughing at their excitement. Nikki jumps first, plummets downwards, hits the water and keeps going down. Fleur hauls her up to the surface and she opens her mouth and screams with joy.

Fleur sits her on the edge of the pool and swims back to the middle for Saffie. Saffie leaps and lands almost into Fleur's arms and Fleur scoops her up before she sinks. The onlookers round the pool clap their hands; it is an amazing sight to see toddlers jumping from the diving board.

'We did it! We did it!' they both cry.

Fleur swims to the edge and pulls herself out and sits next to them. 'You're so brave! I'm so proud of you!'

'Now you! Now you, Mummy!'

Fleur looks at them, small brown bodies, wrists and ankles round and babyish still, their fair hair plastered to their heads. They could both swim before they could walk. They have no fear of the water, no fear of anything. She is suffused with love, overtaken; wants to pull them to her and bite into those plump legs and arms, bury her head in their wet little stomachs.

'OK. But go back to the rug and get your armbands first.'

She watches them run noisily away over the grass; watches heads turn as they always do at the two identical little figures. When they return she blows up their bands, then blows a raspberry on each brown stomach making them shriek.

'Go and sit on the edge of the shallow end, you noisy little girls, and don't jump in until I've dived and I'm in the water. You know the rules. I mean it. If you jump in before I'm in the water, no more diving board.'

The twins nod solemnly and Fleur walks away and climbs the ladder to the top board. Over to her right the sea glitters over the Straits of Malacca and sounds from the naval base below reach her. It is late in the afternoon and a cooling wind is coming from the sea, ruffling the palm trees, touching her wet skin like a whisper. Colours are softening over the grass and families, some with amahs, sit scattered on towels and rugs around the pool, reading, talking quietly, and waiting for the men to finish work and join them.

Fleur stands poised, eyes almost shut, dark hair, dark skin, in a white bikini. She raises her arms, thinking about her movements and the alignment of her body as only a dancer does. She pauses, the diving board rocks, and then in perfect slow motion her body bends, jumps and turns in a perfect arc as she dives, breaking the water with hardly a splash.

She isn't aware of the watchers, of the men turning from the bar, of the women stopping for a moment, of the children, their mouths open in admiration. She is only aware

2

of this small act of precision reminding her of what her body can do.

When she surfaces, the twins are swimming like small, fat beetles towards her, racing to see who can get to her first. She laughs and propels herself towards them and when her feet touch the bottom she holds her arms wide, turning her face upwards away from their splashes. They grab her arms.

'I won!'

'No, I won!'

'You both won,' she says, clasping them to her. 'Now let's go and get dry because Daddy will be here any moment.'

She plonks them on the side and they start to pull their armbands off. When she looks up David is standing in his uniform watching them, his eyes shielded by dark glasses. Her heart turns over as it always does when she sees him from a distance. She thinks, '*Oh God, he's mine.*'

The twins haven't seen him yet and Fleur knows why he hasn't called out. He likes to watch them. He likes to watch them when they are unaware because he too cannot quite believe in this happiness.

She smiles and the twins turn to see who she is smiling at, then squeak and jump up and run across the grass to him. He scoops them up and walks towards Fleur, laughing.

'Ugh! Horrid, beastly little wet rats.'

'No, no! Peapods. We're peapods.'

'You jolly well are not! Peapods are nice and dry and green.' He drops them beside their armbands, takes off his dark glasses and bends and puts out a hand to pull Fleur out of the water.

'Hi, you.' He kisses her nose, his eyes amused, and Fleur wants to wind her arms round him, press her body to him; the feeling is visceral and overpowering.

'Are you going in?'

'Yes, I'll cool off for ten minutes while you get these rats dressed. Can you get me a beer, darling? I'm parched.'

He walks back with her across the grass where the shadows are lengthening and goes to change. Fleur dresses the twins and gets out their colouring books. She walks over to the outside bar to get them cold drinks and the twins turn and watch her.

She has wrapped a thin, filmy piece of material across her hips and people turn as she passes. The young Malay waiter who is clearing the tables hurries back to the bar so that he can serve her. He carries the tray all the way back across the grass for her and places it on the table beside the twins.

'Hello, babies,' he says. He says it every time and they say in unison,

'Not babies.' And he laughs and gives Fleur his glittering smile and swaggers laconically away.

Fleur lies on her stomach in the last rays of the sun, soporific, listening to the different voices coming to her as the day fades. She can hear David's voice faintly talking to someone as he swims. They will be talking helicopters or flight rotas or new pilots or the boss.

The twins move closer, their warm bodies touch her on each side. Saffie has her thumb in her mouth. They are both getting sleepy. Fleur puts her arms around them both.

What should she wear tonight? They are driving into Singapore with friends to have a meal and walk around night markets before going dancing.

How many times has she worn the green Chinese silk dress? It is ages since they've been into the city . . . maybe she will get some material for a new dress . . .

4

'I love you, sweet peas,' she murmurs, drawing the twins even closer so that they seem welded and part of her.

'Blub you.'

'Blub you, Mummy.'

The day is drawing to a close. People are leaving. It is the gap between afternoon and evening when only the single officers prop up the bar for a little longer before they too go and change for dinner. She hears Laura's voice in her head.

'You're throwing your life away. I can't believe that after all those hard years of training you can just . . . give it all up . . . What a waste! You're a born dancer . . . You'll regret it, Fleur. One day you'll wake up and regret it . . .'

She hears David return, pick up a towel, drip near her feet. He takes a deep drink of his beer. He is humming under his breath.

Fleur smiles. *I don't regret it, Mum. I've never regretted it for one single second. I'm so happy I want to burst.*

As she thinks this, she remembers someone saying, *Never, ever say out loud that you're happy because a jealous God will hear and strike you down.* The sun goes suddenly, slips behind the sea and all is black and white.

I didn't say it out loud. I only thought it so it doesn't count.

Fleur sits up and David smiles. 'I guess I'd better swallow this beer and get my three sleepy women home . . .'

ONE

I saw so clearly the hollow grave on the edge of the jungle and the small skeleton curled inside it that I woke up screaming.

Jack erupted from the pillow in fright and switched on the lamp.

'God, Nikki.'

His startled face peered at me, still full of sleep. I clamped my hand over my mouth willing the image to fade.

'Sorry,' I whispered, but my whole body was shaking and I felt icily cold.

'That must have been some dream. Are you OK now?' Jack rubbed his hand up and down my arm to sooth me but it had the opposite effect and I shrank away, back under the covers.

Jack turned to look at the clock. It was four-fifteen.

'Oh God,' he groaned. 'I've got to be up in two hours.'

'Sorry,' I said again, trying to stop shivering.

'I'll make you tea,' he said in a resigned voice. 'I might as well. I'm never going to get to sleep again.' He got out of bed. 'It's bloody freezing in here.'

He wound a sarong around his naked body and went to the window which was wide open and shut it.

'I wonder why it's so cold? I'll come back and warm you up . . .' He paused, staring at me worriedly. 'You've only had bad dreams since you got pregnant, haven't you?'

I nodded and he grinned at me. 'I'd better start monitoring what you eat for supper.'

When he'd gone the room was still, but it was full of something too, full of the cold darkness that was Saffie. Saffie, desperately trying tell me something. Why now, after all these years, when I had run so far and thought the past was settling into something I could just about manage?

Of course, she was always with me, each and every day, because she was my twin and her likeness was mine. Of course she was with me, a shadow, a mote in my eye, there on the turn of a stair, on the end of a street, waiting.

But I had never known her frightened before. She had never called out to me in my dreams as she was doing now. Nothing should hurt her. She should be safe.

I carried new life in me and I felt full of dread. I tried to tell myself that terrifying glimpse of a grave was something I had watched on the television and nothing to do with my sister.

As she faded the room warmed, and when Jack came back with tea and dry biscuits I was able to smile. He kissed the top of my nose and climbed back into bed.

'Thank God, it's warming up,' he said.

'Thank you for the tea.' I smiled at him gratefully.

'No worries,' he answered sleepily, and I knew in a moment he would be asleep again, leaving me to wait for the birds and the sun creeping up over the bay.

An hour later I slid out of bed and pulled my clothes from the chair. I went into the bathroom and dressed quietly and pattered downstairs and out into the new day. I walked down the garden and the dew was heavy and cold and drenched my feet. The bay was full of yachts below me and the sea beyond the oyster beds was the deepest blue, yet summer was beginning to fade, the height of the season was over and soon Jack would be able to relax a little.

In England the worst of the winter would be over and sliding into spring and my mother would be leaving her London garden and making her way inexorably my way. I dreaded it. I dreaded the thought of her here in New Zealand, in our small piece of paradise. I wondered suddenly if that was why I was having bad dreams. If the dread was manifesting itself in my sleep, because it was difficult to articulate to Jack, to explain how I felt about my mother.

He looked at me in a certain way when the subject of her came up, a little shocked and uneasy, as if mothers were sacrosanct, and my not wanting to see her was breaking some taboo. And the worst thing was, I knew he would be charmed by her.

TWO

Fleur finished packing and sat back on her heels. She longed to ring her daughter to say, *Let's try hard. I haven't seen you for years, darling. Just a few days together, then I won't see you again for heaven knows how long . . .* but she dared not risk it. She closed her last piece of hand luggage and walked slowly round the house wondering if the distance between them, literal and resonant, would ever end. Perhaps Nikki's pregnancy would change and warm her somehow. A pregnancy Fleur would have known nothing about if she had not rung her daughter. It was still hard to bear the thought of Nikki living almost as far away from her as it was possible to live.

Fleur was planning a trip to New Zealand on the trail of Hundertwasser's architecture as part of her dissertation and there was one of his buildings quite near where her daughter lived, in Kawakawa, a public lavatory, and Fleur wanted to see it. If she had rung her daughter and said, *Can I come and see you?* Nikki would have made excuses about being in the middle of a busy season, or that she was just about to take off with Jack, or, *Frankly, it's not convenient just now.* So making Hundertwasser her reason for visiting was the only chance Fleur had of catching a glimpse of her troubled daughter for she had always refused to foist herself upon her.

Nikki was amused by the fact Fleur was a mature student, but she had never troubled to ask her mother about her paintings, which Fleur had surprisingly started to sell for quite large sums.

Fleur missed Fergus. She missed his love and encouragement, and somehow, when he was alive, the shadows could be kept at bay, for he had been a part of them and they had come through that awful time together.

They did not hide it away, that tragedy so long ago. They took it out sometimes in the dead of night and turned it over yet again to see if they could find some clue, if the shape of it could change. But it never did, and the best they could do, like so many other people who had to go on living a whole long lifetime *afterwards* was to carry it forward with them, haul it after them like a dead weight, until it became part of them and absorbed into the people they became.

Saffie was the first thing Fleur remembered when she woke and the last thing she thought about before she slept.

Nikki had given her and Fergus a hard time. Fleur was unsure how they had survived, but they had. Fergus had died suddenly, three years ago, leaving Fleur abruptly without warning, and for the first time in her life she was completely alone.

When Fergus retired he had turned his architect's eye to painting. He had gone to classes and turned out pleasing little watercolours. Small paintings of the garden and of their holidays by the sea in Cornwall; of Tuscany on their last holiday together.

'I have an eye for detail and can copy, that's all,' he said to any compliments. 'To an untrained eye I might seem proficient, but this is strictly painting for my own pleasure.'

When he died, Fleur had the paintings of Tuscany framed and they now hung on the wall outside her bedroom. They reminded her of a happy time but also of the random cruelty of life. They had both felt young still, with plans to travel now that they had the time and money. There were so many things to do and places they had never seen. As well as shock, Fleur felt cheated of all the years she should have had with Fergus.

He was able to join his father's firm when he'd left the army but he'd had to retrain as an architect, five long years when they were relatively hard-up. Fleur had to qualify too, to teach dance professionally, and without the help of both sets of parents they would not have survived.

Fergus was an imaginative architect and had worked long and hard to become successful. He'd relaxed a little as the money began to come in, then his father died and he had to take over the firm and his hours became even longer, until he suddenly realised he didn't want to do it any more. He wanted his life back. He wanted to see more of Fleur and travel and enjoy the money he had made. He sold out and retired with huge relief and whirled Fleur away to Italy. Eighteen months later he was dead.

One night Fleur had gone to his little studio and stared at an empty canvas. She had picked up a brush and some of his paints and had simply thrown the colour of her grief and anger at the canvas. She had never looked back. It had released something inside her and she went each day to the place where Fergus seemed nearest to her. She painted her loss instinctively without thought until her work seemed to coalesce into form and meaning: canvases covered with strange abstracts with a

12

hidden power that gave way to something gentler and infinitely lonelier. It was these paintings, full of the loss of him,
that got her a place as a mature student at a college of art.
Her world changed abruptly, and slowly became full of new
and different people and a life that challenged.

She found, left to her own devices, that she was quite
practical and deft with her hands, and now the hands that
changed light bulbs and fuses also made pots and jugs and
little bowls. She loved the feel of clay, the excitement of
moulding something from nothing, and the bright fiery
colours she painted on canvas and clay were the colours of
her childhood; the colours of the east.

Fleur wanted Nikki to see the person who had evolved
from years and years of dependency, to approve of the person
she had become.

It had taken her a long time to decide whether she could
bear to fly via Singapore. Just the name of the city on her
lips made her shiver and ache with longing, but with fear
too. The Singapore of her memory would have turned into
somewhere unrecognisable, would have a different identity
to the place of her childhood and youth. A city of memories where everything changed in the blink of an eye. From
light to darkness.

Every morning of her life Fleur turned Saffie's photo
towards her; a missing child forever caught in childhood.
There was rarely a night when Fleur did not wonder where
her daughter's body lay or worry about the possibility that
she might live in some distant, alien culture, brought up
with unknown people with little memory of her birth and
a long-ago family who loved her.

It was the not knowing. The certainty, as the years went
by, that they would never know, which haunted and
maimed the lives of Fleur and her surviving daughter.

But it was Fleur that the long, relentless shadow of guilt fell on. She was their mother and her mind and heart had been on other things; on David. She had not taken care of her children. Haunted with misery, she had left them to roam free. She had left them to chance, ignored their safety, and something random and terrible had swooped.

It is this that my daughter can never forgive.

THREE

Singapore, 1976
The monsoon was coming. The wind was rattling the shutters, catching the chimes outside Ah Heng's window. They swung and jumped and clashed in a mad little Indian dance. The strings would get all muddled and Saffie knew she and Nikki would have to untwist them in the morning.

The smell of rain filled the dark room, reaching up the stilts of the house, rising up from the damp earth full of bruised frangipani blooms and dead leaves and small branches of trees.

Saffie lay still, listening for the sound that had woken her. She was facing the open door, staring at the closed shutters that kept out insects and the great blind moths as big as sparrows who threw themselves out of the dark into the light, their fat little bodies hitting the lampshades; their dusty, fluttering wings falling into the twins' hair, jumping across the surface of their skin like mice.

Saffie could hear the familiar sound of cicadas, but there wasn't the heavy warmth of a coming day. Her feet touched Nikki's feet at the other end of the bed. She did not think her sister was awake, but she could not be sure. Nikki's breath could be held, like her own; Nikki could be silently listening too.

Suddenly Saffie heard again the sound that had woken her. She saw the shadow of her mother in the corridor that was a balcony during the day when the shutters were thrown back against the house each morning. Fleur had opened a shutter and was leaning out into the dark, listening, looking upwards to the stars that filled the hugeness of the night.

With a lurch of sickness Saffie knew. Daddy was not home yet and she strained like Fleur for the sound of helicopters overhead. She could hear her mother's voice keening. It was this soft, monotonous sound that had woken her, that and her mother's fear. It shimmered across the night and reached both children, touched them with cold fingers and they shivered at their mother's terror.

'Oh, God!' Fleur whispered. 'Oh, God in heaven. *Please. Please.* Let him come in safely. I beg you, God.'

Both girls sat up abruptly as one. Stared at their identical selves.

'Daddy!' they whispered and reached for each other, catching their mother's panic.

At that moment they heard the aircraft engines. Behind dense cloud came the faint sound of rotary blades. Clear, like knives cutting through the blackness, the sound of helicopters rumbling and whirring their way home. Tail-lights winking and blinking like comforting fireflies through the purple massing clouds, which were growling with thunder and bursting with violent wind and rain.

Saffie and Nikki leapt out of bed and ran to their mother.

'Hurry!' they called out into the night. 'Hurry, hurry, Daddy. Hurry, Fergus . . . Hurry, everyone . . . the storm is coming. Hurry, hurry before the lightning comes . . .'

16

The sound of engines was louder now, near to them, and suddenly out of the clouds, in formation, five helicopters appeared out of the night.

'Hurrah!' Saffie and Nikki shouted. 'There they all are . . . hurrah!'

'Shush, darlings. Shush! I need to listen.' Fleur's voice was trembling.

They watched as the helicopters hovered over the airfield. One turned in a circle as if testing the power of the wind and then dropped slowly at an angle to land at the airfield beyond their sight.

The next two helicopters were being buffeted up and down and they too circled quickly, one after the other, well apart, and turned and dropped from sight into the darkness.

'Three down!' Fleur let out her breath like a sigh. A violent damp wind wrenched the shutter from her hand and it crashed back against the house, and then the rain came in slanting, weaving arcs, blowing crossways, bringing great suffocating black clouds which obscured their vision.

A white streak of lightning shot into the night making the children jump back. They all heard but could not see the fourth helicopter drop from the clouds. The engine was making a lot of noise as the pilot searched for the airfield lights below him.

The last helicopter emerged from cloud and circled. *Daddy.* It seemed to the twins to move nearer to the house, as if to say, *I know you're watching . . . I'll be home in thirty minutes, Peapods.*

Daddy was always last down. *It is like being the captain of a ship*, he'd told the twins. *Your men's safety comes first.*

They saw the red flickering tail-light against the lightning as the helicopter hovered, tried to turn and drop out of the savage wind to land. But it was impossible. It was caught as the eye of the storm lifted and threw it about the sky like a toy. Pilot and machine were suspended and buffeted against a backdrop of lightning shooting and cracking across the sky like fireworks.

The helicopter looked pathetically small as it was thrown about the sky like an unbalanced bee and tossed this way and that. Fleur and the twins held their breath in hypnotised terror.

'Land, Daddy. Land!' Saffie cried out into the night. Nikki gripped the windowsill as they watched the tail rising, tail-blade whirring frantically as the engine screamed.

'Holy Mary, mother of God . . . *Please* . . .' Fleur was crying over and over. She clutched the twins, held them into her, gripped them so tightly she hurt, and her eyes never left the sky.

'David . . . David . . . I'm willing you down . . . You can do it. I know you can do it . . . Come on, David . . . please, darling, get her down . . .'

Something terrible was gripping Saffie's stomach in a cramp so painful she wanted to fall to the ground. Nikki was sobbing, still clutching the windowsill. They were only five but they both knew, like their mother, that their father was powerless to do anything to save himself, because he no longer had control of his machine, which was turning upside down and falling out of the sky and spiralling down to the ground so fast that if they'd blinked they would have missed it.

Already, far away, they could hear the sound of sirens. They heard the explosion as the aircraft hit the ground when it was out of sight. They saw the flames leap upwards into a sky cracking with thunder. They could not move, Fleur, Saffie and Nikki. They stood watching the sky where the helicopter had been a moment ago.

A long way away a telephone was ringing and Ah Heng ran in her little backless slippers to answer it. Still, the three figures stood, unable to take their eyes from the empty sky that was growing light now. The rain blew in great gusts sideways, filling the monsoon drains, flushing the snakes out of the dry collected leaves.

Into the dawn, low on the horizon, there suddenly sailed one small pink cloud. Fleur stared and stared at it. She said in a strange thick voice, 'Twins . . . look . . . see? That cloud . . . Daddy will always be there to look after us. Always.'

Saffie reached behind Fleur for Nikki's hand. They stared at the cloud in silence, their small bodies trembling, unable to entirely comprehend that their father was so suddenly dead. They did not want a pink cloud. They wanted their big, laughing, silly, whiskery, safe daddy, who called out each and every day, 'Hey! I'm home! Where are my little peapods?'

Far away on the Chitbee Road they could see the military car containing the padre and the commandant and the military police making its way down the long road to their house.

'Missie?' Ah Heng touched Fleur's arm, took the twins gently from her, holding them to her. 'You come away from window now. You cold. You come away. I make Missie tea. Army men coming.'

But Fleur could not take her eyes from the cloud that was fading to orange and had only been the reflected colour of the flames.

'You will always be with us to keep us safe,' the twins heard her whisper. 'Oh, David . . . David.'

But their father was not there to keep them safe. Did Nikki blame Fleur for what happened later? Was she angry

19

with her? Yes, she was. If you had children you must look after them, no matter what happened to you or however sad you were. You must look after them and keep them safe forever, because you were their mother and if you didn't, who would?

FOUR

'What time is your mother's flight from Auckland?' Jack asked me at breakfast. He was standing at the sink, buttering toast.

'Five o'clock, I think. I'm going to check in a minute. It's OK, Jack. I can meet her on my own.'

'No, Nik, we'll both go. I'll make sure I've finished by four; it will give us an hour to get there. Just be ready, we don't want her standing around jetlagged waiting for us. Did you tell her to stay in the main airport until it's time for the flight to Kerikeri? That other terminal is the pits.'

'Yes. I e-mailed. It'll be a miracle if she's got to Auckland and not sailed off to Hong Kong by mistake . . .' I joked weakly. 'I don't think she's travelled so far on her own for a long time.'

Jack gave me one of his looks. 'Well, she's had the courage to stop off in Singapore on her own so she can't be quite as dumb as you make out . . .' He paused and I waited. 'Your Mom is staying two nights, just two nights, Nik. Surely it can't be too hard to be nice to her for a fleeting visit.'

21

He's right, it shouldn't be too hard, but it will be.

I was aware that the fault lay with me, that I was carrying a perceived injury long after it should have healed, that my feelings were immature, to say the least, in someone of my age. I wasn't a teenager, for heaven's sake. *But there are some people who are so different from you that they get under your skin and make you itch as soon as they appear. My mother is one of those people.*

'Will you try,' Jack kissed me, his mouth full of crumbs, 'to be kind? Or it's going to be embarrassing, especially as she's meeting me for the first time.'

'Of course,' I said, 'Pollyanna is my middle name.'

'Who?'

I grinned at him. 'Just an American goody-goody schoolgirl book.'

When Jack had gone I wandered round the house tidying, trying to see all we had done here with my mother's eyes. Then I took towels up to the spare room, which had its own balcony, and I looked out over the bay and then stared down at the bed my mother would sleep in. It seemed strange to think of someone I hadn't seen for over three years lying there tonight.

Disturbing; a sudden mix of my two, so different, lives. One I had wanted to leave behind me, so that I could be born anew, slough off that old teenage skin and turn into someone else, perhaps the person I was now. I had come so far, to another culture and another continent, and it seemed suddenly as if my mother was following me, as if to remind me of the shadows I left and the person I once was. I didn't want to be reminded.

The baby was moving now and I could feel the tiny flutter of life; a small, tentative movement to alert me to his presence, his curled life within me, slowly growing into the person he will be. And the person he will be will want to know his family and his English roots and his grandmother.

I knew, in the moment I stood by the bed my mother would sleep in, that I wanted them to know each other. I couldn't deprive either of a relationship I had needed in my childhood.

I stared out to the yachts in the bay, beyond the garden Jack and I had created out of jungle, and remembered how hard I sometimes thought my grandmother was on my mother, yet I could do no wrong. I went out onto the balcony and breathed deeply, the sun warm on my face, and I swore that I would try my hardest to welcome my mother. She was obviously lonely without Fergus and seemed to have thrown herself into painting and studying the history of art.

I smiled. Fleur was quite brave really, to start again on something new at her age. *I will be nice. I will.* Jack was right, it was time to move on. After all, I didn't know when I'd see her again.

I went downstairs and put my hat on against the sun and set off for my jungle trail. We had joined an experiment to cull the possums. They were ripping the trees to pieces and Jack and I had placed poison as small enticements, fixed to the trunks of trees.

I wished they weren't so cute. I wished they looked like rats and then I wouldn't feel so bad. But I knew it had to be done, we had more than enough stripped trees that were going to die on our land.

As I walked I felt a sense of achievement; it was an adventure, this life I shared with Jack. There were years ahead of us, preserving and finding new ways of conserving land that could never be tamed, nor would we want it to be. All these acres were becoming familiar, becoming home after years of nomadic existence. I never thought I could settle anywhere.

I hadn't planned to get pregnant, although I knew time was ticking. There was so much to do and pregnancy had reined me in. Jack's face was enough, though, when I'd told him. So instead of gardening in the heat I could only walk round checking things, feeding the hens and gently weeding up near the house, planting rows of vegetables that struggled in the poor soil.

As if by some tacit agreement, neither Jack nor I mentioned it to each other, but we both wondered if our time here would have to come to an end with a child. We lived in the middle of nowhere, miles away from a doctor, school or human habitation. Children needed other children and I didn't want an only child, which is what I had become.

The horror and the loneliness when Saffie disappeared was like losing a limb that went on twitching with the loss of the other half of me,

I feel it, even now.

FIVE

Fleur woke early on the day of her flight to Singapore. She never drew her curtains and she saw it was the most beautiful day. The leaves of the tree outside were motionless. The day seemed to be holding its breath. A blackbird sang clear into the morning against the growl of cars in the distance as the city woke up. It felt like the first day of spring.

Fleur lay looking round her room, where the sun slanted across the floor highlighting the dust motes which hung and floated in the air. She felt a strange sad-happiness, when to be alive was almost enough in the moment of a bird singing; in the moment of sunlight on your hands; in the small awareness of yourself in a new day.

Since Fergus died she had learnt to be still and treasure these mornings, waking alone and listening, really listening, both to the sounds of a world waking up and to herself. The first moments of the day could reveal feelings she could not articulate or write down, but would sometimes attempt to capture in paint.

A lack of professional technique – for Fleur thought of

herself as an apprentice – could not hide the intensity behind her paintings. A fleeting spiritual second could transform a simple painting into a canvas that people stood in front of and gazed at, captivated by the power with which Fleur captured the enormity of loss alongside the budding awareness of something beyond herself that went on moving and growing within her.

The loss of a child ended innocence. To be pre-deceased by your child was the worst that could happen to a parent. It took a lifetime of walking towards a hope of understanding to realise that there was nothing to understand. Sense could never be made of a random wicked and meaningless act. This was the bleak knowledge you carried all your life like a second self, buried, but always with you.

Fleur, triggered by the sudden loss of Fergus, found that she could suddenly translate this knowledge into colour and texture and turn it into something people could relate to. Something they felt in the core of themselves, in the pit of their stomachs, in the ache of their throats as they stood staring at her large, brightly coloured landscapes full of heat and bustle. Their eyes drawn to the one small object or person within the picture that stood quite separate and alone.

Fleur did not know from where her inspiration came. Only that it came from some unexplored source and she painted fast and concentrated, to the exclusion of all else, in the silent nights and into the pale, cold dawn of another day.

As she lay staring at the tree outside her window, she felt as if she had already left this small terraced house and begun her journey of discovery to her daughter and to Hundertwasser's architecture, all without corners, all without angles, all part of the earth and its constant cycle of rebirth. She was aware of why she was drawn to his philosophy and architecture; it was connected indivisibly to her need for reparation with her daughter.

She felt in those first moments of sunlight that she might not return to this small house that she had shared with Fergus for so many years, or that even if she did, everything would be different, never quite the same again. Unease stirred, but she also had the sensation of moving inexorably towards something dark but necessary; that nebulous feeling that something was going to happen.

She got out of bed and pulled on Fergus's towelling robe, caught the scent from a vase of freesias the gallery had sent, which stood on her dressing table. All part of this safe life she led. She padded downstairs and drew back the sitting-room curtains. The man next door was wheeling his bicycle down his path, pausing at the gate as he always did to fix his cycle clips. The teacher two doors down was gunning the reluctant engine of her Fiesta. Fleur found she was listening for it to start and thinking, *This time tomorrow I will be in Singapore.*

Fleur looked down across the glinting wing of the plane onto acres of perfect white cloud the texture of fluffy mashed potato. She remembered as a child the thrill of believing those clouds were solid enough to sit on, that she could have jumped from one floury cushion to another.

The mystery of land mass, ocean and sky from a height never left her. The changing patterns and shape of mountains and desert and the progress of herself encapsulated in tons of moving metal remained a wonder of human engineering.

It was as if, once airborne, between lives and destinations, all normal, taken-for-granted things were rendered, by stress or fatigue, abnormal. As if she was circled by an odd tight silence, worn like a cloak to distance herself, making her progress, a stranger among strangers, infinitely obscure.

Travelling forward through time, arriving thousands of miles into an unfamiliar or distant landscape of tomorrow, imbued Fleur with an almost catatonic immobility and invisibility. She neither moved nor undid her seatbelt but sat and stared out at the wondrous mass of virgin cloud.

An old man on the aisle seat was telling the woman between them how he had built the pipeline down in the vast dry expanse of desert below them in Dubai. For thirteen years he had toiled in the unforgiving sun, taking water to the Bedouins. His skin told the truth of an engineer's harsh life in the sun. Unmistakable patches of skin cancer marked his hands and face like a badge of office.

Normally Fleur would have been fascinated by his reminiscing, but she wanted to remain in her no-man's land, devoid of social interaction, the telling of stories, the re-telling of lives. She loved it when the lights went out, when the blinds went down against the night outside and she could lie tiredly listening to the rustle of passengers, the dull *plom* of the bell as they asked for drinks, the swish of recycled air around the cabin, as inexorably they ploughed through the night sky to Singapore.

Singapore and another life. She thought of David, tried to conjure his face, his voice. But they would not come or came blurred like an unfocused faded photograph. The city contained so much that had been a part of her young life. She had spent time there as a child and a young adult. She had returned there a married woman, carrying the baby twins.

So much happiness. A beautiful couple who had it all.

28

Then, those small, relentless steps that led slowly but surely to tragedy.

Snatches of lines from somewhere popped into Fleur's head . . .

> *When the train starts, and the passengers are settled*
> *   [. . .]*
> *To the sleepy rhythm of a hundred hours.*
> *Fare forward, travellers! not escaping from the past*
> *Into different lives, or into any future;*
> *You are not the same people who left that station*
> *Or who will arrive at any terminus*

A sense of smell could unlock memories faster than the blink of an eye. Fleur could not tell what would leap out at her when she stepped into the shimmering heat and smell of a city where so much of her life had unfurled faster than she had had the wit to stop it.

SIX

Singapore, 1966

When Fleur saw David for the first time he was sitting on the edge of the pool at the Tanglin Club in Singapore City. She thought he was possibly the most graceful man she had ever seen. After her brother and the spotty youths she had travelled out from England with he seemed like a god.

She was fifteen and home for the long summer holidays. Her father, Peter Llewellyn, was colonel of a regiment on a three-year posting to Singapore. It was his second posting to the Far East and Fleur and her brother, Sam, had grown blasé with flying back and forth from boarding school in England. It was Singapore that felt like home.

They had both pretty much done their own thing that summer as their mother, Laura, bored with army life, was studying for an Open University degree, and she trusted Sam to keep an eye on Fleur.

David was on his first posting as a subaltern. He was dark and immensely charismatic rather than good-looking and he always seemed surrounded by teachers, nurses, or young service wives. He noticed Fleur, however, watching him covertly. She was still all angles, like a colt, but she walked like a ballet dancer and had a hint of the exotic, even at fifteen.

Fleur had her mother Laura's dark skin, inherited from a French grandmother, that tanned easily, and a way of rolling up her hair like her mother in a quick and particular French way. Sam's skin was fair like his father's and he moaned about it.

Fleur loved the water and both she and Sam were excellent swimmers having been taught professionally by a Singaporean coach. Peter had insisted on lessons for both his children as he loved sailing. People would stop what they were doing to watch Fleur dive. She would take time to position her limbs in the same way she perfected her dance steps, and once committed her body would arch and spring and break the water almost soundlessly.

David thought her dive was the most perfect thing he had ever seen. He watched her shrugging off Sam's friends and the schoolboys of her own age. She seemed perfectly self-contained and content with her own company. He was amused to see that, young as she was, she attracted the attention of the young naval officers who sailed into the naval base on the frigates, as well as the young army and RAF officers serving in Singapore.

They were all fairly cautious for she was the colonel's daughter, but Peter Llewellyn was not a fierce man, he was more like a vague scientist than an army officer. He was popular with his subalterns, and underneath his slightly bumbling exterior lay a first-class brain.

At weekends the family would drive down to the naval base for the swimming pool, evening barbecues, and films.

It was less stuffy than the Tanglin Club, which had more than its fair share of aging expats and high-ranking service wives who loved rules.

The Officers Club with a large pool faced out to the Straits of Malacca and looked down on the harbour and dry dock below. When the frigates were in, the navy would throw constant parties and Fleur never lost the thrill of being piped aboard. She would walk with Laura in front of Sam and her father, male eyes swivelled their way. The ships were often at sea for some time and any woman from fifteen to fifty was made to feel glamorous and witty. Sam was allowed to drink moderately as he was nearly eighteen. Fleur was not and Laura watched her like a hawk.

It was an incident at a cocktail party on board a small naval frigate that brought David and Fleur together. As they were piped aboard the sun hung low over the Straits, the sky flaring and fired by scarlet and orange. When darkness came, it came swiftly: no dusk, just velvety blackness. Fleur and Sam stood with a group of young sub-lieutenants drinking on the top deck. Her brother was eagerly discussing sailing, and Fleur, a little awed by so much attention, was swallowing a mixed-fruit cocktail rather fast as she practised the art of flirting.

She caught sight of her parents circulating from time to time and was impressed with her mother's practised habit of throwing back her dark hair and laughing hugely; of putting a hand lightly on a young man's arm and leaning towards him to catch his words, as if he was the most fascinating man in the room.

Fleur wasn't quite ready for that yet, but she did practise the head-tossing and smiling up into young, tanned faces. The more glasses of fruit juice she had the better she seemed to get at this. A small warm wind blew in to the harbour bringing with it the smell of spices and petrol and rotting vegetation. A plump sub-lieutenant kept topping her up from a jug snatched from a passing waiter. Sam, suddenly aware of Fleur flushed and laughing louder than usual, moved over to her.

'Fleur, you're not drinking, are you?'

'No. Just fruit juice and mint. Promise.'

'OK.' He looked at her closely for a second and then turned back to the group of young men. Fleur leant over the rail and looked down at the dark water. It looked invitingly cool.

'Do you ever swim from the ship?' she asked one of the naval officers.

'Bit of a way down,' the plump one said, laughing.

'It's not that far,' Fleur replied.

Plump officer stared at her lazily. 'I can't see a girl doing it.'

Fleur looked down, feeling dizzy, but it did not seem that much of a leap. No more than a diving board. She moved forward away from the crush of people.

'You think I'm too scared to jump?'

'I'll put a bet on it.'

The other officers stirred uneasily. 'Come on, let's go below and get something to eat, Fleur. Take no notice of Billy Bunter.'

'Of course she won't take any notice. She's a girl.'

Fleur moved fast, climbed the rail and put both her legs over. She wasn't going to dive because her skirt would come up over her head and that would be undignified. She felt no fear at all, just exhilaration. She leapt into space.

The officers hurtled to the rail and looked down. One moved to the jug and picked it up and smelt it.

'You stupid bastard! You've been giving her Pimms. She's only a kid . . .'

David, making his way towards the group, saw Fleur leap over the side and plummet downwards. He took in the empty Pimms jug and the guilty and furtive fat officer. Fleur hit the water and disappeared. Someone was already undoing a lifebuoy. David leant over the rail with the other men, waiting for her head to appear. It did not.

Fleur, plummeting through dark water, wondered vaguely but without panic why she was still effortlessly headed downwards. It was not an unpleasant feeling, just interesting.

David threw his jacket off and dived, closely followed by the fat officer and Sam.

Everyone else held their breath. Senior ranks, alerted, moved to the rail with sudden alarm, demanding to know what the hell was going on.

Underwater, David saw Fleur now beginning to rise to the surface. He grabbed her and hauled her upwards, helped by the fat officer. As her head rose above the water she sobered abruptly, took a huge shaky breath, choking.

Sam grabbed her under her armpits and kicked his way back to the ladder, where two naval ratings lifted her up onto the deck and wrapped her in a blanket. Laura bent to her daughter, relieved, angry and embarrassed in equal measure.

The captain, furious, quickly assessed the situation and sent his junior officers to their quarters until he could deal with them. Peter Llewellyn turned to him without raising his voice.

'If I accept an invitation I do so in the knowledge that my family are guests and as such my daughter is perfectly safe. Fleur does not drink. She knows that if she drinks she will be barred from all parties. There is a difference between high spirits and mindless stupidity. I do hope that your officers will be made fully aware that their crass behaviour could well have resulted in my fifteen-year-old daughter being drowned.'

He turned, white-faced, and gathered his wife and children. The party came to an abrupt end. Uncomfortable, people drifted away, back down the gangplank to the club where they could eat dinner and gossip about the evening.

Peter Llewellyn turned to David. 'Thank you, David. You acted quickly. Go to the M.O. and get yourself a jab. The water is polluted. I'll see you tomorrow.'

'Sir,' David said quietly, unnerved by his colonel's anger, which he had never seen before.

Fleur was being bundled into the car, still not entirely sober or realising quite what she had done. Sam said miserably, 'Dad, it wasn't Fleur's fault, honestly. There's so much fruit in those Pimms that you can't taste the gin. Fleur doesn't even like drink.'

Laura, getting Fleur into a hot bath soon afterwards, did not want to know the details. Her two concerns were the fact that they had been the centre of a stupid and avoidable incident and Fleur, by leaping inanely into the polluted water, had caused this. She was abrupt and short with her daughter.

It was Annie, the amah, who took Fleur hot chocolate and her father who sat on her bed while she wept with humiliation. Peter adored Fleur. He did not want her to grow up too quickly but neither did he want to deprive her of having fun. He wanted her to look back on this time in the Far East with excitement. His children were almost grown

35

up, would soon be gone. This would be the last posting they would all have together.

He also believed that people were basically decent. Tonight had been gross stupidity, not evil intent, but he advised Fleur to be more aware of the things young men got up to and what they handed her to drink.

'If it had been one of Sam's friends, I guess I would have been on my guard, Dad. But I was with you, so I didn't think . . .'

That was precisely why her father had been so angry.

'I've rung the doctor,' he said. 'Go with your mother and get a jab tomorrow, just to be safe.'

'Oh! Why did I jump? So stupid! Everyone will be laughing at me.'

'No, they won't,' Peter smiled. 'Sam's friends will envy your panache and bravery in leaping that far for a bet.'

But Fleur was not thinking of Sam's friends, she was wondering what Lt David Montrose thought of her.

The next morning the plump naval officer appeared outside Peter Llewellyn's office. He apologised profusely. He had called to let the colonel know he was resigning his commission and that no other officer had been involved.

Peter, looking at him after a night's sleep, thought this penalty a little excessive for one evening's intoxicated foolishness. He invited the captain of the frigate up to the mess for lunch and they decided on a regime of a hundred hours of punishment watches and that his promotion would be delayed. He had jumped in the water after Fleur and he was deeply sorry.

Laura invited David over to their quarter in Singapore for supper to thank him. He brought orchids. Small bee orchids for Laura. Pure white for Fleur. She took them to her room and put the vase on her dressing table. They lasted a long time.

Peter and his subaltern discovered they had a shared love of classical music. After that night David would drive from the naval base to go to concerts with Peter and Laura. He started to sail with the family at weekends and sit and talk to Sam and Fleur at the club barbecues.

One weekend there was a film of *The Tale of Two Cities* on at the naval base. Fleur, sitting with Sam, thought with a jolt how like a young Dirk Bogarde David was. That thing they did with their eyes, half-closed as they watched you. How when they said something quite innocuous it could sound like a caress. The something gentle but stomach-churningly sexy about the movements of a man who had a beautiful body.

Yet there was also something trustworthy about David. It was why Laura and Peter never worried about Fleur or Sam when they were with him. Swimming, sailing or dancing with the young, David could always be relied upon to see them safely home.

When Fleur was back at school in England, she lived for the Easter holidays. When she returned to Singapore after her sixteenth birthday, the mouths of the men and boys round the pool literally dropped when she appeared. She was not a sweet schoolgirl any longer and Laura saw this immediately. Saw the *knowingness* in Fleur. The innocence of being an attractive child had flown. She had become, overnight, it seemed to her parents, a stunningly beautiful young woman, quite aware of the effect she had on men, young or old.

Oddly, Fleur realised with a pang, her budding new confidence in herself seemed to distance David, as if he too was unnerved by her rapid transference from sweet adolescent to full-blown feminine beauty. It was years before she understood the dilemma she posed for David by growing up so quickly.

SEVEN

At lunchtime I locked the house up, drove round to the marina and sat waiting for Jack. He had rung to say he'd taken the afternoon off and we were going to have lunch together on the seafront in Paihia. I sat in the shade of a tree, a book in my lap, watching the Maoris who were often there diving for oysters off the concrete pier, collecting them in great piles to cart away in their aged pick-ups.

Petrol from the boat engines lay in purple-green pools on the surface of the water, but it did not seem to worry them. They called out cheerfully to their beautiful raggedy children who watched with their legs dangling in the water, their white teeth suddenly dazzling at some private joke.

A young Maori boy was poling an ancient canoe around the edges of the bay in the shallows by the trees, bending and digging his pole into the mud, his arm muscles flexing as he began to make it skim across the water, gaining confidence and pace with each stroke.

Out of nowhere came a memory. So slight it was a floater dancing in front of my eyes; a second, a fleeting second of remembrance. A long, empty beach at evening and a

Malaysian fisherman poling fast across the horizon as the sun faded. He was silhouetted in black, like a cut-out against the dying sun, before he disappeared into the suddenness of a tropical night. Suddenly, behind me a shadowy figure appeared from nowhere, sliding past me away fast into the darkness; gone before I could turn.

The image faded abruptly leaving me full of unease. I saw Jack coming towards me and I got heavily to my feet and walked towards him. Whenever I saw him from a distance I felt a rush of gratitude. He was a lovely, uncomplicated man who made life easy; made loving effortless.

We got to Kerikeri early and Jack immediately got talking to people he knew, not difficult in a small place with a tiny landing strip. I paced up and down watching the sky, imagining Fleur emerging from the plane, getting into our ancient car, viewing our house for the first time. I wanted the time to come and go in a flash, leaving us as we were, content and hidden in our own lives, without any outside interruptions to halt the succession of each day.

The speck in the sky appeared and everyone stood looking skyward, jangling car keys, waiting. There were mutters and sometimes ribald murmurs. Most families, it seemed, had wanted and not so wanted visitors about to descend from the small jaw of the aircraft.

Jack threw his arm around me as the little two-engined plane circled and landed. Steps were wheeled out, and as the aircraft door was thrown open I realised that I was hardly breathing. Would Fleur be first out? Last?

People descended singly, blinking as they emerged. We watched everyone get off the plane and still we stood staring at the now empty doorway, waiting, but my mother did not appear.

'Oh dear,' Jack said.

'Oh God. I might have known.'

'Did you check she was on this flight?'

'Yes. I also checked her flight from Singapore was on schedule.'

'OK. Let's go and talk to someone at the desk.'

The girl looked down her list. Yes, Mrs Campbell was on the passenger list. The girl got up and went out and talked to the two pilots and then came back. Mrs Campbell had not taken the flight from Auckland, despite calls over the Tannoy.

Was it possible, Jack asked, for her to make a telephone call to see if Mrs Campbell had been on the flight from Singapore to Auckland?

The girl looked irritated as I rummaged in my bag for Fleur's flight number from Singapore. She obviously wanted to go off-duty. 'I'll try, but you might have to do it yourself from home . . . the lines get busy.'

'That would be great of you. Melanie, isn't it? So sorry to be a nuisance . . .' Jack said smoothly, giving her his most toothy and boyish grin. It did the trick.

She spoke on the phone for some time, obviously being transferred from one department to another. Then she looked at us and nodded. 'Oh,' she said. 'Oh.' She shot me a look. 'Yes. Someone's here in Kerikeri to meet her. Her daughter. Yes. OK. I'll put her on.' She handed me the receiver.

'Hello?' I said. 'I'm Nikki Montrose, Mrs Campbell's daughter.'

'Hi there.' The Kiwi voice was relaxed, wanted to re-assure. 'Now, Mrs Montrose, try not to worry, perhaps there is a message waiting for you at home. Mrs Campbell was on the passenger list from Heathrow to Singapore but she was not on the second leg of her flight from Singapore to Auckland.'

'Did she book in for her flight to Auckland from Singapore airport? Did her luggage have to be offloaded when she didn't board?'

'No. The information I have is that she did not return from her stopover in Singapore and the flight left without her.'

'Oh God,' I said.

'Could I have your home telephone number, Mrs Montrose? If we hear anything we'll contact you straight away, but what I advise is for you to contact her stopover hotel. Do you have the name of it?'

'Yes. It was the Singapore Hilton. It's Miss, by the way, I'm not married.'

'I'm sorry' the man said 'to hear that, Ms Montrose.'

Humour was the last thing I felt like responding to. I also caught a quick flash of regret cross Jack's face, because I didn't want to get married.

'It could be your mother has been taken ill or missed her flight for some reason and is booked on a later one . . .' I could hear him fiddling with his computer. 'She is not on any of the flights out of Singapore tonight or tomorrow . . . Sorry, I don't think I can help you further at the moment . . .'

'Thanks . . . you've helped all you can. Thank you for your time. If you hear anything you will contact—'

'Of course. No worries. Good luck, Ms Montrose. I'm sure you'll find your mother safe and well. Old people do go astray, you know.'

I laughed as I put the phone down. Fleur, old! Never. But she was vague.

We thanked Melanie and left the now deserted little terminal. As we drove slowly home I didn't know what to

42

think. I didn't know whether I was annoyed or anxious.

'It seems you were right, Nik, she has gone walkabout.' Jack looked at my face. 'Darlin', you really are worried something's happened to her?'

'I was being facetious before, Jack. Fleur is perfectly capable of travelling long distances. She spent her whole childhood doing it. How can you miss a plane on a stopover? A bus picks you up and deposits you, bang, at the airport. She knew we were meeting her. If something has happened why hasn't she rung us?'

'As soon as we get home we'll ring that Singapore hotel. There may be a message waiting for us.'

But there wasn't. Dark seemed to descend quickly and the house seemed oddly stilled. We had been poised waiting for Fleur. I didn't want her to be ill and alone in some huge hotel full of strangers.

I rang the Singapore Hilton and could not make the first girl understand what I wanted and needed to know. I could feel my voice rising and Jack took the phone and calmly went over it all again. Then he put his hand over the mouthpiece.

'They're getting the manager.'

Jack repeated his message once more and then listened. I watched his face change and he flashed me an anxious look. He gave the man our number and said, yes, we would ring later. He put the phone down and came over to me.

'Your mother booked in for one night only . . .' He hesitated. 'She didn't catch the airport bus when it came and no one could find her. Her luggage is still all in her room and she hasn't booked out of the hotel. No one has seen her since early yesterday morning.'

I stared at him, felt the blood drain from my face. Something really had happened to Fleur.

Jack took my hand. 'I'm going to run you a bath and then make you toast. You're getting into bed. Do you hear me? We've had one fright with the baby, we don't want another . . .' He paused.

'What?' I asked. 'What is it?'

'The manager is going to contact the police if she doesn't return tonight. We're to ring the hotel in the morning. They are going to ask Fleur to ring us immediately if she comes back.'

My back ached and Jack ran me a bath and made me get in it. I was glad to be in bed. He came and sat on the edge of it with toast, which we shared. Then he brought the phone upstairs where we could hear it and I checked my mobile was switched on. He went for a shower and then got into bed and held me tight, and even though he warmed me I could not stop imagining all the terrible things that could have happened to Fleur.

Jack always could fall asleep straight away and he did tonight. He had been up since 5.30. I lay there against him thinking it served me bloody well right. I had not wanted my mother to come and now she was probably dead in some alleyway in Singapore. Or . . . Or what? If she had been taken ill she would have had her passport on her, and hotel and flight details. If she was in hospital we would know by now. *Which meant she was in trouble. Or dead.*

I shivered and carried on circuitous conversations in my head. It was a long time since I had prayed. I tried to remember what my mother had said to me on our one and only telephone conversation, how her voice had sounded, and I couldn't.

If my mother was dead, I would be to blame for not checking all her plans in detail, like any daughter would have done. For not phoning or texting or letting her know

44

she could contact me and not feel a nuisance. For not monitoring her progress thousands of miles towards me. For not caring enough; for being wickedly self-absorbed and childishly selfish.

Could it be she had gone looking for some piece of architecture and got lost or gone further than she'd meant to? Or maybe her phone had been stolen and she couldn't contact us. Maybe she had met an acquaintance or colleague and was staying with them. I was clutching at straws.

I lay very still with a terrible sense of prescience. More than that, fear lay under my skin as if something dark was crawling my way. Jack breathed beside me and the night stretched on and on and the dawn came, surprising me with its suddenness.

The phone went and I leapt upright. It was a Detective Sergeant James Mohktar who spoke perfect English. He was ringing from the Singapore Hilton. He asked me if I was Mrs Campbell's next of kin. Her luggage was still in her room and her disappearance was worrying. Had she contacted me? Was there any place I could think of that she might have gone to?

No, I told him. She had not contacted me and I had no idea where she could possibly have gone. 'She once lived in Singapore a long time ago, but she doesn't know anyone there now. I'm very worried, this is not like her, or the fact that she hasn't been in touch . . .'

There was a pause and then the detective said, 'You are advising me that Mrs Campbell is definitely missing and that you have no explanation whatsoever for her disappearance?'

'Yes, I am. My mother was flying out to us in New Zealand via Singapore. She caught the plane from Heathrow to Singapore, but did not catch the second leg of her journey

45

to Auckland. She was then due to fly from Auckland to Kerikeri where she knew we were waiting to meet her. If she'd missed her flight or was ill she would have let us know.'

'OK, Mrs Montrose. We are going to make a search of the hotel now. My men will make inquiries to try to ascertain her whereabouts and safety and which member of staff may have had a conversation with her and who saw her last. Then I will ring you again . . .' He paused. 'If we do not find your mother, I am afraid you must fly to Singapore to register her officially missing and identify her belongings. She did always carry her passport about her person?'

'Yes,' I said. 'I'm sure she wouldn't have left her passport in a hotel room. She would have kept it with her.'

'We will' the detective sergeant said, 'maintain hope, Mrs Montrose, that there is a rational explanation. I will ring you this evening. Try not to worry. Good day.'

I crumpled on the edge of the bed, Jack's anxious eyes on me. Was God or fate visiting some sick and terrible retribution on me? Was my mother too going to disappear without trace? Her body never found, so that I would never know what happened or where she had gone, who took her or why?

Just like Saffie. Snatched from under our noses; disappearing from us without trace twenty-eight years ago.

EIGHT

It was time to leave for the airport. Fleur walked round the army quarter which would soon be empty of all their personal things. She moved slowly, touching the heavy mahogany furniture, staring past the small Malay house that chimed in the window of the twins' room, the sound as familiar as breathing in the easy, somnolent days spent there.

Far below her came the dull thud of the naval base and the hot morning breeze brought to her a vague smell of sea mixed with frangipani blossom from the garden. Fleur stood looking out, invoking the image of David moving through the house with her.

Surely if she closed her eyes for a moment she could shift time back, change by sheer will the sequence of events. Make it all a bad dream. A small tragedy you spot suddenly in a paper, the abrupt end of someone else's life.

The sun flowed across the polished floor and touched one arm, making the other instantly cold. She shivered and moved to the front of the house. There it was, the black car moving sleekly up the road towards her, small pennant flying. Fergus would get out, immaculate in his starched uniform, looking as pale and stunned as Fleur; a familiar presence to take them to the airport and the long journey home to bury David.

Fleur turned and walked through the house and down the steps from the kitchen, and stood watching the twins and Ah Heng crouched outside the amah's room. Ah Heng was filling little bags for their journey and the three of them squatted outside her door on the concrete, heads bent together, chatting in Cantonese like noisy sparrows. From her open doorway Chinese pinkle-ponkle music issued softly.

Two fair heads, one dark smooth one. Ah Heng, feeling Fleur's stillness, looked up and in that fleeting unguarded moment Fleur saw the bleakness in the amah's flat, impassive face. The two women stared at each other, accepting an ending where nothing in either of their lives could ever be the same again. No contentment so taken for granted; no happiness so whole.

In lives at each end of a cultural divide, they would, Fleur knew, remember in quiet moments their innocent rivalry for the twins' love. Here in a house that had been filled with the cheerful life of Master and husband; a place the three of them had experienced together the thrill and joy of the twins, the flourishing of small lives.

'Time, Missie?' Ah Heng broke the silence.

'Yes, Ah Heng. The car's coming up the road. Saffie, Nikki, come on, time to go.'

The twins looked up but hung on to Ah Heng. Their mother had an unnerving listlessness, a restless preoccupation with something that lay beyond them. It was as if she could no longer see them, as if they had suddenly become frighteningly invisible.

Ah Heng gathered their bags and led them firmly up the steps past Fleur, through the kitchen to their bathroom where she made them use the loo and washed their hands and faces one last time. She checked that the small jumpers she had bought them were still in their cases. Missie had a habit of changing over the clothes she bought the twins from Chinatown. She led them down the front stairs to the open front door where the black official car was crouched, waiting for them.

Mohammed, the driver, had stowed their luggage in the boot. Fergus stood beside Fleur. He was watching the twins with Ah Heng. The children seemed passive, too devoid of emotion. Had Fleur given them something?

Ah Heng let go of the children's hands and moved towards Fleur. 'Missie take care. Missie have chil'ren think about. If Missie no come back to hand house over to army men, Missie write me all news of babies, please.'

She held out both hands and Fleur took them, clasping them tight, and tears sprang up between the two women.

'I have to come back, Ah Heng. There is an army memorial service for Master . . .' She hesitated. 'I will leave the babies in England . . . I think it is best . . . I don't want them to have to say goodbye to you twice . . . and . . .'

Ah Heng nodded. 'Yes, Missie. I stay here. I clean house. I wait till you return. I help you hand over to army men . . .' She pulled her hands gently from Fleur's.

Fleur whispered, 'Ah Heng, you must look after yourself. I know the High Commission want you back. You must leave when they need you . . .' Her voice broke. 'Ah Heng, thank you, thank you for everything . . .'

'Missie go . . .' Ah Heng turned away in misery and bent to the twins and held them hard as Fergus gently pushed Fleur into the back of the car. Ah Heng hugged them tight to her and closed her eyes to breathe in their skin. She placed her small, flat nose to their cheeks, took a huge breath, so that they were with her always, clear as their laughter, the childish smell of them. Her babies captured forever, not only in the photographs she would display in her next job, but hidden inside her always.

Fergus went round the car, picked the twins up quickly and placed them in the back of the car with Fleur. Then he went to sit by the driver. 'Drive, Mohammed. Drive away quickly.'

Mohammed started the car. Ah Heng stood like a statue, hands clasped to her cheeks, when suddenly the rear door of the car was thrown open and the twins leapt out screaming like small banshees. They rushed at Ah Heng, threw themselves at her, clutching her black baggy trousers, hanging on to her legs.

'No . . . Heng . . . Heng . . . No . . . Heng . . . You come too . . . You come . . .'

Ah Heng folded to the ground in a fluid movement, holding them to her, and her tears spurted, cascaded down her face, soaking the heads of the children.

'Shit.' Fergus leapt out of the car, followed by Mohammed. 'We should have left five minutes ago.'

They tried to tear the twins from Ah Heng but they kicked and screamed hysterically. In the car Fleur sat immobile, staring straight ahead. She could not take any more.

'You . . .' Mohammed suddenly commanded the amah. 'You come airport with English babies . . . You calm . . . You tell babies must be good for English Missie or their dada not pleased. Come! You come, please, or I not get to airport in time.'

'It's a good idea,' Fergus said quickly. 'Would you mind, Ah Heng? We'll see you home again . . . We must leave now.'

Ah Heng glanced in the car at Fleur's blank white face. 'I come. I lock up quick.'

In the car Ah Heng wiped the twins' faces. They had stopped crying and she put her arms around them and whispered to them in Cantonese, admonishing them softly. *'You're big girls. No more crying. Look at Mama. She's very brave, yes? Well, twins too must be brave, take care of Mama for Ah Heng. Who takes care of Mama, if you do not?*

'Ah Heng wants letters to say you are being good girls, then Heng will know you are very grown-up children and Heng will be very happy you are no trouble for Mama. This is what your dada would want . . . and who knows? Ah Heng's brother might come to England, and bring Ah Heng to work in cousin's Cantonese restaurant . . . Who knows, twins might come back to Singapore one day to see Heng. Heng is always here. Ah Heng will send Mama her new address. No more now. No more crying or Heng will get cross. England is a very good place. You will be very, very happy with your grandparents in the big English house . . . You'll see. You listening to Ah Heng?'

'Yes,' Nikki said.

'Yes,' Saffie said, putting her thumb in her mouth.

Ah Heng took it out again. 'You too big girl for that. You no do. I tell you . . . crooked teeth . . .' And she held them close and rocked them to her as the car purred along.

In the mirror Fergus saw that Fleur was still looking blankly out of the window. She was leaving all the comforting to her amah. She did not look, touch or reassure the twins. She did not feign cheerfulness or bravery. Fergus felt unease. Those little girls had just lost a father who idolised them. The life they were leaving was all they had ever known. Had Fleur even acknowledged her children's loss? Or was she only capable of feeling her own?

If I long to comfort my godchildren, how is it Fleur can bear not to?

The coffin was waiting. The RAF plane to Brize Norton had already loaded its normal passengers. A small contingent of top brass and David's squadron were waiting to march David to the plane, on his last journey home.

Ah Heng handed the twins out of the car to Fleur, who took their hands like a robot. The twins turned once to blow Ah Heng a kiss with their hands, their lower lips wobbling, and then they turned back and walked towards the coffin, which was being slow-marched to a Scottish lament to the rear of the plane.

Fleur, Saffie and Nikki all shivered in the heat. Like a sleepwalker, Fleur shook hands and accepted the words of condolence and comfort said all over again. Fergus hugged her briefly and painfully and for a moment Fleur clung to him.

'I wish you could come to the funeral.'

'So do I, Fleur. But we'll all give David a wonderful memorial service when you come back.' There was a big exercise coming up in Malaya and it was impossible for Fergus to leave now. He was doing David's job as well as his own and one of the squadron pilots was still in hospital. 'Take care. I'll see you in two or three weeks.' He shook her gently. 'The twins need you . . . You'll have help keeping them occupied on the plane. I'll ring Laura and Peter when I get back to the mess to say the flight has just left.'

'Thank you,' Fleur said dully.

Fergus suddenly wanted to shake her, wanted to say, *This is me. For God's sake, Fleur. React. The man we both loved is dead and he was a huge part of my life as well as yours. Don't shut your children out . . . or me.*

As the coffin disappeared into the bowels of the plane Fergus felt like weeping. 'Keep an eye on her,' he said to one of the air stewards, as Fleur and the children climbed the steps into the plane. 'She's still in shock and I'm not sure if she is capable of looking after her little girls.'

'Don't worry, Sir,' the corporal said. 'We've got army wives on board. We've also made arrangements for the stops at Gan and Cyprus. The colonel's wife is going to be with her.'

Fergus walked back to the car and stood to watch the huge plane prepare for takeoff. The heat beat down and drenched his uniform, shimmered over the tarmac in the lee of the plane revving up and moving noisily along the runway, gathering itself for flight.

Last week he and David had played tennis. They'd swum together at the club . . . But that had been before the barbecue . . . the barbecue where Fleur had worn the shimmery red dress to shock. And it *had* shocked the older officers' wives, and caused admiration and envy in almost everybody else.

At first, David had been highly amused at her entrance, had let out a whistle of pride. Fergus had felt startled, almost dismayed. Fleur was making a sudden statement. Her beauty hit him between the eyes, but this wasn't the Fleur he knew. She was glittery and hard and . . . hurting. It had been disturbing. As if that night she had to prove to David, and perhaps to him, the power she had to attract. It had been awful watching them hurt each other and using him to do it. He loved them both.

He watched the plane carrying his friend's body take off in a roar over the paddy fields, signalling an ending: to everything.

Ah Heng, in the back of the cool, air-conditioned car, watched her babies fly away in a plane like a heavy, pregnant bird. The sun radiated in waves over the ground where it had been standing. She watched the glint of silver in the sky until it was a speck and wondered if she would ever fill the hole that was opening making each and every breath painful.

Every time a British baby left it hurt, but this time it tore out her heart. There were no babies in her next job, back in the city with the British High Commission. No babies at all.

NINE

As the plane started to descend for Changi airport, Fleur looked down, but the paddy fields had gone. No black-clad figures, knee-deep in water, bent to the rice in their wide-brimmed hats.

Yet, excitement gripped her. If she closed her eyes she could almost be a child, a young wife again, with a safe, happy life and children before her.

The smells as the doors were thrown open were as she remembered. Shimmering wet heat, petrol, and spices. No frangipani this time; the vague, pervading scent of blossom was missing.

Fleur sat in an airport bus as the rain sprayed out from the wheels, splashing cyclists. The luggage, balanced precariously at the front, wobbled and swung behind the driver. The heat was swallowed behind cloud and air-conditioning. The other passengers were as dazed and tired as Fleur, and the bus was oddly silent.

Fleur, looking out at a changed landscape, still felt she knew the basic geography of it. She had driven so often on this Changi Road, to the sailing club, to the military hospital, to see friends. She supposed all the buildings must still be there in a different guise. Was the prison still standing; the atmosphere around it heavy with despair and death; full of the ghosts of captured servicemen imprisoned there by the Japanese in the Second World War.

As they reached the outskirts of the city she recognised the long Bukit Timar Road and thought she remembered some of the older buildings hidden beneath and between vast skyscrapers. Land reclamation started so long ago had continued and the city had spread out into places once underwater. Spread out and out and up.

The bus weaved in and out of the fronts of hotels, dropping passengers and their spreading pools of luggage in front of ornate glass doors with tall turbaned Indian porters. Fleur and two couples were the last to be dropped off at the Hilton in Orchard Road. An old couple who looked on the point of collapse and a young, possibly honeymoon, couple. They all smiled wanly at each other, tiredness and jetlag making everything distant.

The young couple hauled their suitcases up the hotel steps before the porters had time to rush out with their trolleys and admonish them for even thinking of seeing to their own luggage. Fleur and the old couple stood waiting, knowing, unlike England, that their cases would be loaded carefully onto a trolley, and when they had checked in they would be seen efficiently into the lift and up to their rooms.

Once in her room the young Malaysian porter showed Fleur how everything worked and she dived into her bag to tip him, trying to find her Singapore dollars. The porter held his hand up. 'Later, later, you tired, Mem.'

Fleur smiled gratefully and thanked him. *'Terima kasih.'* He gave her a wide smile. *'Sama-sama. Selamat tidur.'* *'Selamat tidur.'*

Night was approaching. Fleur went to the window and looked down on Orchard Road, at the streams of traffic heading home or into the city to eat and shop. The pavements were full of people and the volume would increase as the night wore on. Singapore was a city for serious shoppers.

She had wanted to be in the centre of the city where she could walk to shop for presents for Nikki and Jack. Right here, in the centre where, even after all this time, much would be familiar. Fleur smiled, leaving the curtains open, and went to the fridge and took out water. Then she had a shower and lay on the bed, the hum of the air-conditioning masking the noise of anything outside the room.

Fleur knew she must not sleep or she would never come up from the depth of jetlag, but she closed her eyes and let her body relax. She longed to phone Nikki, to say, *Here I am in the Singapore Hilton and so, so looking forward to seeing you the day after tomorrow, darling; to meeting Jack; to looking at your lovely face, which I miss every single day* . . .

But she couldn't. She had brought a phone that would work anywhere in the world, but she could not ring her estranged daughter. There were no small intimacies or concerns or chit-chat that could be exchanged as comfort. Not yet.

It was the thing Fleur missed most of all with the death of Fergus, having anyone to tell, *I got here! I'm fine! You needn't have worried. Really, the journey was wonderful . . . no problems at all.*

The room hummed around her. She knew she must get up if she wanted to go out into the streets before she collapsed. So strange that hotels could be the loneliest places in the world when they contained hundreds of people.

She dressed quickly in clean clothes and went out into the corridor. There was a lounge eating area on the same floor which served snacks and light food. Fleur ordered a coffee and helped herself to some fruit and nuts beautifully laid out on a table. She went and sat in a corner where she would not be self-conscious on her own and looked out at the night.

As she stood in the lift going down to the foyer the old couple joined her. 'We're just going to have a quick look round the hotel and call it a day, we're much too tired to explore tonight.'

Fleur smiled. 'I'm just going out for an hour or so.'

'Well, you be careful, on your own . . .'

'I think,' Fleur said, 'Singapore is probably the safest place I know. Certainly safer than London. Sleep well.'

She swung out of the glass doors and down the steps into the street and turned right and walked slowly up Orchard Road. She wanted to buy Nikki a Chinese blouse, green silk. All the little night markets seemed to have disappeared, to be replaced by glittering designer shops and huge stores. There was even a Marks & Spencer. Fleur, tired, did not think she could tackle working out the currency tonight. She would scout and return in the morning. She walked, jostled and pushed by the good-natured crowds. There were no rickshaws any more and she was glad. She used to be horrified at the huge varicose veins that stood out like spreading roots of trees on the rickshaw driver's legs.

She stood on a corner waiting for the lights to change and suddenly saw, across the road in a space between the shops, a children's play area and some market stalls. She crossed the road with the surge of people and went to look.

There it was, pale green, the perfect Shantung blouse with small daisies embroidered on the front. Fleur held it up to judge its size. Of course she couldn't be sure, but it seemed to be about right. She saw it had a price tag on and hesitated to barter. Perhaps people no longer bartered?

Did she have enough Singapore dollars? She opened her wallet to look. The small Cantonese stallholder touched her hand. 'I take card. You have this one too, velly good for you. Good colour for you.' She took up a red blouse and held it against Fleur.

Fleur bought both blouses and a length of batik for a sarong for Jack and paid with her credit card. She was feeling sick and dizzy now with the heat and the crowds and she turned back towards the hotel. Even at this time of night the sweat trickled down the inside of her shirt and thin trousers.

Back in her room she made tea, nibbled a biscuit and fell into bed feeling pleased with herself. She had at least small gifts to give to Nikki and Jack. She fell asleep almost instantly.

In the morning Fleur woke disorientated and went to draw the curtains. The steamy rain of yesterday had gone and the day glared and flashed against the window. She felt excited and rested. She had the whole day, until four thirty, when the airport bus would come to collect her. She could do anything she liked.

She made coffee, showered quickly, and put on a thin dress against the heat outside. She opened the glass doors and walked out onto her balcony that looked down on Orchard Road. She leant out and watched the cars snaking along bumper to bumper through the city and saw what you could not see from the road.

A line of trees edging the pavements made a long green snake through the heart of the city, as if the trees had sprung from the roots of the buildings, so that the city could constantly be reminded of the jungle from which it had sprung.

Hundertwasser! Fleur felt astonished to see so clearly and by chance a view he must have looked down on, here or in some other eastern city that steamed with heat and vibrant colour. The ghosts of the jungle and dead tribes rising from the pavements in leafy green, their wavering branches, the arms of the dead, re-created to live again, to breathe again in the heart of a city. Forever alive, forever continuing the pattern of life. A city that had once been jungle.

The Garden of the Happy Dead.

If I had not come, if I had not stood on this balcony eight floors up, I would not have seen so extraordinarily dramatically what Hundertwasser meant and what he practiced so clearly in his colours and architecture.

She smiled, drinking in the snake of green trees below her, a wavy line through the flash of metal cars and spirals of buildings. She could have read and read and studied and stood in front of one of his paintings or buildings, but she might never have glimpsed the exactness of meaning, that bolt of sudden understanding of something deep and fundamental which drew her and thousands of others to his work and philosophy.

Fleur turned away, back into the room. It was like a small sign from the gods. Hope for her and her daughter; new life in the grandchild to come. She ate a quick breakfast and took the lift downstairs. The young Malaysian porter stood by the huge glass doors. He beamed at her.

'*Selamat pagi! Apa khabar?*'

Fleur beamed back. '*Baik.* OK. *Terima kasih.* Can I walk to the Botanical Gardens from here?'

'Yes, Mem, turn left out of hotel. About fifteen minutes' walk.'

'*Terima kasih.*'

'*Sama-sama.*'

Outside on the steps she blinked in the glare and put on her sunglasses. She turned left, waited for the lights and crossed the intersection. The heat bore down on her. Fleur lifted her arm for a taxi. She could not walk far in this heat without melting and she wanted to explore the gardens.

The taxi turned off Bukit Timar Road and into a wide road full of colonial-type buildings that had probably been embassy houses. At the end of one leafy road stood the Botanical Gardens with its gated entrance. Fleur remembered none of this. The taxi took her inside the gates and dropped her in front of the building where groups of taxi drivers waited for fares. She walked through the entrance and inside.

Years ago, there had been no formal entrance. Fleur remembered entering from a small side gate off a busy road. It must have been at the other end of the gardens. It had been more of a park then; people picnicked on the grass. There had been one small place to eat and buy drinks. Amahs and Indian ayahs pushed prams or ran after toddlers and flitted like exotic butterflies round the small paths through the trees. There had been a fountain and in the pool fat yellow fish hid behind lily leaves. There had been monkeys swinging from the trees and down beside you to pinch your food. Grumbling and fighting up in the branches, their tails switching, their voices screeching ominously above you. *There had been a man in uniform leaning against a tree by the fountain, waiting for her.*

Fleur's heart pounded in memory as she walked the wide tended paths that were all signposted now. Large glasshouses stood on a hill and a new pavilion was being made. The grass was neatly kept and there were fewer trees to hide in the shade. Fewer places to hold hands when you should not; to kiss, shaking with the possibility that all might become well and whole again if you did not think, if you pretended for an afternoon away from the army base, away from the uniforms, in this one anonymous place in the centre of a city. If you clung to the only sure and safe person in a life so suddenly turned on its head.

Restaurants and cafés were now placed strategically in clearings. There was no anonymity any more. Wealthy Europeans and Chinese walked together, pushing expensive buggies full of children down the wide cleansed paths. It had all been sanitised and commercialised. It was beautiful still, but the gardens had lost their mystery. Without the monkeys and the deep shade of trees and the hint of danger, it was a place that could have been any botanical gardens anywhere in the world.

Fleur made her way to the Orchid House and bought a ticket. Instantly she was back in the army quarter in the naval base with Ah Heng bringing orchids back from the market and placing them in Chinese vases all over the house. Ah Heng arranging them just so, her stiff little back and dark glossy hair drawn back in a bun, bent to the blooms, her face inscrutable.

She took some photos, unable to compete with some Japanese tourists who had cameras the size of matchboxes. She stood still, watching water trickling on polished stones and small tendrils of ferns arranged against trees. One orchid stood in a wooden vase by a sculpture.

Ah Heng had slept in a little room in a block behind the kitchen with a lavatory and shower. Her small shuttered room had contained so much: an aged sewing machine, materials bought in Chinatown, chairs of ironing ready to bring into the house, toys and books for the twins. Baskets of personal things, hanging chimes, but always, always flowers for luck in a little wooden vase outside her door.

The heat trickled down the inside of Fleur's dress. She was not used to the humidity any more and her tongue stuck to her mouth. She had left her bottle of water in her room. She made her way slowly back to the café she had seen. The gardens were not the same, but she was glad she had come; they were still an oasis in the middle of the teeming city; still somewhere you would come for peace again and again.

She bought a cold drink and ordered nasi goreng. She glanced at her watch. Plenty of time; she had nothing to pack. Everything was still in her suitcase. All she had to do was change into trousers and check out, and then she would wait in the foyer with her book for the airport bus.

This time tomorrow she would be with Nikki. The Chinese waitress flip-flopped over with her food. Fleur got herself another drink. The nasi goreng was wonderful; familiar. Ah Heng had made it once a week, usually when David was flying, because it was light and Fleur and the twins loved it. She smiled as she remembered how proficient their tiny hands were with chopsticks, which they used long before a knife and fork.

The couple at the next table got up to go and Fleur leant over to pick up a paper in English they had left behind. It was *The Straits Times*. She flicked through the pages looking for headlines that used to make David and Fergus laugh when she pointed them out. AN AMOK CAUSES PANIC IN CHINATOWN. BUSINESSMAN CHARLIE CHAN FOILS INDEFATIGABLE ROBBERY.

She turned another page and another, smiling. Suddenly a small headline with a photograph caught her eye, near the bottom of the page. She started to read it. Her heart jumped

63

painfully making breathing difficult. Her hands began to shake and her eyes became blurred with shock. She placed the paper flat on the table, her food forgotten. She blinked and made herself read the words over again, very slowly, sickness rising up in her throat.

She placed her hands over the page and stared down at them as they trembled over the print. She thought for a second that she would pass out and she gripped the edges of the table until her knuckles were white. She made herself breathe again. Breathe.

The gardens and the people around Fleur receded, leaving her beached and isolated at her small table. She did not know how long she sat staring down at her hands. Then, infinitely carefully, she tore the page out and placed it in her bag. She paid for her unfinished food and walked to the entrance.

Taxi drivers called out to her: '*Datang . . . Datang . . . Teksi . . . Teksi, Mem? Hotel? Restoran? Shops?*' She walked past them, stumbling, blind and numb to anything but that terrible small and lonely image etched indelibly on her heart.

TEN

'No,' Jack said. 'Nikki, there's no way I'm letting you fly to Singapore on your own. You're seven and a half months pregnant and you shouldn't even be flying. I'm coming and nothing you say is going to make any difference.'

'Jack, listen, you should be here when the charter boats start to come in. It's the end of the season and what if my mother suddenly turns up . . .'

'Sorry, Nik. You're my priority, you and the baby. Both Neil and Rudi can manage the boats without me and Dad says he will fly down with mum and stay in the house if the boys have any problems.'

'But, it might just be a complete misunderstanding with mum . . .'

'Nikki, your mother's left all her belongings in a hotel in Singapore. We've heard absolutely nothing for twenty-four hours.'

Nikki closed her eyes. 'Oh, God. I'm so frightened for her.'

'I know you are. So don't push me away, Nik. We're in this together and we'll find out what's happened together.'

He pulled her to him and they stood in the middle of the room listening to the bamboo chimes clunking outside in the garden, heads turned towards the sea glinting in the bay.

Nikki gave in with relief. 'OK. We'll both go. Thanks, Jack.'

'Will you try to stay as calm as you can? I'm really afraid of you losing this baby.'

Nikki turned away from him and took the coffee pot off the stove and poured him coffee. She took it to the table and sat down. 'I want to say something.'

Jack sat opposite her, pouring milk into his coffee and wondering what was coming.

'Jack, pregnancy isn't an illness. I'm resting and taking all the care I can. I want this baby as much as you do but I have to go to Singapore and find out what's happened to my mother. It could be that she's dead, that something terrible has happened. I have to deal with that, pregnant or not. *Please,* if you come, just be there with me, don't add to the things I must worry about. I have to have blind trust in this baby going full term. That it is my karma . . . whatever happens.'

Jack looked at her. He loved her intensely, in a way she probably did not yet love him. Nikki had been marked by watching her father die and losing her twin. She had been scarred in ways Jack was still discovering. Every now and then he had a glimpse of her bravery and of her apparent ability to just accept passively whatever fate might land at her feet.

Sometimes, Jack thought, this passivity could be mistaken for a lack of hope. He wanted Nikki to believe in their future together; in the life they were building here. You had to have faith that sometimes things did come right despite the odds. He saw this as his job, to keep faith for the woman he loved.

Secretly, he thought karma was a cop-out, an excuse for not acting. Sometimes you had to fight for the life you wanted. He got to his feet and bent across the table to kiss her nose.

'I'll go and see how soon we can get a flight to Singapore tonight.'

'I'll go and find our rucksacks.'

They smiled at each other. Below them, a motor boat full of tourists wrapped up in wet weather gear shot out of the harbour across the bay to *The Hole* at speed. Their screams of mock terror and excitement were drowned by the sudden burst of the engine and did not rise up from the water to reach them. The speed in the lazy stillness of yachts at anchor seemed out of place, the long white wake disturbing the acres of blue. Then the sound faded and was gone. Peace. The sea straightened out again into glassy stillness.

Nikki moved around the house touching things uneasily like a cat marking a territory she was afraid she might never return to.

Detective Sergeant James Mohktar, a Chinese-Malay, met them at the airport. Nikki stared: he had the most extraordinary and beautiful face.

He drove them straight to the police station. 'It is just for the paperwork, Miss Montrose. Also, we have not quite finished with the hotel room. You see we must explore every avenue . . .'

Nikki went white with shock. *They must think Fleur is dead; they are treating the hotel room as a crime scene.*

James Mohktar, watching her face, said quickly, 'We have

no reason to think the worst, Miss Montrose, this is just normal procedure. The hotel will need the room back and before your mother's belongings are removed we have to make sure there is no clue there to her disappearance. At this stage do not get too alarmed, *lah*? Sometimes people on long journeys get disorientated and lost. Let us hope we find your mother safe and well very soon.' He glanced at Nikki's protruding stomach. 'Now, there are some questions you can help us with and then we will drive you to the Singapore Hilton to rest. I believe you have booked into the same hotel as your mother?'

'Yes,' Jack said. 'We thought it would be practical.'

He wanted to say, *Look, my* wife *is pregnant. Can't she rest before you bombard her with questions?* But he couldn't, and he did not like to say *girlfriend* or *partner* because he was unsure how this Asian policeman felt about Nikki being pregnant and unmarried.

D.S. Mohktar asked Nikki all over again about Fleur's exact travelling plans. Was Mrs Campbell meeting anyone on her stopover here? Had she any worries? Was she a confident traveller? Was she in good health? Had Nikki got a recent photograph?

Nikki had only one recent photo of her mother, taken at Fergus's funeral. She had brought it with her and she took it out of her bag and handed it to the Detective Sergeant. She had asked someone to take this particular photograph because her grandparents had flown over from their retirement in Cyprus for Fergus's funeral and Sam had flown back from Australia. The family had all been captured together, a rare thing.

Fleur was dressed in black, her dark hair streaked elegantly with grey. Nikki had thought when she saw her mother again, *God, she even goes grey elegantly. No aging pepper and salt for Fleur.* Her mother had lost weight. She had shadows under her eyes and her cheekbones had become more prominent, yet there was something ageless about her.

Mohktar stared down at the photograph. This woman was younger than he had expected and she was still attractive. It made his job easier because she would not have gone entirely unnoticed, but it also increased the chances that something had indeed happened to her.

'We will need to keep this photograph and have copies made, Miss Montrose.'

Nikki nodded. He asked her when Fleur had lived in Singapore. He asked her about the army connection and if she had kept up with any expatriates still living out here. Nikki told him she couldn't be sure because she had been living in New Zealand for the last four years, but she had never heard her mother mention still knowing anyone in Singapore.

Was her mother depressed after the death of her husband?

Sad, yes; depressed, no. She had taken up painting. She was studying art as a mature student. She was travelling again.

Was the object of her journey to see Nikki?

Partly, but she was studying the painter and architect Hundertwasser who had lived in New Zealand. She had been keen to see some of his buildings . . . That was one of the reasons for her journey to New Zealand.

'She was definitely travelling alone?'

'Yes. But I think she was meeting up with a friend or fellow student in Auckland, later on . . . after she had stayed with us . . . but I'm not sure.'

'You have the name of this friend?'

'No. I have no idea who it might have been. I've lived abroad for a long time. I don't know my mother's friends.'

'When was the last time you spoke to your mother? . . . How did she sound? . . . She did not ring you from her hotel in Singapore to say she had arrived? Was this unusual? . . . How close are you to your mother? . . . Do you have siblings?'

'No,' Nikki said. 'There's just me.'

But James Mohktar thought he caught a flicker of something in the woman's eyes. He saw also that she was growing paler and paler with tiredness. He said, 'OK, *lah*. Enough for now. We will go to your mother's hotel room and then I will let you rest.'

'Are you OK?' Jack asked Nikki anxiously as they got into the police car.

Nikki tried to smile. 'I'm OK, just tired. The police are only doing their job. Actually, I'm surprised they are spending so much time on this. I thought a missing western woman wouldn't be high on their list of priorities. I'm impressed.'

Jack didn't say what had crossed his mind. That the policeman was sure this would turn out to be a murder inquiry.

Nikki stood looking at Fleur's belongings sitting in the impersonal hotel room, just as she had left them. Cosmetics and washing things in the bathroom, case open but fully packed. A dress and a pair of trousers hanging in the wardrobe; a pair of comfortable shoes beneath, obviously ones she wore on the flight. A paracetamol packet on her bedside table next to a half-finished bottle of mineral water. The small clock she carried everywhere.

Her book and the vague whiff of Fleur's scent. Nikki moved closer to the bed. *Mourning Ruby*, by Helen Dunmore. On the cover, a small girl in a red dress was running through autumn leaves. She had plump brown legs, small feet encased in plimsolls.

Mourning Ruby.

The pain was like being hit suddenly with a cricket bat.

Fleur, like Nikki, still mourned. Each and every day of her life.

Mum. Mum.

Nikki crumpled on the floor and wept.

ELEVEN

Fleur's only instinct was flight. Blind flight towards a place that had lain in her mind all these years. Distraught, fighting panic and finding herself back on Orchard Road in the noise of the traffic, with the crowds jostling and banging into her, she lifted her hand for a taxi.

'The railway station, please.'

As they sat in traffic she felt as if she had been thrown suddenly into a bad dream. She wanted to wake up. She wanted to wake up and find Fergus beside her, gently nudging her awake, saying gently, *Fleur, Fleur, you're dreaming.*

She stumbled out of the taxi and into the station. Hardly coherent, she asked if there was a train to Port Dickson.

'Only to Seremban. Then you take taxi or bus to P.D. You go now, left, to the other side of station. Quick, train coming.' The Chinese man in the ticket kiosk flapped his hand vaguely to her right and an incoming train.

Fleur ran for the nearest platform and waited for people to pour off, then she climbed in. The carriages were old and people pressed and pushed behind her to get on. She found a window seat and sat down. Too late she realised she had

72

no water. Maybe someone would come round with drinks. She tried not to think about her dry mouth. The carriage was rapidly filling up with Malays and Tamils; all talking and laughing, bowed down with shopping and going home to their kampongs.

The noise rose as the train departed and Fleur closed her eyes against the curious glances at her.

The train moved sluggishly through the outskirts of the city and across the causeway into Malaysia, and Fleur, exhausted, slept. When she opened her eyes again people had grown quieter, dozing in the sun which slid off the paddy fields and cast shadows across bent figures in a scene so timeless Fleur could have been a child or young wife again.

She remembered looking down from the plane carrying David's body home and watching the rice fields disappearing as the plane rose upwards. She had sat on that long journey home in a catatonic and bemused disbelief that he was really dead.

It had been spring when she and the twins had flown back to England to bury David in the place he had grown up in, the place where his parents still lived. That little middle-class village had remained a microcosm of the past even then, with its tiny roads and steep banks littered with creamy primroses.

It had been spring in the tiny churchyard, and, as David's coffin was lowered to the bugler's lament, Fleur had looked round for a moment at the graves and the stunned mourners. She had clutched the hands of the twins and thought, *how can this day be so extraordinarily beautiful?* How can the trees and hedges burst with new life when David is dead? When I will never recover from the horror of his death? When his life ended after an argument, when I had no chance to tell him he had nothing to fear, nothing to be jealous of. I loved him. He was the father of my children and I would always love him. *Always*.

It was the dichotomy of a world so new and green and perfect and the bleak finality of David being lowered forever into the ground to the trembling notes of a military bugler that had struck her so starkly that day.

In his parents' cottage a cherry tree was bursting into pink, and bluebells shone in a haze of blue and white in the orchard. David's mother and Fleur's were offering plates of tiny canapés round and gracefully making small talk as if it mattered. *As if it mattered*. It is what they did, her parents' generation. They never showed their grief, it just wasn't done. It was true of the army too. Other ranks could yell the place down when they had their babies, officers' wives bit their lips.

That day of the funeral someone had thrown the French windows open and Fleur saw David's father standing with his back to the house, whisky clasped between his hands, for a moment totally unable to exchange inanities. She had walked out to him and he had wrapped his arms around her and in all the beauty of his garden they had rocked and rocked together, mourning, mourning the loss of the centre of their universe. The waste of a young life.

Stuart Montrose had whispered. 'It is the worst, the very worst thing of all to outlive your child. It is the thing that breaks your heart.'

Fleur turned again to the landscape outside the train window. In the distance where the rubber plantations had once stretched as far as the eye could see now lay palm oil trees. As a child and a young wife she had found them eerie. On the long, long, straight road to the coast her father would stop so that they could all pee behind a tree, and if Fleur had not been desperate she would never have entered the shade of the rubber trees. The rubber tappers, their faces hidden by scarves, moved silently, sliding from tree to tree, emptying the rubber from the small tap on the trunk and moving quickly on to the next tree, like shadows or ghosts.

Fleur knew her fear was due partly to the stories her father had told her about the communist insurgents of the 1950s when plantation owners and managers had been attacked and killed, but she always found the stillness of the rubber plantations sinister and in some way threatening; a place where people could hide and pounce. The palm oil trees, with their thick green fronds, softened the landscape, their shape curving like the tops of pineapples.

After David's funeral, Fleur had lain motionless in the dark, one twin each side of her in the lumpy bed. Saffie placed her fingers on her mother's ribcage to see if she was still breathing. Her fingers felt, under the cotton nightdress, the flutter and throb of Fleur's heart. She wanted to whisper to Nikki over her mother's still form. She wanted to feel her sister's warmth seep into her. If Mum died there would be no one, only their grandparents. They would have to live in this horrid village and probably go to boarding school.

Saffie trembled with fear of the future. Would they have to stay in this cold house of long corridors and draughty rooms? Here in this rolling garden full of huge fir trees that shaded the lawns and made you shiver? Where the roses smelt in the middle of the day but there was no scent of frangipani wafting in on the morning wind; no white frangipani petals covering the lawns. There was no familiar sound of the *kebun* brushing the bruised petals up with his long, slow, indolent sweeps.

No bougainvillaea climbed the walls of this house in a great purple cloud. There were no sounds of cicadas in the night or Ah Heng's high cackling voice coming from the kitchen. Saffie ached with homesickness: for the Chinese chimes moving imperceptibly in the draught of the shuttered windows; for Ah Heng just a shout away.

Home; where Daddy had been, his laughter filtering through the rise and fall of sleep, making you smile as if you were awake. His laugh mixed up with the sound of music, of people chatting and partying.

Saffie thought of his largeness, remembered his happiness just beyond the darkness of the room making you safe to turn and sleep again. She strained for the memory of his face. She could remember his smell: soap and tobacco. She could remember the feel of him, the strength of his brown arms . . . but she trembled in case she forgot his face . . . Singapore . . . the safe place where Daddy had been.

Her face, curled upwards towards her mother, was becoming wet. She touched her cheek. These were not her tears. She was not crying. She reached up to touch Fleur's face. Her mother was weeping silently, motionless. Her chest was not heaving, her mouth was not open; she was crying without sound, tears cascading out of the sides of her eyes. The pillows and her nightdress and Saffie's hair were becoming soaked. Saffie did not know anyone could cry this quietly. She heard Nikki whisper in the darkness,

'Mummy, Mummy, don't cry. Please don't cry.'

Saffie leant up on one elbow. 'It's all right . . . we're here.' She got out of bed and padded across in the dark to the dressing table to get a box of tissues. She handed Nikki a bundle and together they tried to blot Fleur's eyes and cheeks and neck until she slowly became aware of them, came back from a long way away and registered their distress.

Saffie thought, *Mummy doesn't even know she's crying.*

Fleur sat up and wiped her face and blew her nose, looked down at them, one each side of her. 'Cuddle up, darlings, cuddle in close, you're both frozen. That's it; pull the covers up to our chins . . . that's right. Now we're like dormice . . .' She held the children to her tight, rubbed her chin over their smooth hair that smelt like hay, murmured to them to sleep, that it was all going to be all right.

'Mummy, do we have to stay here?' Saffie whispered. 'In this house?'

'No, darlings, we're not going to stay here.'

'Where are we going? Can we go home?' Nikki asked.

'We can't go home, darling. All our things have to be packed up and Ah Heng has to go and look after a new family. I have to go back to hand our house back to the army and Grandpa thought we might all go and have a last little holiday in Malaya . . .'

'Where we used to go with Daddy?'

'Yes, in one of the rest houses in Port Dickson.'

'With the round baths, where the water comes out of a big plug and goes all over the floor?'

'That's right. Does that sound like a good idea?'

'With Grandpa and Grandma, or just us?' Saffie was unsure she wanted them to come. On the other hand, it might feel safer.

'I like just us,' Nikki said quietly. But she could not help wondering if her mother was going to be like she was now or like she had mostly been since they got back to England. Would she see and hear them like she did tonight? Or would she go back to a place where they could not reach her, when sometimes she looked as if she didn't know them any more? As if she had gone somewhere else and forgotten all about them.

'Of course they are coming with us, darlings. But after the holiday we're going to find a little house together, just us three. OK?'

Saffie could feel her heart swelling with a strange sad happiness because Mummy was holding them and for the first time the dark felt safe again.

'You will stay with us all the time? You won't ever go away and leave us in this house on our own, will you? You won't leave us even for a minute?' Nikki asked breathlessly.

Fleur bent to her and kissed the top of her head with sudden passion and then did the same to Saffie. 'My silly little peapods, of course I won't leave you. There is just the three of us now and we'll stick together always, won't we?'

Nikki smiled and curled in for sleep. 'Yes.'

Saffie could feel her mother's body going slack as she fell asleep. After a moment she whispered, 'Nikki?' but no one answered. Nikki too was asleep.

Lying in the dark, Fleur's breath moving her fingers like the quiver of leaves, Saffie heard a fox bark suddenly out in the garden. It was a primeval sound that made her heart jump. She squeezed her eyes tight shut, wanting to sleep too. She thought it was the loneliest sound she had ever heard.

The train slowed and stopped at a junction. Fleur smelt betel nut and curry powder and the musty smell of live chickens carried in cages. She felt a nudge and a fat smiling Malay woman with a child was holding out her bottle of water. Fleur took it gratefully, drank and then handed it back. The woman shook her head, showing her she had another bottle. 'You keep. You keep.'

Fleur thanked her and leant back and closed her eyes.

After the funeral she had flown back to Singapore with

the twins and Peter and Laura There was an army memorial service and a quarter to hand over . . . and then . . .
*And then I let it happen. I let my child die for one selfish
craving for oblivion.*

The train shunted forward again. It seemed to stop at
every single station. Fleur sat up and looked out. The day
was ending. The carriages were emptying. People were leaving the train in droves now.

The Malay woman and her child had gone. *They were
still travelling inland.* Her heart jumped; she must be on the
wrong train. Oh God, where was she going? She shook with
jet-lag and tiredness.

A large Indian with a purple turban was watching her
with gentle eyes.

Fleur lent forward. 'I think I'm on the wrong train.'

The Indian smiled. 'I *was* wondering, Madam. You are
on what we call the Jungle Railway all the way to Kota
Bharu. Mostly workers travel this line. The journey from
Singapore takes fourteen hours, no less! Where is it you are
wanting to be?'

'Seremban. I must get off there for Port Dickson.' Fleur
fought panic.

'Well, Madam, the next stop is Mentakab. Here you must
get off immediately for the next stop is Jerentut. There is
nothing in between. I am afraid there will be no train back
to Gemas tonight. This is where you must return to catch
the train to Seremban.'

He watched Fleur's face. 'Madam, do not worry.
Mentakab is where I alight. I will show you to the best
place in Mentakab to stay and then in the morning you will
catch a train back to Gemas and there change for Seremban.
All will be well. Do not be afraid. I fear you are a little
unwell.'

The Indian accompanied Fleur off the train and took her in a taxi to a small guest house belonging to his sister. *Very good and very clean.* It wasn't, but Fleur was grateful. She lay on the hard bed, stiff with anxiety, beyond tiredness, unable to sleep or shut her mind to the image she had seen in the paper. She was hardly aware of where she was.

Early the next morning the Indian took her back to the station and made sure she got on the right train to Gemas. His sister had changed some of her Singapore dollars for her, and given her Malaysian ringgits.

'I am sorry,' she said. 'I have so little money on me to thank you for your kindness.'

He drew himself up with dignity. 'Madam, I do not wish for payment for helping a lady in a foreign land.' He smiled, 'I hope soon the thing that troubles you will disappear.'

'*Terima kasih.* Thank you.'

'*Sama-sama.*' He smiled. 'You speak a little Malay?'

'A very little. *Selamat tinggal.* Goodbye.'

'Goodbye, Madam and *Selamat jalan* to you. Do not forget Gemas. Change at Gemas.'

The train drew out of the station taking Fleur backwards to Gemas, when all she wanted to do was travel forward to the sea. To reach the place where she could grieve silently and alone. Just for a moment to feel the warmth of a life lost. Just for a moment.

TWELVE

The name *Montrose* was niggling at James Mohktar as he drove home that night. It registered with him, seemed somehow familiar. *It is an English name*, he told himself, *and you are bound to have heard it before.* Yet as he lay beside his wife and listened to her even breathing in the dark, intuition told him it was important, this nebulous something he could not recall.

He said to his inspector the next day, 'Have you heard the name Montrose before?'

Inspector Chan pursed his lips and thought about it. 'No. Should I have done?'

'I don't know. Something I can't remember. Annoying.'

The phone rang and Chan picked it up. The day had started. Mohktar walked down the corridor to his office. He opened up his computer and then thought, *How long ago did this missing woman live here? Twenty-eight years? Long before we were computerised.* He would need to get someone to check the archives, find out how far back files were transferred onto disc and then search through old cases concerning Europeans or service personnel to see if that

81

name came up. He got up again and went to find constables Ahmed and Singh.

Detective Sergeant Mohktar had given the hotel permission to move Fleur's belongings to our room. Her room was then cleaned and hoovered for the next guests; all trace of Fleur was extinguished.

I woke before Jack and got up quietly so I did not disturb him. I bent over the small pool of my mother's belongings. Two Chinese blouses beautifully folded, one red and one green. A length of batik. Presents for me? I opened the small overnight case again. Just her book, washing things, nightdress and underclothes. A white shirt, summer skirt and sandals.

Fleur only had her handbag with her. No change of clothes and nothing to sleep in. Fear caught at me once more in the silent room. Fleur had so obviously meant to return to the hotel because she would never have gone anywhere without clean underclothes.

Jack woke and sat up, fighting to get his bearings. He saw me sitting on the floor among Fleur's belongings.

'Come here.' He held his arms open. I went over to him and he wrapped his arms around me. 'Don't think the worst. Don't give up hope. I was thinking: do you think your mother might have had a sudden reaction to being back in Singapore? Do you think coming back triggered something unresolved? Could she be wandering about the city not knowing what she is doing?'

I sat up. 'It's possible. That could be it, Jack. She might still return here to the hotel.'

The phone rang. It was DS Mohktar. He asked me if I was rested. He would like to see me in an hour if that was convenient. He had witness statements from other guests in the hotel that he would like to go through with me. They had circulated Fleur's photograph to all city patrols and they were hopeful that something positive would come from this.

Mohktar caught up with us in the breakfast lounge. Apparently an old couple Fleur had made conversation with had reappeared from three days in Kuala Lumpur. They had been on the same flight from Heathrow and also on the airport bus. They had talked briefly to Fleur in the hotel lift the night they arrived. She told them she was going out for an hour or so. They remembered distinctly because they told her to be careful, a woman on her own, and she had replied that Singapore was one of the safest places she knew. They had not seen her at breakfast the following day, but the honeymoon couple, now in Penang, had, although they had not spoken to her.

The waiter on this eighth-floor breakfast lounge had served her coffee and croissants and one of the porters had seen her go out that morning by the main entrance, cheerful and seeming fine. She had asked him the way to the Botanical Gardens. One of Mohktar's constables was down in the gardens now, making inquiries with the staff.

'So, Miss Montrose, your mother was not in a distressed state when she left the hotel that morning. The porter says she seemed happy. He described your mother very well and was able to give us a good description of what she was wearing. He particularly remembers her because she spoke a little Malay and he was impressed . . .'

Mohktar's phone rang, and as he answered it I thought that I would like to speak to the people my mother had fleeting contact with. He was listening intently to the person on the other end of the phone and his eyes, watching me, changed suddenly as he fired questions in rapid Chinese.

When he came off the phone he was silent and Jack reached for my hand as if he too expected bad news.

DS Mohktar continued staring at us, his expression unreadable.

'Constable Ahmed is on his way here. He has some information for me. Also, I understand that a girl serving in the café in the gardens thinks she might have served your mother, at about twelve thirty, before her shift ended. The woman talked to her about how the gardens had looked many years ago, and appeared normal and relaxed . . . So, if we assume that your mother was going to return to the hotel in time for her flight bus to Singapore airport, whatever happened occurred after twelve thirty p.m. . . . *Lah*?'

At that moment an Indian policeman walked into the room. He held a file of papers in his hand and he glanced at me curiously as he placed the foolscap in front of Mohktar.

Mohktar read without expression for five minutes or so and the tension felt unbearable. Jack held on to my hand, but despite the air-conditioning my hand in his grew slippery with anxiety. Eventually Mohktar looked up. He smoothed the first piece of paper for a moment as if gathering his thoughts then he met my eyes and said quietly, 'You did not think to tell me, Miss Montrose, that your father was killed here in Singapore in a helicopter accident in 1976?'

My throat felt dry. I suddenly saw how relevant to Fleur's disappearance that accident we had all watched a lifetime ago must seem to the detective.

I looked at him. 'I'm sorry. It was so long ago and my mother has had another life since then and another marriage. I don't think her disappearance now is connected to my father's accident, really I don't . . .'

But I was shaking because I knew what other memories might have been invoked and I did not want to talk about them. I did not want to conjure them up from the darkness inside me. I did not want to voice and make commonplace what was just one more case to these policemen, not a monstrous thing they carried round inside them like a wound.

Jack stirred uneasily and the two policemen did not take their eyes from my face. James Mohktar leant forward suddenly.

'Miss Montrose, you had a sister, did you not?'

I nodded and Jack moved imperceptibly closer.

'Five weeks after your father was killed your sister went missing from the government rest houses in Port Dickson. She was never found, was she?'

How quiet the room was now, and the air-conditioning made my bare arms cold. I shivered. I looked down at my hands. At the small eternity ring Jack had given me instead of a wedding band.

'Her name was Saffie.' The ring glinted as I spread my fingers. 'We were five. We never knew what happened to her. We had to leave her here. We had to leave her behind when we left . . . No one could find her. Not your police. Not the military police. Nor the detectives they sent from England. She was never found . . . my twin.'

There was silence. Then Sergeant Mohktar said gently, 'I am very sorry, Miss Montrose. I am so very sorry.' He rubbed his forefinger along his top lip as if he was suddenly missing a moustache and he fiddled with the papers in front of him. 'You must agree that the death of your father and sister and your mother's sudden disappearance are most likely to be connected?'

His mobile rang again and, sighing, he answered it. He swung round and said something to his constable in rapid Malay. Then he got to his feet. 'Please excuse . . . We will

85

be back in a few moments . . .' He clicked his fingers at the waiter. 'Bring more coffee here . . . cold drinks . . . *Lah*!' And swiftly the two policemen left the room.

Jack turned me to face him. I felt icily and strangely calm. 'They know something, Jack.'

'Yes,' he said. His face was pale too and I suddenly thought how awful this would have been if I had come alone, without him. If I was about to be told that something dreadful had happened to Fleur I would have heard it alone. All my family would be gone; all gone in this one country, as if Singapore held some awful thrall and threat for us.

I leant against him. 'Jack,' I said. 'Jack . . .' But I could not find the words to tell him I loved him . . . that if he had not insisted on coming I would be here now on my own.

Perhaps he knew, because he met my eyes and said, 'Nik, we'll meet whatever's happened together. I'm sure your mother wouldn't do anything foolish, whatever memories Singapore invoked. She wouldn't do that to the daughter she loves.'

I held his eyes and I knew what he said was true. I thought of the two silk blouses lying beautifully wrapped in our room. They were not the act of a woman swamped by memories, but of a woman full of love and anticipation; a woman who was about to become a grandmother.

Then I had another thought. 'Jack!' I clutched him. 'It isn't Singapore City that holds ghosts . . .'

But I did not have time to finish for Sergeant Mohktar came back, his face grave, and sat down again opposite us. I saw that he was not quite sure how to begin. Then he said slowly, 'We think it possible that your mother might have gone over the causeway into Malaysia, Miss Montrose . . .'

'To Port Dickson?'

'Yes.' He stared at me. 'It is where your sister . . .'

'Disappeared; most probably died,' I finished for him.

DS Mohktar was holding a newspaper and he turned it nervously in his hands. 'Miss Montrose, we think your mother might have seen this article in *The Straits Times*. The waitress in the Gardens confirmed she saw her reading a newspaper.'

'What is it?' I reached out my hand for it, but the Detective Sergeant would not let me have it.

'Miss Montrose. A few days ago a workman discovered a shallow grave in Port Dickson on the edge of the jungle near where the old government rest houses used to be. It contained . . . the bones of a small child.'

I took the newspaper gently from Mohktar and I looked down at the page he had been holding. I saw a crime scene. I saw ticker tape and policemen. I saw people in white disposable overalls crouching near a small shallow grave. I saw the headlines that Fleur, turning a page, must have seen.

SMALL BODY FOUND IN SHALLOW GRAVE

THIRTEEN

Fleur had been watching the changing skyline without realising they were nearing Seremban and what had once been familiar territory. She had thought as they neared the coast that she would recognise the contours and shape of the land. She knew that the west coast would be dramatically changed and commercialised; that it would have expanded out of all proportion to her time here twenty-eight years ago, but she could not, somehow, make the leap from the place that still lay in her head.

When the train reached Seremban, Fleur got out and stood on the platform. She shivered with tiredness in the hot morning sun, an English woman without luggage.

It was a tiny station on the edge of town. Taxi drivers lounged by their cars ready to swoop. Fleur felt relieved that she had thought to change her money to Malaysian ringgits in Mentakab. She walked out into the blazing sun and straight into a waiting taxi. As soon as they reached the town she asked to get out. She was stiff with sitting and wanted to walk. She found herself in a dusty road full of small shops where Indian stall holders lolled in doorways calling out to her, their wares spilling out onto the pavement.

As Fleur turned a corner she saw the bus station and a bus with Port Dickson written on the front. She stopped, undecided. She felt thirsty and unwell and realised she could not go on without sleep. She went into a store with a fridge full of cold drinks and bought one. Then she walked on, still ignoring the persistent shopkeepers.

She went into the first small hotel she came to and asked for a room. A Chinese woman eyed her curiously, took a key from behind her and showed her into a spotless room with a shower. It had no view except a high wall with a narrow row of houses behind it, crowded and leaning together like bad teeth. The room would have been claustrophobic for any length of time.

The woman told her she must fill in a form with her name and passport number and Fleur asked if she could sleep first, indicating tiredness by placing both hands against her cheek. The woman nodded and asked her if she wanted tea.

When it came the woman had placed thin pieces of bread and butter on a plate and the kindness brought tears to Fleur's eyes. She showered, washed out her underclothes and placed them in the sun over the window ledge. She climbed into the cool bed, the noise of the air-conditioner masking the sounds from outside, and lay on her back feeling dislocated.

The image of the small grave was etched clearly behind her eyelids. But so were other memories, stirred by the heat and smell and sounds she had almost forgotten. It seemed possible, to go back, to go back and start again and be more careful of the life she had had, the life she had lived out here in the heat and the dust and bustle of a foreign posting.

It was not that she had been unaware of her happiness then, it was that she had wanted too much. She had wanted perfection and there was no such thing, it did not exist. Human beings were flawed, you had to accept what you had, not try to improve it.

Why couldn't you have had this wisdom when you were young, when you needed it?

David seemed suddenly near her in the room, as if he too had been conjured here by the possibility of finding their lost child. She could see his face, clearer than for years, young, still young of course. It was difficult to age while the memory of David remained young and vital. She turned over on her side, heavy with exhaustion, and let the memory of their time together play across her brain until she fell into a troubled sleep.

Mersing, Malaya, 1968

In the Easter holidays Laura and Peter arranged a house party in Mersing for the Easter weekend. Ten friends rented three rest houses near the beach. They were a mixed group of young officers and teachers and a couple of older friends of Peter and Laura's.

The plan was to catch one of the small boats across to the island of Palau Tioman, take a picnic and spend Easter Sunday swimming and diving down to the acres of coral that lay beneath one of the most beautiful islands in the world.

The boats chugged across the aquamarine water full of noisy singing people and diving gear. The boatmen deposited them in the shallow translucent water and waited while they waded back and forth to the beach carrying their picnics and diving equipment. Then the boats turned and disappeared to the horizon to fish and sleep and wait for evening.

Diving canisters, barbecues and drink were held aloft out

of the water and lugged ashore, and the parties broke up roughly into age groups and spread around the small curved beach under the shade of palm trees.

Peter and Laura were conscious of days like these drawing to a close. They wanted to make the most of the time they had left because they had been posted to Aldershot and it was still a shock.

'We've been incredibly lucky up to now,' Peter said to Laura as he stuck beer cans in the shade. 'It could have been worse.'

'Not much!' Laura retorted, but she knew he was right. They had had some wonderful postings.

'It's certainly going to be a short sharp shock for Sam and Fleur,' Peter added. 'Aldershot doesn't quite have the cachet of the naval base, does it?'

Laura laughed. 'No bad thing, darling, they have had a magic three years, perhaps it's time real life reared its ugly head. Sam's really going to miss his sailing, though, and David and his group of friends.'

They both looked across at their children spreading rugs and towels out under the bent palms. Sam and Fleur, dreading an army quarter in England, were making the most of their last Easter holiday. They both sailed with David most weekends from the naval base or raced from Changi yacht club and Sam seemed to be spending a lot of his holiday setting up his summer crewing with some of the subalterns who were also returning to England.

'Fleur is going to feel adrift too,' Peter said. 'Especially with Sam off to medical school. That little crowd seem to do an awful lot together. I must say I've been very lucky with my subalterns out here.'

He was watching his daughter, knowing she considered her world was going to come to an abrupt end when they left. David had another five months in Singapore and then could be posted anywhere.

Laura, following his eyes, sighed. Poor Fleur! She was far too young to interest David. He was always surrounded by pretty girls and was constantly teased about it by the other officers. 'I think we're going to have problems with Fleur when we get home.'

'Oh, Laura,' Peter said mildly.

'Darling, Fleur has always been able to twist you round her little finger. She has such talent and is capable of working so hard when she wants to. I hope she doesn't just throw it away.'

'Let's wait and see. Fleur must live her own life, darling.'

Peter knew what was bugging Laura. She was working for a degree she might never be able to use. It was likely that from Aldershot he would be posted to Northern Ireland where she would not be able to work for security reasons. For the first time he had begun to sense a resentment that seemed more and more directed at their daughter, who might casually turn her back on her own chance to excel.

He handed Laura a cool drink. 'To this lovely day, surrounded by our friends on one of the most wonderful, unspoilt islands it is possible to imagine.'

Laura lifted her glass, met his eyes and smiled. *He was right. How gently he managed to reprimand her.* 'And to our two, who I do love, you know,' she said quietly. 'Are you going to dive?'

'I certainly am. I wish I could tempt you. The coral is out of this world. See you later, darling.'

Peter hopped away over the hot sand towards the group standing by the diving canisters and snorkelling equipment.

Fleur never dived because despite being a good swimmer she hated anything over her face. Her father had tried to get her to go down with him over the years but at the last moment she always tore off her mask. Fleur was convinced she had absorbed Laura's fear at an early age.

That Sunday as Sam and David prepared to dive, Fleur hovered beside them wistfully. She hated to miss out on anything.

David was watching her. 'Come down with us, Fleur? You're missing an amazing experience. Sam and I'll look after you.'

Sam looked up. 'She won't come, she's claustrophobic.'

Fleur hesitated. 'I'd like to . . . it's just . . .'

'Come on, have a go. Come down with Sam and me,' David coaxed.

He held out his hand and Fleur, her mouth dry, reached out to take it. He helped Fleur into a buoyancy control device and handed her a weight belt. Then he started checking all their equipment. Sam, who was ready first, bent and helped her with her flippers, then adjusted her mask and snorkel. When David was ready he gave her the thumbs up sign and Fleur stood anxiously between them.

David told her to breathe from her regulator until they were in deep water then switch to her snorkel to conserve air as they needed to surface swim before descending.

All three flapped sideways into the water, Sam and David grinning at her encouragingly. They started to swim as soon as it was deep enough. A little way out Sam signalled to her and both he and Sam checked her equipment again and then each other's. Fleur tried to ignore the panic that threatened to send her swimming madly for the shore.

Sam indicated that she should deflate her device and exhale. Fleur hesitated. David touched her arm and gave her the thumbs up again, and trembling, she began to descend feet first with Sam and David each side of her, all adding small amounts of air as they neared the bottom.

Once she was underwater and she could see the bright fish and Sam's and David's legs securely each side of her, Fleur tried to relax. The mass of coral lay beneath her, alive and intricate, the patterns of it causing waving shadows on the seabed; a great mountain of faded pink and white. Small, brightly coloured fish darted in and out of her legs in this silent world and Fleur was enchanted. David took her hand and pointed with his other hand to show her rays moving delicately through fronds of seaweed like dancers.

Fleur, gripping David's hand, turned this way and that in excitement. Her fear all these years had made her miss out on all this. Now she knew why people became hooked on diving; it was a different world, an unknown and unmapped place, full of unexpected and undiscovered wonder. When they surfaced she felt euphoric. One of the teachers was waiting for her diving gear and she peeled herself out of it and turned to David, laughing.

'That was out of this world! Amazing! It was incredible!'

Sam surfaced and grinned at her. 'I told you! Think what you've missed all these years!'

David, sitting in the shallows, smiled and handed her a small pink piece of coral.

'There you are, to remember your first dive! Have you got rid of your fear? Will you dive again?

'Oh, yes! Well . . . I will if you or Sam are with me.' She took the small piece of coral, self-consciously. 'Thanks.'

David smiled. 'It takes guts to conquer a fear, Fleur.'

They moved back to their party. Fleur picked up her towel and threw it around her. She placed the small piece of coral safely in the pocket of her canvas bag.

Sam handed David a beer. 'What do you want to drink, Fleur?'

'I'll have a glass of wine, please.'

Sam grinned. 'Here you are. You've certainly earned one.'

Fleur went and sat beside David on her towel. He was smoking a cigarette and he idly touched the goose bumps that stood out on her arms. 'You got cold down there.'

He reached behind him and wrapped his blue shirt around her shoulders. He pulled her thin arms into the sleeves and bent to do up some buttons as if she were a child. He was very close and Fleur stayed still, willing herself not to tremble as his fingers touched her skin. He looked up and met her eyes, held them in sudden amusement, then bent swiftly and briefly kissed her mouth. It was small and firm and salty.

The men began to barbecue and the groups drifted towards the smell, lugging their towels and drinks with them. Laura got Fleur to help with the plates and bread rolls, and as the last divers came up the sound of beer bottles popping got louder and the conversation ebbed and flowed between bursts of laughter.

After everyone had eaten, people moved up into the deeper shade of the trees and lay sleeping or reading. Fleur had moved her towel to the place she always lay, under a scrubby palm where, when they were younger, she and Sam had swung Tarzan-like up on the rope that had always been there. She had had two glasses of wine and although she opened her book she fell asleep on her stomach.

When she woke, David was asleep beside her. Surprised, she gazed at his face, glad of the rare opportunity to scrutinise his features. His eyelashes were long and dark and thick, making tiny shadows underneath his eyes. He had sweat on his forehead and top lip . . . His lips were square, with tiny vertical lines. *Just right lips; neither too full nor too thin*. Fleur longed to touch those lips with a finger.

She knew his face well and yet not at all. She wondered how you changed things. How you made someone notice you in a different way, not as Sam's little sister or the colonel's daughter. How you changed from being a girl he saw often yet did not see at all, to the Fleur she really was.

At that moment he opened his eyes and saw hers fixed on him alarmingly near. Their eyes locked. Fleur held her courage and his gaze. The moment was thick with intent. Then, David slowly grinned, reached out with his finger to touch her nose and sat up, yawning.

The light was changing over the sea, less harsh, turning mellow and golden, lighting up the water in little sparks. People were swimming to cool down, splashing each other and calling out. Peter and Sam were preparing to dive again. Fleur watched her father pulling on diving gear. Laura was nowhere to be seen.

David turned to her. 'Going into the water?'

Fleur nodded and they stood up together and ran over the hot sand into the clear, translucent sea.

They swam out and then lay on their backs in the water, soporific and happy. Around them little clumps of swimmers and couples paired off in the late afternoon, not wanting the day to end, lying close on beach mats, huddled sleepily in the shallows on their stomachs.

'I can't believe I won't be flying out or coming here ever again,' Fleur said. 'I can't believe that next Easter and the long summer will be spent in *Aldershot*.'

David swam towards her. He laughed at her solemn face. 'By this time next year you will have moved on, Fleur. You'll be worrying about A-level results and your end-of-term show. You'll have boyfriends milling around you and a whole exciting, unknown life stretching ahead. Maybe you'll come back one day and revisit Mersing with friends . . .

This, now . . . these days in Singapore will fade into a lovely dream. They'll never leave you, but maybe they won't seem quite real.'

Fleur trod water facing him. 'They'll seem more real than any other part of my life,' she said vehemently. 'Sam and I won't see you for months. You can say all that because you're not leaving yet and you know you might be posted back here one day . . . At times like this I hate being an army family and having to pack up and begin all over again with new friends. I long to be one of those boring families who live in one place with the same set of friends from kindergarten to university . . .'

'Rubbish! Of course you don't!'

He pulled her towards him to hug her, her face was so suddenly forlorn, and they trod water together and nearly sank. Laughing, they both swam in until their feet could touch the bottom. In shallower water Fleur turned and held on to his arms.

'David? I don't know if I want to take A levels. I don't even know if I want to go on dancing either. Laura would have a fit if she could hear me.'

'She certainly would!' David held on to her waist lightly. 'What do you want to do with your life, then, Fleury?'

Fleur looked him straight in the eyes and twined her legs around his waist under the water. 'I want to marry you and have your babies.'

David, startled, stared down at her and then twirled her round, roaring with laughter. 'Do you indeed?'

Fleur would not let him get away with passing it off as a joke and moved her hands up round his neck. 'I mean it,' she said softly. 'I mean it.'

'You're only seventeen,' he said carefully, smiling gently into her eyes. 'And far too lovely for me.'

Fleur reached up and kissed his mouth, pressed her small dancer's body against him. 'No,' she whispered, 'but I suppose you're too lovely for me. You've got all those teachers . . . especially that blonde one who was all over you in the boat. Have you taken her out?'

'No, I haven't.' David gently disentangled Fleur from him, glancing quickly towards the beach. Embarrassing if Laura and Peter saw their teenage daughter wrapped round him.

'I'm not a child,' Fleur said, knowing exactly why he was holding her away. She felt a moment's triumph because she had caught something in his eyes and knew she had aroused him. If he had thought of her as a little sister he didn't now.

'You certainly are not!' David said. 'You're a little hussy. Race you back up the beach!'

He had been amazed to be stirred by her slim little body which he knew so well. Amazed and a little startled. He let her words lie there, new and shiny and intricate, but sharp too, and enticing, like coral.

FOURTEEN

I gathered up my mother's things and put them in with our luggage in the hired car. Inspector Chan had asked the local Malaysian police to look out for Fleur in Seremban and Port Dickson. Detective Sergeant Mohktar had travelled ahead to Kuala Lumpur where there was a main police station and would join us in Port Dickson later in the day. Apparently he had grown up in the Seremban area and been a cadet all those years ago when Saffie had gone missing. He had remembered our name and the incident of a small English child disappearing, and the fact that she had never been found and that no one had been arrested for the crime.

I liked James Mohktar, a man with gentle eyes. I thought he looked more like a priest than a policeman. Jack had bought a map and as we set off through the traffic I tried to breathe deeply to contain my anxiety. I kept thinking of Fleur making her way to that small grave, alone.

It was stupid but I wondered if she would think that those old colonial rest houses still lay on acres of empty coastline. Jack had used the hotel computer and all we could see were rows and rows of hotels and complexes.

I imagined her arriving in a place that must have been clear and vivid in her head and finding a modern world had erupted from the empty paradise she had left behind. The deserted beaches would be gone and the spaces filled with concrete buildings. The jungle that met the edge of those government rest houses would have been beaten back to make way for water sports and rampant tourism. I saw her baffled and alone, not knowing in which direction to turn, the compass of her memory and imagination muddled by progress and a world that had moved on. I wanted to be there before her and it wasn't possible.

Jack had ordered an air-conditioned car. The journey into Malaysia had the unreality of a strange dream and the same sense of urgency. Jack kept glancing at me surreptitiously, and although it was cool inside the car the heat beat down unbearably and shimmered on the busy road ahead and glittered on the windscreen.

I had a sense of familiarity as we drove past the few rubber plantations left. I remembered suddenly the big black Humber my dad used to drive and this long, empty road to Malacca and Port Dickson as Saffie and I played I Spy. In those days there wouldn't be another vehicle on the road for miles. I saw again the flash of white from the trees where the tappers collected the milky rubber and the shadows and sunlight flashing and flashing as the car purred towards the coast.

At midday I began to feel nauseous and knew it would get worse if I didn't eat. Jack immediately turned off for the nearest town, which was called Palah, and we found somewhere to have a meal. I stopped feeling sick but I did not feel well. My head ached and the sweat ran down my legs and arms.

Jack watched me. 'I'm going to book a room somewhere so you can lie down until it gets cooler, Nik . . .'

He waited for me to say I felt fine and would he please stop fussing, but I didn't. I needed to lie down.

The room was basic but clean. I took my dress off and lay on the bed thankfully. Jack went to find me bottled water. I lay there worrying, glad to let my guard down while he was gone. I was anxious for my baby. I was anxious for Fleur.

I must have slept because I was woken by voices outside my door. Jack was talking to someone. I struggled up on one elbow in a befuddled state, wondering where I was or what time of day it was.

Jack came in, sat on the bed and felt my forehead.

'You're cooler now. You had me worried. You were running a temperature and you've slept so heavily and for so long. Four hours! I phoned Mohktar to tell him where we were. He was a couple of hours behind us and he's stopped off to see how you are. Nice guy. We've found a doctor to take a look at you.'

I felt embarrassed. 'Jack, there's nothing wrong with me. I'm just hot, pregnant and anxious, that's all. The doctor will think it's a total waste of time.'

'Just let him take a look at you, please.'

I leant forward to kiss him. Sweet, protective Jack. 'OK.'

The doctor was Chinese and spoke poor English. He nodded at me and felt my forehead and pulse. Then he examined me thoroughly. His hands were small and gentle and I knew immediately they were safe and knowing.

When he had finished he gave me a searching look and went outside. I heard him talking to James Mohktar who translated for Jack. Then he came back and looked down at me.

'You sleep tonight. Travel tomollow. Short distance to Seremban. Baby OK. You must rest each day. Maybe baby come early. You small ploblem . . . you see doctor before fly home . . .'

'Thank you,' I said. 'Thank you for coming.'

Something like a shadow of a smile flitted briefly across his face and he nodded to me and left.

Jack came back and sat on the bed again. 'He thinks you might have a slight problem with your placenta which might affect the birth. He said you must mention this to your own doctor on your next check-up . . .' He grinned at me, looking relieved. 'But we have a healthy baby and he has prescribed some Chinese medicine and ordered you not to strain yourself or overwork . . .'

I stared at Jack and laughed. 'I think he was probably being ironic, Jack! Have you seen some of the pregnant women here? I saw an Indian woman in Singapore on a building site carrying bricks! She looked as if she could give birth at any moment. Me, overwork!'

I got out of bed and pulled my dress over my head and we both went out to talk to James Mohktar. We sat at a street café in this village that seemed to be a place people passed through rather than stayed. Jack ordered cold beer and Mohktar and I had icy fresh orange juice.

Mohktar spoke rapidly to the waiter and delicious small eats arrived. He smiled at me and pointed. 'Those are spicy, maybe too hot for you. These you like, I think . . .'

'You grew up in this part of the world?'

'A little further up the coast, near Kajang,' Mohktar said.

'Will you see your family tonight?' I asked.

'No. Tonight I drive to Seremban and Port Dickson to talk to my colleagues. Your mother must have travelled by train, local or express, because we have been in contact with all taxis and car-hire firms in Singapore. She will have had to alight at Seremban and catch the local bus or taxi for

Port Dickson. It may be that your mother will approach the police herself . . .'

His eyes rested on my face for a moment. I thought I knew what he was thinking. If Fleur had managed to locate the site of the grave, she would not find the small body still there. She would have to contact the police . . . if she was thinking straight.

Jack got up and walked away to pay the bill.

'Try not to worry, Miss Montrose. We will find your mother very soon.'

'The place where they found the grave, what will . . . ?'

'The site will be secured, Miss Montrose. There will be a policeman on duty while evidence is gathered and to prevent any access. The local police have been alerted to your mother's plight and will contact us as soon as they have a sighting.'

I met his eyes, suddenly realising that I was so sure that the body in the newspaper would be Saffie's that I had not even given a thought to the fact that it could be some other missing child.

'It is possible that it might not be my sister in that grave, isn't it?'

James Mohktar looked down at his hands for a moment. 'Yes, it is possible,' he said. 'And you should bear this in mind, Miss Montrose . . . Local children also die or go missing . . .' He paused. 'But . . .'

'Do you know something?'

He looked at me. 'I understand from my colleague in Kuala Lumpur that they are sending two men down with files from the Seventies. And they have been in contact with the British police, so . . .'

'They must believe it is my sister?'

I was suddenly cold and goose bumps sprang up on my

arms as if the shadow that was Saffie, long dead, had reached out to touch me. 'I'm sure it's her . . .' I met his eyes. 'I've dreamt about finding her since the moment I became pregnant.'

'All cases of missing children in the Seremban area over the last twenty years will be investigated. I am afraid you cannot take it for granted it is your sister, Miss Montrose,' Mohktar said quietly.

Jack had come back to the table. 'I need to be in Port Dickson,' I said to him urgently. 'Please let's drive on. It's not far. I must find Fleur. I've slept all afternoon, I won't sleep tonight . . . you know I won't.'

I felt Jack look over my head at Mohktar. Mohktar leant towards me. 'Miss Montrose. By the morning I will know more. You will not reach Seremban or Port Dickson before dark. It is much better you stay here and rest and drive on early tomorrow. I can phone you if there is anything you should know or if they have located your mother. I think you should do as the doctor tells you.'

Jack was looking anxious again. I gave in.

'OK,' I said to Mohktar. 'But please promise you will ring if you find out anything, however small?'

He smiled. 'I promise. Now I will leave you.'

He shook our hands and we watched him drive down the one little dusty road. It felt rather as if our only friend had disappeared.

FIFTEEN

Fleur woke in the small, shuttered room and knew immediately it was late. She could feel the warmth outside, heavy and waiting. The room smelt of electric mosquito repellent. She threw the shutter open and the heat hit her in a wave and shimmered off the rooftops outside. She looked at her watch; it was nearly half past ten. How on earth had she slept so long? Her throat was dry and she picked up the telephone to order coffee then went into the shower.

She felt as if she was someone else. Why had she stopped here? She felt anxious, desperate to be on her way. The Chinese woman knocked on her door and brought her a tray with tea and anaemic-looking scrambled egg and bread. Fleur could not eat it. She filled in her visitor's form, put her things together quickly, paid her bill and, thanking the small, impassive woman, she left the hotel and made her way to the bus station in a state of urgency.

A bus to Port Dickson had its engine running and Fleur hurried across the square and climbed on. It was half-full of people and of fowl alive and dead from market. Old women with string baskets full of soft scarlet tomatoes and small local bananas sat and watched her impassively.

The driver took her offered Malaysian ringgits and poured coins back into her hands as he too looked at her curiously. She did not look poor and she was not a young backpacker, why did she not catch a taxi?

Despite the running engine the bus did not move off and Fleur realised the driver was waiting for it to fill. Her heart sank. The heat trickled down the inside of her dress and she was just checking whether she had enough money for a taxi when, at last, with a blast of its horn the bus slowly rattled out of the small town onto the main road, kicking up dust and sounding as if any moment it might splutter to a halt.

The driver let people out of the doors at regular intervals and they melted into the shady trees that lined the road, off towards their *kampongs*, into little clearings in the jungle, carrying their live chickens and fruit and brightly coloured rolls of cloth.

At times, the bus stopped and waited on the highway to pick up people, and Fleur thought it was the longest, hottest, smelliest journey she had ever taken. When at last they rattled into Port Dickson she felt sick with relief.

The taxi drivers watched her, but she had no idea where to go. She closed her eyes for a moment and when she opened them they focused on a hoarding. *Selamat Datang to Blue Lagoon Hotel.*

'Blue Lagoon Hotel, please,' she said to the taxi driver. It would do for tonight while she got her bearings.

At the reception desk she told the sultry Malaysian receptionist that her husband was coming later with her luggage. The girl took ages checking her form, looking at her passport, and finally smiled sweetly and wished her a happy stay with Lagoon Hotel.

In her room Fleur looked down at the curved manmade lagoon with its carefully positioned palm trees. It was not very blue. All these years later, how was she to recognise the coastline and the wild places she had walked with the twins? This hotel was too near the town, the colonial rest houses had been further down the coast, she was sure of this.

She went down in the lift and ordered herself a strong coffee. Then she crossed the road to the little row of dusty shops. She bought herself odd underclothes with her card, two cheap tee shirts, a length of material to use as a sarong and a batik bag to put them all in. She went to the pharmacy and bought a toothbrush, toothpaste, soap and shampoo. Some instinct also made her buy some medical supplies.

She walked round the man-made lagoon onto the beach and looked both ways but did but recognise any landmark. Nothing was familiar. All was high-rise hotels and large swimming pools. The sea looked grey and uninviting. The afternoon sun beat down on her relentlessly and soaked her clothes. She felt sick and giddy. Going back up in the lift she had to hang on to the sides as waves of dizziness swung over her.

Was she ill? In her cool room she showered, made tea, then drank the miniature brandy with ginger and two paracetamol tablets and fell onto the bed.

Through the darkness of sleep Fleur still felt the motion of the train carrying her slowly towards her dead daughter. The fear of not finding the place where she lay haunted her until memory surfaced and the world outside her room turned again in to a beautiful lonely stretch of beach below the government rest houses.

All those hundreds of little wooden steps she had watched

Ah Heng help the twins down. At the bottom they would run laughing through the sand full of tiny spider crabs that ran ahead of their small feet.

Their beach ended at Tanjung Tuan lighthouse bordering the state of Malacca. Away in the distance, the land curved and became jungle. They used to climb up to the lighthouse to get the view out over the glittering water of the Malacca Straits.

In the dark, Fleur sat upright. It was night and sounds outside were hushed. Now she knew the direction she must take. She pulled the sheet up to her chin and rocked gently as the awful image kept at bay all these years surfaced again.

Saffie's hand in a stranger's. Fleur never saw his face, only the back view of him leading the small child away from her towards the jungle where the monkeys cried out and chattered like overexcited children.

The hand was dark, always dark in her mind, and Saffie, her small hand in his, felt no danger. She skipped, her blonde hair bobbing as she walked beside him, wondering what he was going to show her in the long hot afternoon when the grown-ups slept and made love and children should have been safe with amahs.

Fleur shivered and her guilt, forever with her like a second skin, surfaced in a cold layer of sweat. That long ago afternoon she had slept the drugged irresponsible sleep of a selfish woman who had put her own needs before those of her children. She should have made sure they could not leave the room . . . She should have kept them both safe.

Fleur faced once again in the dark Saffie's sudden and inexplicable disappearance. She thought about her last lonely and trusting walk to the edge of the jungle, to this moment now, when her small skeleton had been found in a hidden grave. She saw the curled little body, all bones intact, in foetal position, the same position in which she had lain beside Nikki in Fleur's womb.

Why now? Why had Saffie's body not been found before? How was it that she had not been taken by animals, all identification of her long gone as her bones were spread about the jungle?

Someone had placed Saffie in that shallow grave. She had lain alone, for a long, long time.

Dimly, Fleur realised she was feverish. She turned and thrashed in the damp bed, neither asleep nor fully awake, until stomach cramps forced her out of bed. She sat up, shakily, realising with a sinking heart, that this was not tiredness or jet lag, she was ill.

She staggered to the bathroom and was sick. She made herself get under a cool shower, then wrapped herself in the hotel bathrobe and switched up the air-conditioning. She went to the small fridge and got out a bottle of water, checking that the seal was intact. She had not eaten anything except toast so it had to be the water, possibly the Malay woman's on the train.

Fleur knew there was nothing she could do until this passed. She swallowed two codeine tablets and got back into bed. For hours her stomach contracted painfully and she staggered to the bathroom and back until she was shaking with exhaustion. Finally, she fell into a deep sleep and slept all that day, only waking to sip water. She was aware of someone knocking to clean her room and then go away again.

Fleur slept through the next night and woke in the unfamiliar hotel room with a cry in the early hours of the morning. Her fever had gone and her stomach was merely empty. She remembered where she was with a start. It was cold and she turned the air-conditioning off. A picture of the twins kissing on a dry lawn with Ah Heng standing in the background against a great burst of bougainvillaea stayed painfully with her.

She showered, made tea and ate the packet of biscuits on the tray. In the mirror she saw a thin, pale and haggard woman and turned quickly away. Fleur dressed, gathered her things into the Malaysian bag and left it on the bed. She went downstairs where, even in the early hours of a new day, the hotel breathed and lived a life of its own. She ignored the glances of the Malay girl on duty and went outside and woke up a sleeping taxi driver and asked him to take her to Cape Rachado.

As they drove, the sun was edging up over the sea in a familiar blaze of beautiful bruised colour. Fleur ached to be at the place where her daughter had been pulled from the earth. She needed to see and touch and gather up Saffie's remains, to keep them safe; to take her on her long journey home.

She did not stop to think that it might not be Saffie that the workmen had found, but someone else's child. It never entered her head that the white bones found lying in that small grave were not her missing daughter.

SIXTEEN

James Mohktar stood looking down into the shallow grave. The ticker tape attached to metal rods surrounding this tiny piece of jungle blew gently, drooped and made the site look forlorn and forgotten. The colour of it jarred against the merging greens; a flash of white and red, signalling alarm.

Dawn was coming. In the distance, beyond the trees full of monkeys screeching noisily, lay the sea. Mohktar sat on a boulder and poured himself tea from a flask. It was like being a child again. He missed these familiar sounds living in the middle of a city. Cicadas you could hear everywhere, even in a town, but you could not listen to the distant sound of the jungle coming alive and stirring with vibrant morning life.

He thought of the tiny room he had shared with his brothers and sisters in the *kampong*. His parents still lived in the same house near Kajang, but now, because of the erosion of the forest, the life of the river had changed, and each year when the rains came the *kampong* would be flooded and swirl round those little atap houses on stilts. His brother's children would gaze down at the muddied water and fish with bamboo rods and hurl down objects with glee to watch them float away.

The sun came now, edging up over the water, bringing with it the heat of a new day. His mobile telephone rang suddenly, jarring the peace, making him jump. He answered it abruptly.

'*Alamak*! Ya?'

Mrs Campbell had been found. She had apparently stayed the night in Port Dickson and had risen early and got a taxi, but they had not located the taxi driver yet to find out where he had taken her.

'Okay,' Mohktar said. '*Tidak apa-apa*. Never mind. I stay here. *Selamat tinggal.*'

The sun touched his hands through the trees. The clearing in the stillness of early morning had a pervasive and lingering aura. Not so much evil intent as a thing unfinished. James Mohktar thought about his small son. He could not bring himself to imagine evil coming to him. Could not bear to think either of his death or of a world in which he would have to live without his child.

Instinct had made him come here and instinct made him wait. It would have been easier for Mrs Campbell to go to the police, to ask exactly where the small body had been found and if it was European, but he did not think she would. In her place he would come here. She would come here first. Mohktar was sure of it.

He saw her alone in a foreign city staring down at the photograph of the grave and believing with absolute clarity that her small daughter had been found.

Far away down on the road he heard the faint sound of a car, possibly making for the lighthouse.

*　　*　　*

112

Fleur asked the taxi driver to wait or come back in an hour. She turned and climbed down the steep steps to the beach. She felt breathless and heady. The sun flaming across the sea warmed her cold limbs. At the bottom she turned left and walked slowly, looking up at the new red-tiled houses on stilts where she was sure the government rest houses had once perched on the hillside. Because of the steps she could just about work out where they had stayed that last time in Malaysia. There had been five rest houses along this stretch of coast and over the years she and David had stayed in all of them.

After David died, she had stayed with Peter and Laura in the one nearest to the beach. There had been only a few steps down to the long stretch of sand, much easier for the twins to play there.

Fleur marked her progress across the sand, seeing the twins' little fat feet running after the spider crabs which scuttled in small waves before her now. Ahead of her lay the rocks and boulders at the end of the beach and then a steep track up to the jungle path which led to the lighthouse.

It was odd to see the beach shops; the water sports and holiday complexes set back on the road. A different world. She could hear voices and the sounds of people cleaning and sweeping leaves from the hotels, getting ready for the first guests to rise and take breakfast.

She pulled herself upwards, shivering slightly at the thought of the darkness of the trees above her. The photograph was indelibly imprinted in her mind. She knew those small bones would have been removed. She knew the jungle would swiftly cover over the grave; that the only marker would be gaudy ticker tape to say where a dead child had lain.

She moved out of sunlight into shade. Above her, unseen,

she heard monkeys swinging from the branches and letting them go with a screech. This had always been an eerie place, lonely and haunting, full of exotic birds calling out into the silence. She climbed on and saw ahead of her trees toppled, their roots skyward and raw on the hillside as the undergrowth was cleared to make jungle walks past the lighthouse. Who had found the small grave she was making her way towards? A Malay workman resting in the heat of the day? A walker or a tourist? Looking at the devastation made by the bulldozer, it seemed to Fleur surprising that it had not razed all evidence of the hidden grave forever.

As she rounded a corner she saw the ticker tape and stopped abruptly on the path, her breathing laboured and painful. She inched forward towards the metal posts and looked down on a grave full of leaves and dead branches.

She imagined the curled bones of her child lying among the bared roots of the trees and the small insects that must have moved invisible and sure over her face, crawling over her skin as she lay cold and still in the undergrowth.

'Saffie.' A small sound escaped and her legs folded under her. She crumpled in the clearing silently, her eyes gazing downward to the place where her child had lain.

She is calling my name. Over and over she is calling my name.

Nikki! Nikki!

She is in some place where light can only filter through the darkness of trees. Water glints on the near horizon. I run towards her, to a place icy, stark and lonely as death. I run towards her but the landscape fades and disappears with Saffie in it. She is swallowed into darkness and I am the one left searching and calling . . . calling out her name.

It is always the same. I run towards Saffie but the dark

*landscape fades ahead of me into blackness and she fades
with it. I can never catch up with her. She just disappears.
I can never catch up with her no matter how fast I run.*

I wake to an overpowering sense of loneliness.

James Mohktar watched the small woman. He did not want
to startle her but he must now make his presence known.
He stepped from the shadows using her name in an effort
not to alarm her.

Her head swung round and her hands flew to her mouth
in fright.

'I am Detective Sergeant James Mohktar, Mrs Campbell.
We have been searching for you. Your daughter is very
worried.'

He flashed his card at her and she stared at it in incom-
prehension, then up at him. His face was gentle and her
fear subsided. He put out his hand to help her up and she
took it. She had the air of someone who was suddenly unsure
who they were or how they came to be in this place.

James Mohktar said again, 'Your daughter has been very
anxious for you, Mrs Campbell. I came here because I
believed this to be the place you might come. I would like
you to come with me now to Seremban. It is there we can
explain to you . . . what was found here.'

Fleur shivered as if waking up. She met his eyes. 'You
found my five-year-old daughter here. I know this.'

'Mrs Campbell, we will have to do DNA. tests before we
know for certain it is your daughter. Come, my car is a little
way only, up on the road. Let us go to telephone your other
daughter, to tell her that you are safe.'

Fleur closed her eyes. 'Nikki! Oh . . . God . . . I . . .
What was I thinking of?'

Mohktar reassured her quickly. 'It is okay, *lah*! Your

115

daughter flew to Singapore when you went missing. She is on her way here as we speak.'

Sitting in the back of James Mohktar's car, Fleur said inconsequently, 'I asked a taxi to wait for me, further down on the road.'

'I will speak with him as we pass. Do not worry.'

Mohktar spoke into his crackling phone in rapid Malay and then he dialled Nikki's mobile phone. She answered breathlessly. 'Yes?'

'Miss Montrose, we have found your mother. She is safe and quite well.'

'Oh, thank God! Can I speak to her?'

Mohktar turned to Fleur. 'Will you speak with your daughter to reassure her you are safe, please?'

Fleur hesitated and then nodded and reached out for the phone.

'Mum?'

'I'm so sorry, Nikki . . . I . . .'

'Don't be sorry. It's all right. Please don't be sorry. I'm just so relieved you're safe . . .' Nikki's voice quavered. 'Mum, I'll be with you in about two hours. Wait till we get to you . . . don't do anything on your own . . . I want to be with you . . . We'll . . . do this together, OK?'

'Thank you.'

Fleur's voice sounded so old to Nikki. Old and defeated and without hope.

SEVENTEEN

When the call came from DS Mohktar to say he had found my mother I was sitting up in the chair waiting for morning. Jack was still fast asleep and I had shaded a lamp and begun to read Fleur's Hundertwasser book.

Of course, I knew a bit about him. There is a public loo in Kawakawa that attracts a lot of Germans and I had gazed at his prints in touristy shops. He was one of those painters you stared at for a long time, revelling in his sense of colour without really understanding what he was about; a painter you knew you would return to one day to delve deeper.

My mother had left notes to herself among the pages of his book and I found these sometimes as revealing as the paintings themselves. She had marked one page in the book that had a painting called, *Half Siena, Half Paris*. It had obviously resonated with her and reminded her of Singapore, with its sprawling mix of races and cultures.

The painting was of a view, as if looking down upon a city full of tall buildings of differing architecture; a strange, uncaptured image of two cities in one place. The text suggested that the painting was meant to convey an impression of a place that never was, yet contained some source and emotion from both cities.

I stared down at tall buildings jammed together, all human nature behind a myriad of windows laid bare, filling the time and space.

I felt, without seeing the original painting or a large print, the aching loneliness of a polyglot of human beings milling round in Hundertwasser's make-believe city, just missing something essential which might have connected them as they lived crammed and hemmed-in without space to breathe. Lonely, like inhabitants living behind any façade, in any city, anywhere in the world.

But who was I to interpret this guy's work. What did I know?

Fleur had scribbled on a file card: '*A multi layer of images. Mixed lives, different cultures; giving permission for schizophrenic mingling of one person living many lives. All there in one place, a hundred cities, all the lives you've ever led in one lifetime. All the different people you've been. And how strange it would be, to hear yourself described by other people – to this person, you – who have little idea who you truly are at all, yet sometimes know too well the way you are perceived. I see myself too clearly through my daughter's eyes – the dart of hurt – because I know a ring of truth. This shallow self I was. Yet I have become wise enough to know I will never shift her image of me. It is set in Singapore and the unchanging landscape of her childhood. There it is, literally written in blood; the mother I was, not the woman I became or the woman I am now.*'

My hands shook as I read my mother's words. She was right: I didn't know her any more. I had taken trouble not to and now it might be too late. Who on earth was she, this middle-aged woman reading Hundertwasser and taking a degree?

Not my mother. Not Fergus's wife, that's for sure. So who had evolved from a decade of playing the pretty little woman needing a big strong man? And how had it happened without me noticing? The answer was clear enough: my total self-absorption and years of studied disinterest.

Did it always take tragedy to know the thing you had so carelessly lost? All my life I had carried the suspicion, no, the *knowledge*, that her affair with Fergus had caused my father's death that dreadful night of my childhood. This I had pieced together over the years, and from listening when I shouldn't to my grandmother, Laura. I had carried this information like a little stick I never mentioned. And boy, had I used it.

I wanted another chance. I desperately wanted another chance. That was when my mobile phone rang and James Mohktar told me he had found Fleur.

When we arrived, Fleur and DS Mohktar were still in Seremban Police Station. They were sitting in a stuffy little room with a ceiling fan. There was another fan on the desk moving stale air around. It was a deeply depressing room.

Mohktar got to his feet in relief and smiled at Jack and I. Fleur got up too, and she seemed so small and bewildered it made my heart jerk with pity and an urge to protect her. I saw her so rarely I had not watched her age and it was a shock to be confronted with the fact that she was, inevitably, older.

I went over to her and took her hands awkwardly. 'Mum? Are you all right?'

She tried to smile. 'I'm all right, darling, but how about you? I hear you had a bit of a fright?'

119

'It was nothing, just the heat. I'm fine.' I looked at her face; it was drained. 'You're exhausted. You need to sleep.'

'I have slept . . .' she said vaguely, '. . . it seems to make no difference . . .' She looked past me at Jack.

'Oh!' I said quickly. 'Mum, this is Jack.'

Jack stepped towards her and took her hand between both of his for a second and then stepped back. He didn't say, 'Glad to meet you . . .' He didn't say anything trite and I really loved him for it.

Mohktar coughed gently. 'Mrs Campbell, if you can just answer some questions; Miss Montrose too. We need a DNA sample from both of you and then I will try and arrange accommodation for you.'

A Malay inspector came in with a record sheet. He spoke hardly any English so Mohktar translated. The few questions he asked were about the past, about Saffie and when we were last here in Malaysia. Could we remember which rest house, the date, the time, the year? It was as if they needed to verify that we were who we said we were. Fleur's eyes did not leave the inspector's face.

Those hours when Saffie disappeared were a blur to me, frightening, like a dream, not quite real. I could not remember the sequence of what happened in the hours and days afterwards. Fleur remembered every little thing.

The Malay inspector got up and smiled at us and said something in a different tone of voice and Mohktar translated.

'Inspector Ibraham says to tell you he is most sorry for your tragedy in losing your daughter and for your sadness about the small body found. He says every effort will be made to verify the identity as quickly as possible to avoid more pain. He urges you to relax as much as possible in this lovely place and accept our hospitality and help. If there is anything that you need you must immediately let us know, *lah*?'

We both smiled at the inspector and thanked him. He left us and an Indian lady doctor came and took Fleur and me away. She took swabs from our mouths and two minutes later we were back with Jack and Mohktar. Of course I understood DNA, but I felt amazed that this quick little swab from the inside of our mouths would determine our link with some small bones found in a shallow grave.

Mohktar was on the phone and Jack came over and put his arm around me. 'He's trying to find private accommodation for us, where we won't be bothered by any press or interested voyeurs. It would be better than a hotel, wouldn't it?'

'Oh, God, yes. Don't you think so, Mum?'

'Yes, I do. How kind of him.'

Mohktar put down the phone and beamed at us. 'We go now to look at this bungalow I have found for you. It belongs to my mother's aunt. She normally rents it to visitors but she had cancellation. It is not so very modern, but comfortable I think. Come, I take you, and if you are not happy we think again.'

'I am sure it'll be wonderful,' Fleur said, almost in her old voice.

She got into Mohktar's car and Jack and I followed in the hire car. We drove out of Port Dickson and stopped at Fleur's hotel, collected her few things and paid the bill. We drove for a few miles before turning off on the coast road towards Cape Rachado and the lighthouse. I tried to remember. I tried to remember us all purring down here in Dad's car, but I couldn't recognise anything at all. That time had long gone, it lived on only in my head.

We bumped down a track that ended in a small car park.

121

'We cannot get any nearer, I am afraid. I think we leave your luggage in the car until you have seen. It is important it is all right for you. That you can feel relaxed while you wait for events to unfold.'

We walked across the sand to two wooden bungalows set above the beach a little way apart, much like the rest houses used to be. James Mohktar confirmed that the rest houses had lain in the curve of this beach. To the middle and further end lay the new – to us – hotels and self-catering accommodation.

We walked up wooden steps to a veranda. The shutters were thrown open and the windows had mosquito screens fitted. Memory stirred, and with it a little thrill of remembered childhood, the excitement, the possibilities of a holiday exploring. I glanced at Fleur and she smiled and moved with me through the door.

We both stopped dead. It was full of old army-issue rattan furniture and faded chintz covers. Orchids stood in a vase on the table and a small woman in a faded coloured *sam foo* stood nodding and bowing to us in the corner.

Mohktar talked to her in rapid Malay. I heard Fleur say under her breath, 'Oh, God, it's like coming home.'

Mohktar said, 'This is Ah Lin. She will look after you and cook if you like to stay.'

'It is perfect, DS Mohktar,' Fleur said. 'Isn't it, Nikki?' She smiled at him. 'I think you knew it would be.'

Mohktar said gently, 'It was how the rest houses were, I think. My aunt bought these two bungalows long ago, before the tourists came. My uncle worked with army supplies, as you see, and bought up surplus when the British moved out. I was only afraid it would remind you too much . . . of those last days here, Mrs Campbell.'

Fleur turned to him. I thought for a minute she might

122

cry. 'You are very thoughtful. That last time here is always with me . . . But a modern hotel would feel more alienating and foreign than staying here. Thank you, it's just what we need, a place to be private.'

Jack and Mohktar went to get our luggage and Fleur and I looked out and down at the stretch of beach, silently watching small children run across the sand, just as Saffie and I had done so long ago. Fleur said suddenly, 'It's a good thing none of us can know what lies ahead, isn't it?'

I moved closer. 'Mum . . .' But I did not know what to say. I couldn't find the right words.

She turned from the sea. 'It's all right, darling. I'm not going to fall apart. I'm not going to go to pieces. It was the shock of picking up that paper, the total, unexpected shock . . . Most of my life I've imagined someone knocking on my door in London to tell me that Saffie's body has been found somewhere and I always knew I would have to fly immediately to that place . . . in a totally irrational need to be near her. I felt the same terror of not being *here, with her* when I saw that photograph. I just flew . . . without a thought for you or for anything . . . I'm so sorry, darling . . .'

'Don't be sorry. I would have done the same and we're both here now, aren't we?'

'Yes, and it's so good to have you here with me.'

'You know, Mum, that it might not be Saffie . . .'

Before I could say any more Jack and Mohktar were back with the luggage. Fleur's dress looked crumpled and worn and I knew the first thing she would do was throw her clothes off, shower, wash her hair and dress in clean, spotless clothes. Then she would look like my mother again.

The amah brought out a jug of iced water and freshly squeezed orange juice and placed it on the table. She spoke rapidly to Mohktar and he said, 'Ah Lin will cook you a

123

light lunch before you rest. She will cook for you while you are here and if there is anything you do not like or cannot eat you must tell her.' I handed him a drink and he drank it down in one. 'I must go. I will be back later. Here is my mobile telephone number. OK? Do not hesitate to ring if you have need. Rest now . . .'

I walked with him out onto the veranda. 'How long will a DNA test take?'

'It depends on how busy the lab in KL is, but not long, Miss Montrose, maybe twenty-four to forty-eight hours only . . .' He held out his hand as if for comfort and I took it. 'Miss Montrose, are you hoping it is your sister or will you be relieved if it is not?'

'I want it to be Saffie. I want an end to the not-knowing.'

'Mrs Campbell too, I think?'

'Oh yes.'

He let my hand go. 'Try not to worry, Miss Montrose.'

He turned and started to walk across the sand and I called, 'Thank you . . . for everything.'

He turned round and flashed me his wonderful smile. 'My pleasure.'

Jack was leaning against the wooden railings. 'He's one of the good guys. You OK?'

I went and leant against him. 'I'm fine. I just want to know as quickly as possible.'

After lunch Fleur went to her room and I fell asleep next to Jack, who was lying reading. The waiting was going to be awful. I thought I wouldn't sleep, but I did.

EIGHTEEN

Fleur could not sleep. She paced, got up to drink water from the fridge, lay down with her book, kept reading the same line. She closed her eyes, tried to banish the memory of that small grave and could not. How was she going to feel if it was not Saffie? Relief that it was not her daughter buried in that lonely place for all those years? Or terror that it was some other child and that she and Nikki would never discover where Saffie lay?

She turned under the overhead fan in the hushed, hot afternoon and the silence pressed in upon her, weighing her down with the memory of that last time, sickeningly clear as if it had been yesterday.

The mosquito net stirred in the draught from the fan, ballooned gently round her like a parachute, and she was back, back in another room in a dusty wooden house long demolished.

Two weeks after the funeral in England Fleur flew back to Singapore with her parents and the twins. They had all stayed with David's colonel and his wife. Fleur had wanted to go back to their quarter, but Peter had vetoed it. Ah Heng was no longer sleeping there and it would be traumatic for Fleur and the twins to return there without David and Ah Heng.

The pilots in David's squadron and their wives were a close family unit and Fleur knew there would have been gossip. She and David had rowed publicly the night before he died. But when she returned to Singapore, people went out of their way to approach and reassure her.

'Fleur, we all row,' her friend Lucy said. 'Please don't let it eat you up. Everyone knows how close you and David were. You adored each other . . . It's just made the . . . losing him worse for you . . . Just keep remembering how good you were together . . .'

Fleur wondered how she was going to get through another emotional ceremonial church service. The English funeral had felt unreal, but this packed army church full of uniforms and unfailing support was harder. David had been a charismatic and popular officer and the anguish and shock his sudden death had caused in the other pilots he worked with did not seem to have diminished in two weeks.

So many people had an anecdote, an incident they burnt to relate, and Fleur sat next to her father twisting her hands, dry-eyed, listening to every word as it took her back vividly to the man she had lost.

One of the pilots who had been flying with David on the night of the storm was still in Changi Hospital. He sent an emotional tribute from his hospital bed. He had managed to crash-land his helicopter just before David came down.

But it was Fergus who made people weep with his happy and funny memories of a man who had been his friend as long and as far back as he could remember. Fergus had also flown that terrible night and felt the sharp guilt of a survivor.

Peter, feeling Fleur begin to tremble, reached for her hand. Her eyes were riveted to Fergus's face, but Fergus could not look directly at Fleur in case he broke down.

Laura had not come to the service but had stayed behind to look after the twins. They were too young to attend another tribute to their father, to be constantly reminded of all they had lost.

Everyone went back to the colonel's house afterwards. He and Peter had decided the house would feel more personal than the mess. It stood on stilts, high on a hill looking directly out towards Malaysia. Bougainvillaea coated the front and from the lawns behind the house they could all watch the sun set behind the horizon.

Fleur went straight up to the room she was sharing with the twins because they would not sleep without her. It faced the garden and the sea. Voices floated up to her, glasses clinked, people laughed and called to one another as they faced the bruised and magnificent setting sun. Somewhere, far below her, she heard the twins' voices.

Fleur knew she must go down. She could not stay here safe in her room. She wanted to turn and run; to find a little nest for herself and the twins and hole down and let the world go on turning without her. She did not want her father's anxiousness or her mother's restless sympathy. She did not want to go downstairs and be brave and bright and not let herself down.

She felt a blind terror of the future and what it now held. She was left with two little girls and no money. They had lived on David's income. Her money from teaching dance, with no formal qualifications, was pocket money. There would be a small army pension, but not enough to bring up two children. She had never worked for a living. She had married David.

She would have to go back downstairs or someone would come looking for her. She could see groups of people glancing back towards the house as if wondering where she had got to. There was Fergus and a group of David's friends standing awkwardly on the lawn. Fleur swallowed. *Fergus*. How strained and unreal things were between them. They were both shrouded in a deep and separate misery.

Fleur turned from the window and made her way down the wide staircase. As she emerged into the last golden rays of the sun, she caught Fergus's eye as he stood by the swing with the twins. Had he been waiting for her? She almost ran for his bear-like hug. *But she couldn't. She had hurt him*. She hadn't set out to use him to wound David as David had wounded her, but that is what she had done. In a way she had betrayed them both.

She held Fergus's eyes for a moment and he lifted a hand and she lifted hers in reply. The three of them had been too close for a permanent rift, but they both needed time to heal. How ironic, she thought, that when we both desperately need the comfort of the other, it is the one thing impossible to give. As she turned, she saw Laura standing very still watching her, her expression unfathomable.

Laura was standing talking to a small group of subdued officers and their wives, while keeping an eye on Saffie and Nikki. Where had Fleur got to? Was she wrong to feel irritated by her daughter? She knew she was. For heaven's sake, they had only buried David two weeks ago. But these were his friends, *their friends* and Fleur should not just disappear and pretend this was not happening. She wanted Fleur to be brave and show her friends what she was made of, not leave her and Peter and the colonel and his wife to it.

People had come to honour David and to show solidarity. Fleur should be down here, dignified and present.

Laura felt anxious by her daughter's crippling lethargy. Peter had always made life easy for Fleur, spoilt her. She had a nagging premonition that would not leave her, and guilt, because she knew her sympathy and love should be maternal and unconditional.

Laura was devastated by what had happened and shocked to the core by David's death. She and Peter could not have had a better friend or son-in-law. She had considered Fleur too young and immature for David and she had been proved wrong. Fleur and David had had a wonderfully happy marriage.

But now Fleur had to be courageous because she had two children and their lives must be put above her own. Her own distress should be secondary to their security, even if this meant Fleur had to feign a stability and bravery she did not feel. Nikki and Saffie needed something to hang on to. A future that was not too frightening without their father.

This was just not happening. Fleur seemed completely detached from all that was going on, especially with the twins. She was going through the motions of caring for them but she was distant and unreachable most of the time. The twins panicked and clung and then turned reluctantly to their grandparents.

Laura watched Fergus pushing the twins on an old swing. He was making them smile, despite his own obvious misery. *Children could not live with unremitting sadness, it weighed them down, suffocated their innate sense of life.*

What were they going to do with Fleur after the holiday in Malaya? Peter had to return to Northern Ireland. It was a worrying time for him out there. Laura felt torn between a husband she wanted to be with and her daughter, who suddenly found herself a widow at barely twenty-five and who needed her far more than Peter at the moment.

I shouldn't even hesitate – Peter is quite capable of living in the mess for a while. She was being selfish. Her life was being interrupted again. She had just got a part-time job in the army library – not much, but something – and she was tutoring privately, A-level English. She had waited all her life to do something in her own right.

It seemed to Laura that she had led a life full of halted expectations. A hundred homes, a million coffee mornings and dinner nights saying and doing the right things. Being nice to people she often had nothing in common with, because it helped smooth the way for Peter's career.

Peter had never asked her to do anything she was not happy with, but it was what she expected of herself. Behind her back Laura had sometimes been accused of being the one with the ambition. She felt no resentment while she was doing what was expected of an army wife. It was when she looked back; looked behind her at the years since the children had left and remembered the thrill of her degree. Now it seemed a faded and rather pointless piece of paper. Like something secret or precious placed in a drawer and years later drawn out with only the shadow of a memory of why it had been so important.

Laura was not so selfish that she did not ache for her daughter or grieve herself for the loss of a young life. But she could not live Fleur's life for her. She could not take David's sudden death or the aftermath from her. She could not make this terrible tragedy go away. Fleur had two dependent children. She was responsible for them. She was a grown-up. Laura and Peter could not take this hurt away.

David was no longer here to make all the decisions, to shelter her, like her father had, from all that she did not like. *Grow up. Please grow up and show us what you are made of. Surprise me. Make me wrong. Make me proud of you.*

Laura walked towards the twins and Fergus. In the night Saffie sucked her thumb and cried out for Ah Heng. Nikki lay for hours with her knees drawn up to her chin, motionless. Turning, she caught Peter's eye across the garden. He was signalling that one of them should go and see where Fleur had got to. Laura smiled. Peter, despite the dangerous and thankless job he was doing, was still the gentlest man she knew.

At that moment Fleur emerged from the house. She looked so young, and despite her thinness and the sallowness of her dark skin she was effortlessly beautiful, her movements languid and graceful. The twins, with a small cry of joy, left Fergus and ran across the lawn towards her. Laura felt love for her daughter well up inside her. *I'm hard on her. I always have been. Did I want another son?*

She smiled at Fleur. 'Darling, are you all right?'

She turned and followed her daughter's eyes. She was looking at Fergus and Laura suddenly caught the expression on Fergus's face. Unmistakable. My God! He was in love with Fleur. Laura felt an icy finger run down her spine. Was guilt contributing to both their misery?

Laura had seen it all too often. An exotic posting, pretty wives and too many single males; a recipe for disaster.

Peter was walking across the garden towards them. 'Darling, are you bearing up?' he said to Fleur when he reached them. 'People won't stay too long, you know. Everybody just wants to feel they are supporting you . . . If you can just manage to say hello and thank people for coming . . .'

'We'll stay and circulate with you . . . You don't have to

131

stay talking . . .' Laura grabbed a drink from a passing waiter and handed it to Fleur. 'Have a drink, Fleur . . . it will help . . .'

Laura's voice sounded as it always did. She surprised herself. She and Peter walked across the lawn with Fleur between them, but the small chink that had opened and warmed towards her daughter closed sharply again. David had deserved better than a flirtatious or unfaithful wife.

Peter had rented one of the government bungalows in Port Dickson for two weeks. They could reach Sam in Penang easily from there. They had booked the holiday in Penang some time ago and were meeting Sam and his girlfriend on their way home from Australia. Sam had done a year in a Melbourne hospital and had spent six months travelling before now returning to London and medical school.

Peter and Laura had hoped Ah Heng would go with them to Port Dickson before she started her job with the High Commission, but Eldest Brother died suddenly the day they flew back and there was a huge Chinese funeral that could go on for days.

After a week at Port Dickson, Fleur seemed more herself. Peter and Laura had no way of contacting Sam or any idea where he was coming from so one of them had to go to Penang to meet him. Sam, out of reach, did not even know David was dead, and Peter and Laura were reluctant to leave a message at the hotel. It would be too much of a shock.

Peter had not wanted to leave Fleur, but Laura would not travel on her own and he was torn. Fleur had assured them both she would be fine. She had to get used to being on her own. Of course they must meet Sam. She was OK. She could cope. Honestly . . .

They had left her reluctantly. There were no phones in

the rest houses, which were quite basic, but there were other young families occupying the bungalows along the coast who promised to keep an eye on Fleur and make sure she did not feel lonely.

They had left her for twenty-four hours. Peter never forgave himself. Laura had to remember for the rest of her life, that she had, as always, made Sam her priority.

Port Dickson, 2004

At four o'clock Fleur gave up trying to rest, pulled her dress over her head and went and sat on the veranda, watching families beginning to trickle back onto the beach.

Ah Lin immediately materialised with a tray of tea and a piece of cake and nodded to Fleur to eat it. 'I make,' she said, smiling.

'Thank you. It looks lovely,' Fleur said, knowing she would have to eat it or smuggle it in to Nikki.

The amah disappeared again on backless little shoes and Fleur felt a lingering *déjà vu*, evocative as a sudden drift of familiar scent when someone passes. Sight, smell, sound; if you kept quite still you might almost believe it was possible to step back into your childhood . . . that sure, safe place where nothing threatened.

But you could not go back. Nor could you edit your life and take out that one second of total irresponsibility.

Fleur trembled, clutched her hands together . . . That day her parents left for Penang, one of the wives in another rest house, someone she hardly knew, had come round to see if she was all right. She had drunk two strong gins, even though the other woman was pregnant and not drinking.

After lunch she had taken the twins into her own room and put them in her bed for the long, hot afternoon. She had asked the amah to stay in the house, to be there in case they woke before her. The twins had gone instantly to sleep, and, longing, craving for oblivion, she had taken some strong codeine, thinking:

If I just take these maybe I can sleep too and then I can get through the evening. If I can only sleep and blot everything out . . . just for a couple of hours, I'll be all right . . . That's what I'll do . . . I must sleep . . .

Fleur moaned, lifted her face to an evening breeze from the sea. She felt the creak of the wooden floor expanding as it cooled. A chit chat dropped from the ceiling and ran along the balcony rail and away. The cicadas stepped up their noisy rhythm as the sun sank and the shadows lengthened.

Somewhere in the house she heard Jack and Nikki begin to move about. She heard the thin trickle of a shower and the clink of crockery from the back kitchen. She absorbed these sounds like sun upon her skin. She saw her younger self, dry-mouthed, crouched, waiting. Waiting in a wooden house for the torches on the hillside to bring back a frightened little girl who had wandered too far from home.

She had the sensation of having never left this place, that a piece of her had remained forever here, absorbed and held, a ghost in the fabric of a wooden house. Part of the shadows . . . waiting.

NINETEEN

I wondered if DS Mohktar had pulled stings because he arrived the following morning as Fleur, Jack and I were having breakfast. We watched him walk across the beach towards us and my heart began to hammer and sweat trickled down the inside of my dress.

I glanced at Fleur. She had gone suddenly grey and her hand trembled as she replaced her coffee cup. Neither of us took our eyes off Mohktar as he came towards us, as if we could gauge by the way he walked what he was going to tell us.

Jack looked anxious and placed his hand over my arm.

When Mohktar reached the wooden steps to the veranda he stopped and said quietly, '*Selamat pagi.* Good morning.'

The amah was pulling up another chair and she placed a cup of coffee on the table for him, before disappearing.

Mohktar did not sit. The tension coming from us all must have been intimidating. He looked at us with his kind eyes and with his hands on the back of the chair, he said gently, 'I come to tell you that I have early this morning the result of the DNA test.'

Fleur was so still beside me I thought she had stopped breathing.

Mohktar's eyes rested on us both, then he turned to Fleur. 'The DNA was a match. It is your daughter, Mrs Campbell.'

The words hung in the air, filled the silence. None of us spoke. I heard the sound of the sea and children a long way off and a radio somewhere.

'Thank you, DS Mohktar.' Fleur's voice was small and far away too.

Jack poured me a glass of water and wrapped my hands round it and made me drink. 'Breathe, Nikki. Take a deep breath.'

Fleur turned to me. 'Darling . . .'

'I'm fine. I'm fine,' I whispered, and I did breathe, made myself breathe. In. Out. In. Out. Then I said, 'When can we see her?'

Mohktar was watching me. 'We must drive to Malacca, Miss Montrose. This is where your sister is.'

I turned to Fleur. 'Let's go now.' I heard the urgency in my voice. 'We should go now.'

'I think later this afternoon would be cooler for you, Miss Montrose.'

Jack said quietly, 'Nik, it's not sensible for you to travel in the heat of the day.'

'It's not nine o'clock yet, Jack,' I said abruptly. 'And if anyone suggests I rest any more I shall scream!'

Mohktar said quickly, smiling at Jack to take the sting from my words, 'We have one air-conditioned car in the police pound at present. If I can obtain this car, the drive to Malacca would be no problem, I think? It is not far, it takes about forty minutes only.'

Fleur smiled at him. I was surprised how normal her voice sounded. 'It would be wonderful to have an air-conditioned car, DS Mohktar. I think Jack and I would feel much easier about Nikki. If you can spare the time, it *would* be good to go this morning. Please, sit and have your coffee before it gets cold . . .'

I stared at my mother. How was it possible to keep to the niceties when she must be in turmoil? I've never been able to. Jack was watching me. I got up from the table and walked inside and he followed me. Outside I heard Mohktar talking on his mobile phone.

I turned to him. 'Jack . . . sorry, I didn't mean to snap.'

'Don't be silly, darlin' . . . I just wish I could take this from you, and I can't.'

'You're here,' I said. 'You're here and it makes a difference . . . I can't wait till this afternoon, Jack. Fleur and I have waited so many years . . . I need to see for myself that Saffie is really dead.'

The small skeleton was almost intact. They had laid the bones of my sister as she had been found, curled for sleep. The Indian pathologist told us they had taken great care with her. They had been sure that the bones fitted the profile of a small European girl aged about five years, who must have died about twenty-five or so years ago, and the DNA had confirmed it.

The room was cool and Fleur's hand in mine was icy but did not shake. We could not take our eyes from the tiny skull, turned sideways still. They had asked us if it was a good idea to see her. They said: *Why not remember her as she was, alive and happy?* The living child my mother and I carried around with us every day of our lives. But when there has been no body, there has been no death that you can really believe in. At first you carry hope, then when that dies you think of her somewhere else, *but alive*. Kidnapped

137

and living with strangers. At least I did. I made up another life for Saffie for years and years. I thought of her with people who loved her, where happiness was possible. And then as I grew up and that slid from me I prayed that she had not had time to be too frightened. I hoped only that death had been quick and that she had not been aware it was coming.

I needed to see concrete evidence that I had been a twin. That once, long ago, I had another part of me that was inseparable, for sometimes it seemed only a lovely dream that I conjured from loneliness. In that terrible, swift and sudden end to Saffie's life a part of me died too.

I moved forward to peer into the hollow eyes that once had eyes like mine and I bent to my own skull and felt the rustle of unease ripple round a room that was so silent it felt surreal.

We were one, Saffie. We were one and the same, you and I.

Lying safe in Fleur's womb we lay curled together, submerged and sealed in warm, protective water. We could have been fraternal twins, but we were one egg which split in two. Conceived together; just a speck of a billion sperm, random eggs that swam upwards making us identical.

Even when you died I thought we could be one again. I made myself believe that by sheer will I could conjure you to me. I put on your blue cotton pyjamas. I pulled my hair up in that old blue band of yours, just like you used to do.

I went to the mirror. See? See? Who is to say this is not you, Saffie? Who is to say that this is really me? No one! No one! I can re-create you. I can be you and you can be me. I can do it. See, Saffie, how I stand before you in the

mirror in these blue pyjamas you always wear. I am you,
Saffie, and if I am you, you cannot be dead . . .

Fleur touched me, pulled me gently away from that
small, fragile skull, from the bones of a child who died
long ago.

'Darling . . . Come away now. Enough. We have seen . . .
and it is real to us now after all this time. Come away . . .'

I turned to her, mystified. *How can I leave her? We have
only just found her.*

The child in my womb kicked hard and I drew in my
breath, put my hand on my stomach and felt the strange
urgent movements of my baby turning. It was like coming
back from a long journey to some dark place and I breathed
deeply and started to shake and was led quickly away out
of the room.

Outside, Jack leapt up and came to me, held me to him,
and I was so cold that my teeth chattered, making a noise
in the silence. I hung on to him as darkness came rushing
sickly upwards.

The journey home passed like a dream as we sped past old
colonial buildings built from mellow stone, places we might
have visited long ago. They thought I would be hot but the
car was cold . . . so very cold . . .

I woke to find myself in bed. The room was dark and I
had a cover over me. The shutters were open and outside I
could see the sky livid with the sun setting. Somewhere, not
too far away, I could hear soft voices talking earnestly.

I looked round. I did not know how I'd got back here
or how long I had slept. I lay still, and the dark thing I
knew was waiting for me edged nearer. The same thing
that had waited unseen in the corners of my grandparents'
cold bedroom in England; a thing I could never remember

when we returned to their house without Saffie.

On my tongue now was our secret language, Saffie's and mine. I thought I had forgotten it, but now I found my lips forming the question.

'Meit to?' I whispered into the shadows.

'Favlo!' came the reply like a breath. And there she was by the window, her hair in a ponytail, wearing the faded cotton dress with the tiny pink flowers on. My dress. I wore pink. Saffie wore blue.

I sat up, leant forward to see her face, but as always it was in shadow. She stood there quite still but she did not move my way. I wanted her to stay. I needed to see the expression on her face, needed to see if she smiled or was sad. Mostly I needed to know, and dreaded knowing, if I would see her last expression of fear imprinted forever upon her features.

I pulled the cover back and swung my feet onto the floor and I saw her shake her head slowly once.

'Pinot. Pinot,' I begged. 'Don't go, Saffie. Don't go.'

I think she turned or the shadows in the room changed. I saw her face briefly and there was no expression there at all. Yet the room was full of her pleading. Then she was gone.

'Saffie!' I whispered. 'What is it? What do you want me to do?'

Beyond the shadows, beyond the mosquito screen in the window, I saw the frangipani trees moving as the wind got up. I thought I heard the faint sound of crying, but I couldn't be sure.

Fleur was impressed by Jack. She had expected a rather detached man's man, but she saw immediately he was a gentle person and very protective of Nikki.

Her daughter's reaction in the pathology department had alarmed Fleur. It was as if Nikki had immediately regressed, frighteningly quickly, to the days after Saffie's disappearance. Twenty-eight years had not diminished Nikki's loss or prepared her for the finality, the evidence of Saffie's death.

Fleur got up and went to the door of the bedroom where Nikki was sleeping with the help of a relaxant from a soft-voiced Indian-woman doctor. Safe for a pregnant woman, she had assured Jack.

Nikki lay in exactly the same position on the bed, heavily asleep. Fleur moved back along the veranda and sat down with Jack again. She had been jerked out of her own shock by Nikki's distress, but she was fighting exhaustion.

The small bones of her child, curled as if for sleep, remained behind her eyes like a clear photograph through all that she was saying to Jack. Seeing Nikki pregnant and vulnerable, her detached and cool exterior blown away, Fleur realised that all these years Nikki had maintained a furious defence against a loss she had had to endure but had never come to terms with.

She said, as she looked at Jack's worried face, 'Twins, especially identical ones, are immeasurably close. Closer to each other, in a way, than they are to their parents. I learnt, when I had Nikki and Saffie, that I could never be cross with one twin or the other would be outraged. Sometimes you could never be sure which one you were talking to because they liked to play games. I used to dress them in different colours so people would not get confused, but they would swap their clothes around and imitate each other's mannerisms, so from a distance even David and I had trouble knowing who we were talking to . . .'

141

She met Jack's eyes. 'Of course, as they grew up it would have got easier and easier as their mannerisms and characters developed . . . but . . .'

Jack leant towards her. 'I can't imagine what you must have felt in there . . . or what you're feeling now, Fleur. Nikki gave me a hell of a turn back there. She's not the fainting sort . . . but she's not having an easy pregnancy.

'Even after all these years, it is your daughter and Nikki's sister in there and I don't know how I could expect any different. It's still a terrible shock and time doesn't change that.'

Nikki has touched gold with this one and I thank God for it, Fleur thought.

'Would it have been better never to know?' Fleur seemed to be talking to herself. 'Or is it better to be confronted by the evidence of my child's death after all this time . . . You see, I dread . . . if they can tell, somehow, how she died. Jack, I'm sorry, I've had it. I'll have to go to bed.'

Jack leapt up. 'Of course. No worries. You look all in.'

Fleur's face was ashen and drawn and she seemed very small. Her dark hair, flecked with grey, was clipped up in the way Nikki sometimes clipped hers, elegantly with a tortoiseshell clip.

'Good night. I hope . . . Try and sleep. I'll keep an eye on Nikki.'

Fleur smiled. 'I know you will. 'I'm so glad she's got you, Jack. Good night.'

In her room, Fleur, trembling, pulled a nightdress over her head, climbed under the mosquito net and slid between cool cotton sheets.

She slept for minutes at a time but kept waking, her mind

throwing up images and memories she would rather had remained buried.

If only she could have that time again; change the sequence of those long, dark days that led resolutely from one tragedy to the next.

TWENTY

James Mohktar shook hands with the English detective who had flown out from London. He had brought a short stack of files dating back twenty odd years. Gordon Blythe was about to retire but had been a young military policeman at the time of the disappearance of the small army child in 1976.

He had no illusions as to why he had been spared to resurrect this old case. By the time he returned to London he would only have a few months to do. He had been let out to graze.

'Detective Inspector Gordon Blythe,' he said, shaking Mohktar's hand.

'*Apa khabar*? How are you, Inspector? I hope your accommodation is satisfactory and you have recovered from your journey?' Mohktar asked politely, glancing at the older man's tired face.

'It'll take a day or two for that,' Inspector Blythe said. 'But it helped having a night in Singapore.'

James Mohktar had expected to be recalled to Singapore himself, but Inspector Teddy Chan had agreed to leave him in Port Dickson as he had established a rapport with the family. He also came from the area and was familiar with the families of some of the locals who had been questioned at that time. He would be useful to Inspector Blythe.

Mohktar doubted he would be able to help as he had only been a police cadet in 1976, but the disappearance of a European child had shocked this small state at the time and people did remember it.

He had moved Fleur, Nikki and Jack to a different location at the quieter end of the beach, purposely, to protect them from any press intrusion. He had managed to prevent them seeing the local papers, which once the DNA had been formally established were free with opinions as to what might have happened all those years ago. They also offered various gory theories about child trafficking and what sort of person might have perpetrated the crime. Some of the papers had also published the names of local men who had been questioned but released at the time.

'If you could plough through these old reports with a couple of your men, I will do the same with your old case notes, Detective Sergeant,' Blythe said. 'Bearing in mind the Met aren't going to leave me here indefinitely, so time is vital.'

Mohktar smiled to himself but said politely, 'Indeed. But you must bear in mind that we are not in England and people here rise early but do not work in the afternoons in the heat of the day, Inspector. Here is also a small provincial force so our main help will come from Kuala Lumpur. All these records have come from there and there is only one policeman left in the force who was involved in this case and he will be our link with KL.

'Good,' Blythe said. 'I presume that it will be almost impossible to determine how the child died after all this time?'

145

'I believe it is doubtful,' Mohktar said. 'Unless the bones show specific breakages.'

'What was the mother doing in Singapore? It seems odd that she was here when the body turned up after all this time?'

Mohktar was unsure due respect was being given to Mrs Campbell and her dead child. But perhaps it was the English way.

'Mrs Campbell was on her way to see her daughter in New Zealand. She had a stopover in Singapore and she saw *The Straits Times* with the article about the grave, quite by chance, *lah*? When she went missing the hotel rang us and we contacted her daughter who flew to Singapore immediately. I believe it to be a sad coincidence that the lady arrived as the body of the child was found in the clearance of that piece of coastline.'

'I am not sure I entirely believe in coincidences,' Blythe said. 'How come the child's body was still intact and in one place in the jungle after all this time?'

'It had lain, or been pushed, under rock in a natural underground cave. It had also been wrapped in something; many fibres of material were found on the body. If the driver of the machine had not stopped for the call of nature, the child's body would never have been found.'

He looked at the English policeman. 'Do you really expect after all this time that we will find out what happened, Inspector?'

'Unlikely,' Blythe said. 'But maybe we owe it to the family to have one more try. I have a list of all the Europeans staying at the government rest houses in 1976, plus a list of local Malay and Chinese working or living there.'

'You would like me to look into the whereabouts of any locals who were here at that time?'

'Yes. I know it's time-consuming, but . . .' It was also complicated, Blythe thought, by the fact that some families had brought their own servants on holiday.

The two men looked at each other. It all seemed a prodigious amount of work for an uncertain result. He had not been sent to solve the case, Blythe thought, but more to close it. He shook himself out of his jetlag. He shouldn't have agreed to come if he had such a negative attitude.

James Mohktar opened his palms. 'Inshallah. We must investigate. It is what we must do. A small child died long ago. No one has paid for that crime. We must do our best for the family, *lah*?'

Blythe looked at Mohktar startled. It seemed they had the same opinion of their chances of success.

'If I could meet Mrs Campbell and her daughter . . . Is it her husband with her?'

Mohktar looked disapproving. 'They do not marry and she has a child on the way. But he is a nice man, I think.' He got to his feet. 'I will now go and see how they are, and to arrange a time for them to meet you.'

Blythe nodded. 'I will make a start on these reports.'

As the Malay sergeant left, Blythe thought he seemed efficient but rather too sensitive to be a policeman. He opened the first report, trying not to feel he was on a wild goose chase, which is what Mrs Blythe had called his sudden departure as she crossly cancelled their weekend in Brighton.

It was almost worth having jetlag to get out of Brighton.

He looked down at the Military Police report with the names of the forces families staying on this coastline twenty-eight years ago. He had been unable to gather any information from the army. Two of the army detectives were now dead, one played a minor role and the last could not be found.

How this small piece of Malaysian coastline had changed. He got up and went to the window of the basic office. He looked out on the dusty street where market traders called out in front of their fruit stalls piled spectacularly high with colourful fruit. Durians, water and honey melons, oranges and limes, small sweet bananas and papaya. Bicycle bells rang, taxis hooted at pedestrians and a small child sat on a wall playing with or tormenting a thin, hungry-looking kitten.

Chinese and Malay voices, shrill and high, echoed into the square, mingling with Indian music playing from one of the dusty shops selling rubber flip-flops and cheap tee shirts and skirts.

Heat and dust and a life where all the days inexorably melt into the next, Inshallah, as the Malay policeman would say.

He could hear the noise of the small police station around him and away from the ceiling fan sweat began to gather under his armpits and over his chest and across his back. The morning had hardly started. Hastily he went back to the desk and looked down at the names on the first page.

Rest House 1
Sqn Ldr Richard Allis. Mrs Barbara Allis.
Grp Capt. Andrew Morris. Mrs Alison Morris.

Rest House 2
Colonel Bill Dury. Mrs Christine Dury. Saul aged four. Susan aged six months. Amah Ah Ming.

148

Rest House 3
Four teachers: Miss Tessa Brown, Miss Natalie
Clarke, Miss Anna Wilson, Miss Daphne Broadbent.

Rest House 4
Capt. Alex Addison. Mrs Beatrice Addison
  (pregnant).
Major Gardam. Mrs Elizabeth Gardam. (British
  High Commission.)
Mr Andrew Right. Mrs Paula Right. (Civilian friends
  living in Singapore.)

Rest House 5
Brigadier Peter Llewellyn. Mrs Laura Llewellyn.
Mrs Fleur Montrose.
Twin girls: Saffron and Nikki Montrose.

There were photographs of the small family as they once
were, all smiling. The two little girls were identical; the man
pictured was handsome and laughing. The woman was dark
and young and attractive. As he stared down at them it all
flooded back, the inexplicable suddenness of the child's
disappearance, the second bleak tragedy of that poor
woman's life.

Something rekindled and stirred in Blythe, as it always
did. The theory at the time was abduction for some nefar-
ious means by persons unknown. The child was blonde and
pretty and European and had seemingly disappeared from
the face of the earth. Mind you, police methods had
improved hugely since the 1970s.

How had the woman borne it, all these years, never knowing what had happened to her child? And what about the
twin, now grown up and expecting a child of her own?

Blythe knew that he and the woman and the surviving twin, despite the intensity of emotion engendered at that time, would have passed each other, without recognition, on a London street. Yet here they all were once again in the same place, twenty-eight years older, desperately hoping for the answer to something it might be better never to know.

TWENTY-ONE

I had thought about finding Saffie almost every day of my life, and now, when it had finally happened, it was not at all as I imagined it. All my childhood I willed myself to believe that Saffie was leading a strange foreign life somewhere and one day I would be walking down a street, a long way from home, and I would catch a glimpse of her, grown-up and happy, brought up by parents who paid someone to snatch her because they couldn't have children of their own. Or perhaps taken by a family who came upon her by chance and wanted her so badly they carried her away with them, but not to do her harm . . . just to have her live with them.

Oh, I had a whole safe world for Saffie, a place where, when I was angry with my mother or Fergus, I would join her, with her new parents who gave her everything her heart desired. In my imagination she would turn as I ran after her and her face as she saw me would widen and she would immediately know that this was why she cried in the night, *this* was why and where her unbearable sense of loss came from. *Me.* I was the missing link in her perfect life. I was the missing piece.

As I grew up the tale I comforted myself with seemed unlikely, faded, and became a thing I could not hold on to. I had to make the hole inside me bearable and I turned my back on Fleur. But not Fergus. I had been appalling to him when he and Fleur married, but I couldn't keep it up. He refused to dislike or cease to love me, whatever I said or did. In the end, I guess he became as much my father as my real father had been for those short first five years of my life.

I'd blocked all thoughts of Saffie in case I lost my mind. I pretended to outsiders that I was an only child. I longed for a sister or brother but it never happened. I used to hear Fleur crying and Fergus comforting her. No one knew why she couldn't conceive, but my mother believed she was being punished for not looking after Saffie; punished with no more children.

I asked to go to boarding school and I broke Fleur's heart, I think. And there, in the dark of an anonymous place, in the rows and rows of beds and muffled sobs, Saffie came to me. Sometimes she just sat on the end of the bed, the shape of her comforting me, making me feel less alone. Then, as I got older, she would arrive randomly and suddenly. All my life it seemed to me as if she was trying to tell me something. No, not just trying to tell me something *but leading me somewhere or to someone.*

Now, I knew. It was here, to this place where she left us. But how would I ever understand what she wanted me to know?

I felt cold with fear at the thought of what that understanding might mean. We both used to know what the other was thinking. Sometimes we spoke the same thing at the same time. If I had a stomach ache, Saffie would get unwell too. If she got a fever, my head throbbed. If she had lived I know we would have felt each other's labour pains.

But I do not want to go through her death. I do not want to know how she died. I am afraid of her fear and dread her last moments which Fleur and I have thrust away from us in order to go on and live our lives.

James Mohktar brought the English detective, who had flown out from London, to the house late in the afternoon. Inspector Blythe had been a young military police detective twenty-eight years ago before he joined the Met. He and Fleur stared as if they should remember each other, but how could they? Look what time does, it changes us inside and out. Fleur had been a young grief-stricken widow. Inspector Blythe had probably been an ambitious and keen policeman.

My mother was now a middle-aged woman with a sad and pretty face. Blythe was a man too heavy, grey with jetlag and a resigned expression, and yet I saw something pass between them, they did recognise each other. *I suppose it is our eyes that never change and always give us away.*

James Mohktar and Inspector Blythe wanted Fleur to go through the list of the names of people who had been staying at the other government rest houses when Saffie went missing. The names, of course, meant absolutely nothing to me. I couldn't put faces to them even if they sounded vaguely familiar.

Blythe wanted to know if Fleur had been particularly friendly with any of them, or if my father had, and if she knew where any of them were now. There were photographs of them taken twenty-eight years ago. I watched Fleur as she spread them over the table. From the open window the smell of frangipani was pungent and I had sudden *déjà vu,* a strange, dizzy catch of forgotten memory as I looked down on a photograph of a young man in uniform. Then it was

153

gone before I could hold it, but my hands on the table shook and I did not know why.

James Mohktar noticed. I knew by the very slight movement of his eyes away from Fleur's hands sorting the photographs to me. Fleur laid them out across the table.

'Those are my parents, of course. I don't suppose you remember them?' she said, touching the photographs of Gran and Grandpa. I stared at them. They seemed young too, although of course they must have been middle-aged. Their faces were blank with shock, their eyes clouded. Fergus told me once that they seemed to age with terrifying suddenness after David and Saffie went. My grandparents have always blamed themselves for leaving Fleur alone to go and see Sam in Penang.

'I do remember them,' Inspector Blythe answered quietly. 'I felt a profound respect for both of them. They were both dignified and helpful, despite the tragedy that had befallen you all.'

I watched the colour seep into Fleur's cheeks. I do not suppose she was able to be either dignified or helpful. Guilt combined with shock and panic must have pulverised her. Pity welled up inside me and I reached out to touch her arm. God! How I had judged her all these years. I thought of Jack dying and shivered. Fleur had still been reeling over my father's sudden death; how on earth could she have borne Saffie's disappearance.

Jack was over by the window, sitting looking out, not quite knowing if it was appropriate to leave me and go outside and walk. He was not part of this past of mine. Mohktar, as if sensing this, walked over and sat by the window with him, watching us.

Fleur looked up, surprised at my touch, and gave me a small smile. Then she went back to the names and photographs.

'I don't think I can add anything more now, after all these years, than I could at the time,' she said, staring down at the photographs of people still young. 'We knew the Allises only vaguely, from parties. David would have known the husband, Richard, rather better, from flying. The Morrises we did not know at all.'

The inspector leant forward and rearranged the photographs under Fleur's hand into the rest houses where they had been staying.

'I know it must seem pointless, Mrs Campbell, when people and places have faded over the years and we are going over the same ground again, but humour me. It refreshes my memory as well as yours. You would be surprised at the odd relevant things the brain retains . . .'

Fleur looked at him, started to say something and then changed her mind.

'The Dury family my parents knew quite well. I didn't as they lived in Singapore, not at the naval base. The teachers I knew by sight and had chatted to, that's all. The Addisons, I hardly knew, but Alex flew with David. Beatrice had been a QARANC, an army nurse in Changi, I think. They had only been posted in a few months. Beatrice was pregnant. I was told Alex stopped flying after the accident and went back to his regiment.'

She leant back in her chair. 'I know nothing about anyone else. You know what it's like, Inspector, you're posted and then move on, you lose track of people. You can't be bosom friends with everyone. I knew no one in the other rest houses really well. I was there with my parents. It isn't that I mind doing this, Inspector; it's just that it does seem pointless.'

The inspector turned to me and swivelled the photographs round to face me. 'And you, Nikki, any fragment of memory? I know you were only five, but children are very observant.'

I looked at the photographs but nothing came. Whatever sliver of memory there had been earlier had vanished. I shook my head. 'Isn't it far more likely to have been an opportunist? A local person meeting my sister suddenly out there in the afternoon?'

Inspector Blythe did not answer. James Mohktar got gracefully to his feet. He smiled his gentle smile and we all seemed to relax; he had that sort of effect on people and I was very glad he had stayed here.

He looked at Fleur. 'How are you feeling, Mrs Campbell?'

'I'm fine,' she said politely, as English people always do. 'Thank you.'

'And you, Miss Montrose? I do hope you are feeling recovered?'

'I'm better today, thank you.' I got up heavily and went over to Jack and leant against the chair he was sitting on. He put his arm round where my waist had once been.

Fleur got up too and went to the fridge and got out water and fresh orange and poured five glasses for everyone without asking. As she handed a glass to James Mohktar and Inspector Blythe, she said 'Saffie's body has been found and that is all I can think about at the moment. I'm unsure what going over old ground can possibly achieve after all this time, except to bring back bad memories for me and my daughter.'

The Inspector said quietly, 'Mrs Campbell, we did not have a body twenty-eight years ago. We had almost nothing to go on. We are waiting to see what the pathologist can tell us about the manner of your daughter's death.'

'And what,' I heard myself say suddenly, my voice odd and high, 'if we would rather not *know* the manner of Saffie's death?'

156

There was silence in the room. The inspector got up. 'We will leave you in peace now.' He looked at me. 'I am sorry; this is very hard for you both. Because we have to ask questions doesn't mean we are unaware of either of your feelings, I assure you.'

At the door, Mohktar hesitated. 'I will come back to see you this evening.' He smiled at us anxiously and then both men left.

'Shall we go out and walk for a while?' Jack asked after a minute. I nodded, but Fleur said, 'You two go, I'll join you in a while.'

I hesitated, unsure whether I should leave her alone but sensing Jack's restlessness.

'Go,' Fleur said, and I knew she wanted to be alone.

Jack did not speak as we walked. I looked around me; there were no landmarks I recognised. The deserted paradise I had kept in my head all these years bore no resemblance to this new resort, apart from the crabs. Water sports had sprung up at the other end of the long beach, and the jungle behind it had made way for hotels. The sea was no longer aquamarine, but a dirty grey as if someone had taken a stick to the ocean floor.

I wondered what was going to happen next. Did we wait to hear what the pathologist had to say? Would Saffie's body be returned to us? How long would Inspector Blythe stay and make his inquiries?

I wondered what James Mohktar thought and I decided I would ask him.

Suddenly, incongruously, making us jump, Jack's mobile phone rang as we walked towards the far end of the beach to the rocks, towards the place Saffie had been found. He dug it out of his pocket and held it to his ear. I could tell from the way he paced it was going to be something serious. He turned back towards the guesthouse we were in and covered the phone. 'I'm going to have to go back and get my diary, Nikki. Someone's pranged one of our yachts. I need some telephone numbers.'

'Oh, Jack!' I said. 'Which one?'

'Nik, it doesn't matter which one. Don't think about it. Are you coming back or staying out here?'

'I think I'll stay out here for a while.' I was hot, but I did not want to go back inside. 'I'll go and paddle, watch the windsurfing for a bit. I won't be long.'

'OK,' he said, distracted, already moving away. I walked on towards the sea and a small breeze caught my hair, but it was not cooling. I stopped and looked back at the modern buildings dotted at various angles along the cliff. At the far end, long, wooden steps led down to the beach, and at once I remembered Ah Heng leading Saffie and me down them from the rest house, making us hold her hands. They were steep and to a small child they seemed to go on forever.

I can smell the oil she put on her hair. I can see the smooth oval of her brown face and her spotless white sam foo *that she changed every afternoon after her shower, and the black baggy trousers she used to make herself on the old sewing machine in her room.*

I remember the way she would bend to lift both of us up together and how we clung to her when we were tired and how she scolded Saffie for sucking her thumb.

When Saffie disappeared Grandpa sent an army driver to bring Ah Heng to me. I would not let anyone else touch me. I screamed if they tried. She sat guarding me for two nights, making me sip water, and when everyone slept I crawled onto her lap and would not let her leave me.

Then we had to say goodbye to each other, all over again.

I wonder what happened to that little Cantonese person

we loved so much. We never knew how old she was. Would she be dead? Had she returned to her province in Canton or was she still with her second brother's family in Chinatown, a very old lady, cared for because all her life she had given half her wages to her family.

Something was tugging me away from the sea and the people in the distance, and I turned, aware of where I was going. I walked to the rocks and began to slowly climb the steep slope to the path that led to the lighthouse.

I had forgotten what it felt like to move quickly or to feel light. My body seemed to belong to this baby housed inside me, not to me. I felt I might never regain the freedom of my limbs again. I stopped and took a drink from the water bottle and sweat ran down the inside of my dress and down my legs.

I took it slowly, and when I reached the top the shade of the trees was wonderful. I could hear the distant sound of monkeys and the cicadas were loud and overpowering in the stillness. A huge butterfly landed on my hand and I remembered the moths, the huge moths Saffie and I hated when they got into the house at night and Ah Heng had to shoo them out of the open shutters.

The silence, the absence of people, seemed profound up here. It was an early morning or an evening walk. The main path had been cut through the jungle long ago and the trees above it had formed an arch of leaves in which the sun filtered down in flashes of light and shade.

I walked slowly, aware of the drop in temperature. I felt as if I must make this journey to the place Saffie had been found. I knew the only danger now was in my head and the amount of truth my heart could cope with.

I walked on for five minutes or more, deeper into the forest which would end in the lighthouse. Then I saw her in front of me, flitting among the trees, dancing almost, turning every now and then to see if I was following. She was wearing the cream dress with little pink flowers; my dress.

My heart lurched painfully and I longed, in that second of seeing her in that familiar dress, to be a child again, to go back, back to the time of happiness when she was always with me, each and every day.

I hurried in case she disappeared again and I peered anxiously among the trees for another glimpse of her, but she stayed resolutely ahead of me, the whiteness of her dress leading me onwards, and I began to walk with dread, my breath getting quicker and harsher. I felt chill on my arms and legs and began to look behind me, listen for the crack of a twig or a footfall against the backdrop of jungle sounds.

I wanted to stop. I wanted to turn back to the sunlight and the cries of people having fun on the beach; to the ordinary safety of the real world. I stared ahead and fleetingly caught the expression on Saffie's face, her mouth open in surprise, her eyes wide with fear, then she was gone and my mouth was so dry I could not swallow. I tried to open my water bottle but my fingers were trembling and I dropped it.

I bent to retrieve it and as I did so I felt suffocated. I could not breathe, it was as if someone had placed a hand over my mouth and nose and I frantically twisted my head and gulped air so that I would not pass out. The pressure on the back of my head and neck was unbearable and I moaned with fear and cried out.

Then, it was over. I could breathe again and I knelt on the path taking deep breaths. I knew Saffie had gone. I got clumsily to my feet knowing what was round the corner.

There it was, well off the path in a small clearing, the sad remnants of ticker tape and the gaping upturned boulder which had housed her cold and lonely grave.

TWENTY-TWO

Fleur took a deep breath in the empty room. It seemed a very long time since she had been alone. She did not move for some minutes after Jack and Nikki left the house. She closed her eyes against the bright sunshine and concentrated on slowing her rapid heartbeat. Sounds and smells drifted in and turned in the air. Chinese music and chattering rose and fell with the smell of the sea; curry; seaweed.

Fleur wanted to fly away somewhere safe with the small bones of her lost child; to mourn again for a life so carelessly lost. She wanted to wrap and comfort Saffie in a warm, soft blanket and rock and rock her in a shady place, to keen in peasant fashion and hold her child as safe now as she ever could be.

Not goodbye; not yet. Not a resting place, but a private lament, easily resurrected because it had never left her, its ceaseless cry had lived on in the folds and creases of her life, touching and colouring everything she did, tingeing all she was.

Saffie.

To think of her end was too hard, it made Fleur's limbs

twitch and her throat constrict. It made her heart feel it would burst from her chest. She knew that this way madness lay. She got up and went to the window and looked out at the distant sea. It seemed that her life was vanishing again in the moment of shimmering heat and that everything between that time of horror and this moment now, here in a room alone, was disappearing once more, like her life with David and the twins had vanished long ago.

She suddenly heard Fergus's quiet voice: *'Fleur, you can go on and on blaming yourself for the rest of your life, like a monk whipping himself until he draws blood. Or, you can accept the fact that someone wicked took Saffie's life while you slept, and you slept because you were human and grieving for someone you loved. You are not responsible for Saffie's death.'*

'I contributed to her death and nothing can change that.'

'Oh, Fleur! You can't keep five-year-olds under lock and key. You did not take Saffie's life. Someone else did that and he could have done it at any time . . . anywhere. How on earth were you to know there was any danger in that peaceful backwater? It was not Peter's or Laura's or your fault . . .'

Of course, in the end it did not matter what anyone said because you knew the truth of a thing in your heart. But you had to go on living and breathing and getting leadenly through the days if you had other children, and Fleur knew she could not have done that without Fergus.

She had not heard Jack coming back looking anxious with his mobile in his hand. He entered the room and Fleur jumped and turned her face, naked with sorrow, and Jack, seeing it, suddenly thought: *What on earth does losing a yacht mean against Fleur and Nikki's horror?*

'I'm sorry. I didn't mean to make you jump,' he said.

162

Fleur tried to smile. 'I didn't hear you, Jack. Is something wrong? Where's Nikki?'

'She stayed on the beach. I've just got a call on my mobile. Someone has holed one of our boats . . .'

'I'm so sorry, Jack—'

'Fleur,' he interrupted. 'It's nothing . . . a yacht can be mended . . . You look . . . all in. Can I get you something?'

'No, I think I'm going to go and lie down for a bit. It's coming up for midday, Nikki should not be out in this heat.'

'I'll go back and haul her in, I promise.'

'Good.' Fleur smiled vaguely at him and went into her room, thinking as she lay thankfully down on her bed, *Poor Jack. Catapulted into a tragedy not his own. How the past goes on and on changing the shape of our lives.* She wondered how Nikki had been when she met Jack? Had the loss of Saffie affected their relationship, or had Nikki managed this time, in a new life, in another country, to leave the shadow of her twin behind her?

Fleur thought of all the disparate men Nikki had brought home from university, as if to illustrate clearly to her mother what her life was turning out to be. *Look . . . all I can manage is to form relationships with no-hopers, men with towering personality disorders.* Many had been laughably dreadful.

Fergus, ever patient, had given her a year and then he had driven down to Bristol without telling Fleur. He had had enough of Nikki punishing her mother for a perceived wrong she would not let go of. He had caught her with an entirely reasonable set of friends in her rented house. Friends who had no trouble meeting his eye and were perfectly articulate. The life she wanted them to believe she was leading bore no resemblance to the actual one she was living in Bristol.

When her friends had gone out of the room, he had, he told Fleur, laid into her for the first time in her life. He had told her to grow up. He'd told her that tragedy happened to other people too, or hadn't she noticed? She had no right to decide Fleur must be punished for the rest of her life, or him, for that matter. She had no right to judge a past that was *not hers* and that she knew little about. She could either make something sensible of her life or screw it up. He told her he was not going to stand by watching her intent on wrecking their lives as well as her own, and she could keep her so-called *friends*, wherever she found them, to herself from now on . . .

He told her they both loved her very much and it was at that point the tears began to trickle out of the corners of her eyes, but she neither made a defence nor uttered a word.

She had not come home for months. Then she had turned up for Christmas with a South African girl. She had been polite and distant and told them that after her finals she was going to work for six months on a National Park project with this girl's brother, near Johannesburg. She had sent postcards regularly, saying little, and sometimes she had written to Fergus excitedly about her work. That had hurt.

After her degree, Fleur had never been certain what Nikki was doing or where she was. She travelled and seemed to try so many things, but she always moved on. *Chasing herself*, Fergus said sadly. *Never stopping for too long in case she catches herself up*. Then she would have had to face Saffie's death. Accept it.

Eventually she did a navigation course in New Zealand and helped sail ocean-going yachts from boatyard to wealthy owner. She still sent postcards from wherever she was. But postcards can say little, except where you are.

* * *

Jack made telephone calls back to the Bay of Islands, rang his marine insurer in Auckland and then his father, who promised to go and view the damage. He could not afford to be anything but pragmatic about this, but it could wipe out his profit for this year if it was contested.

He went out again into the heat and saw Nikki coming towards him slowly and heavily across the beach. Jack, screwing up his eyes, thought he was in danger of forgetting Nikki's normal quick, fluid movements. Her hat shielded her face but as he reached her she looked as sad as Fleur.

He put his arm around her and she leant against him, and together, without speaking, they went back inside the house. The amah had laid out salad, fruit and bread and a rice and fish dish. As they came in she nodded at them, pointed at the food and smiled, urging them to eat.

Nikki sat at the table under the fan and Jack went to the fridge and got her cold water to drink. He dug himself out a beer. She drank greedily and asked, 'Where's Fleur?'

'She's resting. We'll save some lunch for her, shall we? We can put it in the fridge.'

Nikki looked down at the table. She was about to say she was not hungry but decided Jack would make a fuss. He helped her to a small portion of fish and rice and she put some salad onto her plate thinking she could hide her food under it. As if reading her mind, Jack said softly, reaching out to touch her stomach, 'Nikki, you have a seven-month baby in there.'

She met his eyes, annoyed. Did he ever think of anything else? 'I'm hardly likely to forget it, am I?' she snapped. 'I'm moving about like a beached whale.'

He stared down at her face, drawn and pale against the natural tan of her shoulders, and wished this hadn't happened; that her sister's small body had never been found.

He wished with all his heart that they were back home, which seemed, at this moment, a hell of a way away.

'Anyway, tell me about the phone call. What's happened?'

He sat down and picked up his fork. 'Someone pranged *Blue Fish* as they were trying to moor next to her in the marina. There was a swell on and she took quite a lot of damage . . .'

Nikki looked up at him, sorry for her earlier bad temper. 'Oh, hell! Why did it have to be our newest yacht? Jack, listen . . .'

Knowing what was coming, Jack said quickly, 'It's OK, Nik. Dad's going to fly down and check the insurance and everything for me.' Yet his guilty heart had leapt at the thought of going home to all that was familiar, where he could *do something*.

Nikki, staring at the face she loved, felt equally guilty. She longed to be on her own, to take out, privately, the familiar wound that coloured everything.

She had felt pity for Fleur that morning, and now, strangely and suddenly, the bitterness she had fought all her life with her mother was beginning to seep slowly back. She felt confused and exhausted and craved space, even from Jack.

They stared at each other for a moment over their uneaten lunch, each hesitating to be truthful. Then Nikki reached out to take Jack's hand.

'Jack, go home. Go back, darlin', and look after things there. Fleur and I have to wait for Saffie's body to be released. We will be perfectly OK here on our own. There is James Mohktar and now the inspector . . .'

'Nik, you'll soon be beyond the safety regulation to fly . . . What if you get ill here and I'm miles away? I need to be with you . . .'

166

'Listen, Jack. I could get ill at home when you are over at the marina. We live miles away from anywhere. You could say I'm safer here with Fleur . . . and nearer to a doctor.' She leant forward. 'Let's take a day at a time, Jack. You're needed back home. I must stay here with Fleur. You must trust everything will be fine with me and the baby, worrying all the time is not going to help. Please . . . will you think about it?'

Jack nodded. 'All right. Nikki, stop playing with that food and go and rest.'

Nikki smiled. 'Will you thank the amah and ask if some lunch can be saved for Mum?'

'I will.' He got up and kissed her forehead. 'Try to sleep. Go on, I'll bring you cold water from the fridge.'

'You're a very sweet man . . .'

'Go, woman, or I'll be forced to carry you . . .' He made a face and clutched his back and Nikki laughed. 'Don't rub my size in . . . so cruel . . .'

At the door, she turned. 'It isn't that I don't want you here, Jack . . . It's just . . .'

'I know,' he said gently, handing her a bottle of cold water. 'I know.'

When she had gone, he thought: *This is not my story. I have no place here. This is something that happened to the woman I love, a long time ago.*

Nikki and Fleur needed to be left alone to come to terms with this; Jack was sure of it.

When James Mohktar returned that evening and sat with Jack out on the balcony while the two women showered, Jack felt he could voice his thoughts. Mohktar smiled his priest's smile and said, 'It is hard, I think. You are torn. Your woman is having a child. But maybe Miss Montrose and Mrs Campbell need to be alone together to talk over their lives at that time, *lah*?'

Jack was unsure whether Mohktar was talking as a policeman, hoping they might remember something vital if they concentrated, or if he was being an astute judge of character.

'I will make sure they are taken care of. We do have good doctors here you know. It is a tourist area, so English is spoken.'

'Oh, I'm sure,' Jack said hastily.

'You must decide. But if you wish, I could find out what flights there are out of Kuala Lumpur to Auckland?'

'Could you? That would be great.'

Fleur and Nikki came out of their rooms looking rested and cool. Jack's heart missed a beat. Nikki looked so young and pretty and he thought, *It is as if our future hangs in the balance; as if I know somewhere inside me that she might never return to the life we have together; that this terrible thing that happened so long ago might erupt once more and destroy us.*

Mohktar, watching him, said very quietly, reaching out to touch Jack's arm, 'Your woman is having your child. Neither distance nor the past can change this fact. Inshallah. God willing.'

And the strange policeman moved from the veranda into the room where the two women waited anxiously for whatever he had to report.

TWENTY-THREE

Jack flew to Auckland from Kuala Lumpur twenty-four hours later. He felt guilty relief not to be sitting on his butt doing nothing, but going home where he could be of some use. Driving through KL brought back memories of student days. He realised how caged and restless he had felt in the small rest house with two grieving women, but he left Nikki with a heavy heart.

After Jack had driven off in the hire car the wooden house seemed still and empty. I felt a surge of loss for the largeness of his presence. But if I couldn't sleep I could roam the house at night without alarming him, and I felt my limbs begin to relax at the thought of time alone trying to understand how I felt about everything.

Fleur and I were suddenly awkward with each other. Jack had acted as a buffer without either of us being conscious of it. The heightened emotions of Fleur's disappearance and the relief at finding her safe were slipping away from me. I felt the old vague irritation creeping back, the childhood suspicion that she might be playing a role.

It was the unpleasant side of me that I would have hated anyone to suspect I had, especially Jack.

Fergus said once, 'You judge your mother so harshly, Nik, it takes my breath away. Fleur loves you unconditionally whatever you do, whatever you say to hurt her, as I do. How sad you are unable to suspend judgement for even a second, to understand the person she is.'

My feelings towards Fleur have always yoyoed frantically. Yet the relief in finding her safe and alive had been over-powering. In those dreadful moments in the pathology lab I didn't want anyone but her, not even Jack. And now? Now I had no idea how I felt about anything except this aching sorrow under my ribs and an anxiousness that would not go away.

Fleur knew exactly how her daughter was feeling. If Nikki had ever shown open love or need for her, or sudden under-standing, it was certain to be followed by puzzled regret. It was inevitable that Nikki should automatically revert to a position taken long ago in childhood. A perceived injury as familiar as a playground chant, repeated often to make it true.

Even if Nikki, as a mature adult, could now recognise that the flaws she saw in Fleur were part of being a human being and making mistakes, to let it all go and move on meant she had to question the persistent and uncertain stand she had taken; the childhood she had shaped; the life she had determined for herself.

Fleur longed for the easy intelligence of Fergus, who had understood them both better than anyone. Who had been able with quiet insight to lay in front of her the substance, the reality of his and Fleur's love that had survived so much.

'You have to take responsibility for your own life and

170

your own mistakes,' he had said. 'It was to betray yourself, twist your own motives, ruin your life and the lives of those nearest to you if you believed you were responsible for the actions and emotions of other human beings.'

He had clinically laid before Fleur the facts of their life together; why it had happened, that attraction between them. For Fleur to have a future, to have a life with him, a life that must always hold regret and sadness, she had first to put away that terrible burden of guilt; for herself as well as Nikki.

They had managed, despite their difficulties with Nikki, to have a happy and close marriage. Except that there had been no children with Fergus, and oh how she had longed for more children. Nikki, the only child, had become Fergus's child, and in the end his unfailing patience had been rewarded with her love.

Fleur, walking alone on the beach as the day cooled and the colours changed, preparing for the dusk that would come quickly, felt surrounded by shadows from the past. David, whose face she struggled now to remember. Fergus, always present. Ah Heng. The twins; as they were, running towards the misty ocean in tiny shorts and nothing else. And her parents, the background for this life she had led here.

Peter and Laura! Fleur realised that she must let them know about Saffie. They could get English papers in Cyprus and it was possible they could come across an article . . . She turned and hurried back to the rest house. She must ring them. They were old now and becoming frail. How would they cope with the news after all this time?

Fleur was relieved it was her father who answered the phone. She told him quickly and briefly, trying to keep the mounting emotion out of her voice. Peter was shocked. He had to go and sit down.

171

'Oh my dear girl . . . how dreadful for you . . . after all this time. Oh dear. I am so sorry . . .'

'Dad, I don't want to upset you, I just thought you ought to know in case you saw something in the papers.'

'Of course we need to know, darling, and from you. Don't worry about upsetting me; it's you I'm worried about. Shall I fly to you? Would that be a comfort?'

'No, Dad. Bless you. Nikki's here with me. It's too far for you and there is nothing you can do. We have to wait for the pathology report. The police here have reopened the case. A detective who was on the original case has been flown out from London.'

'Good heavens. What on earth do they hope to find after all this time?'

'I don't know, Dad.'

'Bloody awful for you and Nikki.'

'Yes. But it's so good to see her. She's asleep at the moment, or you could talk to her.'

'I'm so glad she's with you. How is she?' Peter asked carefully.

'Heavily pregnant, poor girl.'

'Bad timing, all this . . .' Then, aware of what he had said, Peter added hastily, 'I mean, darling, extra hard for her and a worry for you . . .'

'I know what you meant, Dad.'

A long pause and then Peter said, 'Fleur, can they tell, after all this time, how my lovely granddaughter died?'

Fleur swallowed. 'They don't know yet.'

'Oh, how I wish we were with you and not so old . . .'

Fleur smiled. 'I know you're there, that's what's important.'

'I'll ring you tomorrow . . . my darling Fleur.'

Tears sprang to Fleur's eyes. As she replaced the phone Ah Lin put her head round the door to say that supper was

172

ready for the Mems. Fleur went to find Nikki. She was lying on her bed trying to read, but actually watching the ceiling fan go round.

'Nikki, I think the little amah might commit hari-kari if we miss another meal.'

Nikki half-smiled and got up awkwardly. 'OK.' She actually felt hungry.

As they were eating, Fleur said, 'I spoke to your grandfather earlier. I was worried he might read something by chance. He was very shocked, he wanted to come rushing over to us like the cavalry.'

'Typical Grandpa. Sweet of him. Did you speak to Gran?'

'No, she wasn't there. Grandpa sent his love; he's going to ring tomorrow.'

Nikki looked up. 'James Mohktar was going to come this evening, wasn't he?'

'Perhaps he has nothing to tell us, darling. I'm sure he'll ring.'

'Mum?' Nikki said, suddenly putting her knife and fork down. 'Do you want to know how Saffie died? Would it be better not to know?'

Fleur's heart did a painful flip. How direct Nikki was, she had almost forgotten. Fleur was groping around, trying not to think, unsure what she hoped the pathologist would tell them. Eventually she said, 'I don't know, Nikki. If the pathologist has no idea, I think I'll be relieved. But . . . I'll go on being haunted by not knowing. If she can somehow tell . . . I have to then ask if it was quick . . .' Her voice wavered. 'How much Saffie would have known . . . and I don't know if either of us could bear to hear it.'

She looked up and met Nikki's eyes. They seemed to fill her face.

'I don't want to know, Mum. I don't want to know.'

Nikki's hands on the table trembled and she clutched them to her, not wanting Fleur to see.

'Nikki,' Fleur said quietly. 'You don't need to know . . . Oh, darling . . .' She longed to rush round the table and hold Nikki but something in her daughter's face forbade it. 'I wish this hadn't happened now, when you are so pregnant and vulnerable.'

'Just wish it had never happened, Fleur.' The words burst out of Nikki.

Shocked, Fleur's hands flew up to her face. 'Don't you think I wish that every single day of my life?'

Oh, Nikki. Nikki.

At that moment they both heard someone outside and there was a short knock on the open door and Inspector Blythe entered without waiting for an answer. Both women wondered how much of their conversation he had heard.

'Good evening,' the inspector said, smiling at the two women. 'I'm sorry, am I disturbing your meal?'

'No,' Fleur said. 'We've finished. Can I offer you anything?'

'A beer would be great, if you have one.'

'I think Jack left some in the fridge,' Nikki said, going to get him one.

'I'm having difficulty getting used to this humidity,' Blythe said genially. 'I suppose,' he looked at the two women, 'you're both thoroughly used to it?'

'Not really,' Nikki said coolly. 'I'm used to the heat but not humidity.' She had the distinct impression the inspector was playing for time.

The inspector took his beer gratefully. The question the women dreaded to ask him hung in the air.

'Inspector Mohktar is on his way. How have you both been? Did your . . . Jack catch his flight safely?'

'Yes. He rang me from the airport in KL.' Nikki glanced at her watch; Jack would be in mid-flight. All at once she longed to be home and moved and sat by the window looking out at a large moon silhouetted above a black sea. Did the bloody man have something to tell them or was he going to make small talk all evening?

Fleur too was beginning to wonder if Blythe's visit was purely social. Perhaps he was bored in his hotel room.

'Have you been interviewing local people, Inspector?'

'We've been gathering all relative information from various sources and asking any local people living here at the time to contact us. Can I ask if either of you have thought of anything that is not in your original statements, that on reflection might help?'

Fleur and Nikki shook their heads. He's clutching at straws, Nikki thought, and he knows it.

'Will you excuse me?' she asked. 'I'd like to go out and get some air. I'll walk along the beach for a while.' She turned to Fleur. 'I won't be long.'

Fleur opened her mouth to say, *Be careful in the dark and mind the steps*, but shut it again, knowing what effect her fussing would have. She saw the inspector had noted this and she felt irritated. She went to the fridge and poured herself a glass of white wine. Then she took a deep breath.

'Inspector Blythe, does the pathologist know how my daughter died?'

Blythe met her eyes. 'Mohktar drove up to the pathology lab this afternoon. He's not back yet. The pathology report should have been ready this evening. He will be here any moment and then we will know more . . .' He hesitated. 'I came ahead to see how you and Miss Montrose were feeling . . . It is a long time ago, Mrs Campbell, and painful for both of you. I was unsure whether it was the right time for either of you to hear any stressful details of your small daughter's death.'

'My daughter being so obviously pregnant, you mean?'

'James Mohktar told me she had been unwell on the way here.'

'Yes, she was. It's why I worry . . .'

'Of course, it's natural.'

Fleur folded her fingers round the cold glass. 'I think I need to know the truth about what happened to my daughter, Inspector. I thought I wouldn't be able to bear it, but I think I owe it to her . . . now we have found her again.'

'I rather thought that was what you might feel,' Blythe said gently.

Fleur saw suddenly that he was a kind man who had come ahead to pave the way for unpleasant news. He had asked for a beer to dispel the obvious atmosphere in the room as he entered it; to try to put them both at ease.

'I don't think DS Mohktar will be long. I hope I'm not keeping you from anything.'

Fleur smiled. 'No, of course you're not.'

There was a little silence and then he asked, 'So, you flew from London via Singapore to visit your daughter who is living in New Zealand?'

'Yes. To see Nikki and also to look at some architecture; I'm doing an arts degree at an advanced age.'

The inspector smiled. 'So do many other people, a great deal older than you. Well done, I say.' He paused. 'When did your daughter settle in New Zealand?'

'About four years ago.'

'This is your first trip out to visit her?'

'Yes.'

'You must miss her. Does she fly home to see you?'

Aware of where she was being led, Fleur said, 'My

husband died three years ago. Nikki came home for the funeral.'

'She got on well with her stepfather?'

Fleur's eyes reflected a sudden rush of anger. *Don't even go there*. 'He was David's best friend. He was the twins' godfather, so he knew the twins even before my husband was killed. Fergus and Nikki adored each other. Fergus was closer than I am to my daughter.'

'Why is that, Mrs Campbell?'

'Nikki blamed me for Saffie's death.'

'Because you slept that afternoon?'

'Yes.'

'She made a judgement at five years old?'

'No, not at five years old, Inspector. Not straight away. The blame and sorrow grew slowly over the years. She was totally adrift without her twin. Our difficulties with her began slowly, thirteen months later, after Fergus and I got married.'

'But if she got on well with your husband, wouldn't she have been happy?'

Fleur met his eyes. 'I can't actually see how my private life is relevant to this inquiry, Inspector.'

Blythe leant forward. 'I'm sorry. I'm not being prurient. You'd be surprised how building up a picture of people involved in a case is incredibly relevant sometimes.'

'Except that Nikki was five years old and Fergus was in Singapore at the time of Saffie's disappearance, so I can't follow your line of reasoning.'

The inspector sighed. 'I guess I was asking if, although she liked her stepfather and knew him well, your daughter resented you actually marrying him and usurping her own dead father.'

Fleur felt a growing respect for this man, he was like a

terrier. 'Yes, you're right, Inspector, she did resent me remar-rying. It took Fergus years and endless patience for her to accept his love. When she did, they never looked back.'

'And you, Mrs Campbell? Did she accept your love too?' He watched her small brown hands that were never still.

'No, she has never been able to forgive me. The twins lost their beloved father, and then you see, in her eyes, I let her sister, her twin, the other half of her, die by my neglect.'

This was too much for Blythe. 'But she is an adult woman now, Mrs Campbell. Someone came along and snatched your daughter while you slept. *You* did not kill her . . .'

'Nikki knows that. So do I. Fergus used to tell me often enough. This trip was . . . full of hope. I was visiting her in New Zealand for the first time, hoping her happiness with Jack and her pregnancy would help us to start again . . . to become closer . . .'

Fleur stopped, then said softly, 'When I first saw her, so worried about me, so concerned, I thought for a while it was all going to be like I had imagined for so long. I felt so close to her on that awful morning in the pathology place . . . But life isn't that simple, is it?'

'No, it's not,' Blythe said. 'We all become entrenched in our assumptions. Tragedy sometimes brings people closer, for a while. But it is the everyday living and loving that's so difficult to keep up, don't you think?' There was some-thing wistful in his voice that surprised Fleur.

'Yes,' Fleur said. 'I do.' She looked down at her glass.

'When you arrived this evening, Nikki was asking me if I could bear to know the truth about how Saffie died. I don't think she can bear it and I'm not sure she should know in her present condition, Inspector, even if she finds out later on.'

'That's why I'm here.' He met her eyes and smiled. 'I think we've just about gone a full circle.'

Fleur smiled back. 'So it seems. Would you like another beer, Inspector?'

Blythe shook his head. He could hear voices as Mohktar and the daughter came up from the beach. He said quietly, for it had to be said if he was going to make any headway on this inquiry, and he was secretly convinced the answer lay in the small, closed army community of that time, 'Mrs Campbell, did you know that about eighty per cent of murders are committed by people known to their victims and their families?'

TWENTY-FOUR

I sat on the rocks at the far corner of the beach. The sea was still and phosphorescent. I remembered the wonder of seeing those dancing silver lights sparkling on the surface of the sea as a child, my fingers in my father's large hand.

The water lapped gently in front of me and I listened to the night sounds, the constant blanket noise of cicadas, the faint screech of monkeys up in the trees on the promontory. The beach was almost deserted, people elsewhere eating and drinking. Some young Malays bent over a fishing boat, sorting a net. They had torches and their voices came to me over the air.

From the nearest house came the sounds of pots and pans and high Chinese voices. The air was heavy and velvet, trapped in the heat that remained long after the sun had gone. The night was like being cocooned in a familiar soft, suffocating blanket. It seemed that if I closed my eyes I could be a child again, lulled to sleep by far-off jungle sounds, by Ah Heng's music and the drone of insects directly below our window.

I thought of Jack. The man I would not marry; whose

child I was carrying. Where would he be now? In the clouds above Auckland? Nearly home. Home seemed at this moment like some remote planet I might never reach again. As if I had been plunged into the past and might be unable to return to what I once had.

On my year out travelling I had deliberately avoided revisiting the Middle East, Singapore, and Malaysia. I had headed for the Antipodes. I was afraid of all this; these familiar and longed-for smells and sounds of my childhood; the essence of those first years of my life, sensations that stay with children forever.

The feeling of loss caught at me, sharp and lonely, the memory of the blessed, endless golden days I had then, in the safety of army quarters with my happy, laughing dad. Real life as a family; two parents of your own, untouched by tragedy, not singled out forever because of a double sorrow that scarred your soul like a birthmark.

Memories grow hazy with time and sometimes we fill them in with the pictures adults paint for us. I did not really remember the long journey back to England after Saffie disappeared but I do remember being back in that house of my grandparents. I hated it and I remember feeling constantly afraid of what was going to happen next.

My mother seemed numb and silent and strange. I could not understand it as a child, but it was in the days when doctors handed out vast doses of tranquillisers and all my mother seemed to do was sleep.

I would go and climb into my grandparents' bed to feel the warmth from their bodies. Mum always seemed so cold. I would pretend in the dark that it was Saffie who lay beside me.

Sometimes I would wake up and Gran and Grandpa would be holding and rocking me. I never knew I was crying.

I cannot remember if it was then that I began to sleepwalk or on another visit to that house. I would wake in the dark on the stairs or downstairs and I always knew in those moments that Saffie was near.

I would see her turn a corner ahead of me, a small, lonely shadow, and I began to believe that she was not really dead but somewhere I could not reach her; somewhere trapped where she could not get back to me. Her puzzlement and fear touched me with icy fingers and I would shake and shake my head over and over and whisper, 'No. No. No. No.' I had to banish the sensation of her frightened and alone. Banish the sickness that rose up in my throat for the dark unknown thing that had happened to her.

I remember vividly the day Grandpa had to fly away from us to join his regiment in Northern Ireland. Someone else large and safe was leaving me. I would go and sit in his small dark study and stroke his sweater, smell his smell of tobacco and whisky which reminded me of my dad, too.

I was too young to understand why, but the atmosphere in the house with Mum and Gran became stiff with resentment and I clung protectively to my mother as I felt Gran's disapproval of her.

Later, when I was older, I realised it was always this way between them; something unsaid that has always unnerved me in its intensity.

One morning I heard them shouting at each other. Terrible words that I could not make sense of and made them both cry. Mum told Gran that she was taking me to stay in a chalet in Cornwall belonging to Fergus's parents while she thought about what she was going to do.

I remember Gran's face as they shouted. She suddenly said.

'David was a wonderful husband and father. He did not deserve to be betrayed by you and his best friend . . .'

We left the house abruptly in a taxi. On the train Mum tried to pretend it was exciting but I've always remembered how long that journey was and how the tears slid down her face underneath the dark glasses she wore when she thought I was asleep.

My grandmother's words stayed with me, lodged just under the skin. I wasn't able to comprehend the meaning fully then, but I saved those words, took them out and repeated them over and over to myself as I grew up.

I looked *betray* up in the dictionary: Deceive, delude, dazzle, beguile, play false, double-cross, distort, falsify, break faith. *Break faith*.

Then I looked up *betrayed* and one word jumped out: *heartbroken*.

We listened to the whispers, Saffie and I, while Ah Heng tried to divert us. Adult conversations *sotto voce* in the stilled and shuttered army quarter when the inquiry into my dad's death was going on.

Was it the weather or had David made an error of judgement in flying home that night? Was pilot error contributory?

Heartbroken. My little private wound grew a healthy scab that I scratched often in the coming months and years. When Fergus and Fleur first got together I made it bleed.

My father was exonerated from any blame, but I remembered. I remembered creeping out of bed one night at one of my parents' numerous parties and watching in the dark and shuttered corridor Fleur dancing with Fergus. Their eyes were shut and their heads were close together as they held each other tight.

TWENTY-FIVE

James Mohktar walked along the beach path towards the house where the two women were staying. As he climbed the wooden steps to the bungalow he could see Inspector Blythe inside talking to Mrs Campbell. The girl was not in the room. Mohktar turned and looked towards the sea. Although he could not see her in the fading light, he retreated back down the steps and walked towards the rocks and the forest path which led up to the lighthouse.

He had not passed her from the direction he had come but he thought she would most likely be at this end of the beach. As he drew near the rocks he saw her sitting very still looking out to sea. There was something alarming, a little unnatural in her stillness. In his experience few people managed to stay without fidgeting or moving their hands for long. This girl could.

He moved warily closer, deliberately advertising his approach so that he would not startle her. 'Miss Montrose,' he said. '*Selamat malam*. Good evening.'

She turned his way. In the dark he could not read her expression, but he felt sorrow emanating from her like something tangible he could reach out and touch.

'How are you?' he asked gently. 'How are you?'

Her hands dropped to her lap as if she was relinquishing something precious. 'I guess I've been conjuring ghosts. It's being here, in Malaysia again. Heat and smell are evocative. They don't change, do they?'

'You had happy times here?'

'Before my father was killed we came here often, the four of us and sometimes Ah Heng, our amah . . .'

The girl smiled suddenly, a sweet smile that changed her face. 'I think when we were small sometimes we loved our amah almost more than our mother.'

'Ah! Amahs spoil us, give in to our childish needs; give us their undivided attention.'

Nikki looked at him, her face still alight. 'Yes, I guess you're right.' She paused and then said, perhaps because it had been on her mind, 'My mother was very beautiful when she was young. Forces wives had the most wonderful time in those days. More freedom, servants, swimming pools, wonderful places like this for holidays. Attention from the navy when the ships came in. Men, my grandmother told me, outnumbered women even with the single nurses and teachers who came out to work. It was all so different from cold army quarters in England . . .'

James Mohktar, alerted to something in her voice, waited to see if she was going to say more, and when she did not he said, 'It is very sad that your happy time as a family was destroyed, Miss Montrose. But it is good that you can still remember those times of happiness.'

Nikki got up. 'They fade. People too. You have to keep conjuring them up from photographs and memory. You become terrified they will disappear altogether as if they had never lived, their faces a blur . . . But it is easier here,

185

in Malaysia. Here the images are clearer. My father and my sister feel nearer . . .' She trailed off. 'Sorry. Did you come to tell me something? Inspector Blythe is with my mother in the house.'

'Yes. I know this.'

They looked at each other. James Mohktar did not want to tell the girl how her sister had died on this dark beach. But something told him he would learn more from her if she was alone rather than with her mother. Together, in that house, the two women managed to create an uneasy atmosphere, and Mohktar wanted to know why.

'Miss Montrose, come, let us walk back to the house. It is late and I must let the inspector know that I am here.'

'You came to get me? You have something to tell us?'

'Yes, but I think it better if I tell you when you are with your mother.'

'I know you're going to tell me how my sister died, but, you see, I already know how she died.'

Nikki's voice was so low that he only just caught her words. Mohktar stopped and looked down at her and quite suddenly he felt chilled. He shivered in the warm night air and wished he had entered the house and not come down to the beach to this strange Englishwoman.

'What do you mean, Miss Montrose? You cannot know.'

She did not reply for a moment, but turned and looked out to sea. When she turned back to him, she said, 'Yesterday I went up the cliff path to the forest. I needed to see Saffie's grave—'

'Not her grave,' Mohktar could not help interrupting. 'It is just the place where she was found. You and your mother will give her a Christian burial and that will be her grave, her resting place.'

It was as if he had not spoken.

'I was walking up the path in the shadows of the trees. I saw Saffie, as I often do, a little ahead of me, as if she wanted to lead me to the right place . . .' Nikki's eyes were intent on his, willing him to believe her. 'Then . . .' her voice wobbled, 'I suddenly felt frightened, as if I heard steps behind me. I dropped my water bottle, and as I bent to pick it up I couldn't breathe. I could not get my breath. I felt as if I was being suffocated . . . I was kneeling on the ground, terrified. Then it was over. I got up and turned the corner and saw the clearing with ticker tape round the hole . . .' She gave a sigh, suddenly exhausted, and then she moved nearer to him and said urgently, her hands on his arms. 'I know. I know that Saffie was suffocated by someone holding a hand over her mouth. She wanted me to know that. She wanted me to know . . .'

Despite the warmth, her hands on his arms were cold and Mohktar felt a superstitious dread in the pit of his stomach.

'The most likely cause of death, Detective Sergeant Mohktar, is suffocation. A hand held over the mouth with undue force. So much force, in fact, that the child's thin neck was broken.'

He met the girl's eyes, hypnotised by a primitive fear of the unknown. His mother believed that the ghosts of their ancestors, their loved ones, were all around them. As a child he had thought so too. Now he did not. He was a policeman.

'Am I right? Is this how Saffie died?' Nikki's eyes on his were bright and insistent.

He nodded. 'Yes, Miss Montrose.'

'So you believe me?'

He did not answer, but took her hands in his and held them firmly for a moment. 'Let us go back to the house;

you are cold and it is late,' he said gently. 'To visit the place where your sister died was perhaps unwise on your own. Imagination plays such a part in what we believe.'

But Nikki saw that James Mohktar was disturbed by what she had said. He let her hands go with a smile, and together in silence they made their way over the sand back to the house.

TWENTY-SIX

Fleur said the next morning, 'Nikki, let's go out for a while, I'm beginning to get cabin fever. It seems cooler today. Do you feel up to walking to the little row of Indian shops near the big hotel at the other end of the beach?'

Nikki looked up from her book. She had read the same sentence fifty-two times. 'I'm not ill, Mum, just huge. Sounds like a good idea.'

They walked across the beach and then turned down a track by one of the hotels and carried on by the road, which led to the small square of local shops that tourists from the hotel considered a bargain after the expensive hotel precincts in Kuala Lumpur. Rows of bright hippy skirts and cheese-cloth shirts hung on racks outside the cramped and hot little shops. Small electric hand-fans whirred inside, only stirring the stale heat and dust until it settled somewhere else. Flip-flops in boxes on the pavements adorned with gaudy plastic flowers lay beside balls and spades and faded sun-creams.

Fleur and Nikki walked slowly, shaking their heads as the shopkeepers called out persistently, each trying to outdo the others. They stopped at a shop with a rack containing

vast quantities of batik shirts and Nikki riffled through looking for one for Jack. Immediately she was surrounded by
whole families. *What size, Mem? What colour? How many
you like? This colour? That colour? This size? That size?*

What am I doing here? Nikki thought, suddenly claustrophobic; buying shirts for Jack when . . . Hastily she
bought two large traditional ones with subdued colours and
she and Fleur moved on.

Out of the corner of her eye Nikki suddenly spotted a
corner shop selling baby clothes. She moved towards the
rail with its tiny shirts and dresses and trousers hung neatly
in rows under the hot sun. She had not bought anything
for the baby yet because she was superstitious and now she
glided towards the shop as if pulled by a magnet.

Fleur smiled as she watched Nikki touch each item with
wonder, fingering the dresses and baby suits with amaze-
ment that any human child could be so minute as to fit into
these Thumbelina clothes.

Nikki had clipped her long fair hair up but strands had
escaped and curled in the heat round her neck and face. As
she made her way dreamily through the baby things a small
smile lit up her face at the prospect of dressing her child in
little garments like these. It was as if this array of baby
clothes had reignited the excitement, the reality of the life
growing steadily inside her.

Fleur, watching her, was suffused with love and pride.
How beautiful Nikki looked bending to baby clothes with
the same concentration she and Saffie had picked out clothes
for their dolls. Nikki's face changed when she smiled, lit up
everything around her. Her blonde hair against her creamy
brown neck was ravishing.

How wonderful she would be to paint, Fleur thought.
How lucky I am to have my lovely daughter here with me.

She saw how people turned and watched Nikki, smiled at her obvious pregnancy and dreamy expression, totally oblivious to them all; bent, intent on a miniscule white dress with pink rosebuds. She took it from the rack and held it up and her fingers trembled.

'Our white dresses. Mine was like this. Saffie's had blue roses. Do you remember you only liked us to wear them on holiday?'

Fleur said quietly, 'How could I forget? Ah Heng brought them back from Chinatown for you both.' Her fingers reached out to touch the dress. 'I was immature and snobby in those days. Ah Heng loved dressing you both in clothes she bought from the markets but I thought her clothes looked cheap so I used to change you back into my clothes in the car as soon as we turned the corner. I kept those little dresses for your holidays . . .'

They both looked down at the dress. Saffie had been wearing the dress with pink rosebuds when she died. Nikki could not put it back. She held it to her, clutched it to her and tears streamed silently down her face. 'Saffie wanted the one with the blue roses because you laughed and said there wasn't such a thing as blue roses . . .'

Gently, Fleur took the dress from Nikki and replaced it on the rack. Then she led her away to an outside café and sat her down. Nikki took a small, battered straw hat from her bag and placed it on her head so that her face was hidden. She blew her nose and said, 'Sorry . . . I wasn't trying to hurt you, Mum.'

Fleur ordered two cold drinks and they came in monster glasses full of watermelon and orange and mint. Nikki cooled her fingers against the glass.

After a moment, Fleur reached out and tentatively took her hand. 'Don't be sorry, I know you weren't, darling . . .

191

I'm just so glad that you're here with me. Nikki, you must try not to let anything spoil the enjoyment and excitement of your baby.'

Fleur stopped because she was frightened of saying the wrong thing; of the small hand in hers withdrawing, snatching itself away. She searched desperately for the right words. She wanted to reach Nikki, to help her understand that life had to go on, had to be lived and loved and enjoyed for the most each day had to offer.

How many times do we have to learn this in one lifetime? Fleur wondered. There was Jack, and Nikki must think of him and her child and a future full of opportunities and good things.

Saffie was dead. She had been dead for a long, long time. *But not to us. Not to us.* The refrain was a familiar wail inside both of them. *It is not Saffie's death now that is going to haunt us but the manner of her dying.*

Nikki looked at her mother. 'When I was a child I used to think about Saffie with foreign parents, unable to speak the same language and terrified. Then, to make it better, I thought of her as eventually having to accept this and changing . . . letting herself be loved by another family, because she must.

'In the night I used to cry thinking of her lying with other people, out there somewhere far away in the dark, trying hard to keep us, her real family, alive inside her head. If it had been me, I couldn't have coped, I would have fragmented . . . gone mental. If it had been me who had been taken I would rather have been dead than without Saffie . . . without anyone I knew or loved . . .' Nikki looked down at her hand in Fleur's and slowly withdrew it. 'Now we know she really did die that strange, horrible afternoon. That all these years she has lain buried underneath boulders up there, under the trees . . .' She gestured up towards the promontory. 'And it seems so lonely a place to die, to lie in the dark . . . worse than if she had been snatched to live with foreigners who could neither speak her language nor understand her. So sad, Mum, I can hardly bear it . . .'

Fleur wondered how many times you quietly died in one lifetime.

She took a deep breath. 'Finding Saffie after all this time is like a nightmare returning, Nikki, but if we dwell on how she might have died . . . it will drive us mad . . . would be . . . wrong.'

'Morbid, you mean?' Nikki's voice had a hint of the old challenge.

'Yes,' Fleur said, firmly.

Nikki, surprised at what she saw in Fleur's face, said, 'Did you feel that Mohktar and Blythe were keeping something from us last night?'

'I don't know, but I don't believe anyone could ever be a hundred per cent sure what happened to Saffie or how she died after twenty-eight years.'

She hesitated, again willing the right words to come; words that Nikki might accept and believe from her.

'I rather think Sergeant Mohktar and Inspector Blythe are gently putting the case to bed rather than reopening it.' Fleur leant forward. Her hands shook and her voice was suddenly croaky with stress. 'We won't be needed here much longer. It's all too long ago; there's nothing left for us to remember. We have to let go, darling. We have to let go . . .'

Nikki's hand flew to her face. 'And leave Saffie? Leave her again? No! She's still trapped here . . . and there's something—' She stopped abruptly. Fleur would think she had lost it.

Fleur stared at her daughter uneasily. 'Nikki, of course

we're not going to leave Saffie here, we're going to take her home and give her a proper funeral. Say our private good-byes at home.'

Nikki said nothing. She had never told Fleur that she saw Saffie. She had only ever told Fergus. Nikki never knew if he believed her. She had wanted to keep Saffie to herself as a child. Fleur hadn't deserved her.

She looked up at the people passing their table without seeing them. Americans, so fat. French, dainty and voluble. English, appallingly badly dressed.

She said suddenly, 'The man who did it will get off scot-free. He might even have forgotten he once killed a child. He's lived a whole life without paying.'

'We don't know he hasn't paid,' Fleur said. 'We don't know he hasn't been haunted by killing Saffie and will be for the rest of his life . . .'

At that moment the Chinese lady from the baby-clothes shop appeared by their table. She shyly handed Nikki a package, then beamed at them both and nodded her head up and down.

'For you,' she said. 'For baby. I see you like.' Then she was gone like a little sprite back into the crowded square.

Startled, Nikki peered inside and saw the tiny dress with the pink rosebuds. She pulled it out and laid it on the table smoothing it out.

Fleur said worriedly, 'You don't have to keep it, darling. The woman thought she was being kind.'

But Nikki was warmed to the heart. 'Oh, I want to keep it. Mum, do you think she knew who we were?'

'Perhaps, darling.' Fleur reached out to touch the dress. 'Nikki, this is your future, this child you're carrying.'

'I don't know whether I'm having a boy or a girl,' Nikki said. 'I didn't want to know.'

'Let's go back to the bungalow,' Fleur said. 'It's getting very hot.'

They both walked slowly across the long stretch of beach back to the wooden bungalow. A hot wind blew from the sea, churning it white and choppy. Sudden clouds appeared in the sky. Both women glanced sideways. Their shadows, elongated across the sand, seemed to have substance as if a third person walked unseen in their footsteps, as she always had.

TWENTY-SEVEN

'Come on, Detective Sergeant, think about it logically. In a crime against a child what is the easiest way of silencing her? By placing a hand across her mouth, of course; and if you keep it there you will suffocate her. Nikki Montrose doesn't have to have second sight to work that one out!'

'Of course,' Mohktar said defensively. 'I know that, Inspector Blythe, but Miss Montrose is a twin and twins have a . . . connection with each other. I know this to be true. My wife's sister had twin boys. One of them got trapped in an old freezer in his grandfather's garden. The other twin was at home with his mother. He started to have breathing difficulties. He knew immediately that his brother was trapped somewhere. He made for his grandfather's house, indeed, it was as if he was pulled by a magnet. The boy was saved in the nick of time.'

'Well, unfortunately Miss Montrose did not have that ability to help us find her twin twenty-eight years ago, or we wouldn't be sitting here now!' Blythe said dryly, then seeing Mohktar's face, he added, 'I'm sorry. I know what you're getting at, Mohktar, and you're right. It's very possible Nikki

Montrose did see or hear something at the time without realising it. She was the first one up and out on the beach by late afternoon. I've asked Mrs Campbell if they could both write down everything they remember now, before they look at their original statements again. I'd like to compare them. May be a waste of time, but there's an hour or so missing.'

He drummed the desk with his fingers. 'A five-year-old has little sense of time. When she was questioned as a child, Nikki said she woke up and her sister was gone. She went out to find her on the beach but couldn't see her anywhere. After a while she went back to her mother's room but she was still sleeping.

'She went out again, hungry and wanting her sister. This time the sun was low in the sky, we established that from her, and when the light began to go she was suddenly afraid and ran to the house to wake her mother.'

'Something might have frightened her out there alone in the coming dark?'

'Yes. I've also wondered why she didn't go to the next rest house if she couldn't wake her mother. Why didn't she go to see if her sister had gone there? She must have seen the lights. They were all army families, people she knew . . .' Blythe pulled the statements towards him. 'Mrs Campbell's parents left early that morning in a hired car to Kuala Lumpur to fly to Penang, and the wife in the next rest house – Beatrice Addison – called in to see if Fleur was all right on her own. She did not leave until nearly two and then Mrs Campbell and her children ate a late lunch.

'The twins always slept straight after lunch at about one o'clock, but this afternoon it was two thirty. Fleur took both children into her room and they were in bed each side of her when she fell asleep. According to Nikki, Saffie woke first and tried to get her to wake up and go outside with

197

her. Nikki got cross, turned over and went back to sleep. The last thing she remembered was Saffie out of bed and pulling her dress over her head.'

Mohktar said, 'There was the Malay girl in the main room. She was asked to stay in the house to keep an eye on the children when they woke. She too had fallen asleep, but she would not have seen or heard either twin as they both climbed out of the bedroom window. She said it was late, about five to five thirty when she took Mem a cup of tea. She did not wake her but left the tea beside her. Neither twin was with their mother, but she heard Nikki in the bathroom and thought both children were in there. She had slept too long so she hurried to her own quarters to shower and change ready to help the Chinese cook with dinner.

'She was not employed as an amah, *lah*? She was just an eighteen-year-old girl who had been asked to stay in the house because of the children . . .'

'I remember her,' Blythe said. 'She was very pretty and very upset. We had to keep reassuring her it was not her fault. I wonder what happened to her.'

Mohktar smiled. 'She is married now with five children and she is rather fat.'

'Oh!' Inspector Blythe smiled back, his memory spoilt. 'So, between about three thirty p.m. and five thirty when Mrs Campbell woke up, the other twin, Saffie, disappeared from the face of the earth. Possibly murdered between the rest house and where we found her remains.'

'Unless she was taken somewhere else and buried there later.'

The two men looked at each other. Blythe said suddenly, 'Do you ever have a strong gut feeling about a case?'

Mohktar looked puzzled. 'Does murder upset my stomach?

Indeed, Inspector, how can it not, especially when a child is involved, when families are destroyed.'

Blythe laughed dryly. 'I meant – and I felt this twenty-eight years ago and I still feel it now – that the answer lies within the army community, not with a local man. Yet they were all officers, they were all acquaintances, if not friends. A sexual motive seems perverse in this setting. And it can never be established now.'

'Unless,' Mohktar said quietly, 'the child saw something she should not have seen on a hot afternoon when she should have been sleeping?'

Blythe looked at him with interest. 'A bit of extramarital activity would certainly not be unknown.'

'It could be that her murder was a mistake, an accident.'

'You mean he did not mean to kill her but was too rough, broke her neck by mistake?'

'Yes.'

'You didn't tell the mother and her daughter that the child's neck was broken, did you?'

'No. It is too much information for them. I see no need unless they ask. I agree with you, Inspector, I too think the answer lies in the British community. It was, and still is, very rare here for a Chinese or Malay to harm a child.'

Blythe got to his feet. 'I'm retiring. I thought on the plane flying out here how good it would feel to solve this last nasty little murder before I go, but we're not going to, you know, Mohktar, we're not going to.'

Mohktar's face was impassive. 'Do not be too sure, Inspector. Do not be too sure. The answer lies in Miss Montrose's head. I feel this.'

Looking down at his handsome, cerebral face, Blythe wished he felt as confident, and yet there was something magnetic and reassuring about this strange Malay detective.

He had come highly recommended and apparently had a nose for odd cases; for getting inside people's heads when all else had failed. But most of all, Blythe thought, this was a man who really cared. A man you could trust.

The two men smiled at each other. 'Inspector, once the child's body is released by the coroner we cannot keep the two women here.'

'I know. That's why I've asked the powers that be not to release her body for another forty-eight hours.'

'It is not long.'

'No, Mohktar, it isn't nearly long enough, which is why I think this case is a crime that will never be solved.'

'I do not yet give up,' Mohktar murmured. 'But soon they must lay their child to rest. I hope this is what they can do.'

'Yes,' Inspector Blythe said. 'So do I.'

TWENTY-EIGHT

When they got back to the house, Fleur went to check her mobile phone for messages. She had left it behind to charge. There was one from DI Blythe to say there was nothing to report today but he and Mohktar would come to the house tomorrow. If they needed anything they must ring immediately. He added that it would help greatly if they could both jot down anything they remembered on a piece of paper, including things that seemed totally irrelevant.

Sam had texted her: *Fleury. Will ring 6 p.m. your time. Sam x.*

As they sat down for lunch, Nikki said, 'At Fergus's funeral, Sam said he was going to try and get home every two years. Be nice for you if he could, Mum.'

'Yes,' Fleur smiled. It had been a shock when Sam had married an Australian and decided to live there permanently all those years ago. They had always been close. He had been the big brother, always there for her, conscious perhaps that he was Laura's blue-eyed boy.

'Now his boys have flown, I think it's going to be easier

for him and Angie to get away. Also, of course, he's conscious of Laura and Peter getting frailer.'

Nikki had seen more of Sam in the last few years than Fleur. Both his boys had backpacked to New Zealand and Sam had flown out to sail a yacht back to Sydney with them. He and Jack had immediately taken to each other. They had sailing in common and a passion for boats, and Nikki saw that Sam and Jack were the same sort of gentle giants with little emotional baggage. Funny; perhaps she had subconsciously been drawn to Jack because she and Saffie had adored Sam when they were little. He used to stop off on his long-haul trips between Melbourne and London to visit them.

Nikki vividly remembered Sam and Fleur clutching each other when Saffie had gone, when they were all back in England. He had held his sister in his bear-like grip and they had rocked together, to and fro, to and fro, in a dark room of that cold house. Nikki had watched the tears stream down Sam's face as he whispered over and over, '*Fleury, Fleury, Fleury.*'

He could not say it was going to be all right or things would get better or time would heal, or any of the clichés people say to one another to comfort, knowing as they speak that it is the tone and texture of their words that register, not the content.

Sam knew, in those searing moments he held Fleur, that his beautiful, happy sister's life was blighted forever by this second tragedy. Here was a sorrow that could never be healed, never absorbed into everyday life.

As they sat at the table, Fleur said suddenly, as if it still hurt, 'If David hadn't died and then Saffie been taken, I don't think Sam would have gone to Australia for good. He couldn't cope with all our combined grief. You, me, Laura and Peter. It was too much; bits of him broke off and fragmented. He had to get away . . .'

'He ran away, Mum. He left us.' Nikki could hear the childish lament in her voice. Sam had been the third beloved person to disappear from their lives.

Fleur looked at her. *He ran away.* In that second, Nikki saw that she had done exactly the same when she couldn't bear any more.

Fleur broke the silence. 'Sam needed to make his own life away from the shadow of mine. People can only take so much unhappiness. I think it was brave of him. He knew himself. He was a happy person whose good nature would have been destroyed if he hadn't got away.'

Nikki thought suddenly: *Fergus was the only one who didn't run, who was steadfast throughout my whole life. And I gave him a hell of a lot of grief.*

'We're lucky Fergus didn't run too, then, aren't we?' It came out before Nikki could stop it.

Fleur could not interpret the tone in Nikki's voice. Then she remembered Nikki's reaction at Fergus's funeral. Nikki had cried silently by day and inconsolably at night. When Fleur couldn't bear the sound any longer, echoing her own grief in the silent house, she had gone into Nikki's room.

'Darling, enough! Fergus would be so upset to see you like this.'

'*I never told him I loved him! I never told him I loved him,*' Nikki had wailed over and over.

'He knew! Nikki, he knew. How could he not know? He loved you as much as you loved him.'

Nikki had not let Fleur touch her, only her grandmother, but she had listened to their words and flown home to Jack comforted by them.

'Yes,' Fleur said evenly. 'We were lucky to have Fergus

and there was rarely a day when I didn't thank God for it.'

Nikki saw her mother's hands tremble as she put down her knife and fork. It was back, this thing between them; this unsaid thing that Nikki had wanted to shriek out at her mother all her life. *Why? How could you love my dad and have an affair with Fergus? How could you?*

Fleur got up from the table to get more water from the fridge. 'If you've finished, Nikki, I'm going to go and have a rest. What about you?'

'I've finished. Can I borrow your Hundertwasser? I can't get into my book.'

'Of course you can. I've got some paper here, Nikki. Will you do what Blythe suggests and write down anything you can still remember?'

'As if,' Nikki said, 'either of us is remotely likely to remember more than we did twenty-eight years ago.'

'I suppose they just want to compare minor details.'

'Or clutch straws. Have a good sleep, Mum.'

In her bedroom, Fleur found the amah had closed the shutters against the hot midday sun and, feeling claustrophobic, she opened them slightly to let the glare of the day slide into the room in a sliver of heat that slanted across the floor. She took her dress off, turned the ceiling fan on, and got under the thin cotton sheet.

It seemed such a long time since morning. The days had a strange lost quality, like a dream, but real too, like slow, somnolent, heavy steps back towards something she did not want to remember. Fleur felt a longing to return to her normal life; the life she had made. To be doing the thing she had set out to do when she started this journey.

The day she left her London house swam back; that uneasy sensation that she would return home a different person.

She closed her eyes, longing for sleep. She reached out across the bed with her hand to touch the empty space the other side.

'*Fergus . . . I miss you.*'

Fergus, who had flown into her life and changed the balance of everything. He had been David's best man at their wedding, but she hadn't known him then. Not then. And she could not possibly have foreseen the future, not on the day she and David got married.

TWENTY-NINE

They married in David's village church with the reception in his parents' garden. There was a marquee on the lawn and the sun shone the entire day.

'*Well it would, wouldn't it?*' someone remarked. '*Lovely couple, picturesque village, quaint church, wonderful house and garden. Fun people. It wouldn't dare rain.*'

Laura flew back from Northern Ireland to help Kate, David's mother, and his unmarried older sister, Cecile, to organise it all. Laura and Peter's house in Hampshire was rented out, and in any case Fleur had always hated it.

David was the golden boy. He had inherited his mother's good looks, while poor Cecile, who patently adored her brother, was shy and plain and had unfortunately inherited their father's features. Life, as Laura remarked at the time, could be very cruel.

David's mother took Cecile totally for granted. Laura could see that clearly without experiencing any revealing insight into the difference with which she treated her own two children.

David's friends and fellow officers had been ensconced

in the local hotel. They had whipped him up to London for his stag night and he had got married with little sleep and a hangover.

Fleur had floated through the hot, dreamy summer day in a private cloud of happiness. In the run-up to the wedding she had not seen much of David as he was completing a flying course with the Army Air Corps in Middle Wallop and she was stuck in army quarters with her parents in Northern Ireland, bored and counting the days. She had escaped briefly to London. Sam was in his second year at Guy's Hospital and she stayed in the flat his Australian girlfriend shared with two other girls and got a temporary job in a wine bar. Sam and Angie were both in medical school, working every hour God made, and Fleur found herself counting the days.

Two weeks before the wedding David got his wings and was jubilant. He was also exultant to be getting married in the village he had grown up in. All he needed now was a good posting and life would be perfect.

They went to Cyprus for their honeymoon and stayed in a villa in the middle of an orange grove with wonderful views of the sea. They dived together and went to clubs and ate out and read and swam in the pool. They lay on the marble tiles on cushions and read trashy books and made love for hours all over the house. To Fleur it was perfect. It was exactly what she wanted; just her and David in the middle of nowhere. She had not had him on her own for months.

He suddenly announced that he had arranged a surprise for the second week because it was her birthday. They shut up the villa and drove up tortuous roads to the Troodos Mountains. As they climbed the air grew cooler until they reached an isolated farmhouse perched on the edge of a mountain with breathtaking views looking out over fir forests.

There were two cars parked outside and David made Fleur close her eyes while he led her indoors. When she opened them in a large, empty room a table had been spread with food and there was a huge cake and balloons. The door burst open and Sam and Angie burst in shrieking,

'*Happy birthday, Fleury!*'

They had been closely followed by Laura and Peter. Her mother beaming, her father, who had been overruled, very unsure this was what Fleur wanted for her nineteenth birthday.

The smile had frozen on Fleur's face, then she had turned and seen David's happiness at surprising her and had hastily acted out a cry of astonished delight. She had escaped to go and shower and change and she had howled silently in the bathroom with disappointment. Honeymoons were *for two*, even if it was her birthday.

It had been a wonderful idea, generously thought out. David had obviously worked hard at this surprise. Local music, food and flowers had been arranged. Everyone had taken so much trouble for her. Fleur knew she was childishly ungrateful, but she had not wanted her wonderful spell with David broken, and it had been.

Her parents and Sam had only stayed two nights and then continued on their own separate holidays. But in those two days, David, Sam and her father had gone off walking and exploring together, leaving the women trailing behind them. There had been *boys'* drinks till all hours, long after the women had given up and gone to bed.

Fleur knew she was lucky to have a close family who loved her and wanted to spend her birthday with her. She felt even more ashamed of her feelings when Sam, who knew

208

her well, said: '*Hope you didn't mind us gate-crashing, little sis. It's just, I guess we are all are going to go our separate ways now. I'm going to travel for a year with Angie, then make up my mind how I want to specialise. Mum and Dad will be posted who knows where next, and the same goes for you and David . . . You and I will have children and I guess we'll never be so close again, will we? You're all grown-up and married now!*'

Fleur had hugged him, looking over his shoulder at the sea glinting in the distance. It wasn't just her and Sam. It was the memory of a particular time they had all had together, her parents and David. The bond they had all forged in Singapore living and working together would never be so close again. This was the end of a happy childhood for her and Sam. This party – her birthday party – had been recognition of this fact. Life was moving on.

When she stood on the steps with David's arm round her and watched the two cars pull away, she wept, unsure why. Perhaps the sudden realisation Sam had given her that all the people she loved had been here in one place together.

She suspected David felt the same. An anticlimax had hung over the rest of the day. They drank a lot of wine at supper and tottered up the stairs to bed and had fallen asleep without making love.

Making love. David had laughed at her: '*You're a little floozy, you*!'

She would wake first and watch him sleeping, aroused by his beauty. His lashes were dark and thick and made shadows under his eyes. His limbs were long and lean and brown. She felt amazed that it was really her in the bed with him. She lay in early sunlight just watching him sleep.

She saw women turn to look at him; their eyes following him around a room. He had a slow, laconic walk and an air of constant amusement which was deeply sexy and Fleur wanted him every minute of the day.

'I'm exhausted!' he would laugh, holding her away. 'You've got the body of a little boy and the voracious appetite of a dancer who's totally aware of her own body . . . not to mention mine! I'll have a heart attack.'

'No you won't. You're too young!'

'I'm getting older by the minute!' He swung her under him.

'I don't think you fancy me, you want a woman with large breasts and child-bearing hips!'

'So why did I marry you, youngster?'

'Tell me why you married me?'

'Because your dad has a wonderful sailing boat?'

'Wrong answer.'

'Well, it must be that I married you because I love you to bits and because I cannot imagine ever wanting to be with any other woman but you, Fleury.'

'Is that really true?' she whispered, thrilled.

He laughed and kissed her nose. 'Of course it is.'

But she had seen something sad or wistful in his eyes for a second, as if he knew she was going to ask for more than he was able to give.

Fleur reassured herself in the following months, ensconced happily in army quarters with lots of other young wives, all complaining in a good-natured way that their men could not talk about anything but aeroplanes. She told herself that it must be his new job; that he'd only just got his wings; that he had to prove himself flying. The fact remained, and she buried it mostly, because she was so happy and David was fun, life was fun . . . the fact remained that David did not want to make love to her as much as she wanted to make love to him.

When he did it was as lovely as ever, but he had rebuffed her very gently a couple of times and it had cut her to the bone. He knew, and was immensely attentive to make up for it, but Fleur realised instinctively her neediness would put him off. She felt almost ashamed of her body and how she felt about him.

When she backed off it was better. He would initiate their love-making. But Fleur learnt in those first few months of marriage that his sexual appetite for her was much less acute than hers for him.

She read magazines: she knew it happened sometimes. People's appetites were different. It wasn't as if he never slept with her. But supposing, and this niggled at her, it was chemistry, and he loved her but she just did not arouse him in the right way, the way he dramatically aroused her.

It seemed at nineteen such a terrifying thought, because she could not change herself physically. But she could grow up: she would try to be more aloof and sexy, more sophisticated . . . more . . . mysterious.

Fleur could not be unhappy. Her days were carefree and effortlessly spent with the other young wives, thrown together and having fun. There was tennis and endless parties or dinners in each other's houses. Those without children roamed around Salisbury together, shopping or going to films.

The men relaxed on their three-year secondment to the Air Corps; the atmosphere was less stuffy away from their regiments. The wives were all of an age, all young, and their lives stretched ahead of them.

Then, Fleur found she was pregnant. It was a bit soon, but to her surprise David was over the moon and a preoccupation with her desirability gave way, for a time, to morning sickness.

Then she started bleeding and was rushed to hospital. They found she was having twins and she was ordered to take three weeks' bed rest in the military hospital with a terrifying army sister who bellowed, *Wife of Captain Montrose* – but never Fleur's name.

After two weeks she could bear it no longer, and David, who was on exercise in Norway, came home and sprung her from the maternity ward one afternoon against orders, and his mother came down to make sure she rested for one more week.

David managed to send her a postcard every day he was away. She found out later that he had written most of them in advance and left them in Oslo for the Norwegian wife of a colleague to post to her each day.

When the twins started moving inside her, David would bend his head to her stomach to feel the movements, and Fleur would sigh and run her fingers through his hair, terrified at her absolute happiness.

She resembled a small whale and the twins came a month early in Tidworth Military Hospital in the early hours of the midsummer solstice and were put straight into two incubators. David was smitten from the first moment he saw them. He was on leave and spent hours sitting with Fleur watching his tiny babies. Nikki weighed just under 4 lbs and Saffie 3 lbs 2oz.

When she was able to come home with the twins, David had to leave for six weeks' flying in Germany. Both their mothers swooped down to help Fleur, who felt frightened and helpless and exhausted most of the time.

When David returned he could not believe how big the twins had grown. He stared down at the two little identical faces in wonder.

'How are we going to tell them apart, Fleury?' he

exclaimed. 'Two sweet little peas out of the same pod! My God, aren't we clever?'

'Incredibly clever!'

He sat on the bed, grinning at her. 'I've got a surprise for you. You're going to like it.'

'What? What?'

David bent and kissed her mouth. 'I've just had my next posting.'

'Quick, tell me!'

'Singapore! As part of the ANZUK force out there!'

Fleur squealed and clapped her hands to her mouth in delight, then threw her arms around him.

'It won't be until early next year,' David said.

'We're just too lucky,' Fleur said, feeling overwhelmed by good fortune. They turned to look at the two babies side by side in their cots.

'It will be like taking our little peapods home, won't it?' David said. 'Back to the place where we met; to the place where you grew up. I don't suppose we'll ever get another Far East posting. We must enjoy every minute, darling; every single minute.'

Fleur sighed, threw herself on the bed and closed her eyes, already feeling the hot wind blowing in from the Malacca Straits. Already seeing a vivid Singapore sky turning orange and black before a blood red sun slipped below the horizon, turning the world abruptly and startlingly black.

THIRTY

Jack phoned me as I lay spread-eagled inelegantly on my back like a stranded lobster. My neck had started to ache and I wondered if it was because of the overhead fan; but if I turned it off I grew red and overheated immediately. His voice pulled me back to the world I had left, a world that seemed as far away as the moon.

'How are you doing, Nik?'

'I'm fine . . . just exceedingly hot.' I heard my own voice sounding short and tetchy with a sharp edge, as if Jack had woken me or taken me away from something I was doing.

'Did I wake you, darlin'? I thought this would be a good time to catch you . . . when you were probably resting . . .'

'It is. Take no notice of me . . . I'm just irritable, Jack. I can't stay cool and it's no fun being me in this heat.'

'I'll bet it isn't. I worry about you, Nik. What—?'

I interrupted quickly. I did not want to talk about Saffie. 'Tell me what's happened with you. Did you get the yacht insurance sorted?'

'More or less. But you know what insurance companies are like. It should be all right in the end but the Aussies

214

made a terrible mess of the yacht. There's a hell of a hole in her stern . . .'

'Were they pissed?'

'Well, of course they deny it. At least I have their hefty deposit which they'll forfeit.'

'Good. How are *you*, darlin'?'

'Missing you. Wishing you and bump were safely home.'

I smiled at the wistful tone in his voice. 'It won't be long. Jack, I don't think there's much more they can find out about Saffie . . . about how she died. We're never going to know what happened. I think Fleur and I both realise that.'

I heard Jack hesitate. 'Could they establish the cause of her death?'

'They think she suffocated.'

He was silent. I knew he wanted to ask how they could possibly know that. I knew he was thinking that it was probably the most palatable cause the police could come up with.

'I'm sorry, Nik.'

'I know . . . Listen, this call will be costing you . . .'

'You are taking care of yourself?'

'I am. My mother is here, remember?'

'How are you two getting on?'

'Oh, we're all right. Jack, I miss you too, you know?'

'I'll ring you tomorrow. Love you.'

'Love you too,' I said. ''Bye, Jack.'

I turned my mobile off and raised myself into a sitting position and drank some tepid water. I longed to sleep but I had begun to dread the nights and I wanted to keep myself awake so that I would be so tired by the time I went to bed I would crash. I pulled the Hundertwasser book towards me, idly flicking over the pages. It was mildly irritating that Fleur knew more than I did about him when there was one of his buildings just down the road from us.

I opened the book at random, flicking through his history and his paintings. His only formal artistic training was a three-month stint at the *Akademie der Bildenden Kunste* in Vienna in 1948. Was this why Fleur had found him appealing: Hundertwasser and his self-trained eye?

He had a home in Venice near the Piazza San Marco where the light, reflecting on the water, the age of the buildings and the colours of clothes hanging on lines in the jumble of the city, had inspired him. '*He found decay strangely beautiful.*'

I thought of the path Jack and I had made in our garden at home. We had wanted to make a circular walk from the house back to the jetty. The land dropped dramatically at the far west end to circle the swamp. Trees rose from the murky water like arms seeking the sun. The shapes of them were eerie, angular and broken, frozen in time and stripped of bark by the possums.

Lichen covered some of the branches in lacy patterns of the palest green and grey, like the faded, tattered clothes on a corpse. The brackish swamp with its rotting logs and grass did not have the easy movement of water; it was still, like the stillness of something thick with decay hidden and clotting underneath its surface.

Jack and I would stop working and stand there motionless, feeling something primitive and ageless. The silence pressed down like the heat, enveloping us, nudging us back to a time when this wilderness ruled, and we both knew that as fast as we hacked a path for some purpose, it would return faster than we could clear, to raze our time there.

'*Hundertwasser believes that within each of us is a*

compilation of memories, sensations, images, dreams and
wishes, which he calls "Individualfilm". In his opinion the
role of art is to bring this material to a conscious level . . .'

I found him disturbing and closed the book and turned
awkwardly on my side. I thought about Mohktar and Blythe
wanting us to write what we remembered of that long-ago
afternoon. Did Fleur and I have locked memories waiting
to emerge after all these years? I did not think it was likely
and somehow it made me uneasy.

I must have fallen asleep because Fleur woke me coming
into the room and the sun had gone; it was almost dark.
She had a cup of tea in her hand.

'I'm glad you slept, darling.'

'I didn't want to,' I said grumpily. 'I'm not sleeping at
night and I was going to try to stay awake in the afternoons. What's funny?'

'You. You always were a little grump when you first woke
up. I'll let you wake up properly.'

She went out of the room and I pulled myself upright. I
drank my tea and went under the shower and washed my
hair. I felt better. The worst aspect of pregnancy, I thought,
was not being able to anticipate that wonderful first glass
of wine.

Fleur had a glass at her elbow and was sitting at a corner
of the table, writing. I didn't disturb her or speak in case
I broke her train of thought. I went to the fridge and got
out a jug of fresh orange juice and then I walked out onto
the balcony, which faced the sea. I didn't want to churn
up my memories of that dreadful afternoon; the exercise
was pointless.

I looked out to sea. There was silver light on the surface
of the water and a small breeze brought in the smell of fish
being barbecued somewhere. A boat slid from behind rocks.

The fisherman was silhouetted against the sky which was lighter than the sea. He poled fast across my field of vision. Black and white; black and white. His arms bent and lifted, bent and lifted as he poled from right to left and into darkness.

My heart beat wildly in my chest. My baby kicked hard and I gave a small cry for at that moment I caught out of the corner of my eye the shadow of a man, slightly to my left, superimposed, for a second in line with the fisherman . . . moving fast, running past me . . . and then I heard the sound of a door opening and closing . . .

Fleur called, 'Are you all right, Nik?' She had raised her head and was looking out of the open door towards me. I turned and something in my face must have alarmed her for she scraped her chair back and came out to me.

'What is it, Nik? What is it?'

I was suddenly cold on this warm night. *So cold*. I shivered and the goose bumps stood out on my arms, and I could not speak and just stared at Fleur, feeling the blood drain from my face.

Fleur caught my fear, bent to me, took my hands in hers. 'Nik, what is it? Darling . . . darling, are you in pain? Is it the baby?'

I shook my head. Took my hands from hers and curled them round my stomach as if to protect the life there.

'No,' I whispered. And I looked at her without hope for I knew now that I couldn't escape what was locked in my head. Saffie wasn't going to let me. There was something I had to act out. There was something I had to remember. I was so afraid that my teeth began to chatter and my knees trembled and then my whole body began to shake and my mother wrapped herself around me as if to protect and warm me.

218

'Not the baby,' I managed. 'Not the baby, Mum. It's something inside my head.'

Fleur lifted her head and her eyes were as dark and frightened as mine.

THIRTY-ONE

Fleur put me to bed. She made more tea and brought me supper on a tray, which I played with. I grew warmer and the fear left me as quickly as it had come. Fleur sat on a chair with her book on her knee and I began to feel like a child again. It was as if Fleur and I were in a bubble together, convalescing, our lives revolving around the comfort of bed as if it was an island no one else could reach. She didn't press me to talk and I couldn't have explained anyway.

She had put an exercise book and a pen on my bedside table in case I wanted to write anything down. I realised that something in Fleur dreaded but needed to know what happened that afternoon and why.

I looked at her sitting in the chair in the half-light. We had thrown the shutters open and there was a moon out there, in a crystal clear sky of stars. If we turned the light on the mosquitoes would have had a field day. The small mosquito coil burning on the bedside table reminded me of Ah Heng squatting on the floor waiting for Saffie and me to go to sleep. The smoke from the coil would waft up around her head, the smell of it so much a part of being young.

I looked at Fleur's face and saw such sadness there, and I wondered, if she could go back, what she would change, apart from the obvious. I could hardly remember her happiness with Dad; I had concentrated on my own memories. Mostly they lived on in photographs and stories. Stories Fergus and Fleur had shared with me to keep him alive for me, to keep him firmly in my heart. And it had.

I was unsure if she had gone to sleep in the chair because her eyes were closed. I said softly, almost to myself, 'If you could go back and have your life again would you wish for a life with David or with Fergus?'

I had wondered this so many times. Fleur and Fergus had been close, like soul mates. They *liked* each other as well as having a love that was unmistakable. I had been too young to know what sort of love my parents had. I only knew that Fleur and Fergus surmounted the sorrow they carried together, the sorrow I added to for most of my childhood. I saw now that their sadness added to the depth of their relationship, to the life they shared together. They never argued about unimportant things and I don't think either of them ever took happiness for granted.

I guess it was why I could not help loving Fergus; despite the fact that I could never understand his lack of integrity when my father was alive. I knew he had saved us, Fleur and me. I knew he was special. He had the sort of loyalty and love that nothing can kill, absolutely nothing. It lasted his whole life. I could see and hear him now, saying, the day I got my degree, *'How lucky I am! How incredibly lucky to have a beautiful and clever daughter!'*

He had scooped me up in a bear hug with one arm, and Fleur, laughing, with the other. They had been inseparable, yet he never, ever made me feel the outsider in their lives.

So I said now, 'If you could go back and have your life

221

again would you wish for a life with David or with Fergus, Mum?'

She looked up straight away. 'Nikki, you know it's a question that I can't answer. You might as well ask me if I would have preferred to be an Eskimo.'

I was glad to hear the exasperation in her voice. It was a pointless, childish question. I knew I had asked it instead of the thing I really needed to know, but did not want to hear. *Why did you fall out of love with my Dad? What happened? What happened in that seamless memory I have of you both?*

In the light from the open window her face was obscured, but I could feel her weariness, a sudden sapping of her strength. I propped myself up on an elbow.

'Mum? Go to bed. I'm all right now, really; perfectly all right. It's probably my hormones.'

She smiled. 'Are you sure?'

'Quite sure. I'm sorry I asked that stupid question. I didn't mean to upset you.'

'I know . . .' She got out of the chair and came to the bed. 'You need to get home to Jack, darling; back to your life . . .' She took a deep breath. 'You *must* look forward, not turn constantly back to the past . . . to a terrible thing neither of us can change, Nik. I suddenly believe it's wrong to think about that afternoon, to try to write anything more down. Leave it. Try now to think only about pleasant things. You, Jack and the baby . . .'

I smiled. It was such a Fleur statement. How can you possibly dictate what your mind throws up? This is the terror of memory; the tiny slits that open to reveal slithers: clear, sharp shards that make you bleed. We both knew this.

She bent to kiss me. 'Good night, Nik. Shout if you need me. Promise?'

222

I reached out for her hand and held it for a moment. 'Good night, Mum.'

When she had gone I turned on my side and watched the sky for a long time. I did not fight sleep. I just lay waiting for Saffie. I knew she was near. I knew she would come.

I pulled down the mosquito net. I did not close the shutters. I liked the sky and the faint scent of sea and herbs on the wind. I moved the pillows to help my aching neck and turned the other way as I felt my child kicking again. I wondered how many of our feelings – love and anxiety – are transferred to the child in our womb.

I slept and when I woke it was the dead of night. The moon had gone, the stars were hidden by cloud and the night was very still. I lifted the mosquito net to go to the loo and then, thirsty, I moved out into the main room to the fridge in the corner. The water was blissfully cool. I poured another glass and took it back to bed. I slept immediately.

When I woke it was no longer night but a hot afternoon. I could tell because the heat hovered heavily outside the shuttered room.

We were both in Fleur's bed. Saffie was sitting up on the other side of Mum, fiddling with her hair. She was awake and bored. She had a small paper flower and she bent to tickle Mum with it, wanting her to wake up.

'Don't,' I said sleepily. 'Mum doesn't like to be woken up.'

'Let's go out,' Saffie said. 'Come on, let's go out and play on the beach.'

'No,' I said. 'Go back to sleep, Saffie, you'll make Mummy cross.' I turned over, away from her.

I heard her get out of bed and go to the door and look out. 'The amah's asleep,' she whispered. 'Come on . . .

Nikki, please come with me. I don't want to go out on my own . . .'

'No!' I said, annoyed. I curled up tight into a small ball, my back touching Mum's. I heard Saffie moving about trying to be quiet. She was looking for her dress. I heard her on my side of the bed picking one up from the floor. I half opened my eyes as she pulled it over her head. It was my dress; it had a tear in the pocket.

'You've got the wrong dress on.'

'Don't care. I'll wait for you . . . ?' she said hopefully.

'In a minute then . . .' But I fell asleep . . .

This time she would not leave without me. This time she made me go with her. She placed the chair under the window and climbed out onto the balcony and I followed. We ducked past the shuttered window where the amah was sleeping and we ran away, out into the deserted hot afternoon.

I ran after her and the tiny colourless crabs ran ahead of us like a little wave, and we laughed and headed towards the rocks by the sea. We had the world to ourselves and we caught hands and ran and jumped in small pools and laughed to be free.

Suddenly, as we rounded a corner there was a man sitting on the rocks. A man with his hands round his knees and a Panama hat on his head and sunglasses covering his eyes. He did not look at me, just Saffie.

'Hello,' she said cheerfully, staring at him.

I don't think he was pleased to be disturbed because he did not answer for quite a long time, then he said, 'Aren't you supposed to be resting?'

'Yes,' Saffie said. 'I can't sleep. I'm bored.'

'Where's your sister?'

'She's asleep and I've got no one to play with.'

224

'I'm afraid I'm no good at playing. I haven't got any little girls.'

'We could walk and see the monkeys.'

'If your mother wakes up and finds you are gone, she'll be worried.'

'Mummy won't wake up. She takes pills.' Saffie moved closer and stared hard at him. 'Were you a pilot, like my dad?'

'Yes, I'm still a pilot.'

Saffie ran in little circles stamping at the crabs.

The man unfolded from the rock. He was tall, as tall as my dad, with long legs. I could not see his face properly but there was something familiar about him. I could see that he wanted to walk away from us. I could see that he didn't want to talk to two children.

He turned and began to walk towards the steps and the forest path and I saw he had a limp as if he had hurt his leg.

'Can I come with you? Can I come with you?' Saffie called, running after him. She smiled her best smile. The smile Dad called our wheedling smile. 'Mummy won't mind if you are a pilot like Daddy . . .'

He kept walking away and he said as we ran after him, 'No, you can't come with me. Go home. Go back to your house now, to your mother and sister . . .'

I was fascinated by his long legs limping fast away. *Long, long legs.*

My heart jumped. I called to Saffie, 'Let's go home. Saffie! We've got to go back . . .'

She took no notice and ran ahead of the man, up the stone steps to the lighthouse. I ran after her into the sudden shade of the trees but I couldn't see her. I darted about, whispering, calling her but she did not come.

The man came up the steps, took his glasses off to wipe them, blinking irritably in the sudden shadow, and my heart hammered. *I knew his face. I knew where I had seen it before.*

He called Saffie too, not her name, he just called, 'Hello' and 'where are you?'

She was waiting at the turn of the path holding fir cones in her hand. 'Here I am! I can walk with you. *I can . . .* We're not allowed to talk to strangers, but you're not a stranger, so mummy won't mind.'

She went closer to him. 'I *think* I remember you.' She said, peering up into his face. 'You were daddy's friend.'

Saffie was lying. She didn't remember him but she did not want to go back to the house.

The man bent suddenly in front of her and held her arms. I ran to her side. *Saffie, come away! Come away!*

'What do you remember?' The man asked and his voice was cold and hard.

Saffie, abruptly subdued, was silent.

'What – do – you – remember?' He shook her, bringing his face close to hers.

I bent to her ear. *'Tell him, Saffie . . . Tell him the truth, you don't remember him at all.'*

But Saffie was frightened now. Her eyes were growing huge with fear at the thing in his eyes.

'Come on, answer me. What were you going to say?' His voice made us both shiver.

I wrapped my arms round Saffie from behind, held her to me.

'Nothing.' Saffie's voice was tiny, like a whimper. 'I want to go home now . . .' She tried to pull her arms away from his hands.

'But I'm your daddy's friend, aren't I? You said so. What

made you think that? What made you think we were friends?'

Saffie looked at him bewildered, her bottom lip wobbling. Little beads of sweat lay on her forehead. 'Because . . . because . . . you flew with my dad and . . .' She stopped as he gripped her arms tighter.

I screamed then. '*She doesn't know! It was me! It was me. I saw you that day. I saw you . . . It was me . . .*'

He did not hear me. He bent so that his eyes were level with Saffie's.

'So you do remember me as your daddy's friend, Saffie?' His voice was soft.

Saffie desperately nodded her head up and down, thinking this was what he wanted to hear. Her face was white and very frightened.

The man straightened up holding on to one of her arms. 'Come along. Can you hear the monkeys? Let's go and see if we can spot some.'

'No! No! I want to go home now. I want to go back . . . Let me go.'

'Sorry. You wanted to walk, young lady, and we are going to walk . . .'

Saffie began to cry, then to kick and scream. 'Let me go! Let me go! I'll tell Grandpa! I'll tell . . .'

Suddenly the man whirled her sharply round and put a hand over her mouth to stop her screaming. I rushed. I rushed between them and held Saffie tight to me and I was screaming too. He was hurting. He was hurting . . . His hand was covering my mouth. I could not get my breath. I could not breathe. I kicked and twisted and the pressure on my neck increased and pain shot through my body. I could not move. Suddenly there was a crack, a painful pop in my neck and darkness came; an endless, endless darkness.

*   *   *

227

'Oh, God! Oh, God! What have I done?' he was saying over and over again. 'Oh God, I didn't mean . . .'

He lifted me, I saw myself dangling over his arms. He carried me into the darkness of trees. He was crying and shaking, I could feel his whole body shaking. 'What am I going to do? What am I going to do? Oh, dear God!'

He put me down on the ground and walked away and I heard scrabbling. I heard him kicking something and pulling and grunting. Then he came back for me and I saw what he was going to do . . . and I screamed.

'Don't bury me. Don't bury me. I don't want my face covered. I don't want to be buried under the ground.'

He drops me with a small sound like a sob and rolls me underneath the boulder and covers me with another stone and I disappear into the earth. I disappear screaming into the earth . . .

Suddenly, Saffie is with me, her arms lift me up and away and we are running, running across the sand, back home to Fleur, and I know Saffie is not so alone any more because I know now. I know what happened.

Saffie had my dress on. Saffie was killed because he thought it was me. He thought I was the twin who saw him that day.

THIRTY-TWO

Fleur knew she would not sleep. She had a shower and climbed into bed under the mosquito net with her books.

If you could have your life again who would you choose, David or Fergus?

It had always been impossible to explain truthfully about the two loves of her life.

How do you explain to your daughter that there are many different ways of loving? That if you are desperate enough to keep the person you love you will compromise, you will do anything to keep them.

Nikki was thirty-three. By the time Fleur was twenty-five, David and Saffie were dead, and her life had been blown apart. By the time she was thirty-three she was living another quite different life.

When she married Fergus he had come out of the army to join the London branch of his father's architectural firm. It was not the gossip and innuendo within the army that drove Fergus out; he could cope with that. It was Fleur's shattered life. Fergus foresaw that Fleur would need a settled base if she was to survive, and a completely different way of life.

He could imagine the effect on her if, on a new posting with him, she was confronted by friends of hers and David. Neither of them needed to justify their relationship, but that would not stop people judging them. He did not want to leave her on her own for long periods, so he also, with regret, gave up any idea of becoming a civil pilot.

He too was grieving for the man he'd known from school-days and through Sandhurst. He had joined a small flying club where he flew for pleasure. He assured Fleur, always, it was much more fun.

Fleur, restless, got up and wandered round the house in the dark.

Death was like the resolute closing of a heavy prison door between you and the person you loved. You could never get beyond the wondering; you could never be sure of the shape of that lost life. You could never be entirely certain of either its substance or what its future would have been.

This prevented you answering anything completely truth-fully because death ended any choices she and David might have had to make.

Fleur liked to believe that they would have weathered the sudden crisis in their lives. Yet she knew in flaring, painful moments of truth that she had been the one without a real choice. David would have had to make the decision. He would have had to decide between his two beckoning lives.

Yet he had died thinking she was the one who had given him an ultimatum, and she hadn't had time to explain. This is what had tormented her. This is what had obsessed her after his death.

She could never undo it, or have that time back to reassure him.

She opened the thin screen door and went out onto the

balcony. *You think wounds heal, but some don't; some never heal.*

Palm trees wavered against the night sky. The sea lay glistening like a thin strand of metal in the distance and the ghost of the girl she had once been rose up to remember the good times here with her parents and Sam, and later with David and the twins. Now she was another woman altogether, here with her daughter to gather up her lost dead child and finally lay her to rest.

How could these two terrible deaths have happened to her? The girl Fleury, who had been full of hope and optimism and passion. Her eyes swept across the deserted beach and up to the lighthouse on the headland.

There, over there, someone casually took the life of a child. My child.

The shock of it never diminished. Fleur let her grief flow through her, as familiar as the blood coursing through her veins. The growing horror when she had been forced to understand that this was not a childish prank but something infinitely more sinister. The torches in the dark; the endless calling of Saffie's name. The Military Police and local police arriving in Jeeps full of men. The loudspeakers; the willing Malay and English volunteers who beat for hours with sticks to the very edge of the jungle and found nothing.

The knowledge that in that noisy cicada-rubbing vegetation, the jungle sprang back relentlessly, hiding human interference as if it had never been. A small body covered forever.

Until now, this moment, when the world narrowed again to a small isolated focus. No David. No Fergus. Just her and Nikki again, walking a dark, familiar path. Just the two of them.

And me.

The flimsy door behind her banged in a sudden breeze and Fleur shivered and jumped at the shadow the palms made over the sand below her. It was as if a small child brushed past her, touching her briefly in a torn dress with little pink flowers.

She went back inside the house to bed, pulling the mosquito net down behind her. *Saffie. Naughty little Saffie.* She let herself wonder for a second how it would have been to have both her daughters, laughing and joking together; married and having children. She smiled at the thought of the endless telephone calls and private jokes and screams of mirth. All the trivial things that families and siblings took for granted. Nikki and Saffie as close as two peas in a pod.

She had to stop herself in supermarkets or on busy streets, when she saw a small child being slapped for being grizzly, for being tired, for being a child. She wanted to scream out, *'Stop it! Don't you realise how lucky you are?'*

She shut her mind abruptly; thought again of Fergus. How good he had been at deflecting this persistent inner voice that pulled her back, back into the shadows of her first life, obsessively going over what she could never change.

THIRTY-THREE

Fleur bumped into Fergus on a flight home to Singapore from Brize Norton. He had been David's best man and at the twins' christening as one of their godfathers, but he and Fleur had never really had a conversation.

David had flown on back to Singapore with the twins. Fleur was recovering from a bad dose of dengue fever and had stayed behind recovering with Peter and Laura. She had spent ten days in a military hospital. Her army doctor wanted to take blood tests and try to stabilise her weight loss before he allowed her to fly back to Singapore.

On that flight home she had the strange light-headedness that comes after illness and excessive weight loss and she felt very odd to be travelling without children.

Both sets of parents had been worried about Fleur and David's decision to extend his tour of service for another two years. Peter believed that three and a half years in the tropics at one time was enough. Health and marriages suffered, in his opinion, in that relentless humidity. It was unusual to be offered an extension, but David's OC had gone sick, and David, as his second-in-command, knew the job better than anyone.

Neither Fleur nor David wanted to come home. To stay meant early promotion for David and he could still fly as well as do an admin job. Fleur was teaching dance twice a week at the International School. The twins would start school next year and they had both jumped at the chance of staying on at the naval base.

The day before her flight home, Sam rang her from Melbourne.

'I hear you've been ill, sis, and look cadaverous!'

'Gee, thanks, Sam. You and Mum are so good for my morale.'

'Are you fit enough to go back? Dad seems very worried about you.'

'Is he? He hasn't said anything. I'm fine now. You know what these tropical diseases are like. It takes time to pile the weight back on.'

There was an unlike-Sam silence and then he said in a different voice, 'Fleury, I don't think it's your physical welfare that's concerning Dad, you've always been skinny. It's what he calls your *"air of sudden sadness"*. Are things OK with you and Dave?'

'Dad asked you to phone?'

'Yes. Because he knows I'm the only one you ever talk to. I want you to know that you still can.'

A lump formed in Fleur's throat and tears sprang to her eyes and ran down her face, surprising her with their suddenness. She did not want Sam to suspect so she coughed and said brightly, 'Dad is sweet. I'm OK, honestly. It's only . . . I don't usually get ill and I guess it depressed me to be left here while David and the twins flew home.'

Fleur had not answered and Sam persisted. 'So, you and David are all right, still happy?'

'Why on earth shouldn't we be, Sam? Of course we are!'

But the damn tears would not stop. They fell onto her hands holding the phone. They were going to make her voice thick and ugly with misery. They were going to give her away.

Sam, thousands of miles away, heard. 'Fleur? You still love him?'

'Oh, yes!' he heard her whisper. 'Oh, yes, Sam.'

'And he loves you?' Sam held his breath. There was the tiniest of pauses. You would have to know and love someone to detect it.

'Yes. He loves me.'

But? Sam thought. Then, *Bugger it! Dad's right, something is wrong.*

'OK . . . Got a pen? Right, this is my telephone number and address for the next three months . . . I'll let you know when and where I move on to. Tell Dave he owes me a letter, will you?'

'Yes, I will. Sam?'

'Yes.'

'I'm glad you rang.'

'So am I. Take care, Fleury.'

'And you, Sam.'

Sam walked away from the phone with a heavy heart. Shit! Dave was obviously bloody well not behaving himself. He had seen so much of it growing up in a foreign posting. Too much temptation and too much heat, booze and bare flesh. Tiny cracks in a marriage would widen in that sometimes vacuous life with too little to do.

He had even watched his parents wobble once. Laura, fed up with the narrow confines of pool, Officers' Club, Mess, wives' club and NAAFI had decided to take a degree, as many wives with half a brain were driven to. She had had the eager and willing help one summer of a young

American professor from Harvard who was passing through, but not quickly enough, it seemed to his father.

Peter, wisely, had merely exaggerated his air of never knowing who was where or why in order to create a gap for Laura. His mother, foiled of drama, had returned, faithful, Sam believed, to the fold and to his father's bed.

He smiled to himself. That had been the summer some naval officer had got Fleur absolutely blotto and she had leapt over the side of a naval frigate causing a terrible fuss.

He remembered his sister turning from a gawky teenager into an absolute stunner. God, how determined she had been to throw away everything to marry David. He remembered his surprise when David had told him he was going to marry Fleur. Fleur had had a bit of a crush, but David always seemed to treat Fleur as a little sister. He had women flocking and a bit of a reputation for pulling.

God! How awful if David had given in for convenience, because it was easy. He got to know us all so well. He, Dad and I just hit it off from the very beginning. But he was very fond of Fleury, who wouldn't be? He must have loved her, but enough? I'm not so bloody sure of that.

Fleur had been fighting the toaster in the accommodation at Brize Norton. There was a large table where you helped yourself. Her toast was burning and wouldn't pop up. It seemed to her the eyes of a million men were watching her struggle with amusement when a hand reached over and whacked the toaster hard, and burnt toast flew out onto the spotless white tablecloth.

'Mrs Montrose, I presume. Trying to burn the building down in a random act of terrorism?'

Fleur whipped round to see Fergus's laughing face.

236

'Oh, God! Thank you! Why are all those men staring? Is it such a heinous crime to burn toast here?'

Fergus grinned. 'Bastards! All of them! They would have come to your rescue eventually, I think. They are staring because you are very pretty and have tight denim jeans on and most officers, wives don't travel in jeans.'

Fleur grinned back. 'For twenty-four hours I am pretending I am not an officer's wife and can wear exactly what I like.'

'Good for you! Ignore the pursed lips of the general's wife as you board!'

'What general's wife?' Fleur squeaked. 'You're joking?'

'Yes!'

They made more toast and sat down together, watched by the watchers. 'You realise this is a scandal in the making before we've even boarded?'

'What, having breakfast together!' They stared at each other and giggled.

Fergus was flying out to take over David's job and one more pilot had been drafted in to help David for a big exercise in Malaya. It was why David had had to fly on home. He had taken the twins back to Ah Heng so that Fleur could rest.

'I was meant to fly in two days ago. David's furious, but I had to give my seat to a brigadier,' Fergus said. 'So fate has decreed we travel together, Mrs Montrose.'

'So it seems.'

Once on board she found she was sitting next to a fat major. Fergus was nowhere to be seen. Then a burly corporal flight-attendant bent to his ear and the major got up grumbling, shot Fleur a hostile look and made his way to the end of the plane. As soon as he'd left his seat, Fergus bounded up and slid into it, breathless.

'You can't sit there, Fergus! It's that grumpy fat major's seat.'

'Not any more. I bribed the corporal to say he had made a mistake with the seating. I told him it was imperative that I sit next to you because you have been very ill and you might throw up all over the place and I was a family friend . . . Fat major is not amused. I was sitting next to the most enormous army sister . . . Hey ho, this is fun!'

Fleur threw her head back and laughed. 'You and David are going to be appalling together! Whoever suggested you became his second-in-command?'

'I did, of course!'

Fleur looked back on that flight home to Singapore as the moment she recovered her sense of humour. Fergus made her laugh. He could make the most ordinary story amusing. They talked and talked about everything and nothing as they headed back into the heat on the long, slow journey via Cyprus and Gan.

Fleur changed out of her jeans at Gan and into a cooler brown skirt with small butterflies on and a cream tee shirt. Something changed in that moment. Fergus, watching her return to the waiting area, was suddenly still, mesmerised by her long, dark hair caught up in a band, by the smallness of her waist and the way she moved, but most of all by the sweet beauty of her face, guileless, it seemed to him, as she walked over to him.

Fleur met his eyes and for a moment was stopped by what she saw in them. They simply stood staring at each other, unable to look away in front of a whole room of people. Then, confused, she sat quickly down and Fergus went away to get her a drink.

Fleur, shaky, thought with a start: *David has never, ever looked at me like that; with blatant, unabashed, open longing.*

Even buying her a drink Fergus turned as if he could not bear to take his eyes off her. Fleur was used to being admired and flirted with, but Fergus's intensity, his air of sardonic amusement on that long, intimate journey home was seductive, made her stomach churn and desire flash through her body, horrifying her. Their naked, mutual attraction was shocking.

When she fell asleep he covered her with a blanket, and left his arm under her head. Fleur thought they possibly learnt more about each other on that strange disembodied journey through space than at any future time. However, it wasn't love; not then. Fergus was too honourable and she loved David.

But David had not made love to her for four months and Fleur was young; she wanted more babies and she had begun to doubt the attraction of her own body. And here, here was someone attractive and funny who thought her unmistakably desirable.

Fleur had been telling herself for months that David had been overworked and strung out before his UK leave. Then she had been ill. Then she told herself it was the excessive humidity that year, and was only to be expected when David had been coping with two jobs while he waited for a replacement. She told herself she was selfish . . . but she knew that the heat had never been a factor in their lives before.

It would have been wonderful to pretend there wasn't anyone else, that David was a man who did not have the same sexual appetite. But she could not pretend this, because instinctively she knew it wasn't true. She watched how he danced, how sensuously he moved, how he touched and charmed and loved and was amused by women.

There was nothing cold and detached about David. He had that effortless charisma and knowledge of his own popularity. How could he not? He had been his parents' golden boy. Good at almost everything and nice with it.

With the right person, Fleur knew instinctively he would be the most passionate lover. That person was not her, and probably never would be. But she never gave up hoping and the excitement of being with him never faltered. He would run up the stairs, calling, 'Where is everybody? Fleury? Peapods? I've discovered a wonderful place for a picnic. We'll go this weekend . . .'

He would hug her and whirl her round. He would gather up the twins and cover them with noisy kisses until they yelled, *'Stop! Stop, Daddy! Stop! Ugh!'*

At night he would fold her in his arms, scoop her to him with a small sigh of contentment.

'You see,' she said to Fergus many months later. 'Everything else was so lovely. I thought I could live with how it was. *If I didn't ask*. I really thought I could.'

Fleur, lying under the mosquito net, remembering, jumped violently at the sound of Nikki's blood-curdling cry.

THIRTY-FOUR

The phone went before DS Mohktar was fully dressed. He expected it to be DI Blythe but it was Mrs Campbell.

'I'm so sorry to call you so early, Detective Sergeant Mohktar. Nikki's asking to speak to you. Something's worrying her but she can't seem to tell me . . .'

'I'll be right over, Mrs Campbell.' James Mohktar experienced a surge of excitement. Then he felt Fleur's hesitation over the line.

'Is there something else I can help you with?'

There was a pause. 'My daughter seems unwell . . .'

'You would like a doctor? Is it the baby?'

'No, I don't think it's the baby. She's just very listless . . . almost as if she's in shock. Perhaps it's something she's remembered. DS Mohktar, I feel very disturbed.'

'Mrs Campbell, I will now immediately call my friend, Doctor Janus. She has seen your daughter before. She is a very gentle lady,' Mohktar said. But he knew it was not her daughter's physical state Fleur was worrying about. 'I will be with you in half an hour.'

'Thank you so much.'

Mohktar shaved and put on a spotless shirt, buffed his shoes and resisted the urge to rush. He had a hard knot of anticipation in the pit of his stomach and he knew instinctively this meant there was going to be something he must concentrate on, something he must be sure not to miss. Rushing would not calm his mind.

In this instance he did not want Blythe with him, and he left a message for the inspector and made speedily for his car. He rang Dr Janus as he drove. Her clinic was on his way and she agreed to check on Miss Montrose before she opened up her surgery. She took her own car and they arrived at the small car park at the same time and walked together to the house.

Mrs Campbell was waiting for them on the balcony. The amah brought out orange juice clinking with ice and they sat at the table outside. Dr Janus was looking at Fleur closely. She was very pale and Mohktar said, giving her his lovely smile, 'Please, before we talk to your daughter, will you tell us your worries?'

Fleur turned the glass in her hands. 'Nikki sometimes gets like this when she has had a really bad nightmare. She wakes exhausted, drained. She has had bad dreams on and off all her life . . .'

'Since her sister died?' Mohktar asked.

'Yes.' Fleur looked up at him. 'My husband was always better than I was at calming her down as a child.'

Because you showed your own fear of her dreams, Mohktar thought.

'So, she had a nightmare last night?'

'I heard her cry out. I woke her up. She was feverish and incoherent. I put the fan on and bathed her with cold water and she eventually became calmer as it got light.'

'Could she tell you what she had dreamt?' Dr Janus asked.

'No. She just lay there shaking, her teeth chattering, but she wouldn't speak.'

'She was afraid?' Mohktar's voice was soft.

Fleur nodded. 'Yes. She was too afraid to speak about it.' She paused. 'It will sound . . . odd to you, I know, but Nikki, as a child, believed Saffie came to her at night. That she could see her and talk to her. Sometimes I think she still believes this.'

Both Dr Janus and Mohktar stared at her. To them it did not seem odd at all. Dr Janus smiled and adjusted her sari. 'Only the western world believes in the impossibility of this. Why should it not be so? Why is it impossible to believe that the dead are not beyond our reach?'

Mohktar said, 'How do we know what is a dream and what is the subconscious mind working in ways we can never understand, Mrs Campbell?'

Fleur looked at them both. This wasn't the reaction she had expected, at least from Mohktar who was a policeman and dealt with facts.

There had been many days over the years when Saffie had seemed near to Fleur. In the moments between sleeping and waking on a Sunday afternoon in an empty house. Looking over a school wall at small children in tiny pleated skirts playing hopscotch on concrete. Listening to Mahler in the garden with Fergus as the sun turned the leaves of the copper beech gold, and in the tiny, visceral moment a small hand slipped into hers. Waking, waking, suddenly in the suffocating dark with your heart banging as if someone had whispered a name in your ear and the thought: *Why? What reason could anyone have for killing you, darling?* As if the clue, the vital clue lay in the remembering.

Dr Janus bent for her medical bag. 'If it is all right with you I will go and examine your daughter on my own.'

243

Fleur nodded. 'Of course. She is in the same room as before, Dr Janus.'

When she had gone, Mohktar said, leaning towards Fleur, 'Mrs Campbell, is it perhaps that you are worried about what Nikki might remember?'

Fleur looked past him at the sea. 'When Nikki was questioned all those years ago she said she got out of the window to look for Saffie. But it was a very long afternoon for a five-year-old to stay inside. We don't know how long Nikki might have been out on the beach. I know she would have got bored. She wouldn't have settled to anything until she knew where Saffie was and what she was doing.'

'The amah said at the time that when she brought my tea in, at about five thirty, Nikki was in the bathroom and she was sure she did not go out again. At the time I believed her, but the amah went off to have a shower, so how could she be sure? The twins were so quick, they darted about like fish . . . what if Nikki had gone outside again and seen someone . . .' Fleur hesitated.

'Someone she knew?' Mohktar finished quietly.

Fleur's eyes met Mohktar's. 'What if she had been confused by the actions of someone she knew behaving strangely?'

'How did she seem when you woke up?'

'Anxious, in case I was cross; desperate for me to wake up. She said Saffie had been gone a long time and something in her voice jerked me awake. I looked out of the window and saw the light was going and I pulled my clothes on and we both rushed out to look for her . . .'

Mohktar watched Fleur's hands flutter and clasp each other.

'This is very hard for you, Mrs Campbell . . . I regret to ask these questions.'

Fleur smiled faintly. 'I know, DS Mohktar, but it's your job.'

Dr Janus floated back and sat down. 'Mrs Campbell, the baby's heartbeat is slightly irregular indicating a measure of distress. I've told your daughter she must stay in bed all day today. I want her to rest. I will come back just after midday and again this evening.' She took a card out of her bag. 'This is my number; you must ring immediately if you are worried. Please do not look alarmed, all the indications are that your daughter has had a fright of some kind and everything will settle down. She seems calmer, but anxious to speak to you, James. This is not the ideal time. On the other hand, she has a need to talk. Please will you go easy, *lah*? Stop immediately if she becomes distressed or unwell?'

Mohktar nodded and got up from his chair. 'I will go now.'

Fleur got up too. 'I'll just go and see if Nikki needs anything before you go in.'

Mohktar said to Fleur quietly as she passed him, 'Trust me, Mrs Campbell. Your daughter's welfare is my priority.'

Fleur nodded. She did trust him.

When she returned, Dr Janus said quietly, 'I have known James Mohktar since childhood . . .' She smiled. 'He was always wise, even as a child. He will proceed gently.'

She placed her hands on the table and stared at them a moment. They were small hands, the fingers thin and neat. Fleur stared at them too. She felt strange and detached, as if she was going to float away.

'I must go and open my clinic.' Dr Janus's voice came from a long way away. 'Even now there will be a queue waiting, squatting outside my door in the hot sun . . .' She gave Fleur a searching look. 'Mrs Campbell, I believe the best thing for you and your daughter is to go home soon.

Nikki will need a hospital examination before she can fly. The longer you leave it, the more risky it becomes. I think a long stay here is unhealthy for both of you.'

She smiled and was gone. Fleur looked out over the beach, mesmerised by two men playing with huge kites: one blue; one red. The amah came out to collect up the glasses.

Fleur smiled. 'Thank you.'

She was watching herself from a distance, detached, but her voice sounded fine. She turned and went into her room and shut the door. Her head throbbed and she took two paracetamol and crawled under the mosquito net and lay on the newly made bed.

She wanted to be home, in London, in her little safe house where she could close the door against everything; where the smell of Fergus's whisky and cigarettes still lingered in the curtains and air of his study. Where she would sit sometimes in his swivel chair to pretend he had just popped out to walk the dog or to buy a newspaper or cigarettes. Fergus. Constant and loving as the seasons.

He isn't here now because all that happened took its toll on him too. He drank too much, he smoked too much . . . he gave too much. He died before he was sixty. And here I am, still alive.

It seemed to Fleur to be the loneliest place on earth.

THIRTY-FIVE

I could hear their voices outside my room and they seemed
to come from a long way away. The ceiling fan stirred the
mosquito net; it moved gently around me like a billowing
white sail. I felt strange. I was in a sailing boat way out at
sea and nothing could touch me. I hovered above myself
for the next thing that would happen. Interested, but
detached.

Fleur came and lifted the mosquito net. 'DS Mohktar is
here, darling. Do you still want to speak to him?'

I turned to her. I was no longer afloat. I could not escape
the words that had to be said. 'Yes, Mum.'

How tired Fleur looked. How thin and aged. I knew I
should get out of bed and wash my face, brush my hair, but
I did not have the energy. Fleur put orange juice on the
bedside table.

'You must keep drinking, Nik.'

She went to get Mohktar and I felt myself tremble. I
turned the pillow to cool my head and sat myself up,
suddenly minding what Mohktar thought of me.

He came in carrying a plate of papaya and melon cut

into small pieces with a sprinkling of ginger over them.

I smiled. 'Ah Heng used to do that when we were children.'

Mohktar smiled back and sat on the chair next to the bed. 'From Ah Lin. To a Malay it is as comforting as your English toast and butter and marmalade!'

I took a piece and he took a piece. He seemed in no hurry and I began to relax as I ate the fruit. There are some people you could believe you had known in another life and Mohktar was one of them.

'Tell me about the place you grew up in?' I said. 'Did you have a happy childhood?'

He hesitated, his dark eyes watching me. 'I had a very happy childhood in a small *kampong* by a river. I ran wild with my brothers. There were many of us and we were poor by western standards but comfortable by our own. My father was a bank clerk and my mother, helped by all her children, raised livestock.' He smiled. 'It was a very ordinary, boring childhood, I'm afraid, Miss Montrose.'

'What made you become a policeman?'

'Perhaps to give families like mine a voice against corruption.'

I waited, watching his beautiful face.

'Two of my brothers were killed by faulty scaffolding. They fell thousands of metres to their deaths. The builder was never prosecuted. He paid off the police and the judge. My mother was never the same again. I was in England at the time, studying. I returned with new eyes and could not go back to the old ways of acceptance of corruption.'

'I could have gone into law, but you see, I like jigsaws. I like the process of discovery and solving and I am not adversarial enough for the law.'

'So what were you studying?' I asked, interested.

'I was studying philosophy and religion.'

I smiled. *So, he was very nearly a priest.*

'An English university taught me much, Nikki. I learnt how good the English are at dissembling. How polite and clever they can be at deflecting interest away from themselves. How hard it is for them to give away their privacy. To grieve openly. To speak of what is in their heart.'

I looked down at my hands. I played with the white linen sheet and the silence I would have to break stretched into a silence I could hear around me. It made me dizzy with the weight of it.

Mohktar waited and I knew he would sit there all day until I was ready. I leant against the pillows and closed my eyes and I was immediately back on the beach running after Saffie towards the lighthouse. I opened them with a jerk, shivering, and stared at Mohktar. He saw the fear in my eyes.

He leant forward. 'Nikki, if you do not know how to begin to talk to me, or you are afraid, just say whatever comes into your head? Your mother told me you could not speak about your dream. Can you still remember it?'

'Oh yes. I remember it.'

'Will you try and tell it to me?'

I reached out my hand towards him. I felt as if I was pleading. 'It felt real, so real. As if it really happened and wasn't a dream. I'm afraid that if I talk about it I will hurtle back to the terror of it. I don't want to go back there . . .'

Mohktar took my hand for a moment. It felt hot and dry like a stone that has absorbed too much sun.

'Nikki, it matters not whether it was a dream or your subconscious, *lah*? Dreams serve a purpose. They alert us to something our conscious mind has recorded but banished or forgotten.'

I shook my head. 'No. It is Saffie who alerted me. Saffie who took me back.'

'For a reason?'

'Yes. For a reason.'

'Then, my dear Nikki, do not try and work it out, just take me where your dream took you. Nothing bad can happen, it is daylight and I am here beside you.'

I turned slightly away from him. *It is daylight and I am here beside you.* He sounded soothing, like Fergus. *Have I stopped still in my childhood? Am I emotionally arrested, a part of me forever wandering as a child, like Saffie?*

I lay trying to be calm. I had to stay very still for a while and Mohktar must have wondered if I had fallen asleep. Then I began to tell him of my dream and he leant forward to catch my words.

'Saffie was here. She came to my bed. She wanted me to follow her. I followed her out onto the beach into the afternoon. It was hot. We ran chasing the crabs towards the rocks and there was a man sitting there on his own smoking a cigarette. He had a panama hat on and sunglasses and had very long legs, like a spider. Saffie said hello but he was not pleased to see us, he wanted to be left alone. Saffie said she was bored and could he play with her. He said he did not know how to play with girls and she should go back to her mother and sister. He could not see me.

'He walked away towards the lighthouse path and Saffie followed him, calling out that she wanted to walk with him to see the monkeys. He told her that her mother would be worried and she should go home. Saffie said Mum was sleeping and then she ran up the steps quickly in front of him and I ran after her, but she had disappeared and I could not see her in the shade of the trees after the brightness. I kept calling but she took no notice.

'The man called out for her too. He was getting cross and suddenly Saffie appeared again in front of him. She was being annoying and dancing round him saying she could walk with him because he knew her dad, she knew he did, because she remembered . . .

'He grabbed her and asked her what she meant and began shaking her, and I tried to pull her away and I kept shouting at her to say she didn't remember him. But she was scared now, very scared, and she went still and silent. I wrapped my arms around her to pull her away and then she started kicking and screaming to get away from him.

'Then his hand was over my mouth and he held it there and I couldn't breathe, and I wriggled and kicked but he would not let me go. He was hurting my neck . . . he hurt me . . . he made me scream with pain . . . he pressed my neck so hard I heard it crack and then there was darkness . . . but no more pain.

'He . . . looked down at me. He was whimpering. He picked me up and I saw myself dangling over his arms and he carried me into the jungle and he . . . he . . . made a hole in the undergrowth. He pushed me down into the darkness between two stones . . . He used his feet to push me down into the ground . . . I was being buried . . . I was going to be under the ground forever . . . I screamed and . . . screamed . . . and Saffie came running and pulled me out of the earth and we ran, we both ran back together over the beach to the house . . .'

'Nikki. OK. Enough! Enough! Open your eyes. Open your eyes.'

My eyes flew open. I realised it was me making those small, terrified noises. *The horror lived on in me.* I could not stop my whole body shaking. I kept my eyes on Mohktar's face as if he could save me. He shivered and the hairs stood out cold on his arms. He leant towards me and lifted me upwards and stared into my face and I do not think he liked what he saw there.

He hesitated for a second and then he sat on the bed and held me up against him, as if the heat of his body could warm me back to this room and to this place. I leant in towards him and he held me, rocking me in silence. I was very conscious of him in the still room. I knew he was carefully going over my words. I knew he was troubled at his own distress as well as mine.

After a while, I whispered, 'That is what happened to Saffie. What I felt, she felt. She was placed under the ground . . . small and alone. It is what happened . . .'

'Yes,' Mohktar said. 'It is what happened.' He rubbed my arms as if to warm them. Then he held me away to look at me.

'Nikki? Why did you keep shouting at Saffie, "*Say, you don't remember him. Say you don't remember him.*" What did you mean? That you *did* remember him? That you had seen him somewhere before?'

I clutched his arms. 'I don't know! I don't know!'

Mohktar laid me gently back on the pillow and took my hands firmly between his own. 'Nikki, *you do know. You do know.* Why do you think Saffie took you on her last journey? Not to punish you for not being with her, but to show you something. *There is something she wants you to remember.*'

I stared past him, willing myself somewhere a long way away. I lay without moving for what seemed a long time. I heard Mohktar swallow. I thought he too was conscious of the silent house and of Fleur somewhere beyond us, stilled and breathless, waiting.

'The dress,' I whispered. 'It was the dress. I always wore

252

the dress with pink roses and Saffie always wore the one with blue. She was wearing my dress, you see . . .'

I felt Mohktar freeze. The very air around us was alive with tension.

He didn't want to rush me. He was trying to give me time to say the words that stuck in my throat. He was so still, James Mohktar, waiting. When I was silent, he said gently but firmly, 'Nikki? You must tell me.'

'She was wearing my dress that afternoon. It had a torn pocket. When he saw her he thought it was me . . .'

'Who? Why did it matter which one of you it was? Where had you seen him before?'

How could a fleeting image lie etched forever on my heart when I did not even understand until now the implications of what I had seen?

I closed my eyes. 'It was one afternoon . . . I was ill. Mum and Saffie had gone off somewhere in the car . . . I think to the dentist . . . I can't remember. I was left with Ah Heng, although it was supposed to be her day off.

'She always slept in the afternoons so she took me to her room, although Mum didn't allow it when she was at home. I had a temperature and I was hot and Ah Heng's small room was claustrophobic. She always closed her shutters and door when she was sleeping. I picked up the dress she had put on the chair for me, the one with the pink rose-buds, and I left her sleeping and I walked across the garden and up the steps which led to the kitchen.

'I was going to my own bed when I heard a noise from Mum and Dad's bedroom. I was so happy . . . I thought, *Mummy's back!*

'I went into the bedroom and the mosquito net was down and I could hear talking and Dad's voice, so I called out and there was this rustling then a funny silence and I was afraid and called out again and Dad lifted the mosquito net and erupted from the bed . . .'

My chest was so tight I couldn't breathe. I could hear little noises of fear escaping from my mouth.

'Nikki!' Mohktar's voice brought me back.

I turned then and looked at him. 'He wasn't alone . . . there was someone else there . . . I couldn't tell Mum, I couldn't. It wasn't a woman, it was a man in bed with my dad . . . it was a man . . .'

Mohktar stared at me.

'Dad's face was frightened, like he was shocked to see me, and he lifted me quickly and carried me out of the room. I turned, clutching my dress, to look back. I caught a glimpse of the man's face before the mosquito net fell. Then all I could see was the man's long, long legs under the sheet . . . right to the end of the bed . . . like a spider. Mum must never know, Detective Sergeant Mohktar . . . she must never know that Dad was . . .'

There was a small movement by the door. It was Fleur. She looked tiny and ashen.

Oh, Mum!

She walked towards us and there was a dignity and grace in her movements that tore at me. She still walked like a dancer.

'Oh, my darling Nik,' she said. 'I knew that David was a homosexual. How could I not know?'

I began to cry. Saffie died because of something I had seen. Because she had been wearing my dress.

THIRTY-SIX

Inspector Blythe was not happy. Mohktar saw that as soon as he got out of the car.

'What the hell are you playing at, Detective Sergeant? Why has your mobile phone been switched off?'

Blythe turned and stalked back into the small hot office. Sweat lined his back and under his armpits. Mohktar thought quickly.

'Sir, may I take you to a very good place to eat lunch? I have not eaten today. There I will tell you all I have learnt today, *lah*.'

Blythe relented, fractionally. 'Yes . . . very well. Let's go. I could certainly do with a Tiger beer.'

As they walked past fruit stalls lined with artistic rows of oranges, lychee, melons and bunches of small sweet bananas, they avoided the bicycles wobbling and overloaded making their way along the road to the nearest *kampong*.

A butcher's shop lay open to the flies, strange thin carcases hung on hooks. Outside, stray dogs hovered and Blythe couldn't help thinking, as they passed, how like dog those carcases looked.

Mohktar wondered how Blythe would accept Nikki's dream version of how her sister died. Would he believe the link Nikki had made about this nameless, but certainly identifiable, army pilot who she believed killed a small child, the wrong child, because of what she had seen one hot Singapore afternoon in a supposedly empty house?

'Well?' Blythe said, as soon as their drinks came. 'Are you going to keep me in the dark or tell me what you have been up to?

Blythe had got through his second beer by the time Mohktar had finished Nikki's story. Mohktar waited. Blythe was thinking, rubbing his fingers up and down his glass, making patterns in the condensation.

'I must check the files, but do you think there is any chance that both twins went out together that afternoon. That Nikki ran back because she was afraid and blocked it out?'

'I am unsure. Mrs Campbell also is wondering how long Nikki was out on the beach that afternoon. Undoubtedly she was frightened, but I do not think she understood why she felt afraid. Now we know why she was confused. But you are not thinking she saw the murder, Inspector?'

'No. I don't think that. If Nikki Montrose had witnessed her sister being murdered she would have been far more traumatised . . . hysterical. But what if she had gone after her sister, followed her a little way, seen the man in question and returned to her mother's bed?'

'Inspector, you were one of the officers who questioned her. She was only five years old but the report at that time says she never wavered or changed what she said about that afternoon to you or anyone.'

Blythe sighed again. 'That's true. But I don't know how proficient we were at questioning children in those days.

She was a very distressed little girl. I don't think we pushed it.'

'If she had recognised the man on the beach with her sister, she would have picked him out at the time. Children are honest, Inspector. I think she has lived with the guilt of knowing that if they had gone out together her twin would not have been killed.'

'Possibly, but not necessarily. I certainly think the murder was opportunist, not planned. But Mohktar, I find it difficult to believe a man would kill a child because of what *she might have seen*. How could he possibly be convinced it was the right twin?'

'Because, apparently, it was of common knowledge that one twin always wore a dress with blue roses and one with pink, it was how their parents told them apart. Nikki says she was carrying her dress with the pink roses the afternoon she saw the man with her father.'

'So he knew the family, but not well it seems. If he had mixed with them socially both twins would have remembered him.'

'I suppose the husband must have made a point of not inviting him to the house.'

'What a damn nuisance you didn't have the photographs of the officers staying at the rest houses at the time with you this morning.'

'Nikki Montrose is not going to forget, Sir, by the morning.'

'Mohktar! We'll go round tonight, get this cleared up . . .'

'Sir. I believe it important for them and for us too that mother and daughter talk tonight. They have much to say to one another. When secrets come out, it is very hard . . .'

'Well, perhaps. Maybe something else will come out of it too. You do understand that all this doesn't *prove* anything. Nikki Montrose *saw* the officer in her father's bed but she did not see the face of her sister's killer. It doesn't make him the same person.'

Mohktar was silent. It was true. A dream, so real to Nikki, was not evidence. He was about to speak when Blythe added, 'On the other hand it's the nearest to a motive we've had. It would have been a terrible scandal in the Seventies. If you had been an ambitious career officer who thought a child was taunting you about where she had seen you before, it might be tempting to grab her on the spur of the moment, in temper . . .'

'And kill her by mistake?'

'Yes. Literally ring her neck. Let's go back to the office and go through the files and check who the high-flyers were. I wonder if it is possible to jiggle Miss Montrose's memory some more.'

THIRTY-SEVEN

Nikki slept for six hours. Fleur too slept for a long time that afternoon. The nice Doctor Janus had seemed more worried about her than Nikki. When Fleur woke it was to a sense of unreality and to the feeling that this moment, as Fergus had warned her, had been inevitable. She had never wavered in her conviction that no one needed to know about David; not her parents, not Sam, certainly not David's parents.

She wanted the twins to keep the memory of the wonderful father David had been. She did not want their time with him spoilt by any shadows. It was no one's business. Both she and Fergus wanted him to remain *David*, not a whispered scandal.

They paid a price for their silence but they expected to. The only thing they disagreed on was explaining to Nikki when she was grown-up. Fergus thought she had a right to know and he felt Nikki and Fleur's relationship might improve if she did know, but Fleur had been adamant.

Frangipani and the faraway cries of children on the edge of the sea came in on the wind. The overhead fan made the leaves of her book flutter gently inside the mosquito net. Fleur felt torpid, her body heavy and lifeless, the heat pressing her down on the bed with the weight of her memories.

That faraway day in a military hospital when she didn't want to know what David was trying to tell her. Refused to listen; did not want to hear any words that might burst her safe little bubble. Then, years later, the moment it became clear, the moment he had told her. The night the sky fell in. When the world stopped for one clear beat of time and was never the same again.

Tidworth Military Hospital, 1971

Fleur was lying in the maternity ward, her feet raised, trying to keep as still as she could, terrified of dislodging the tiny lives inside her. *Please, God*, she kept saying in her head over and over. *Please, God, don't let me miscarry; please let me keep my babies . . . please . . . please.*

The gynaecologist, a colonel, had sat by her bed. 'Fleur,' he said. 'Nature has a way of taking care of things. It's wretched, I know, but if you miscarry it will be because a full term pregnancy is not viable.'

Fleur had closed her ears. *She was not going to miscarry. She was not going to lose her twins.*

David had been flown back from exercise in Norway to see her. She had watched him walk up the ward, his face pale and anxious. She had put out her hand and smiled reassuringly. 'It's OK, darling. I'm doing everything I'm told. I'm not going to lose our babies. Really, it's going to be all right.'

He had taken her hand and held it to his lips, then turned his cheek, keeping her fingers pressed against his face. He had dark rings under his eyes and looked unwell.

'What is it?' she whispered, alarmed by the feel of his hand in hers trembling.

He could not meet her eyes. Fleur suddenly became still. Her body felt as if it was crouched . . . waiting.

'I don't deserve you, Fleury,' he said. 'There's something I need to tell you . . .'

'No!' she interrupted quickly, withdrawing her hand in fury. 'I won't hear it! Whatever it is! I'm trying to keep my babies and I don't care if you've been unfaithful. I don't care what you've done. Go away, don't upset me. Why now? Why try and tell me something *now*, David?'

He got to his feet, wretched. 'Because I'm a selfish bastard. Fleur, I love you to death . . . Of course I haven't been unfaithful . . . I'll come back later.' He had turned and almost run out of the ward.

Fleur had closed her eyes in relief. It was all right, he hadn't been unfaithful and he loved her, nothing else mattered.

On one of the postcards he sent her daily from Norway, he had written:

'Fleury, I was just going through a long night of the soul. Felt I did not deserve you or children. I'm knackered too. New OC is a bastard. It's been a tough exercise out here – longing to get back to you. We've got so, so much ahead of us, haven't we? Forgive me. I love you . . . David.'

From somewhere at the back of the house Fleur could hear the cackle of laughter as the amah gossiped or played mahjong. I am so glad, Fleur thought, that I didn't let him tell me then. That I didn't know for years. I have those lovely few years of not knowing.

But all that time you knew something wasn't right, didn't you, if you're honest? Come on, admit it.

Yes, I knew.

* * *

261

Nikki came softly into the room and looked down at her mother through the mosquito net. It was a double bed and Fleur looked so small in it. The cup of tea in her hand wobbled. *All these years, I had it so wrong. You and Fergus. All that I did to you both. All that I said and you never ever defended yourselves. Never screamed the truth back at me.*

'Mum? Are you asleep?'

Fleur jumped and sat up. 'No Nik. Lift the net.'

Nikki hooked the net back and peered in. 'I've made you a cup of tea.'

'Darling, I should be making you one.'

'You should not! Thank God, you look better. Have you slept at all?'

Fleur smiled. 'Yes, I did. What about you?'

'Mum, it's five o'clock. I slept for nearly six hours!'

'Wonderful! Do you feel better?'

'I'm fine. I'm like Doctor Janus, far more worried about you . . .'

They stared at each other.

Here we are exchanging pleasantries to put off the moment of talking, of going back, of understanding what our lives really were then.

'Can I get my tea and join you in bed, Mum?' Nikki's voice was small and childlike.

'I'd love that,' Fleur said, hearing her voice tremble with hope.

Singapore, 1976

Fleur and David had been to a dinner night and the taxi dropped them off at the entrance to the army quarters as the driver had to take another couple on to the RAF base at Serengoon. They were making their way unsteadily back to their own quarters, singing and giggling as they walked.

It had been a good night and David was particularly happy as he had had a hint of early promotion. He skipped ahead of her, walking backwards serenading her.

'Ssh, you idiot! You'll wake everyone up.'

'Can't I sing to my beautiful wife?'

'No, you can't!'

He grinned, walking back towards her and scooping her up and twirling her round. 'Did I tell you that you looked amazing tonight?'

'No, actually!'

He looked down at her. 'You always look amazing, Fleury. I have to spend all my evenings watching you being ogled . . .'

'Ogled?'

'Yes, definitely ogled . . . I watched you dancing all evening with the leery new doctor . . . and the colonel, and . . .'

'Watched me all evening? I don't think so, Captain Montrose. You, as usual, were propping up the bar with your cronies swapping flying stories, while your poor old wife had to be rescued from sitting like a droopy wallflower . . .'

'Droopy wallflower!' David gave a shriek of laughter. 'The biggest little flirt on the army patch . . .'

'I AM not!'

'You are!'

'Not!'

'Are.'

They were running down the wide road beside the monsoon drain full of dried leaves which would soon be swollen and overflowing when the rains came. A huge moon kept appearing from behind clouds driven by a wind from the sea which brought the scent of oil and seaweed from the naval base below them.

Fleur lifted her long, pale dress and ran behind David in his tight dress uniform, the spurs on his boots making little clinking sounds as he moved. The colonel's car drew level and he wound the window down to the amusement of his driver and waved his finger at them, his voice slightly slurred.

'Time you children were in bed and not causing a disturbance in the gardens of the officers' quarters. Be gone! To bed!'

'Sir! At once!' David picked Fleur up and began running towards their quarters singing the bandolier song.

They heard the colonel laugh behind them and the car purred away. Fleur twined her arms round David's neck and said happily, 'Put me down! You're drunk and you'll fall and break your nose.'

'Shan't.'

'Will.'

David dropped her at the front door of their house on stilts and they climbed the stairs up to the sitting room shushing each other noisily. Ah Heng looked down at them disapprovingly, holding her little backless slippers in her hands.

'Good night, Master. Good night, Missie. Chil'ren sleep all night.'

She hurried away to her own quarters.

'Now,' David said. 'Do I need a little nightcap?'

'No, you do not!' Fleur said firmly. 'It's a good thing you're not flying tomorrow . . . Come on, bed.'

'One small whisky, darling . . .'

'You're going to have a hell of a head in the morning.'

'Officers do not have hangovers. They merely feel the need to move extremely carefully the next day.'

Fleur moved towards him. He looked wonderful in mess kit, meltingly beautiful.

'Just come to bed,' she murmured, kissing his mouth.

He kissed her lightly back, amused. 'By the time you've used the bathroom and hung up your dress, I'll be there . . .'

She left him with the whisky decanter and by the time she came out of the bathroom he was sitting on the bed trying to get his boots off. Fleur bent and undid the spurs and then pulled at his boots so hard he fell off the bed. They both giggled.

'I wonder,' he said, 'how many army wives have pulled their husbands' boots off down the centuries.'

'And the rest!' Fleur said, helping him out of his jacket, undoing his braces and pulling his tight dress trousers with the stripe down the side over his hips and down his long legs.

'What a lovely, capable girl you are!' David murmured sleepily.

'Get in!' Fleur ordered. She poured him water from his jug and he drank two glasses gratefully and fell into bed. Fleur switched the overhead fan off and checked the coil Ah Heng had lit, and then she pulled the mosquito net down and got in beside him.

David scooped her to him and wound his arms around her, as he did every night. He was instantly asleep, but Fleur lay against his body, feeling the warmth of him with longing. Dinner nights were always a hopeless prelude to romance; sex was quite impossible, there was always too much to drink, but oh how she ached to be made love to. She closed her eyes tight, making herself slide into sleep before she sobered up and became maudlin.

She woke early, her back to David, his arm still thrown over her hips. She was unsure what had woken her but she was conscious of David and felt that he was lying awake too, very still. There was something tense in his body and with a surge of happiness Fleur realised he had an erection.

She turned sleepily to him, her body sliding to his, her head buried into his neck. He jumped slightly as if startled that she was awake, then bent to kiss her cheek and the curl of her ear.

Fleur arched, her body trembling as David pulled her small bottom to him and, slowly turning on his back, pulled her over on top of him. Her hair fell around their heads like a curtain, hiding them, locking them together. Fleur bent to his mouth, staring down into his face, his eyes fringed with those incredible black lashes.

She loved him *so much* and kissed him with passion, hard, wanting to bruise his mouth. She was ready, her body throbbing. He turned her head gently and slid from beneath her, turning her over on her stomach, which was what he liked.

Fleur felt disappointment. She loved seeing his face when he came and he rarely let her. Then, feeling his trembling need to be inside her, she moaned gently as he murmured things she could not hear, nibbling gently at the back of her neck which always made her taut with pleasure. They came together and she did not hear what he cried out.

It was so good. So good.

David rolled off her, and Fleur, turning in his arms, longing to prolong the moment of rare intimacy, pulled his face down to hers to kiss his mouth.

He flinched. It was only a tiny, involuntary movement but it felt like a slap. Both their eyes flew open and for a second they stared at each other aghast. Fleur could not read what was in his eyes. Numb, she slowly pulled her body away from him. David reached out to touch her.

'Darling . . . sorry . . . don't look like that . . . I . . . didn't mean . . .'

Fleur waited but he did not know how to finish the sentence. Eventually, she said in a voice that did not sound like her own. 'You dislike me to kiss you like that. I revolt you . . .'

'Fleur, don't be so silly. You're overreacting.'

'Am I?' It was as if Fleur had been blind to the truth and suddenly had bandages ripped from her eyes. 'Am I? You haven't made love to me for weeks, sometimes it's months. You . . . you nearly always turn me over so I can't kiss you. Now I know why. There's something about me that repels you and I didn't realise, wouldn't see it . . .'

The tears were pouring out of her eyes and down her cheeks soundlessly and she turned to get out of bed, to run to the bathroom. David caught her arm and pulled her to him.

'Fleur, listen to me!'

Something in his voice made her freeze. He was very pale, grey round the mouth, almost as if he was afraid. He closed his eyes for a moment, and then he said, 'I love you more than you will ever know, Fleur. Of course you don't repel me. I hate sleeping without you close to me. I love the feel of your sweet little body . . .'

'You *flinched* . . . like a reflex action, just now when I tried to kiss you. I know . . . I know, whatever you say, that my body doesn't turn you on. I've always known it . . . in my heart . . . that you don't really like making love to me. I'm not sexy enough . . . I must have the wrong chemistry.'

She looked up and to her horror she saw tears in the corners of David's eyes.

'Have there always been other women?' she whispered. 'David, I need to know . . . I need to know this now, or I will go mad.'

267

He looked at her then, right in the eyes, and the pain there made *her* flinch this time.

'Darling, I'm gay. I've always been gay. I tried to tell you before . . . I love you, but I'm gay.'

Fleur stared at him stupidly. 'But . . . you married me, we have children.'

He nodded, put his hand over his mouth, which was trembling.

'But . . . why?'

He tried to smile. 'Why am I gay or why did I marry you? I married you because I absolutely adore you. I wanted a wife and children and I thought, I thought wrongly, that I could change, I could deny what I am.'

'But you can't?'

'I've tried. My God, Fleur, I've tried.'

'You bastard! What was I, a social experiment? All these years I've thought there was something wrong with *me*.' She leapt out of bed, pulled a kimono round her and headed for the bathroom. She turned at the door. 'You utter bastard.'

David got out of bed too. They both heard Ah Heng's keys in the lock of the back door. She would bring in tea and papaya. The twins would be bounding in at any moment. They stared at each other.

'Fleur, whatever you, rightly, think of me, I love you. You and the girls are my life. *My life*,' he whispered.

'Where does that leave us?' Her voice was hard.

'I don't know.' He was wretched. 'I don't know, Fleur.'

They heard the sound of small running footsteps and laughter and Fleur turned and went into the bathroom and locked the door and stood leaning against it, eyes closed, her mouth open in shock.

She heard the twins fly into the bedroom. 'Daddy!' they yelled. 'You're still here!'

'Hi there, peapods! I'm still here! I'm not flying today. Come on, let's have brekkie together. Morning, Ah Heng. Missie's in the shower . . . How are you today?'

David. *The same as ever.* Fleur switched on the antique shower and cried silently as the water ran down her face and body. Outside in the garden the *kebun* began brushing up the dry frangipani petals from the lawn and fingering the small, tight bunches of bananas to see if they were ripe. A dog barked somewhere. Ah Heng shouted to Annie, the wash amah, to collect up the bed sheets. A snake slid down into the dry leaves of the monsoon drain, where Indian women in faded saris would soon come to sweep them out. The phone rang. It would be Lucy to say she would pick Fleur up for yoga.

It was an everyday weekday morning; a morning that should have been much the same as any other. Fleur, turning the shower off, listened to all the sounds that made up the beginning of her days. Dizzy and sick, she reached for a towel and sat on the edge of the bath and shivered.

Was this the end of the life she shared with David?

THIRTY-EIGHT

'But it wasn't the end, Mum, was it?'

'No, it wasn't the end,' Fleur said. Naturally she was giving her daughter the edited version. 'Your father went off to Malaya for a week, to join some paras on a jungle course. I think it was the most miserable week of both our lives. I was operating in a dream, taking you both to the club and the library, meeting friends. I couldn't eat or sleep. His words kept going around and around my head. I didn't know what he wanted. I didn't know what I wanted. I only knew that the thought of life without him terrified me; it would be the loneliest place on earth. It's a cliché, but he was my best friend too. I'd known him nearly all my adult life. I adored him, Nik. I absolutely adored him.

'What upset me before, our lack of a real sex life, suddenly seemed unimportant in the light of not having him at all and having my whole life pulled from under me . . .'

'Go on, Mum.'

'He came back looking as dreadful as I felt. Possibly close to breaking point. He stood at the top of the stairs as if he had no right to come into the room or back into our lives.

We just stared at each other for what seemed a lifetime and we both knew without saying a word that we could never live without each other. He needed me as much as I needed him. He held out his arms and that was it.' Fleur closed her eyes. 'The relief, the pure relief that he wasn't going to leave me, that he did not want our life to end, suffocated any other feelings for a while. We packed the car up for the weekend with you and Saffie in the back and headed for Mersing.

'It was strange, we should have gone on our own, there was so much we needed to say to one another and we were quite selfish in those days. We could have left you and Saffie with Ah Heng, but we both needed you with us . . . as if . . .'

'You needed us to validate your marriage?' Nikki asked softly.

'Yes,' Fleur nodded. 'As if we needed our children to make us whole again; to be as we were.'

'But you couldn't be as you were, could you? You couldn't pretend the words hadn't been said, that you didn't know?'

'Of course we couldn't and we both knew that. The only thing we were both sure of was that we wanted to stay together.'

'But Mum, you were still only in your twenties, how could you possibly live without a sex life, and what would Dad . . . do? He was an army officer.'

Fleur looked at her daughter. 'Oh, darling, we had weeks, months of intense discussion on the way we could live together and make it work. We argued; I often felt bitter and betrayed. Then I got a really bad dose of dengue fever and it seemed to lower my resistance to everything. I felt constantly low and depressed. We went home on leave and

271

I ended up in hospital. David had to fly home with you and Saffie without me.

'When I got back to Singapore, in bad moments I accused him of wanting marriage as a shield. In those days if anyone had known about him he would have been out of the army in a flash.'

Fleur smiled, her whole face lighting up. 'But he really did want marriage and a wife and children and a normal life. I never doubted that he loved us all far more than a life he might have had and could have chosen.'

Nikki bit back the thought: *Having his cake and eating it.*

Fleur suddenly remembered, *It was not true, what she had just said.* It was true she'd never doubted his love, but she had agonising misgivings about his control over his sexuality. She tortured herself with the moment of their last love-making, going over and over her waking and knowing in a burst of humiliation that it was not *her* that had aroused him that morning but the thought of some *man.*

She knew he must have been attracted to and possibly unfaithful with men during their marriage. She had considered it in their intense and prolonged conversations into the early hours of the mornings. She was unable to think about it in detail, that was too much to bear, but his faithlessness, in her mind, was always away from the base, for obvious reasons, with dusky and beautiful long-lashed Indian youths. It had never once occurred to her that there might be other homosexuals in uniform.

'Can you live your life in two compartments?' Fleur had asked him.

'You and the twins are my real life, so is the army and my flying. The other is peripheral and . . . occasional.'

Fleur had not yet met Fergus on the plane and she had

said hesitantly, not believing she really could, 'What if I . . .'

'. . . Want to sleep with someone?' His face had tightened.

'Yes.'

'I would hate it. It's totally and completely unfair, but I would be devastated.'

Inwardly and immaturely, she had been thrilled. This was evidence of his love for her; his possession.

'But this is how I feel about *you*, David. It *is* crucifying, but it won't stop you . . .'

Round and round they had gone in desperate circles until slowly they had to let it go before the damage was terminal. They slid back into the life they had had and kept the secret distant and unspoken, almost as if it had never been, or might go away. If you were busy and you partied enough and loved and enjoyed the lives you shared, this was possible, for a time.

In their bed, David tried to please her, to make her happy in a far more conscientious way than he had before. He wanted to keep her there. Keep her his. But the shadow of what she knew came between the moments of intimacy and turned slyly into a thing of impurity and lasting sadness.

'Then you met Fergus?'

'Then I met Fergus. And he was fun too, and made me laugh and . . .'

Nikki smiled. 'He was absolutely wild about you and remained so until the day he died.'

It was true. Fergus had been wild about her. 'We all flirt and are attracted in a passing way to other men; it gives us a little fillip, it's part of being alive and young. I suppose in my case the feeling was exaggerated because I had begun to doubt my self-worth, my own attraction. With Fergus, physically, it all fell into place like a jigsaw I'd known was possible but had never had. It is amazingly seductive to be an object of desire for an attractive and lovely man.'

'So did you fall in love with him and out of love with Dad?'

Fleur shook her head slowly. 'No. I never, ever stopped loving David. I never pretended to Fergus. I knew he loved me, but Fergus accepted I was married with two small children.'

'But he wasn't that honourable, coming on to you, was he? He was supposed to be one of Dad's best friends.'

Fleur made a face. 'What a horrible expression. He never *came on to me*, as you call it, until he discovered David was gay.'

'How did he?'

'He saw David talking to his Indian driver, a very beautiful youth. Something in his body language alerted Fergus and he asked me outright.'

'Had he never suspected before?'

'No one did, Nikki. Your father was not remotely camp. He hated that in gays, as a lot of his generation did in the days before they came out.'

'So Fergus was shocked?'

'He was shocked and immensely angry with David for marrying me. Nik, can you remember your father at all?'

'A bit. I remember him being big and happy and he seemed to me to be always laughing, as if life was one big joke. He was always scooping Saffie and me up to take us somewhere . . . Life with him, as I remember it, was always exciting and fun.'

'Well, that's because it was! He had a gift for making an ordinary day special. Someone once said to me, "*When David leaves a party, the party leaves with him,*" and it was true, darling. Fergus couldn't remain angry with David for long.'

'Did Dad know Fergus knew?'

'I think he suspected, because it was obvious something had changed between them, but he didn't associate it with me. I didn't want to hurt David or cause gossip so I used to meet Fergus in the Botanical Gardens in Singapore. At first we just walked and talked, then . . . I was terribly attracted to him.'

'Then you had a full-blown affair?'

'No. But we would have done, Nikki, eventually.' Fleur got out of bed. 'I need a shower and a glass of wine. Ah Lin is going to put supper on the table any minute.'

Nikki also got heavily off the bed. 'I've had a shower. I'll go and ring Jack. Mum, we don't have to talk about it any more tonight. It's making you sad.'

'Yes, of course it makes me sad, even after all these years. But now I have to think about what . . . what it all might have led to.'

Nikki said quickly, knowing she must deflect Fleur, at least for tonight, 'Mum, I could never be a hundred per cent sure who I saw that afternoon with Dad. I was only five.'

Fleur turned on her way to the bathroom. 'Something is niggling at me, something I should remember. I can pinpoint the moment David changed, was late home more often, seemed distracted, and sadder. There had been a big inter-service exercise on in Malaya. As well as Fergus, who had been posted in, extra pilots had been sent out for a few weeks to back David up and cut down on his flying hours. He came back from that exercise pre-occupied and a little distant.'

'You think he was involved with someone?'

'I think it was more serious than that. I think he might, for the first time, have fallen for someone and shocked himself.'

275

'In a few weeks?'

'I don't know, Nik. Maybe it started on that exercise. Maybe it was someone he had known before. It's possibly why he told me when he did.'

'Oh, Mum.'

'I felt as if everything might slide from under us. Fergus was wonderful; always there . . . just to listen. Then, one day I went into Singapore to buy some material for a dress for a dinner night. I saw this amazingly wonderful red silk and I thought, I'll show him. David, I mean. I had it made up into the most daring dress I'd ever worn. And I made a provocative entrance. I was sick of being sad; I wanted to be happy and young again. I danced all night, especially with Fergus, and I was excited by the sense of power I suddenly had in that daring red dress. A terrific sense of being sexually attractive and the centre of attention.

'David had been hugely amused by my dramatic entrance. I certainly got his attention. But I knew that night that soon I was going to sleep with Fergus. I wanted to . . . I suppose I was beginning to fall in love too.'

'I remember that dress, Mum. You looked amazing. I remember it.'

'Do you, darling?' Fleur was surprised.

'What happened?'

'Fergus was kissing me on the dance floor and David saw us. We looked up and there he was. All three of us just stood rooted without saying a thing. It was an awful moment. David was ashen. He looked at me in total disbelief. He was so sure I single-mindedly adored him enough not to do anything. He turned and went out through French windows into the Mess garden and I went after him. It was as if Fergus and I had stabbed him in the back.

'He kept shouting and asking me how long it had being

going on. I tried to tell him I had not slept with Fergus but he wouldn't listen and I saw that he felt impotent, powerless, because there was nothing he could say or do to put himself in the right.

'Suddenly he went quiet and gave this deprecating, bitter little laugh. He nodded to himself and looked down at me and said quietly, "I think it's called poetic justice, darling. If *I* wasn't married to you I couldn't wish for a greater guy for you than Fergus . . . my old friend Fergus . . ."

'I realised that he thought I was going to leave him for Fergus. He must have seen me and his beloved twins slipping from his grasp. He turned and started walking away from me and I started to run after him and I was screaming, "I will never leave you . . . I will never leave you," over and over, but he wasn't listening any more, he was just walking away from me as fast as he could. He didn't come home that night and the next day he went flying. I never saw him alive again. I never ever saw him again.'

Fleur crumpled onto the floor, her hands covering her eyes. Nikki drew in her breath, the anguish in her mother piercing her like shards of glass. She bent awkwardly to the floor.

'It wasn't your fault. It wasn't your fault, Mum.'

Fleur lowered her hands. 'But it was, darling; that is the point. If he hadn't seen Fergus and me together, he wouldn't have died. He would have taken more care.'

'Mum, Fergus must have said it to you a hundred times. *You don't know that.* Dad was a pilot; he wouldn't have taken risks with other people's lives. A storm blew up. That is what happened. The tragedy is that you *quarrelled* the night before he died. That is the saddest thing.'

'The saddest thing is he died thinking I was going to leave him.'

Nikki levered herself up and sat heavily in a chair. 'Mum,

we can't do this any more. Go and have your shower and I'll pour you a drink. Do you want something stronger than wine? A drink that *talks* to you, as Gran always says?'

Fleur smiled. 'Yes, Nik. I think I'll have a whisky.' She got to her feet. 'Forgive me, darling, you're supposed to be resting. This can't be good for you.'

'It's about time I understood, Mum.'

Fleur turned on the shower and came back into the room. She said desperately, meeting Nikki's eyes, 'It's why I drank that afternoon; why I took strong painkillers . . . I just wanted to shut it all out.'

Nikki held Fleur's eyes and then she said, with difficulty, because it was hard, 'I know, Mum. You were *not* to blame for Dad's death . . . or for Saffie's. Have your shower and I'll find you that drink.'

Gently I shut the bathroom door on my mother. I stood in the empty room listening to the sound of water running and watching the bats swoop in the dark beyond the window.

My heart was filled with an impregnable and lasting sorrow. Indirectly, my dad might have contributed to Saffie's death. *If it was his lover that killed her.* And Fleur would have known him.

As I stood there I saw that when my parents' lives together ended, my dad was only thirty-two and Mum was twenty-five. If he had lived, it wouldn't have worked, their marriage. It couldn't have done.

We would have grown up and been less dependent on him. Mum would have fallen in love, as she later did, and left him for Fergus or someone else. Dad would have got more promiscuous and less careful. Their lives together would have been unlikely to have had a happy ending. *The happy ending that has lived in my head, all of my life, despite my love for Fergus.*

I needed to know that my father had been gay to understand this. But how old and full of remorse I now felt comprehending this simple fact.

I thought of Jack and the inequality of our love. I wrapped my arms around my swollen stomach. Jack had been so patient, waiting and hoping for me to say words that would mean commitment to him, to our child and a life together.

I thought of Fergus, how gentle, in waiting, he had been with Fleur, because he loved her so completely and selflessly. I saw how close they had become, living their lives so *absolutely together* with all its tragedy and joys.

I wanted that. I wanted that with Jack. I was now so sure. My life lay with him and I must ring and tell him this. It felt like my first really considered act. *I was a grown woman.* I was thirty-three years old, much older than Fleur had been in her life with my father.

I would always love the memory of my dad, for it was *my memory*, a large, beautiful man who made us squeal with laughter. A man who never grew old and tetchy. A big solid rock of a man who brought happiness wherever we went. But he was also the same man who, knowing what he was, married a young dancer, let her turn her back on her talent, for him, when he must have known the danger of it. He knew, he knew how much she absolutely worshipped him. He broke her heart, the father I loved. He broke my mother's heart and she never used this as an excuse, not to anyone. She wanted me to keep the lovely dad of my childhood and in doing so nearly broke Fergus's heart too; having to watch me punish her day in, day out.

I remembered how hard Gran had been on her. Laura had considered Fleur weak and feckless. I wondered if

Grandpa had suspected. He was always so close and protective of Fleur.

I walk out into a night that is so warm that the air is like velvet on my bare arms. The sun has left scarlet wavy lines. Dark cigar-shaped clouds tinged with gold hang above a sea that moves imperceptibly from here, small glints lighting the waves.

I stand, holding the rail of the balcony, aware of my hands on the wood, of the scents coming in on the night. Blossom, spices, faint sewerage; Chinese music and high sing-song voices. The ghosts of my father and Saffie seem to hover in the dry rustling of the palm trees.

But what I am really thinking of is the extraordinary courage of my mother. Love and loyalty to David lasted long after his death. I know, too late, it is possible to love two people in quite different ways. One love does not negate the other, but is as much a part of it as Fergus was of Dad's life as well as Fleur's.

I am past tears though not past sorrow. I cannot change my mother's life, but I can change the defiant passage of my own. Each time my child moves inside me I feel closer to understanding Fleur. I cannot marshal my thoughts or understand my feelings in a matter of hours and I know that what I feel now will change into something else. But it must be something that I am able to accept and live with.

All my life I have wanted to go back to a time of safety and happiness, when we were a real family. Mum and Dad, Saffie and me. When the tropical sun shone down but never burnt. When the rains were swift but no one ever drowned in the monsoon drains. When Saffie and I drew little square houses with windows and a garden path with flowers and a matchstick mum and dad with happy, smiley faces.

This is what Fleur was bravely protecting me from the

whole of my life. The moment when you realise none of it really exists; it is just an illusion, the sunshine and the smiley faces. It is what lies behind that counts.

I think of Jack. 'No worries,' he always says, as they do in New Zealand, whatever happens. 'No worries, darlin'.'

Damn. I'm not crying. I'm not.

THIRTY-NINE

Inspector Blythe was waiting for an update from London. He had asked for the current whereabouts of everyone staying at the government rest houses in 1976. He did not care if they were now living in Timbuktu. He wanted them located and their movements traced back from the 1970s to the present day. He wanted to know when they left the forces and why. He wanted to know their progress through the last twenty-eight years, and if anyone was dead he wanted to know where and how.

He got up early to sift through every witness statement. He went over and over their movements that afternoon to see if there was any small thing they had missed the first time round. As everyone, except two of the teachers, had slept in the afternoon, there was little to find.

The two teachers in question had been in Kuala Lumpur for the night so they were ruled out. Of the other two, the only tiny significant paragraph was that one of them, a Daphne Broadbent, had heard running footsteps and a door slamming somewhere. So had Mrs Christine Dury, because she had got up to breastfeed her sixth-month-old baby. But a door slamming somewhere was hardly indicative of murder.

The pregnant Mrs Addison, apart from Mrs Campbell and Nikki of course, had been the last person to see Saffie alive that day. Before Mrs Campbell's parents had left for Penang, they had asked if the Addisons would keep an eye on Fleur for them. Beatrice Addison had gone to see them on her own around lunchtime. Her husband, Alex, recovering from the same crash that had killed David Montrose, had thought it would be better if he stayed behind as his wife was better at the emotional stuff.

Beatrice, being pregnant, had a couple of soft drinks with Fleur. She had admitted reluctantly that Fleur had had at least two strong lunchtime gins, and who could blame her?

Both husband and wife had slept after lunch. Beatrice had slept longer than Alex. He had got up before her to take a walk, but he had seen no one except Major Gardam of the British High Commission, who had gone down to the beach in the late afternoon to swim with Andrew and Paula Right. They had been at different ends of the beach but had waved at one another. None of them had seen anything out of order or vaguely suspicious.

They had been at different ends of the beach. Not near enough to see each other's faces. Not near enough to see if any one of them was behaving oddly.

So . . . nobody had seen or heard anything except the faint slamming of a door. Inspector Blythe wondered what had made two people even mention the door. Because it had woken them? Because it denoted haste and for some reason had alerted them, that non-specific, ordinary sound?

He got on the phone again. 'When you locate Daphne Broadbent and Mrs Christine Dury, assuming that both are alive and still have their faculties, will you make sure they see the statements they made at the time and ask them why they particularly mentioned or remembered the slamming of a door? I want to know what it sounded like. Because the doors out here are very light and made of rattan. I cannot see that the slamming of a door would wake anyone.'

'Inspector, you're talking about twenty-eight years ago, for God's sake!'

'I know I am. But would *you* ever forget a holiday where a small child suddenly disappeared, never to be seen or heard of again?'

There was silence and then, 'No, Inspector. I'll get on to it.' Another pause. 'A thought, Sir. Finding the child's body has been reported in most of the papers here. Not headlines, of course, but I'm wondering if any one of those families who stayed in Port Dickson at the time will get in contact with us.'

'Now that, DS Blake, is a very interesting thought. You might pass it on to the team. We don't want to miss anyone who might ring in. Pin their names up in large letters on the board.'

Mohktar came into the room as Blythe replaced the phone.

'Shall we go, Detective Sergeant?'

'My car's outside,' Mohktar said. He looked at the inspector with an expression Blythe couldn't interpret.

'Is there a problem, Mohktar? Please don't tell me either Miss Montrose or Mrs Campbell are unwell again or the time isn't right. We are police officers, not the confessional.'

Mohktar didn't rise to this. Englishmen often got irritable in the heat. 'No problem, Inspector. No problem, indeed.'

'I'm relieved to hear it. Let's go.'

When they were in the air-conditioned car and purring along the coast road, Mohktar said, 'Today I have a phone call to say the body of the child can be released for burial.'

Blythe turned to look at him. Mohktar's face remained impassive, his long, thin fingers relaxed on the wheel. *Bugger it!* Blythe thought. *Why do I get the impression this man is censoring me gently, for being a policeman, for doing my job?* He remembered his own words on the telephone: *'Would you forget the day a young child disappeared?'*

He sighed and leant back in the seat. This was not a case you could stay strictly uninvolved in. The two of them were both stuck bang in the middle of it, trying to make sense of all the implications that were surfacing, while two women were wildly treading water before struggling for some recognisable shoreline.

He said to Mohktar, 'Please don't inform Mrs Campbell about the release of the child's body before we have gone through that afternoon one last time.' He closed his eyes against the blinding sun shimmering on the tarmac outside and sighed. 'DS Mohktar, I am aware that you probably think of me as an insensitive, foreign policeman but my job is to try and find out what happened here, even if the truth is unpalatable to Mrs Campbell and Miss Montrose. A small child of five was murdered. We owe it to her to discover why.'

A small tic moved in James Mohktar's cheek. It made Blythe uneasy. Mohktar did not reply until they pulled into the car park near the bungalows. He turned the engine off. His movements were slow and deliberate. His eyes followed a grey monkey running sideways across the tarmac to the trees beyond, clutching a baby to her breast, one eye on the car before she disappeared into the trees.

'I understand, Inspector.' Mohktar scanned the rocking branches left by the monkey. 'I do not think of you as insensitive or foreign, but as a colleague. Neither do I forget that

285

I am a policeman or that a child was killed and no one has been punished for her death. I have a son of four and I know how it would be for me if my child were to die a lonely death . . .' He turned and looked at Blythe and the inspector saw an intellect behind his anger which gave him an alarming edge. 'But what we are discovering here is not simple, Inspector. We might suspect a possible motive, but after all this time it is going to be difficult to prove anything. As you say, Nikki Montrose having a dream or believing her sister guided her to the spot to show her what happened is not going to stand up in a court of law, *lah*?

'So, look what we have in evidence. Nikki says she sees a man on the beach in her dream. A man she remembers with long legs. She tells me she follows her sister up into the trees where her sister is killed by this same man. Nikki already knows, because I told her earlier, that the pathologist believes Saffie was suffocated.

'I think about this all night. What if you are right, Inspector, and Nikki Montrose did go out later that afternoon to look for her sister and she saw this man in the flesh, no dream. But fear or guilt maybe has blocked the memory of him out, makes her forget . . .'

'Your point, Mohktar?'

'There is something going on in Nikki's head. Suppose she saw this man after he had killed her sister? I believe there are things she has blocked that are slowly going to . . . to . . .'

'Unravel?'

'Yes, unravel. Nikki could not make sense of something she saw as a small child so she dismissed it. We suspect, because it is the only motive we have, that the person she saw with her father and the death of her sister must be linked. But, Inspector . . . this is what I feel. Mrs Campbell and Nikki Montrose had to go on living their lives after the child died and they have to go on living them now. Would you expose the killer at expense of more pain to those two women?'

'You mean that if it was David Montrose's lover, then mother and daughter will have to acknowledge that not only was the person they loved gay, but that he might have indirectly contributed to the death of one of his beloved daughters?'

'Yes, Inspector, that is what I am saying. I believe this will break their hearts all over again. A future that was possible will become impossible. Nikki Montrose has an unborn child and a man who loves her and a new life in New Zealand. Mrs Campbell has suffered two tragedies. Do we give her another sorrow to take with her into old age and loneliness? Do we do that, Inspector? Do we show her the face of her husband's lover and the man who killed her child? Do we let him destroy her one last time?

'Oh, then we can close the case and go back to our homes and our wives and children and say to them, *Ah, yes! After all this long time, we find the child's killer? Is this not good? Is this what we do, Inspector Blythe?*'

Mohktar got out of the car without waiting for an answer. He shut the door and leant against it, his face to the sea so that the inspector could not see his anger and confusion.

Blythe sat very still as the car warmed up. Damn! Damn! Damn! He was a policeman, for God's sake! He was a goddamned policeman . . . not a psychiatrist . . . not a bloody priest or a therapist or a . . . bleeding-heart leftie social worker. It was his job to protect society, to solve crimes and to bring to justice those who broke the law of the land and transgressed against the vulnerable and innocent . . .

He erupted out of the car and slammed the door. 'So, Sergeant Mohktar . . .' Inspector Blythe was building up his own righteous anger. 'I'd be interested to know the answer to this, given that you're a *policeman*, and from what I hear a good one. How come you can't see that what you've just suggested is totally immoral? It's a policeman's job to put perpetrators of crime behind bars, not to go into the ethics of it one way or another, or delve into the emotional ramifications of either the victim or the villain. *That is not our job*. It is for others: a judge, the Samaritans . . . God.'

Mohktar faced him. 'You think I am unprincipled? I am sorry, Inspector. Do you think it dishonourable to speak my mind or to have an opinion? If being a policeman means that I must cease to care for those I am trying to help, then maybe you are right, it is time I gave up being a policeman.'

He locked the car and both men turned in silence and began to walk over the sand to the house. Blythe hated to be left-footed. He was an old-fashioned, dedicated policeman who was good at his job but certainly no high-flyer. He hadn't been to university like all the young did now and he had occasionally been called unimaginative, but that did not mean he was uncaring. The young always thought they had the moral high-ground and it pissed him off. Right was right and wrong was wrong, and it was no good blurring boundaries or getting too involved. You did your job and you moved on to the next. *That's all you could do.*

All the same, he liked Mohktar and it was a pity to fall out.

'Look,' he said. 'We'll go carefully. I don't want to upset them any more than you do, Mohktar. We'll take it easy, go over it all one more time and then they can go and collect the child's body and return to their lives. There's nothing else for them here. You too can go home to your wife in Singapore. We'll carry on our inquiries in England. I personally am determined to find out who killed this child and ensure he pays for it.'

Mohktar stopped walking. 'Yes, Inspector, I am sure you are right to do so, but I imagine he has paid every single day of his life. I wonder, is there a difference between an evil man who kills coldly and deliberately and a possibly good man who does a terrible, evil thing, by chance, by fear, by mistake?'

'No difference, Mohktar, no difference at all to the person who dies or the people who grieve, or the people who have to live a whole life without the person they love.'

Mohktar abruptly put out his hand. 'I believe we have said all we can say to one another about this bad business, Inspector. I understand and respect your views. I apologise for my extreme viewpoint.'

Blythe smiled and took his hand. 'You have nothing to apologise for, DS Mohktar. We'll have to agree to disagree.'

'Indeed, Sir.' Mohktar flashed him his dazzling and beautiful teeth. 'That is what we must do, *lah*?'

They moved on in silence over the sand, and as they reached the house they saw the two women on the veranda. They were bent together, deep in conversation. Fleur suddenly lifted her face to the sky and gave a small cry of such anguish that both men froze to the spot. Blythe had never heard such a sound.

James Mohktar had. It had erupted from his mother on hearing two of her sons had plummeted needlessly to their deaths as she slept.

Nikki awkwardly knelt on the floor and put her arms round her mother and they began to rock silently back and forth, back and forth, eyes closed, oblivious to the two men.

Blythe turned away, choked, and began walking swiftly back the way he had come across the sand.

Mohktar, looking for a moment at the fair and dark heads pressed together, whispered before he too turned away, *'Inshallah! What God wills.'*

FORTY

When Inspector Blythe and Detective Sergeant Mohktar arrived the following morning before lunch, something seemed to have changed, although I could not tell what it was.

I was worried about Fleur. She was frail this morning and intensely vulnerable. Neither of us had slept much. I heard her wandering about the house making camomile tea as I lay sleepless in the dark. We were talked out; there was only so much we could bear at one time.

Our roles were subtly reversing and I began to regret telling Mohktar my dream. I didn't know how much Fleur had heard because the walls were paper-thin. I had remembered an incident that was cruelly painful to her and she had begun to be haunted by memories during the night.

When the horror of the dream began to diminish I began to distrust it as I often had before, until the next time. I no longer felt that Saffie was near me and I missed her as if somehow she might guide me. I was afraid of a little chink of memory that was beginning to open. I knew I could not control my mind and what it might disclose.

At breakfast, Fleur had suddenly broken down. The thought of someone we knew killing Saffie, someone Dad knew, seemed unbearable, too terrible to contemplate. I made her go back to bed and stayed with her until she fell asleep. She managed to sleep for two hours and was having a shower when the policemen came.

'My mother's very upset today; she's had a bad night,' I said, looking at Mohktar.

'Yes,' he said, as if he somehow knew. 'I am so sorry.'

'We won't keep you long,' Inspector Blythe said. 'I just want to go over that afternoon one more time.'

'What is the point?' I asked wearily.

Fleur came into the room. 'It's quite all right, Inspector. Good morning.' She smiled at both men. 'Let me get you both a cold drink before we begin.'

She seemed to be her old self but I noticed her hands shook and so did the two policemen.

Inspector Blythe laid out the photographs and his witness statements on the table with a plan of the government rest houses showing where each family had stayed and we sat down with our drinks. I glanced at Mohktar he seemed very quiet this morning and I missed his reassuring smile.

Blythe said gently to Mum, 'Will you humour me one last time, Mrs Campbell?'

He took her back over the time Beatrice Addison left us to go back to her own house. They had been staying in the one nearest to us, but slightly higher up the cliff. The Durys were the other side of them on the same level and the teachers were lower down near to the beach, like us, but further along.

'You went to your room with the twins at about two thirty. When you fell asleep, both twins were beside you?'

'Yes.'

He turned to me. 'Can you remember if your mother fell asleep before you?'

'I'm not sure, but I think so.'

'Did you and Saffie go to sleep straight away?'

'I did, I don't think Saffie did, or only for a while.'

'She woke you up?'

'Yes.'

'It was still afternoon, not evening?'

'Yes.'

'How can you be sure, if the shutters were closed? If you didn't get out of bed?'

I stared at him. 'The room was still hot. I was still tired and did not want to be woken.'

'OK. So tell me what you can remember. Saffie got out of bed and asked you to go outside to play with her?'

'She . . . she leant over mum and shook me awake . . . I was cross because she woke me and I turned over. I heard her get out of bed. She went to the window and opened a shutter because it was dark. I knew she was looking for her dress.'

'Then?' I opened my eyes and saw Mohktar was checking my original statement.

'She came round to my side of the bed and picked up my dress . . .'

'How did you know it was your dress?'

'I'd dropped it on the floor beside me and as she pulled it over her head I saw my torn pocket. Saffie asked me again to go outside with her and I said, *"In a minute"*. I heard her moving a chair to the window, but I didn't think she would really go out without me . . . and I went back to sleep.'

'When you woke again was the room cool? Was it evening?'

I closed my eyes again. Despite the overhead fan in the

293

room it was hot and sticky. I felt odd. I thought hard. *No, it was still hot that afternoon and I couldn't find my dress and I . . .*

'Nikki?'

'No, it was still warm. I got up to go into the bathroom, which wasn't shuttered, and I found Saffie's dress there and . . . I put it on . . .'

The sweat began to trickle down the inside of my dress. It was as if a fog that had suffocated that whole afternoon was slowly clearing. 'I put the dress on and then I went back into the bedroom. The shutters had blown nearly closed again and it was dark. I got onto the chair and pushed back the shutters just a little to see out . . .'

I listened to the silence in the room and it frightened me. 'I saw Saffie in the distance. She was running towards the rocks, chasing crabs . . .'

'Anyone else on the beach?' Blythe asked me quietly.

'No.'

'Then?'

'I don't know.'

'Did you go out after Saffie?'

'No!'

'But you had put your dress on,' Blythe said. 'Did you get back into bed with your dress on? Did you leave the shutters open?'

'I don't know!' I shouted. 'I don't know what I did next.'

'Nikki,' Mohktar said gently. 'You do not say these things in your original statement.'

'What did I say, then? What did I say?'

'Nikki,' Blythe said. 'Close your eyes, concentrate. Just tell us *what you remember now*.'

'I can't, it's all a blur. You can't expect me to remember after all this time . . .'

Fleur had been watching my face in silence and she suddenly leant forward. 'Nikki, you're trying to avoid saying that you tried to wake me that afternoon to tell me that Saffie had gone out, but you couldn't wake me, could you?'

Fleur always knew when I was lying or avoiding the truth. The tears sprang to my eyes.

'Did you try to wake me?' Her voice was just a breath.

'No! I didn't,' I lied. 'I know . . . I know I should have done.'

I looked at my hands, then up at Mohktar again and his eyes were not those of a policeman. I kept my eyes on his face and told the truth that was surfacing. 'I remember lying on top of the bed, waiting for Saffie to come back and for the house to wake up. I might have slept for a bit. Then I got bored. I got out of the bedroom window . . . I went a little way down the beach . . . but I still couldn't see Saffie, then . . .'

'Then, Nikki?' Mohktar's voice was soft.

'I saw a man in the distance. He was walking up and down, up and down by the sea . . . as if he did not know which way to go. The sun was going down. He was tall and he made a shadow on the sand . . . like a giant.'

'What did you do?'

'I ran . . . I came back inside,' I whispered. 'I climbed quickly back through the window.'

'What were you afraid of, Nikki? The man was far away across the beach, wasn't he?'

I nodded. I was shaking and felt sick.

'What made you afraid?'

'I don't know.'

'What did you do then?'

'I don't know. I remember going into the bathroom and playing with a clockwork dolphin in the basin. I remember hearing the amah come into the bedroom with tea for Mum. I came out, but she was still asleep . . . so I went to my own room.'

'It was evening by then?'

'Yes. The sun was huge and bright red on top of the sea.'

Blythe looked at his notes. 'But Nikki, your bedroom was shuttered. How did you know where the sun was?'

'I must have gone out onto the veranda . . .' I heard my voice strange and high. 'I think I went out . . . it's hard to remember if it was then or later that . . .'

'What?' Mohktar held my eyes.

I looked away. I was cold and clammy in the hot room as the sweat cooled on my skin and memory came flooding back.

I got up abruptly and went outside to feel the sun on my limbs. I wanted the heat to penetrate my bones. I walked down the steps and across the sand away from the policemen towards the sea.

I could hear children laughing and chasing each other, and Indian amahs ran about with towels, the gold on their wrists and teeth catching the sunlight.

'*Lazy Daddy sleeping in the afternoon! We'd better not tell Mummy, had we? Let's tuck you in, darling, you've got a fever . . . there we are. I'm going to get you a cold drink and a sponge to cool you down . . . back in a minute.*'

'*Daddy, who's that man in your . . .*'

'*Just someone I work with . . .*'

'*Is he lazy too?*'

'*He is not very well, like you, so Daddy lent him his bed for a little while to rest. I don't think we'd better tell mummy had we . . .*'

'*'Cos it's her bed too?*'

'*That's right. So is it our secret, little peapod, yours and mine?*'

*I nod. But daddy's eyes aren't laughing, they look fright-
ened and the sweat is running down his forehead and down
his chest and his hands as he tucks me in tremble and I
don't like this secret and I don't like the smell of Daddy. I
don't like the smell of his fear and of something else which
repels me, but I don't understand why.*

I walked to the sea's edge and I stood letting the water
lap against my ankles. I wanted Jack. I wanted to go home
and see my wonderful garden. I was afraid of my memories and how far they would take me.

I knew Mohktar would come and he did. He took his
shoes and socks off and stood beside me in the water. After
a while, he said, 'You tried to wake your mother more than
once that afternoon, didn't you, Nikki?'

I nodded. Then I said, 'I can't remember if it was after
people began looking for Saffie or before Mum got up, but
I know I went outside and sat on the veranda on a chair.
That sun seemed huge and strange to me. It filled the whole
sky. I knew something bad had happened, really bad. I felt
. . . numb and frightened, but I didn't know why and I
didn't know how to explain to Mum how I felt . . . in the
very depths of me.'

'I watched that sun begin to fall behind the sea and I sat
there looking outward waiting for Saffie to come home.
Calling her in my head like we used to, in the private
language we had, that only she could understand.

'I saw two fishermen across the beach. They had nets and
torches. They got into a boat and I couldn't really see them
properly as the light went. Then they poled across the last
curve of the sun and they were silhouetted, black, like stick
figures across the sky and I . . . I froze with fear.'

My heart hammered as I remembered.

'The fishermen frightened you?'

'No! No. It was the sound . . . the sound coming nearer and nearer . . . but I couldn't leave my chair until Saffie came . . . I couldn't run inside.'

'What sound, Nikki? What did you hear?'

I didn't want to remember. I didn't want to go back. Mohktar took my hands and held them, firmly, facing me. 'Tell me what you heard that night, Nikki.'

'Someone running . . . coming towards me in the dark . . . moaning, gasping under their breath or hurt . . . crying as they ran . . . Then a man ran past the front of the house but he didn't see me in the dark and he began to climb, stumbling up the cliff steps still making odd whimpering sounds as if he couldn't help it. Then I heard a bamboo door in the dark behind me squeak and slam as he went inside one of the houses. The night was quiet again, but the noises he made went on and on in my head . . . like a hurt animal. I couldn't move. I saw a light go on somewhere and the sound of a shower. Then I ran inside to my room because I knew Saffie wouldn't be coming home. Her voice was silent in my head . . . I knew she would never come home.'

Mohktar led me out of the water and I sat down leaning against the rocks because my legs wouldn't hold me up. Mohktar crouched in front of me, his face concerned.

'Why?' I asked him. 'What is the point of remembering now? It's too late. It can only hurt us. Why couldn't I remember at the time?'

'The mind has a way of protecting us.' Mohktar's voice was gentle. Nikki, did you think this man might come for you too?'

It was such a relief to say it. 'Yes! Oh yes.' How sure I had been that he would come for me in the heavy dark of some night.

'Can you remember if this man seemed tall or average height?'

'Tall,' I said, without hesitation. 'He was tall.'

Mohktar said, almost to himself. 'I wonder if that was why those ladies remembered the slamming of the door. It was not the door that woke them, but the odd panic noises they heard in the dark.'

We stared at each other. 'Have I always known who, and buried it?'

'Perhaps.' Mohktar said and his face was sad. He knelt in the sand and took my hand and held it between both his own as if it was something precious. I was so glad of his warmth.

'I am not sure my mother can bear it.'

'I am not sure she should have to.'

I looked at him in surprise. He let go of my hand gently.

'To believe a man is guilty is one thing, but to prove it after twenty-eight years is another, Nikki. It will now be Inspector Blythe's job and that of the English police.'

I smiled bleakly. 'You can go home to Singapore?'

'Yes.' He said. 'And you, Nikki, can also go home. The body of your sister is being released. I heard today. Will you and your mother be able to bury her and move on, do you think?'

'I don't know,' I said. 'I feel confused. I should want justice and vengeance, but all I see is more hurt for Fleur. A part of my mother and a part of me died twenty-eight years ago and maybe something in this man died too. Maybe he has lived his whole life remembering each morning what he did and he has died a little death every day.'

'It is what I believe too.' Mohktar said.

'What is your Christian name . . . your first name? Why have I forgotten?'

Mohktar smiled. 'It is James.'

I smiled back. 'Has it always been James?'

'No, but it was cool to have an English name at school. My mother was a James Bond fan, *lah*?'

I laughed. *I like you, James Mohktar.* Perhaps the thought registered in my eyes for something passed between us, then we both looked away.

He helped me up, smiling at my awkwardness. I said, as we walked back to the house, 'I want to look forward, to be happy or at least *aspire* to happiness. To have the *possibility* of joy and to give it, for once. I want to wake without the shadow and jerk of remembrance. I want to wonder about all the things a new day might bring.'

I stopped in the sand. 'Is it selfish and wicked to want happiness when Saffie is dead?' I touched my stomach. 'I want a happy baby, James. I want a new life. I want to forget and begin again, as if all this . . .' I waved my hand to where all the colonial rest houses had once stood. '. . . and my childhood was a life I once had but can leave behind me. I've spent so long mourning Saffie, blaming my mother. Is it shocking of me to want to move on and away? Is it?'

I couldn't stop the tears. They just flowed out of me and James Mohktar stood looking at me, his beautiful face distressed. He placed his hands on my arms gently.

'Of course it is not wrong. It is time, Nikki. You must bury your sister with your Christian burial service. She is safe now and your love goes with her. There is no more to be done. A man may be brought to punishment or his God may punish him. It is over now. You carry new life. You do not look backwards, you go forward. It is for you to share your life now with those who love you. Yes?'

'Yes.' I said. 'How did you get to be so wise?'

He smiled. 'If I am wise, Nikki, it is through sorrow I learnt. I loved my brothers and I watched the light go from my mother, never to return in the same way; never to light up her face to make her look young again. She lost the smile all people have, that is ageless and comes from the inside; the smile that is the soul and comes from the pleasure of being alive.'

We stood facing each other. I saw that certain people are sent to us. Maybe we have known and loved them in another life. It would have been difficult to feel what I am feeling at this moment with a westerner. We all carry so much baggage and have forgotten the simple, honest emotions and the fact that strangers can connect and touch one another with absolute understanding.

I feel such closeness with James Mohktar and the moment will be etched always on my memory; like a photograph I take out and examine all through my life.

I stood on white sand with an aquamarine sea rolling in behind me. The heat bore down on the houses and hotels in front of me and shimmered above the ground like a mirage. From the backdrop of jungle I could hear birds and the noisy cackle of monkeys. I could hear our hearts beating and the silence stretching into something neither of us wanted to break.

'Thank you,' I whispered.

'There is nothing for which to thank me, Nikki.'

'I thank you for being here and for being you. I will never forget you.'

James Mohktar's face was sad. As sad as mine. 'It is hard to say goodbye to someone you have only just found, isn't it?'

'Yes. It's very hard.'

We did not touch. We looked for a long time to engrave

the other's face upon our memory and then we turned and walked again in silence. Before we reached the house, I spoke, because I needed him to know what was on my mind.

'I would like to bury Saffie in my garden in New Zealand. I don't want to be parted from her again. We live in a place called the Bay Of Islands. My garden slopes down towards the sea and we have this beautiful flower meadow. I want to bury her there and plant trees all round and then build a little summer house over the grave. I want to let the trees and flowers grow through the house and Saffie will become part of . . .'

'The cycle of birth and death?' Mohktar finished softly.

I smiled. 'Mum is studying this painter . . . he was an architect too, called . . .'

'Hundertwasser?'

'Yes!'

'Not so clever of me, Nikki. You mentioned him in Singapore. At university there were many of us who became fascinated by him.'

'Do you remember a painting called *The Garden of The Happy Dead*?'

'I do. And in other paintings too, he has trees and plants growing out of his houses . . .'

'Do you think I'm weird?'

James Mohktar laughed out loud. 'No, I do not. And I do not think your mother will either if she is studying him. In our culture, also, we take many things to the graves of our loved ones. A favourite pair of slippers, sweetmeats, chimes to keep the evil spirits away. Toys. Many of the things the person we loved enjoyed when they were alive. I think it is a . . . God given idea, Nikki.'

'Thank you.'

We were almost at the house. James Mohktar stopped

and turned to me. 'Did you know there is another of Hundertwasser's paintings called *Painting I Made Secretly in the Garden of the Beautiful Girl?*

I smiled. 'No.'

'I think it is all exactly right. Your sister will lie for ever in the Garden of the Beautiful girl . . .' He leant towards me. 'Happiness will come to you, Nikki. I know this, because it lies in your heart.'

Touched, I could not speak.

He smiled. 'I think we say our private goodbye now, for the chance may not come again.'

I did not want to say goodbye. He held out his hand and I took it. His face was the most extraordinary face, beautiful and familiar, and I could read it because it mirrored my own. I shivered.

'In a different time? In a different place?' I asked him.

James Mohktar tried to smile, but this time the smile did not reach his eyes.

'It may be that we have already been there, Miss Montrose.'

'Goodbye, Detective Sergeant James Mohktar.'

'Goodbye, my dear Miss Montrose.'

FORTY-ONE

Fleur said apologetically, 'I'm sorry, Inspector, I think Nikki finds it easier to talk to DS Mohktar without me in the room.'

Blythe cleared his throat. 'Mrs Campbell, I really don't like having to put you through it over and over, but you do see the importance of doing so? You do see how fickle memory is?'

'In my case, Inspector, it is not fickle enough,' Fleur said quietly.

Blythe felt at a bit of a loss; he was a blunt northerner and he did not have Mohktar's gift of empathy, nor his ability to look at a situation sideways on, from everyone's point of view. Yet he was canny enough to realise that a gift for getting near people could play against you and get in the way of objectivity. He was pretty sure that his Malay sergeant was edging along the borderline; *getting too involved*.

Fleur seemed to be reading him. 'I think it helps, Inspector, that your sergeant is a gentle man and also an exceedingly beautiful one, and that he is nearer Nikki's age than . . .

either of us.' She watched his rather pleasant face. He looked a family man. 'The need for children to protect their parents is amazing, isn't it? You must have seen it often. Even a bad parent is better than no parent at all. I'm not a stupid woman. If Saffie had gone out alone without permission, Nikki would have tried to wake me, instinctively.

'Inspector, don't you think I've asked myself *every single day of my life* why I drank that lunchtime? How I could have taken painkillers on top of drink and slept the sleep of the dead and put my children in danger?'

Suddenly, from nowhere a great protective anger took hold of Blythe. He stared at this small woman who had carried her guilt like a stranglehold round her neck for twenty-eight years.

'Mrs Campbell, you are not a bad mother. Nor are you responsible for the death of your child, although I doubt anyone can make you believe it. You did not go to sleep in a dangerous place where harm could come to children. You were staying in a sleepy little Malaysian rest house, surrounded by other Europeans and locals who would not harm a fly.

'You had watched your husband die in a horrific accident. You were still grieving and exhausted. You wanted to sleep, you craved oblivion, you had a drink and you took painkillers, but you also took your children into your own room so that they were near you and asked the amah to stay in the house knowing you needed to sleep. These are not the actions of a bad mother, but of someone nearing the end of their endurance.

'It was unfortunate your parents had to leave you. You might ask them if they have blamed themselves for the rest of their lives. It was unfortunate that the amah slept, but it is the man who killed your child, either by accident or design, that is responsible for the death of your daughter. *Not you*.

Not your parents. Not Nikki who stayed behind with you.
A person, as yet unknown, killed your child randomly and
wantonly while you rested. That does not make you a bad
mother . . . or culpable . . .'

He took a deep breath. 'This is the real world and
parents aren't perfect, just human. We make mistakes, but
we do our best, Mrs Campbell, we do our best for our
children and that's all we can do. We can't foresee what's
coming. We can't protect them from a chain of events that
together produce a tragedy. All we have is the knowledge
of hindsight . . .'

Blythe petered out, astounded at himself. His wife would
have been even more astounded as he was a man not prone
to vocalising his feelings.

Surprised, Fleur could not trust herself to speak. Her
emotions were so near the surface that she had to rein them
in tight; unexpected kindness threatened to tip her over the
edge. She was aware that Blythe was not a man given to
outbursts and she was touched.

She got up and went to the fridge and got out a beer for
him. It was nearly lunchtime and she guessed he could do
with one.

'Thank you, Inspector,' she said as she put the glass down
beside him.

He looked up, slightly embarrassed, and said, quickly,
while he had the courage, 'My eldest son was killed in a
motorbike accident. My wife hadn't wanted him to have
one. I said he could. He tried to race a mate to Cornwall
for a dare. He killed himself and a young girl in a car. For
a while I blamed myself . . . my wife did too. If I'd said no,
he would still be alive.'

'But if you had said no, your son could have been on the
back of someone else's bike, couldn't he.'

'Yes, Mrs Campbell, he could. Death can be swift and random and there is little we can do about that. We're not God.'

'I'm very sorry about your son. A parent never ever gets over losing a child. We carry the loss on with us as part of our everyday lives, don't we? Always there, but unseen.'

Blythe met her eyes briefly. *How aptly she described the beginning of each and every day.* They smiled at each other bleakly and then Blythe lifted his glass of beer. 'To your future, Mrs Campbell.'

Fleur lifted her juice. 'And to yours, Inspector Blythe.'

Blythe hesitated. 'I heard this morning that your daughter's body is ready for release. Sergeant Mohktar and I will accompany you to the mortuary when you are ready.'

Fleur closed her eyes. 'Oh, thank God. We can take her home. I also want to get Nikki safely back to New Zealand. She is over the deadline for flying.'

'You will accompany her to New Zealand?'

'Of course, Inspector. Is my daughter's body still in Kuala Lumpur?'

'Yes.'

'Would it be possible to choose a coffin here, in Malaysia, and take her on the flight with us?'

'We will need to get clearance and the right forms, but of course . . . I am sure the authorities expect it . . . Will you bury her in New Zealand or England, Mrs Campbell?'

'I need to talk to Nikki, but I have a feeling she will want to have her buried in New Zealand, somewhere close by. Twins, especially identical ones, are often symbiotic, Inspector Blythe. The strange bond between them can be alarming sometimes. In life, their need for each other is often greater than their need for anyone else. I am not at all sure this ends with the death of one of them.'

Inspector Blythe looked out of his depth. She smiled at his face. He was afraid of places she might take him and he certainly did not want to go.

'You will be going home too, Inspector?'

'Yes. I will go on working on the case from London . . .' His mobile phone made them both jump. 'Excuse me.' He got up to go to the window.

'I don't care what rank he is,' Fleur heard him say. 'Or whether he is entitled to anonymity under the Northern Ireland terrorism act. Go through the appropriate channels. When I get back I want to interview everyone living who stayed in Port Dickson at that time . . . no exceptions. Is that understood?'

'Sorry,' he said to Fleur as he put the phone back in his pocket. 'Now, I must go and find my sergeant.'

'I can see them walking back now,' Fleur said.

Blythe gathered up his papers and put them in his cardboard file. He stopped and mopped his brow. Fleur, watching, thought how hot and out of place he looked; an English bear of a man. He bore little resemblance to the young, eager military policeman whose life of solving crimes lay ahead of him in 1976.

She wanted to ask him if he had been happy, apart from the death of his son, but knew he would hate such a personal question.

'I am grateful for all the help you have given us, Mrs Campbell. I won't say goodbye, because we will see each other again before I leave . . . but the best of luck to you, you deserve it, and happiness.'

He cleared his throat, embarrassed, and held out his hand. Fleur took it.

'Thank you for your kindness and sensitivity, Inspector. I do appreciate it and all you've done.'

Blythe smiled wryly. 'Never been called sensitive before. I might get it in writing to show the wife.'

Fleur watched him walk towards Nikki and Mohktar. Mohktar held up his hand in salute and Fleur waved back. The two men turned and walked away across the beach and Nikki came on towards her slowly, looking very young, one hand holding her back which was obviously aching. The heat was making her blonde hair stick to her head.

The reality of it hit Fleur for the first time. *I really am going to be a grandmother.* Nikki was carrying a new and unknown life. In a few weeks that life was going to become a small person with its own unique identity. She had lost this daughter of hers for so many years; now she had another chance.

A man known or unknown had killed Saffie in a violent random act. To think, if David had not been gay; if I had not kissed Fergus; if David had not died; if I had not come on holiday with my parents. If I had not slept for one entire hot afternoon– was destructive, and would blight any possibility of future happiness.

She walked down the wooden steps to meet Nikki, and as she did so her mobile phone rang.

'Hi, it's me!' Sam said.

'Sam! I wondered where you'd got to.'

'Ah! I have a pretty good reason for not ringing you when I said I would.'

Fleur felt a lurch of excitement. 'What's that?'

'I've just landed in Kuala Lumpur . . .'

'Sam!' Fleur burst into tears.

'I figured you could do with some moral support. At the very least I can see you and that niece of mine safely home. I'm going to stay the night here, old darling, I'm bushed. I'll drive down to you first thing in the morning.'

'Sam, you couldn't have timed it better.'

'I'm glad. I'll talk to you before I leave to find out exactly where you are. I'll catch up with your news then. Good night, Fleury.'

'Good night, Sam.'

'Good night, Sam,' Nikki called, smiling. She pulled herself up the steps and sat under the fan. 'I'm so tired.'

'Bed, darling?'

'Yes, please.'

'Go straight away. I'll ask Ah Lin to put your lunch on a tray.'

'Thanks, Mum.'

Nikki lowered herself on to her bed gratefully. She did not want to worry Fleur but she wondered if she was going to be allowed to fly home.

She closed her eyes. 'Thank God for Sam,' she whispered before she fell asleep. A family doctor might just tip the scales.

She wanted to take Saffie home. She wanted to go home to have her baby.

FORTY-TWO

I could see Jack below me with Fleur and Sam. He was showing them the new jetty he had started to build while I'd been away. His yacht was moored at the end with the small motor dinghy we used for going across the water to shop. He was taking them across the bay to show them Paihia and I was grateful because I needed to be on my own.

I was like a cat reclaiming her territory. Autumn was beginning, it was cooler and I was determined to walk the boundaries of our land, despite my size. I was so glad to be home. I closed my eyes, wanting to cry with relief. Happiness settled like sunlight, warming me with its reminder of the simple things here that gave me so much pleasure.

The bay was the palest blue and there was no wind and I watched the figures below me get into the small motor-boat. The sound of the engine reached me up here on the hill and I saw three heads turn back to the land, reluctant to leave me.

It had been difficult to persuade them that I would be

311

fine, that they were only ten minutes away by water, and eventually they had understood how important it was for me to have time and stillness alone here. I did not want to hear voices or movement or feel other human beings around me while I chose the exact and perfect place to bury Saffie.

I knew she would guide me; I knew we would choose the place together, so I sat on the hill watching the white wake made by the boat crossing the water, carrying the people who loved and were worried about me.

Singapore Airlines would not have let me fly home with them if Sam had not been with me. Although I had been given a thorough check-up in a hospital in KL and they had judged I was fit enough to fly, especially with a doctor, I was way over the safe period and of course I could not get any insurance cover.

I had to pretend I was not worried about the flight because it was far worse for Fleur and Sam and poor Jack back here waiting.

The local villagers had brought little gifts for us before we left Port Dickson. They had left us alone during our time there and protected us from any intrusion and we were touched by their gentleness and sensitivity.

The Malaysian police in Kuala Lumpur had been wonderful too. They had advised us about the wood for the coffin and made suggestions for how it should be lined. When we had arrived in the city it was all ready. The small coffin had been made beautifully in local wood. It was highly polished and smelt of camphor. There was a small gold plaque: *Saffron Alice Montrose 1971–1976 R.I.P.* There were wreaths of bougainvillaea, orchids and frangipani from the Malaysian Police Federation.

We were escorted onto the plane before the other passengers and a little group of policemen including Mohktar saluted as they wheeled the tiny coffin to the plane. I felt Fleur beside me. We were both remembering Dad's coffin entering the vast cargo-hold of an army flight, long ago, and we moved nearer to one another in silence as Saffie was tenderly carried across the tarmac by a huge turbaned Indian and a Malay officer.

We shook hands with the courteous Malaysian police. Blythe had left the night before for the UK. When I reached James Mohktar I felt such a sense of loss that I was afraid it would show in my eyes. Perhaps he knew, because he was brisk, shook my hand, and drawing me away from the others he took a small box from his pocket and opened the lid.

'These are the smallest pair of shoes I could find. One shoe is for Saffie to guide her safely into the next world, and one shoe for you, Nikki, to guide you forward without her. You think that one shoe is no good without the other. It is not true, for wherever you go in this life she is with you. You will always be one half of a pair and death does not change that.'

I stared down at the tiniest pair of little bejewelled Chinese shoes and then Mohktar put the lid on and folded my hands around the box. 'The reality of your days here will fade like a dream, but the essence of something, of your spirit and your sister's, will remain. You will live on in my memory, Nikki.'

I looked into his strange and complex face. Such a mixture of cultures lay behind his eyes. 'I am so glad to have known you, James Mohktar.'

He smiled. 'Take care, Nikki.'

He turned abruptly away, back to his colleagues, and Sam and Fleur and I boarded the plane. As it motored along the runway I craned out of the window. There was one police-man standing alone waiting for the plane to take off. I knew he would watch it until we were a speck in the sky and then he would turn and drive home through the palm oil plantations on the long, straight road back to Singapore, to his wife and his child.

I sat in the long grass of the meadow and considered the strange intensity and familiarity between us. I knew it would seem unreal as the months passed; all part of finding Saffie in a place that had so many conflicting memories. Mohktar, somehow, has not touched my real life, just enriched it.

If I felt loss, it was for the passing of strangers who would never meet again and a glimpse of another culture which embraced the unknown and unseen and saw it as normal, a link and passage between worlds; a journey from a state of life to an afterlife. Not a death.

The spirit of Saffie will always be with me. Sleeping or waking. I do not need to dream. I do not need to conjure her from darkness and loss. She has always walked beside me, her small feet in sure and perfect time with mine. This was the simple and obvious truth that James Mohktar had given me.

I believe it finally. It is why he passed my way.

I stood up awkwardly. If I turned to my left I could see the tiny clapperboard Maori meeting place where Saffie lay waiting. Candles were kept alight day and night by Maori friends who took turns to guard her so that she was never in the dark or alone. *Tangihanga*, the Maori process of mourning, had begun.

I thought the perfect position for Saffie's last journey to a peaceful afterlife was here where I stood now. The grass was long and the smell sweet, of hay and childhood, of the myriad of possibilities that lay ahead. You could just glimpse our house to the right with the view down the valley. Across the river from our land lay the curve of blue sea with the yachts resting in the shelter of the bay. Beyond, tiny islands lay.

Behind me our land circled and there was no sound but the constant crickets and the kokakos. It was a perfect bird's eye view of all that I loved and the things that made up my everyday life.

We will bury Saffie here.

Sam's boys were going to fly over and help build a small summer house with a grass roof and no straight lines. Inside, I already knew what trees and shrubs I would plant. Manuka, kowhai and ponga, and saplings to grow upright through the roof and windows.

Distant Maori relations of Jack's were coming up from their farm in Whangarel to help too. Gran and Grandpa were travelling all the way from Cyprus to be here.

Saffie will never lie alone again.

I turned from the water and started to walk back to the house and it was then that the first pain came, sharp and urgent, making me double up with the shock of it. I crouched on the ground to get my breath. Sweat broke out on my forehead and fear made my heart hammer.

I must get back to the house. I got to my feet shakily and I felt Saffie's presence suddenly beside me, anxious.

'It's OK,' I told her. 'It's OK. I can make it back to the house . . .'

No!

The word seemed loud in the silence.

No, Nikki. Stay where you are – don't start walking. Ring Jack. Ring him now.

At that moment my waters broke. I got my mobile out of my pocket and I dialled. Jack anwered immediately.

'Nik?'

315

'Jack, please don't panic. Could you come back? I think I've gone into labour.'

Jack panicked. I heard it. Sam came on the line. 'Nik? Where are you?'

I was doubled up again and could not speak for a minute. Sam's voice was calm and reassuring. 'Take deep breaths, that's it. How close are your contractions?'

'Oh, God, Sam, pretty close, about three or four minutes . . .'

'Nik, listen to me . . .' His voice was jerky and breathless and I realised they were all running as he talked. 'Don't try to get back to the house. Stay where you are. Lie down, breath as you've been taught and try to relax . . . We're in the boat now and on our way. OK?'

'Yes.' I could hear the boat engine start up from across the water. Jack was frantically gunning the old engine for more speed. I lay down in the flower meadow and disappeared into the long grass. I felt strange, as if I was floating above myself.

'Are you lying down?' Sam's voice.

I looked up at the sky through my dark glasses. Not a cloud. Very peaceful. I smiled.

'Nikki? Answer me! Come on! Keep talking to us, there's a good girl.'

But I was very sleepy. Then the pain came again and I cried out.

'OK, sweetheart. We're coming into the jetty now . . . Can you still hear me?'

I turned slightly to the phone, sweating profusely. 'Yes.'

'Good. You're doing great. Jack's rung the emergency services. The helicopter will be with us before you know it . . . Nik?'

Everything was beginning to slide away from me . . .

Wake up! Don't you dare go to sleep! Saffie's voice; indignant.

She was always saying that to me. I liked to sleep longer than she did.

Very tired, Saff . . . Just the wind through the grass whispering and then a heavy silence and faraway sounds from down on the water . . .

Jack was leaning over me . . . 'Nikki! Nikki! Oh God!'

Then I heard Sam's calm voice. He lifted the lids of my eyes and then took my hand and listened to my pulse. I heard him rustling with something, then a sharp prick in my arm. I heard him saying to Jack, 'Listen, Jack! Listen! You must keep calm. I'm going to need your help. She's had a small bleed and this baby is going to arrive quickly.'

I began to feel better and opened my eyes.

'Nikki?' Sam's voice was loud. 'Right, sweetheart, we can't do this without you. Stay with us . . .'

The pain came again, violently, and I groaned and passed out. When I came back, Mum was putting a pillow under my head and lower back and covering my legs with a thin sheet. She made me sip water. Both Sam and Jack were talking on their phones. Fleur stroked my hair.

'It's going to be all right, darling. Jack is guiding the helicopter in and Sam is talking to the paramedics. Help is coming.'

I closed my eyes. Jack was giving grid references. 'Yes, there's room to land . . . sloping meadow . . . southwest of Paihia . . . Yeah, that's it! Straight line at twelve o'clock up from the bay. Great. How long? OK. Please hurry.'

I could hear Sam talking on the phone now. 'We need . . . No chance! She won't make it to Auckland, she's dilated. Yes, if we have to . . . but she's had a small bleed. The baby's in some distress . . . Yes, it might be an emergency caesarean . . . if I need to get him out fast. Yes, I have . . . I would appreciate all help pronto . . .'

Baby in some distress. I gripped Fleur's arm, fighting sleep.

I'm going to lose my baby.

'Nikki!' Fleur's voice was firm. 'Come on, darling, you must stay awake. This baby needs all the help he can get.'

I groaned and waited for another contraction. 'You never told me it was this bad!' I yelled at Fleur as she wiped my face. 'Where's Jack?'

Her answer was drowned by the sound of the helicopter overhead and I saw Jack on his trail bike flying by, pointing to the flat end of the field.

'Nikki, I need to see what's happening with the baby . . . OK?'

In a moment Sam covered me up again. 'Nik, on the next contraction, you must not push until I say. This is important . . .'

'Why?'

'It's possible the umbilical cord is caught round his neck.'

'Sam, am I going to lose this baby?'

'He's doing OK so far, sweetie, but we're going to have to get him to hospital pronto. So be brave and do exactly as you're told – even though you'll want to push . . .'

The rotary blades caused a wind and whipped the grass where I lay. It landed noisily and two men in flight overalls came running towards us. They talked to Sam and then one paramedic gave me something to help the pain and put an oxygen mask over my face. 'You're doing good.'

Jack was beside me as another contraction gripped me and I screamed, 'I want to push!'

'No!' three voices said sharply.

'Come on, breathe, darling . . .'

'OK, lady, let's see what's going on . . .'

'Sam!' I gasped. 'The baby's coming, I can't stop it. I can't.'

The pain was overpowering. 'Stop for a sec! Hold still, Nik. OK . . . OK. Now you can push. Push!'

I bore down with all my strength and I felt the baby slip out of me.

Silence. I listened to everyone's quick breathing and frantic movements. *Please God. Please God.* One of the paramedics ran to the helicopter. I looked round. Fleur had her hand over her mouth. Jack was ashen. Then suddenly a tiny splutter, a hiccup, and then a thin wail of fury.

'Atta girl!' a paramedic yelled. The baby was held near my face briefly, so fleetingly, and then placed in something and whisked away as they ran to the helicopter. Sam smiled down at me as I was bundled tight onto the stretcher.

'Well done, sweetheart. You've got a little girl.'

Then they were running with me towards the helicopter and the rotary blades were already starting to turn. Jack climbed in beside me as we rose up from the flower meadow. And that is all I remember.

FORTY-THREE

Fleur and Sam watched Laura and Peter Llewellyn walk off the tiny plane at Kerikeri.

'God, they look old, Fleury,' Sam said. 'Old and tired and small.'

Fleur felt her heart constrict. 'It's all too much for them at their age. It's all too much.'

Sam held up his hand and waved and Laura's face lit up, changed in an instant as she saw her son. Saw only him. Fleur drew in her breath in a stab of familiar but almost forgotten pain. She found her father's eyes and he held them and smiled and all was well again.

Peter held her close for a minute as if she was very precious. 'My beloved Fleur,' he whispered.

Fleur turned to Laura. 'Mum, how was the journey? Have you survived? You look wonderful.'

'Hello, darling. Trust my granddaughter to live in the middle of nowhere! My dear girl, you are much too thin . . .' She took her daughter's arm. 'Fleur, it must have been awful . . . awful. We felt helpless so far away. I don't think we stopped thinking of you and Nikki once.'

Laura's face was anxious and Fleur squeezed her mother's arm. 'Thanks, Mum, I'm fine. It's been wonderful to have Sam. Come on, let's get you into the car.'

On the long drive back to the house, Peter and Laura were too tired to make much conversation, and within half an hour were asleep in the back of the car.

Sam glanced at Fleur. 'It's going to take them a few days to acclimatise. They don't go anywhere now, you know. I don't think they would have survived the journey if they'd had to fly from England. I'm glad we decided to leave Saffie's funeral until next week.'

'Jack says Nikki is still hoping to bring the baby back. What do you think, Sam?'

'Not a chance! She was a prem and is still underweight. It's not as if Nikki and Jack live in the middle of Auckland. Besides, Nikki will still be weak. She haemorrhaged twice. If it wasn't for special circumstances, I doubt they'd let her out of hospital yet, either.'

'We need to bury Saffie, Sam. Nikki won't relax or move on until it's done.'

'I know,' Sam said quietly. 'I know.'

Fleur and Sam had had time to talk while Jack stayed up in Auckland with Nikki and the baby. They had never spent time together as two adults and probably never would again. One night she had told him about David. He had stared at her in disbelief. He had gone through a period of intense hero-worship towards David while he had still been at school, when the few years between them still seemed huge.

'It never occurred to me . . . not once,' he said to Fleur. 'David was always surrounded by pretty girls and flirted all the time. It all makes sense now, how miserable you were when I was in Melbourne. God, Fleur, I wish you'd said something, at least to me. I could have protected you from Mum; she was so hard on you.'

'If you tell one person, Sam, you might as well tell the world. I wanted to protect David and the twins.'

She told him about their time in Port Dickson and how and why Saffie might have died. It was hard for Sam to take this in and he was deeply upset.

'What a brave woman you are, Fleury.'

'I had Fergus for most of my life . . . easier to be brave with him, and now I don't have a choice. I can't let the past destroy me, Sam. I have Nikki and a granddaughter. I have you, and old parents whom I love.'

'I'm glad you had Fergus. My God you deserved him.' Sam had hugged her fiercely, shaken with all the implications surfacing.

Now he cleared his throat and glanced in the back of the car to make sure his parents were sleeping.

'Fleur, I think you should tell Mum and Dad about David.'

'No, Sam, they've enough to think about. They're just too old to take any more.'

Sam looked at her. He just stopped himself saying, *Fleur, what if it becomes public? You'll have to tell them then.*

He had guessed correctly that Fleur hoped the whole thing would go away if she did not think about it.

For heaven's sake, let her bury her child before she thinks about anything else.

He thought about Angie back at the house and the sons and grandsons he adored, pitching in to build this odd summer house for Nikki before she came home. He thought of Jack caught bang in the middle of this tragedy and of the child he and Nikki had nearly lost.

This far-flung family were gathering to mourn for a lost child that was only a whispered legend to his grandchildren.

322

And because Sam was an optimist, he saw in this instinctive gathering of the clan a new opportunity for closeness. For honesty and for a gentle moving on to the next generation, when his children and grandchildren might become closer to Nikki and Jack's children.

It was as if the catastrophe that had befallen Fleur had scattered them all, yet it did not matter how far away you lived from each other, in the end blood counted.

Sam had spent half his life in a vast, often inhospitable and uninhabited country, flying to anyone who needed him. He had learnt to listen to the voices of those living close to the land. Jack had explained about *tangihanga*, the Maori process of mourning. A *tangihanga* was not just about grieving, but about saying goodbye and talking openly about the dead person. It was also a support system for the *whanau pani* – the bereaved family. A time where family ties were strengthened and lost relations welcomed.

Sam had smiled as he listened. It sounded far more sensible than therapy with strangers. It seemed to him that there might be a mysterious pattern to life. Saffie would be buried far from an Anglo-Saxon graveyard, in a place of sun and water. There would be no sad grave to keep, just the growth each year of new life springing from the earth of the meadow.

We named the baby Alice. She weighed nearly 5 lbs now and had a shock of black hair which the nurses said she would probably lose. She was a little fighter and she had no intention of losing her grip on this world.

I could hardly bear to leave her to fly home, but I had to. Laura and Peter had travelled so far. Angie, Sam, their children and grandchildren had lives they must get back to. And Jack's family were slowly gathering from across New Zealand.

All the bachs on our land, usually kept for visitors, were full. Jack had spent the last three weeks travelling back and forth from Kerikeri to Auckland while Sam held things together at home.

Before the small plane landed in Kerikeri I turned and saw the weariness in Jack's face. Love for him gripped me, terrifying but real.

'Jack?'

He opened his eyes.

'Will you marry me?'

I watched the grin spread across his face.

'Mmm,' he said. 'I'll have to think about it.'

'Don't you dare play hard to get!'

He leant over to kiss me. 'Pot and kettle come to mind? Yes, all right, I'll marry you . . . I think it would be churlish to refuse.'

'Thank you.'

'No worries,' he said, pretending to pick up the paper and read.

I laughed. He still had that stupid grin on his face.

Laura lay in the bath in her granddaughter's bathroom which had a clear glass window reflecting the blue sky and the sweep of the bay below the garden. The day was warm, like an English spring or a Cyprus winter, but Laura felt cold and very old.

When the water lost its heat, she got up and wrapped herself in a large towel, shivering slightly and once dry, she pulled on her dressing gown again.

Reluctantly she met her eyes in the mirror. It was a defining moment. She was forced to face herself: to admit to the horror of having got something so wrong. She did not like the person she saw. Her voice of long ago clamoured in her head as if it was yesterday.

She was back in that cold Berkshire house she and Peter had never felt at home in and had sold without regret. Those awful words she had shouted at Fleur after Saffie disappeared and they returned to England. She had always remembered the scene but did so now with brutal clarity.

Peter had just returned to Northern Ireland and they were all missing him acutely. They did not know how to fill their days, she and Fleur; they could not talk but circled each other in limbo, a sort of suspended animation. Life seemed to have stopped for Fleur and for Laura too and she resented it and was ashamed.

One morning, out of the blue, Fleur had announced that she was taking Nikki to a chalet in Cornwall belonging to Fergus's parents. Laura had been furious. 'Look, Fleur, I've stayed behind to look after you and Nikki. I could have gone back to Northern Ireland with your father if I'd known you were going to take off.'

'Well, now you can go and join Dad and not feel full of resentment.' Fleur had retorted.

'You are in no state to look after a child on your own; you can't even look after yourself.'

Fleur had turned and run upstairs with poor little Nikki scrabbling worriedly up after her. Laura could not leave it. She had followed Fleur upstairs and watched her angrily throwing things into a suitcase. Peter had given Fleur his car and Laura thought she meant to drive to Cornwall.

'You can't drive, Fleur. You're drugged up to the eyeballs.'

Fleur had looked up and said in a voice Laura had never heard before. 'All my life you have told me what I can't do, what I'm no good at. Even now, even now! I'm *not* driving. I'm going on the train. Fergus has offered to drive the car down for me next weekend.'

Laura had felt sudden righteous outrage. 'You mean he'll be staying there with you?'

Fleur had looked at her with an expression as cold as the inside of that house. 'Fergus is coming down with his parents and they are all staying with friends nearby for the week-end. He flies back to Singapore on Monday. They are all trying to be helpful and kind, not judging me the whole time. You can never think the best of me; it's just too difficult isn't it? Even in these moments when I need you more than I ever have . . . you are resentful.'

She clicked the suitcase shut. 'Go to Dad.' She said quietly. 'Book your flight to Belfast.'

Laura had been smitten. She sat heavily on the bed. 'I'm not resentful about not being with your father, Fleur. For heaven's sake, you are my priority. I am trying . . . it's just . . .'

'You blame me for . . . Saffie?'

'Of course I don't! How could I?'

'What, then?'

'I guess it's to do with trust, Fleur. Trust and betrayal.'

Fleur had gone very still. 'Spit it out.' She said. 'It has sat there unsaid ever since Dad left.'

Laura had taken a deep breath. 'You had a husband who adored you and was a wonderful father. He was our friend too, your father's and mine. He did not deserve to be betrayed by you and his best friend.'

'This is what you believe?'

'Yes, I do.'

'Why?'

'Because, Fleur, it was being said all over the mess.'

'Why, then, it must be true, Mother! Dad heard it?'

'Yes.'

'Did he believe what he heard?'

'I don't believe he did.'

Fleur stood in front of Laura pale and still. 'You know absolutely nothing about my life or my marriage to David. I betrayed no one and neither did Fergus. He was a true friend to David and to me. Do you know, Mum, at this moment I don't like you very much . . .'

Then she had called a taxi and gone, leaving Laura with a bitter taste in her mouth: a raw feeling that however justified she had felt in saying the things she had to Fleur, she had misjudged the moment.

Laura put her hand up to her face and found she was crying. She sat on a small white chair in the bathroom and cried silently. *Misjudged! My God! I've spent a lifetime doing it.*

Peter was sitting up in bed when Fleur carried up her parents' tea. She could hear her mother in the bathroom.

Peter patted the side of the bed. 'Come and sit for a minute, darling.'

Fleur sat. 'You're looking better, Dad.'

'I should jolly well hope so after three days doing absolutely bugger all. Your mother's her old self, though, so watch out.' He looked at her. 'How are you really, Fleur?'

'I'm OK, Dad, really I am.'

'We are worried, your mother and I. What about when you get home to England to an empty house? Bit different then, we are all so far away from you.'

'Dad, I've got my painting and friends and . . .'

'We wondered if you would think about coming to live in Cyprus, near us, darling. You can get wonderful villas with a pool.'

'Dad, that's a lovely thought, but my life is in London.'

Her father nodded. 'I suppose you're too young to bury

yourself. It was just a thought. I miss you, Fleur.'

'I miss you too, Dad.' She looked at his face. 'Oh God! Sam has told you, hasn't he?'

'Don't be angry. I'm so glad he did. You see, I wondered . . .'

'Did you?'

'Yes. But then David married you and you were so happy I knew I must have got it wrong. We did have homosexuals in the army, more than you would suspect. But they didn't usually marry or come out. I guess if they were ambitious they were discreet and then they just got more like crotchety old women, like we all do . . .'

Fleur smiled. 'Not you, Dad.'

'I thought when Sam told me, what if I'd warned you, even if you'd been furious with me. But you see, Fleur, I had no real evidence, it was just a feeling.'

'I wouldn't have listened, Dad. I'd have thought you were making it up. You know what David was like with a room full of women, he could take his pick.'

Hearing her mother moving about, Fleur said quickly, 'Does Mum know?'

'No, but I think she should know . . . for obvious reasons I won't go in to . . .'

'Dad, I don't want her to feel guilty, it's a long time ago and she's old and frail.'

Laura came out of the bathroom in a pretty, flowery dressing gown, smelling lovely. 'Not that frail, Fleur.' She put her vanity case on the dressing table and Fleur saw how carefully she was made up. Too carefully. Had she been crying?

Laura met her daughter's eyes. 'I overheard Sam and your father last night. They thought I was asleep.' She sat on the end of the bed, facing Fleur. 'To say it was a shock would be a vast understatement and I deserved to hear it in the way I did, with no preamble or forewarning. I'm not a frail old woman, Fleur, but a wicked, wicked one who rushed to judgement and never even considered she might have got it wrong. Not only did I judge you, I judged Fergus . . .'

She bit her lip. 'You see, I never thought for a moment you had it in you to be so brave or loyal, to keep silent for a lifetime. And now this, with Saffie . . . Look at you, still so brave, with a frightening strength and dignity.'

She held out her hands in a misery so abject Fleur could not bear it. 'I have the most lovely, talented daughter with a gift for loving beyond anything I am capable of, and instead of recognising that, I have spent years blaming you and I've lost you.'

Fleur took Laura's hands and held them. 'Mum, you haven't lost me. I'm still here, as I've always been. I don't blame you. How could you understand something I wasn't prepared to disclose?'

'Because I should have known you, Fleur. That is the tragedy.'

'Mum . . .' She turned to her father. Peter saw Fleur could only cope with so much at one time and this wasn't the moment for Laura's unburdening.

Laura immediately saw this too. 'Darling, I'm sorry. We'll talk another time. We must have everything ready for Nikki and Jack. What time are they due?'

'Not until about five p.m. Sam will drive to meet them. I'm going to take breakfast to the men up at the summer house now and see how they're getting on. See you both later . . .'

Fleur backed out of the room and ran down the stairs and into the kitchen. She gathered up the basket with flasks of coffee and bacon rolls and flew out into the overcast

329

morning. She took huge gulps of air and made herself observe everything around her as she walked, trying to drag her mind away from so many conflicting emotions, trying to ignore the knot of pain which never lay far away from the surface.

As she climbed to the flower meadow she could hear the sound of voices and hammering and someone singing. She looked around her at the vast swathe of uncultivated land sloping down to the swampy river and out to the bay and thought of Nikki's life here. So different, so unimaginable, all this space and wilderness, unless you saw it for yourself.

How independent people had to be to live here, thrown on their own resources. It was miles to the next human habitation and Fleur wondered how quickly Nikki had adapted to the loneliness. If she had embraced it first as an escape, and then come to love and feel part of it all because of Jack.

She looked out over the water. Peaceful. Always moving. She had forgotten how much she missed living by the sea, living by water.

Fergus. Fergus. Did I tell you every day how much you meant to me? How I loved you? It's hard, it's so hard without you.

She thought of the little chalet house his parents had once owned down in Cornwall. *Blue on blue of sea and sky where your heartbeat settled to the pulse of the ocean.*

Fergus had loved it. It was where he had begun to paint. After his parents died they had mostly rented it out but they had tried to go each year. She had not been there since he died.

I could try it. I could rent out the London house. It came to her in a flash. There was a thriving arty community down there. She saw the glittering arc of blue sea and sky in front

330

of the house. She saw the surfers swooping in on great waves as the sun set. She remembered the throb and shush of the sea, soothing and continuous as she lay in the dark.

She wanted to wake again to the sound of water. She wanted to live swallowed by sea and sky where the space and silence made room for her. A place to draw breath, to live the sort of life she must live, on her own now.

As she came to the top of the meadow she stopped at the almost biblical scene in front of her. Sam, his two grandsons and two highly tattooed Maori boys with brightly coloured bandanas were laying turf in strips on the soiled roof of the structure. Fleur had seen grass roofs in the Outer Hebrides and she stood watching, fascinated.

On Nikki's instructions Jack had planted two saplings inside the house, their branches leaning out of the windows each side of the doorway.

Fleur smiled. *Tree tenants.* All the young had been pouring over her Hundertwasser books, wanting to surprise Nikki, but also fascinated by his innovation which made so much sense to the environmentally conscious New Zealanders and Australians.

Hundertwasser had returned to New Zealand in the Seventies where he bought a dairy farm in the Bay of Islands somewhere. He had planted thousands of trees from all over the world. When he returned to Europe he had the idea of planting *tree tenants* through windows on the Via Manzoni that could cope with the run-off water and return greenery to the city and cleanse the air and purify water. This was their rent, more valuable than human currency.

Fleur smiled. At the time Hundertwasser had been here in New Zealand, she had been a young woman in Singapore.

She walked on towards the summer house, and seeing

her with a basket of food the four younger men waved and stopped working. Sam turned and grinned.

'I see! Tools down and everything stops for food, does it?'

Fleur threw a cloth over the grass and laid out their breakfast. The four boys threw themselves down beside it. 'Great! Thanks, Fleur.'

Sam called her over and took her into the summer house. They had dug a hole half a metre deep for the tiny coffin. Pots of small indigenous trees lay waiting to be planted in the new earth.

'I don't know how purist Nikki wants to be, but the wooden coffin won't biodegrade instantly, Fleur. Has she realised that?'

'Yes she has. But the wood was chosen with love and help from the Malaysians. It's a non-durable hardwood. We both want to keep it.'

Sam touched her arm. 'I hope Nikki won't go on being obsessed with Saffie's death. I hope this place is not going to become a shrine but something that evolves and changes and eventually goes back to nature . . . in the spirit Hundertwasser intended.'

They moved out into the sun again and walked slowly towards the boys.

'Sam, I think she's going to be all right. Nikki has a child now, and Jack, and a future here. She's chosen a place where Saffie can be a part of her life . . . part of all this . . .' Fleur waved at the acres of trees and land all around them.

Sam threw his arm round her. 'It's all a bit of a mixture and New Age for me . . . Christian, Maori . . .'

'Rubbish!' Fleur said, wrapping an arm round his now ample waist. 'You understand this constant fusing of cultures and beliefs perfectly well. The young do it all the time . . .

I've heard you talking to Jack and the boys.'

Sam grinned and turned her to face him. 'Fleur, I want you to come out to Australia once a year. I mean it. I miss you. Let's try to spend some of each year together. I'll even build you a house with a tree tenant.'

Fleur laughed. 'How about every other year? You come to see me one year and I'll come to you and Angie the next.'

'Done!' Sam let her go and peered down at the picnic. 'I sincerely hope you guys have left me something to eat,' he said to the youths lying on their backs in the flower meadow.

FORTY-FOUR

We decided that the perfect time to bury Saffie would be at dawn when the sun rose on a new day. Often a mist would hang over the water and I would feel as if we were on an island cut off from all other human habitation, until the light filtered through making strange mountain shapes that evaporated in the heat of the day. I wanted the sound of seabirds calling and to hear the kokakos and takahe singing in the trees and scuttling in the undergrowth.

I wanted a tranquil, *given* morning to lay Saffie at long last to rest, and I got my wish.

We all made our way up the hill in the dark. I had found thick church candles and we shielded them from the wind in tubes of glass and they lit our way from the house to the flower meadow.

I was still weak from losing so much blood, and Sam helped me on one side and Jack on the other. When we reached the top we lit nightlights in the summer house and I looked down into the earth where Saffie would lie, part of our garden and forever near me.

We stood back and waited and soon we heard the low

sound of Maori singing and saw the small candlelit procession making its way downhill from the tiny meeting house to the water. The *tangihanga* was moving our way and the sound of their voices rose eerily in the dark. They were carrying Saffie down the valley to the river. There they would cross the water in small boats to our side and take the path Jack and I had long ago hacked out of wilderness. They would carry her up the steep path to her last safe resting place here.

The summer house was beautiful. More '*of the earth*' and perfect than I could have imagined. The boys had immersed themselves in the spirit of all that I had hoped, and they had built the tiny house with thought and love, these cousins I hardly knew.

I looked over at Fleur. She stood a little apart from us, small, very still, listening to the singing, watching the candlelit group flickering their way towards us. I could not see the expression on her face but the way she held her body tight into itself I knew her feelings were sharp and impenetrable. She was not crying. *There is a pain worse than tears: it is the burden you carry to death. The shock you never lose; the death of your child.*

I thought about Alice and shivered violently.

I let go of Jack's arm and walked towards her, but Gran was quicker. She placed Fleur's arm firmly in hers, her old hand covering Mum's. I saw Fleur glance at her in surprise, then she saw me and held out her other hand and I went to her and took it and I wished with all my heart Fergus was still here to stand with her instead of me.

We stood close together, three generations of women, as the little procession topped the rise and came towards the summer house. Gently they laid the coffin down in the grass in front of the house and the priest began to pray, and as he did so the first rays of the new day began behind the trees, filtering light to us in long shafts between the branches.

Fleur and I had chosen Saffie's favourite hymn and prayer. '*All Things Bright and Beautiful*' and the prayer '*Gentle Jesus Meek and Mild*'. Gran had taught us this prayer long, long ago, one Singapore Christmas, in a different life we once shared. Ah Heng made sure we said it every night before we slept.

Sam's boys chose a piece from Kahlil Gibran and read without self-consciousness or embarrassment. Our Maori friends sang for us, *the whanau pani*, the bereaved. They had not left Saffie's *tupapaku* alone once in all the days I had been in hospital.

I read a small piece from Fleur's Hundertwasser book. I wanted everyone to understand what this place was, what this funeral meant. Not a shrine, but a part of us all.

'*Everything is alive constantly, only transformed into other forms . . . A person should be buried only half a metre below the surface. Then a tree should be planted there. He should be buried in a coffin that decays so that when you plant a tree on top, the tree will take something out of his substance. When you visit the grave you don't visit a dead man, you visit a living being who is transformed into a tree. You can develop a beautiful forest which will be more beautiful than a normal forest because the trees have their roots in the graves. A fantastic place where you can live in constant contact with life and death . . .*'

My memory house. Containing Saffie and our private world of childhood. A place where we shared a secret language and the same face and our hearts beat in unison. Where we jumped from high boards into blue pools and raced each other to the side before we sank. Where the worst thing in the world was to be separated.

One day this small house will return to the earth as if it has never been; but out of the windows trees will have sprung.

When the moment came, Jack stood close beside me. We took Saffie inside the summer house and laid her in the place we had made for her in the ground, and the autumn sun began to warm the land as we knelt beside her. Fleur laid sweet peas on the thin coffin and I placed one gold Chinese shoe from the small box I held.

The priest blessed her, whispered, '*God and peace be with you*' and we sent her on into the next world.

We covered Saffie with earth and while the Maoris swayed and sang softly of things I did not know we placed our plants into the new turned soil. In the spring they will flower and the saplings will have thin branches stretching to the sky and the palest green translucent leaves.

In the spring I will bring Alice and it will be a new year of a new life. Fleur is part of that life; part of Alice and part of me. I will never let her feel alone again and neither will Sam. Fleur protected me and now it is my turn to protect her. We have both come home, Saffie and I. We have both come home.

In the spring I will bring Alice.

EPILOGUE

The man folds the newspaper carefully into its natural creases and leaves it on his desk. His study overlooks the garden and he goes to the open French windows where the scent of tobacco plants is overpowering.

He stands leaning on the doorframe staring out into the darkness. He brings his hand up to his face to brush away a moth and realises that his hands are trembling and his mouth is dry. Fear lies like ice upon his heart. The velvety night of summer draws him out of the light. He walks across the grass to the shelter of the apple trees near the old summer house.

As he turns he sees his own footprints on the damp grass, walking away from the house, and it seems to him they belong to someone who has already left. As if he is no longer a part of the lives in the lighted drawing room where he can see his wife and eldest daughter watching television, unaware of him out here in the garden.

Upstairs, in the spare room, his small grandson lies asleep.

Standing under the trees a terrifying lethargy overtakes him and he shivers violently. He crosses the lawn again and goes back to his study. He cannot distract himself from the dreadful consequences of his discovery. It is a stark fact that makes all reasoned dialogue with himself meaningless.

His daughter calls, 'Good night, Dad,' as she goes upstairs. His two black Labradors fill the doorway looking expectant, waiting for their last walk.

He pours himself a whisky and sits down again, his back to the newspaper. The dogs move towards him, puzzled by his silence, and he strokes their smooth heads. He holds his glass up and examines it in the light as if surprised how quickly it is emptying. He can hear Beattie plumping cushions, switching the kettle on, turning off lamps.

She comes to the door. 'I'm going up. Will you be long?'

'No, not long. I've just got a couple of letters to write and then I'll walk the dogs. I'll try not to wake you,' he says as he always says, but something in his tone alerts his wife.

'Are you all right, darling? You seem sad suddenly.'

He looks at her open and still guileless face. 'Oh, just middle-aged angst . . . you know . . . if you could have your life again the things you would change. The things you would undo.'

'What would you change, Alex? An army life?'

'Maybe. Or a less selfish life. A more secure and settled life for you.'

Beattie comes back into the room. 'You're talking rubbish. I've had a wonderful life. So have the girls. How many women get to be a general's wife with all the privileges? Now get your letters written and walk the dogs and come to bed.'

She kisses his nose and he catches hold of her hands. 'You always were the strong one, Beattie. A general's wife had to be his PA, admin officer and a hundred things besides. I got there with your help; because of you . . .'

'Piffle! This is so unlike you. You were fiercely ambitious, even when I first met you . . .'

She stops, remembering his sudden breakdown after Malaya. He had still been recovering from the accident that killed David Montrose and the tragedy of that poor child tipped him over the edge. *That poor Montrose woman.* It is a time neither of them ever refers to. She had to cover for Alex for months or he would have been discharged or deemed medically unfit to fly. As it was he had abruptly given up flying and changed regiments.

'Don't be long. You look tired,' she says, all at once feeling anxious.

'I won't. Good night, Beattie . . . God bless,' he adds softly.

He pours himself another whisky and swivels his chair round to his desk. He writes four letters, seals the envelopes and lays them neatly in formation on the wooden surface.

He finishes the bottle of whisky and then with unsteady fingers pulls the newspaper towards him. He turns to the page and he is back in the horror of that time and place in Malaya.

So small the grave.

He unlocks the small drawer in his desk, closes the French windows, calls his dogs and lets himself out of the back door. He walks down the lane that runs past the house towards the wood. He moves without a torch, deep into the heart of it; he knows the paths by heart and heads towards the river. The dogs, surprised at this change of routine, shuffle happily beside him sensing rabbits.

The man is not in the woods of the English countryside but back in the heat and smell of that place and that time. The heat, the beautiful laughing man wrapped around white linen sheets under a mosquito net, their limbs entwined.

Their flying suits thrown off, in a heap on the polished floor. They are abandoned in the supposedly empty house. Wife and children are at the dentist. The Amah is on her day off.

They are unaware of the sick child, not at the dentist but waking beside her sleeping amah. She calls out suddenly from the other side of the mosquito net, grizzly with fever, waking them. *Thank God, only waking them.*

He watches the man leap from the bed, pick up his child, make a joke to the child, who is pointing. 'Who's that? Who's that in your bed, Daddy?'

'He's not very well . . . like you. He is having a little rest because he's going to fly with Daddy later. He's going to borrow our shower now to cool down.'

'Oh.' The child loses interest quickly, turning away, clutching her dress with one hand and her father with the other . . .

As they stand on the tarmac waiting for one of the helicopters to be serviced they cannot look at one another. The man he loves turns to him, his face wretched.

'We stop it here; now and for good. I have a wife and children I love and you have a pregnant wife.'

'I don't love her.'

'Then you should. This is wrong. We can't risk what happened this afternoon ever again.'

'There are hotels. Singapore is a vast city, David.'

'Sordid, and there are eyes even in crowds. Do you want to be disgraced and drummed out of the army?'

'No, I don't. But I don't want to deny what I am, either.'

'Well . . .' David laughs bitterly. 'I'm afraid this is the British Army and you chose it, so grow up and accept things as they bloody well are. I love flying. I love my wife and kids and I am not throwing it all away for . . . anyone.'

341

He turns away angrily and Alex calls out, stung, 'I'm not *anyone*, and you bloody well know it. You're just less honest than I am. *You are what you are.* You cannot deny your nature any more than I can. This is not a miserable, guilty one-night stand. Oh, you can dance with your beautiful wife all evening, but it was me your eyes were searching for last night and this is how it will always be for you . . .'

'Get off my back, will you, Alex?' David faces him. 'I've told you how it's got to be and you'll thank me later, believe me. You're far more ruthlessly ambitious than I am. Let's fly. The planes are ready. Get your arse in gear.'

He turns and starts to walk across the airfield.

'Do you know what they are saying in the mess?' Alex shouts, running desperately after him. 'That Fergus is fucking your beloved wife . . .'

David swings round so fast Alex didn't see the blow coming. Then he marches off to his plane and climbs in.

That evening David's wife wears a red dress. That evening David watches Fergus kissing her . . . and so does he.

The storm caught them a few minutes before landing. He climbed out. David did not. The man shivers and feels in his pocket. *Funny how you keep things, just for the sake of it, never thinking you will have real need of them.*

When he gets out of hospital he is on sick leave and he and Beattie go to Malaya. It is like a sick joke. David's widow is there with her parents and children. He keeps out of the way; watches those twins in near panic from a distance.

He is out smoking and pacing on the deserted beach going over and over what he said and what he should not have said to David.

If only the house really had been empty. If only the child

342

had not caught them. If they had not had a row; if he had not yelled the things he had David might not have tried to get home. He would not have been so furious with Fergus; he might well have laughed the kiss off. Instead he had a burning need to get back to Fleur and punch Fergus on the nose.

David might still be alive if he had kept his mouth shut . . .

'Hello,' a small voice says. *Here she is*. Oh God. His mouth goes dry and sweat runs down inside his shirt. He feels a sudden terror of exposure. His flying, his army life, his marriage, his reputation . . . all blown away. He understands what David felt now and he was damn right to feel it.

Is it the same twin? He sees the white dress with the pink roses, the one she had been clutching that afternoon, and he hears Beattie's voice.

'*So sweet those twins! Even their parents can't tell them apart. They have to be dressed in different dresses . . . one wears pink and the other blue . . . isn't it killing?*'

He will never know how it happens. He tries to get rid of her, tries to shake her off, but she will not leave him alone. She remembers him all right. She remembers it was him with her father. She dances around him as if to taunt him, smiling, and her smile seems to him innocent but *knowing*. He feels blind anger as he pulls her along, then . . .

He has to stop her screaming. He puts his hand over her mouth and somehow the thought comes and he leaves it there. She is a small child and he has large hands.

A moment; a moment only. A rush of insanity and it is done. He is safe. His life is safe.

He buries her. He buries her deep; turns and runs and his leg throbs painfully.

It did not happen. It did not happen. It never happened. Not to him. It is someone else's tragedy. Not his. He never left the beach. He saw nothing. No, no one suspicious.

He helps them search. He even helps them search.

When the detectives are flown out from England he waits for them to come for him. All his life, really, he has waited for the knock on the door. It never came. That life faded. He retired. Terrible things became something that happened to someone else; a different, younger, fiercely ambitious self . . . but a man who would once have given up all he had for a life with the man he loved.

Yet, from the moment his first daughter is born he thinks about that child every single day of his life.

The child had looked up at him bewildered, suddenly terrified. Little beads of sweat lay on her top lip. Her fear had ignited something in him, something primitive and powerful. A predator sensing blood. One single evil moment that bleeds into the rest of your life, the horror of it dormant but pervasive, preventing happiness, preventing peace.

He leans against a tree to steady himself. Raises his hand. Opens his mouth. The shot rings out and lifts the crows from the treetops. The dogs race back from the shadows to the body lying in the bracken and stay with him all night until Beattie comes looking for him.

A story started long ago, finally ends. At the other side of the world, in a garden with no straight lines or angles, just the wild curves of land and blue sea and sky, a child is being laid to rest and another life is just beginning.

A note on the painting
The Garden of the Happy Dead

Hundertwasser: Human Architechture,
In Harmony with Nature

Here an ecological burial method is already anticipated. In it the dead are buried in harmony with nature and creation, integrated into an ecological whole, returned to a higher order. In this way there would be no more cemeteries, but just a respected sanctified nature which goes on reproducing with trees growing out of people where there are no dead, only life. This I called the *Garden of the Happy Dead*. The spiral is a symbol of the cycle of death and re-birth, of eternal life.

ENJOYED THIS BOOK? WHY NOT TRY OTHER GREAT HARPERCOLLINS TITLES – AT 10% OFF!

Buy great books direct from HarperCollins
at **10%** off recommended retail price.
FREE postage and packing in the UK.

☐ **Sea Music** Sara MacDonald 0-00-715073-3   £6.99

☐ **Another Life** Sara MacDonald 0-00-717577-9   £6.99

☐ **The Lady and the Unicorn** Tracy Chevalier 0-00-714091-6   £6.99

☐ **Moonshine** Victoria Clayton 0-00-714344-3   £6.99

☐ **Clouds Among the Stars** Victoria Clayton 0-00-714255-2   £7.99

☐ **The Tea Rose** Jennifer Donnelly 0-00-715556-5   £6.99

Total cost _____

10% discount _____

Final total _____

To purchase by Visa/Mastercard/Switch simply call
08707 871724 or fax on **08707 871725**

To pay by cheque, send a copy of this form with a cheque made payable to
'HarperCollins Publishers' to: Mail Order Dept. (Ref: BOB4),
HarperCollins Publishers, Westerhill Road, Bishopbriggs, G64 2QT,
making sure to include your full name, postal address and phone number.

From time to time HarperCollins may wish to use your personal data
to send you details of other HarperCollins publications and offers.
If you wish to receive information on other HarperCollins publications
and offers please tick this box I

Do not send cash or currency. Prices correct at time of press.
Prices and availability are subject to change without notice.
Delivery overseas and to Ireland incurs a £2 per book postage and packing charge.